THE
RIVER
KILLINGS

MERRY JONES

St. Martin's Paperbacks

This is a work of fiction. All of the characters, organizations, and events portrayed in this novel are either products of the author's imagination or are used fictitiously.

THE RIVER KILLINGS

Copyright © 2006 by Merry Jones.
Excerpt from *The Deadly Neighbors* copyright © 2007 by Merry Jones.

Cover photo of bridge and rowers © Corbis
Cover photo retouching by Shasti O'Leary Soudant

Library of Congress Catalog Card Number: 2006005613

ISBN: 0-312-99863-5
EAN: 978-0-312-99863-9

Printed in the United States of America

St. Martin's Press hardcover edition / October 2006
St. Martin's Paperbacks edition / December 2007

St. Martin's Paperbacks are published by St. Martin's Press, 175 Fifth Avenue, New York, NY 10010.

10 9 8 7 6 5 4 3 2 1

To Robin, Baille and Neely

ACKNOWLEDGMENTS

I owe thanks beyond words to my agent, Liza Dawson, and to Thomas Dunne, Marcia Markland and Diana Szu at Thomas Dunne Books. They are dream-makers.

Thanks also to:

Vesper Boat Club, Masters Rowing Association and Win Tech Racing, organizations that have made it possible for me to become part of the rowing world.

My first coach, Kay Mac Donald; my first doubles partner, Ellen Carver; my first mixed-quad racing mates, John and Alexis Franklin; my favorite cheerleader, Gus Constant; Chicago River Rowing founder, Susan Urbas; Schuylkill Navy Commodore Clete Graham; renowned boat producer, rower and coach Drew Harrison; relentless Masters rowers Lee Barber, Michael and Patti Glick, Davinder Singh, Maria Raymond, John and Catherine Holdsworth, Red and Sarah Sargent, and the many other awesome rowers, coaches, referees and officials who frequent the Schuylkill River.

My mom, Judy Bloch, and my sister, Janet Martin, for their quiet encouragement and pithy wisdom. Nancy Delman for her dark humor and our scintillating walk-and-talks on the lake. Jane Braun for sharing belly laughs and oldies even in the toughest times.

Lanie Zera, for her insightful reading, her morale boosts, her enduring spirit and her company at too infrequent trips to the spa. Sue Solovy Mulder, Michael and Jan Molinaro, Sue Francke, Ruth Waldfogel and Steve Zindell for nurturing enthusiasm and precious friendships.

Sam the Corgi for keeping guard under my desk as I wrote.

My daughters, Baille and Neely, for teaching me so patiently in ever-changing circumstances what it means to be a mom. Also, Baille for rowing and racing a double with me and Neely for making her own good choices.

My husband, Robin, for closely reading and commenting on every draft of this book, and for rowing with me in all kinds of weather, moving our boat together along the river of life, one stroke at a time.

My late dad, Herman Bloch, and late brother, Aaron Bloch, for showing a young child the importance of imagining, and for leaving me with so many rich memories.

ONE

The water gleamed silver and black like a stream of mercury winding through the night. The almost full moon and the traffic lights on Kelly Drive spilled some light our way, and Susan had clipped a red blinking flash onto the back of her spandex top. Even so, as we shoved off the boathouse dock, we were clearly alone on the inky river, only a thin layer of carbon fiber separating us from the chilly waters of the Schuylkill River.

For June, the night was unnaturally muggy. The weather had been abnormal lately, the air swelling, sticky and humid, with temperatures in the high eighties too early and for too many days. After sunset, the air had begun to cool, but it hung heavily, as if exhausted from the day.

Maybe I was projecting; I was drained, having spent a long, stifling day at the Institute, finishing paperwork and saying good-bye to patients, some of whom wouldn't be there anymore when I returned from a two-week break. My head was crowded with their incomplete art projects and unfinished therapy programs, and I wanted simply to collapse at home, sorting myself out, chilling under a ceiling fan.

By contrast, Susan had taken the day off, staying in her air-conditioned Center City home, supervising contractors who were putting in skylights and redoing the deck. She'd been desperate to get out of the house and singularly unmoved by my claims of fatigue.

"The water's completely calm," she'd promised. "The row will be easy and quiet. The river will be empty—no coaching launches to speed by and wake us. In fact, there won't be any other boats out at all."

She sounded pleased, as if being the only boat on the river in the dark was a plus. Frankly, I was uncomfortable rowing at night. The water was too black, too silent. Rowing on it seemed risky.

I'd tried to put up an argument. "Susan, we're still novices."

"Exactly. That's why we should go now, while it's quiet. It'll be easier water than during the day. Trust me."

I'd sighed, still resisting. "What am I supposed to do with Molly?" Molly was my six-year-old daughter. So far, she'd usually been at school when we rowed. Or, on weekends, she and Susan's daughters Rollerbladed or rode bikes along the river on Kelly Drive. But at night, what was Molly supposed to do? Nick was working late again, and with Angela off on her honeymoon, I had nobody to baby-sit.

But Susan had been undeterred. She'd offered to bring two of her daughters, Emily and Julie. "They'll all stay at the boathouse," she'd said. "They'll watch TV in the lounge for an hour."

"What about Tony?" Tony Boschetti was the boathouse manager, and we'd heard that he wasn't happy about members leaving their children alone there.

"Screw Tony. They'll stay in the lounge. They won't bother anybody."

She'd had me. Molly and Emily were best friends; Julie was older, almost eleven. They'd be fine. After all, we'd only be gone for an hour.

And so, despite my reservations, I'd agreed to go. We'd left the girls in the lounge with sodas and bags of popcorn, then gone down to the deserted dock, gotten into the *Andelai* and shoved off.

Susan was energized. In just a few months, she'd become an

avid, if not particularly skilled, sculler, bringing to rowing the same relentless fervor that she applied to the rest of her life. Susan did nothing halfway; if she wanted to swim, she threw herself wholeheartedly, headfirst, into the pool. Somehow, she successfully managed her marriage, her three daughters, her active criminal defense law practice, her volunteer work at a homeless shelter, her second term as PTA president, her position with the Neighborhood Town Watch, and her never-ending process of redecorating her home and preparing not just healthful but delectable meals for family and friends. Sculling was merely the newest of Susan's many passions, and I knew from past experience that it was best not to interfere; for a time, she would be utterly consumed.

It was all Nick's fault. Nick was the man I'd been seeing, and he'd been rowing since high school. The first thing he did when he moved to Philadelphia the year before was to buy a new sculling shell and join a boathouse. And as soon as the winter ice had thawed, he'd begun rowing. Nick rowed when he was stressed or fatigued, when he needed to think or relax, when he needed to work off frustration or uncertainty. He rowed at all hours, often before dawn, and in all weather. When Susan had complained that her thighs were getting flabby, Nick suggested that she take up rowing. Before I knew it, Susan had signed us both up for a Learn-to-Row class. I'd never have taken the class on my own, but Susan had insisted. Rowing would be good for us—less fattening than going to lunch, less expensive than shopping. Besides, she'd argued, fortyish-year-old women like us needed to take action to resist rolling midriffs and the tolls of time.

In the end, though, I took the class not because of anything Susan said, but because I was curious. What was this sport that lured Nick out of bed before the sun was up? For years, I'd been intrigued by the long, sleek shells on the river, the elegant sway of the rowers, the synchrony of their oars. I'd wondered what it would feel like to be one of them, gliding on the water with silent strength and grace. But I'd been an innocent. I'd had no idea how all-consuming this new hobby could become. Or how it would change our lives.

By the time our six weeks of Learn-to-Row classes had ended, Susan had become addicted. She'd urged me to join Humberton Barge, one of the oldest rowing clubs on Boathouse Row, and she insisted that we practice daily, preparing to compete in the Schuylkill Navy Regatta, the first race of the summer.

Susan may have been the instigator, but, in my way, I'd become hooked, too. We'd even hired a coach, the controversial but esteemed Preston Everett, to work with us twice a week. A former Olympic champion, Coach Everett had the reputation of being both the most cantankerous and the most capable coach on the river. It had been Coach Everett who'd assigned us our boat, a double named *Andelai*. And it had been Coach Everett who'd assigned us our positions. As "bow," Susan was to steer the boat and give commands; as "stroke," I was, basically, to keep quiet and obey her.

This arrangement suited Susan perfectly. She enjoyed talking without interruption on any subject that breezed through her mind. As we rowed, she often commented on the natural environment, the lush foliage along the banks, the egrets and loons, the turtles, the ducklings. Depending on her mood, she would rave or rant about her husband, Tim, and any of her three children. She talked about the clients she was defending, the rabid ferocity of prosecutors, the shoulders of the contractors working on her house, the price of slipcovers for her sunroom sofa, a new chili recipe that was rich with chocolate, the outcome of her impending mammogram, how much weight she'd gained or lost, the burgeoning sizes of her teenage daughter's bras. She saw her role as bow as a license to speak uninterrupted for as long as she wanted about anything. Mostly, I tuned her out. But buried in her monologue were occasional directions about rowing the boat, so I had to tune in at least marginally.

We shoved off the dock, gliding gently away from the glowing lights of Boathouse Row. The water was smooth and sleepy, a dark mirror for the lights, and the boat slid along smoothly, undisturbed, leaving a rippling triangular trail. Rowing at night, I thought, might not be so bad after all. It was peaceful. Romantic, in a way. Maybe Nick would row with me some evening. I pictured it, the two of us alone on the river under the dreamy moon.

"Half-slide in two," Susan called. "And stop splashing."

Splashing? I wasn't splashing, or I hadn't thought I was. But I didn't say anything. Coach Everett had been very clear about in-boat behavior. The bow, and only the bow, was to speak. The bow was in command. Everybody else was to keep silent, backs straight and eyes focused forward. They were not even to turn their heads.

"Watch your oars," Susan ordered.

Watch them? What was wrong with them? And how could I watch them if I wasn't supposed to turn my head?

"Why?" I called as I rowed, aware that, by speaking, I was breaking a cardinal rule. "What's wrong?"

"You're still splashing."

I was? "With both oars?" I had to shout; the river was quiet but Susan was behind me, and I was faced away from her. And, along this stretch of the river, sounds of traffic on Kelly Drive and the nearby expressway muffled our voices.

"Sometimes," she shouted back. "And watch your slide."

My slide? The slide is the part of the stroke when the legs bend as the rower's seat moves up from bow to stern. But what about the slide was I supposed to "watch"? Was it too fast? Too slow? Too early or late? Why couldn't she be specific? Was she being deliberately obtuse? Never mind, I told myself. Let it go.

"And relax your shoulders."

Oh, boy. We hadn't rowed five hundred yards yet. Was Susan going to comment on my every move for six more miles?

"Watch the splashing," she shouted, "and give me pressure on port. More port. Give me more port."

I gave her port, thinking about what else I wanted to give her. After we passed under the Girard Avenue Bridge, though, Susan changed her approach. "We have to relax," she said.

We?

"Our shoulders are tense."

She'd begun referring to us as a single being.

I took a deep breath, trying to focus, to inhale the warmth

and calm of the night. The clear sky. The glassy water. Anything but the cloying commands of the bow.

"We need to sit up tall," she said.

I closed my eyes, centering myself. Coach Everett had told us to row with our eyes closed so we could sense the boat moving in the water. I closed mine to escape the squawking in the bow. No good. Susan kept it up. She began to narrate each stroke, start to finish, in an annoying singsong cadence.

"Hands away fast. Swing with our bodies. Now, slow slide. Roll our oars early. And catch."

Okay. I'd had enough. "Susan," I called, still rowing, "can we just row?"

"What?"

"Please. Just steer the boat and call the drills. Can you not talk so much?"

"I'm the bow. I'm supposed to tell you what to do."

"But you're talking nonstop. I can't focus on rowing. All I can think about is you, talking."

"Excuse me?" She was appalled at my insubordination. Stunned. "I can't believe this. Let it run." That means stop rowing.

Our oars slapped the water as we floated to a stop. I twisted around to face her.

"What's your problem, Zoe?" Susan demanded. "You don't like me being bow? I didn't ask to be—Coach Everett made me bow."

"I have no problem with you being bow—"

"Obviously, you do. You can't stand not being in charge, even in a damned boat. This is about your control thing, isn't it?"

Oh dear, she was making it personal. She knew me too well, knew what my issues were. "Susan, no. It's not about me. I don't need to be in control—"

"Really? Not about control? Then what? Your trust thing? You don't trust me to be bow. Is that it? You don't think you can rely on me?"

I closed my eyes and took a deep breath. "Susan. This is not about trust or control. It's not about me. I really don't mind you being bow. I just mind you being the bow from hell."

Oops. That was harsh. I felt her recoil, wounded and defensive.

"How am I the bow from hell?"

"You criticize my every move—"

"No way—I do not—"

"Oh, please, Susan."

"I'm just doing my job. I'm responsible for how the boat moves."

"You want to move the boat? Focus on your own rowing instead of mine."

"My rowing? What's wrong with my rowing?"

The conversation wasn't going well, but I couldn't stop myself. "We're both beginners, Susan. Neither of us is perfect."

"I didn't say I was—"

"But you blame me for every little wobble."

"That's absurd. I do not."

Alone in the middle of the river, we scrapped like an old married couple. Susan was my best friend, and I knew the fight wasn't worth it, but I was tired and cranky. We kept it up, jabbing, bickering, getting nowhere and behaving badly.

"How about we both just shut up and row," I finally said. I sat in the ready position, waiting for a command.

"Fine," she answered. "You want to row? We'll row." Susan glowered at me. I knew because I could feel her glower burning my back. "Is it okay with you if I ask you to please sit ready?"

Uh-oh. Her tone was both sarcastic and ominous. I didn't know how, but she was going to make me pay for complaining.

Sure enough, she began calling drills, steadily increasing our power and stroke rate, trying to exhaust me and prove who was in charge. I didn't challenge her again, didn't make a peep. I was going to prove I could perform at least as well as she could. So, when she called, "Take it up," I cursed silently but took it up, pushing harder with my legs and swinging my body. Oddly, the harder I pushed, the more I enjoyed myself. My strokes became smoother as we gained momentum. The boat gurgled, leaving a bubbly, moonlit trail. Our oars clicked into place with each stroke, and we began to soar upriver, swinging together, pushing, feeling the burn of our muscles and the potential of our combined power.

Lungs searing, we sped under Columbia Bridge and reached the tip of the overgrown pile of rocks called Peters Island. Halfway up the island, I was about to die. Susan had proved her point. She'd won. I had to stop. I tried to say that I needed to stop, but I didn't have enough wind to talk. Susan yelled, "Take it up. Full power for forty."

I'd had no idea that Susan was that sadistic. But my pride or my temper kicked in, and I didn't give up. From some remote sector of my being, I pulled out more energy and rowed faster, pushed harder than I'd imagined possible, using my body weight as leverage against my oars. The boat took off. It skimmed the water, speeding ahead. We passed the woods of Peters Island in a whoosh.

"Keep it up," Susan huffed.

I kept the rate up, legs and thighs aching, blood surging, lungs bursting. Lost in rhythm and exertion, I rejoiced in the wind, the glide. I had the impression that we'd left the water, that we'd begun to fly.

Apparently, Susan was similarly absorbed; she didn't call a warning. Maybe she hadn't looked ahead. Or maybe, in the darkness, she simply hadn't seen anything that low to the surface. But, when we made impact, our boat lurched so violently that I flew off my seat. I stopped rowing midstroke, but my oars crashed into Susan's. The boat shuddered, and we dipped dangerously to port.

"Shit," Susan shrieked. "Hold still; don't move."

I squatted, trying to balance, not able to get back onto my seat. We were tipping at an impossible angle. Slowly, I turned my head to look over my shoulder. Susan's starboard oar stood erect in the water, definitely out of reach. She'd lost hold of it; its blade was entangled with mine, and both were caught in a mass of what looked like floating cloth. I couldn't see what we'd hit, couldn't turn far enough around.

"Zoe—stop. Don't move."

"I'm not moving."

"Don't turn around. Set the boat."

"I can't set the boat—my oar's stuck with yours."

"Oh, shit—hold still." Cursing, Susan flailed at her starboard oar, trying to grab it, inadvertently knocking my oar deeper into the water, rocking the boat, tipping us even farther.

"Susan—stop—we're flipping—"

Susan stopped. In fact, she held completely still. "Dear God," she breathed. "A floater."

"What?"

"We hit a floater."

Slowly, careful not to shift my weight, I turned to look. At first, all I saw was bloated cloth, lumpy yards of it, adrift on the water. Then, near the surface beside our oars, I made out a dim opalescent oval bobbing with the movement of the river. I stared, focusing, and the pale oval took on definition. It had features. Eyes, a nose. Lips. Hair that disappeared into the dark water and reemerged, washing against its skin.

"Oh, damn." I don't know who kept repeating that, Susan or I. Or maybe both of us. For a timeless second we sat, not moving, tilted at an unmanageable angle, staring at the body, balanced precariously at a forty-five-degree angle, our oars tangled up with a dead woman's dress, our minds racing to figure out how to right the boat. Soon, though, we grasped the grim reality: It was too late. Any movement we made would disturb our delicate balance and flip the boat. In fact, even if we made no movement at all, we couldn't maintain our balance much longer. We'd tilted too far. There was nothing we could do. We could reach for our oars or not; either way, we were going over.

For endless seconds, our boat hung tenuously as if holding its breath. Then, gently, teasingly, it rolled over, spilling us into the chilly black water of the Schuylkill.

TWO

I went in sideways, bumping into my oar handles, hearing Susan's shouts muffle as I submerged, realizing only after I'd sunk that I was trapped in the boat—my feet were fastened into the shoes. I dangled upside down in cold water, realized that I was going to drown, and I panicked, thrashing blindly through long thin vines, river plants that curled around me, entwining my head, my arms. I began to choke. Then, as if from a great distance, I heard a man's voice—Coach Everett's? He was hollering commands, telling me what to do. I stopped thrashing and held still, listening. "Pull the shoe flaps," he yelled. Of course. The shoe flaps. They're Velcro. I reached up through the tangling vines to my feet, found the strings and yanked. The Velcro peeled open; my feet came free. And so did I. I dropped out of the boat. The water swallowed me, and I swallowed it. Murky river water flooded my nose, my mouth, my hair, my pores. I fell deeper into dark water, certain that I was going to die.

Somehow, it wasn't as bad as I had imagined. In fact, the water felt cool, soothing. It moved gently, enclosing me, and I suddenly understood that the river was alive, seducing me as it tugged me down, welcoming me into itself. Drowning wasn't so bad, I thought. It was soft. Hushed and womblike, the water caressed me, comforted me, tempting me to stay. I considered giving in to it, but the air left in my lungs must have lifted me and I surfaced, shocked at the sudden assault of air, the harshness of sound, the brightness of night.

Then I remembered. Susan—where was Susan?

"Susan!" I called, but all that came out was a gurgle and a cough. I treaded water, calling again, hearing no answer but the splashes of water around and under me. Dear God. Where was she? I called again. Still no answer. Maybe Susan had been stuck in the boat as I had. Maybe she'd been hurt and couldn't get out of her shoes. Couldn't surface. Oh, Lord, where was she?

I hung on to the inverted hull, dunked under it to feel for Susan, and, shoving away the oars, I bumped into someone. Susan? I surfaced, gasping for air, grabbing a limp, slippery arm, blinking water from my eyes. In the moonbeams, clutching the woman in my arms, I swept her hair off her face. It wasn't Susan. I saw instead the bloated features and blank eyes of the floater. Shuddering, I shoved her away, but she was heavy, wouldn't budge. I pushed her again and she floated back again, rocking beside me like a playful inflatable float.

"Susan!" I yelled again but heard no reply, just more splashes of moving water. I edged away from the corpse, still holding on to the hull, and reached out, feeling the water, waving my free arm back and forth, up and down, finding nothing. I let go of the boat and went back under the surface, reaching, rotating, sweeping with my arms until, a few yards away, I found her hand under the surface. I grabbed on to her and tugged, disturbingly aware that her hand didn't grab or tug back. Susan's hand merely sat in my grasp, passive and lifeless.

"Susan," I breathed, tugging at her arm, pulling her toward me. I swam under and behind her, shoving her upward, boosting her face so she could breathe, encircling her head with one arm to keep her mouth and nose above water. Her hair floated against my face, into my mouth, as I kicked back toward the boat, awkwardly backstroking with my free arm. I was tugging at her, grunting, out of breath, amazed at how heavy she was. A few more strokes, I told myself, and I'd be able to reach the boat. To catch my breath and revive Susan. On my next stroke, though, my arm smacked something long and solid, too smooth to be a log. I spun around, came face-to-face with a foot, a leg, an entire woman. Oh, God. Oh, God. Another one? I thrashed, still holding on to the person I'd thought was Susan, who still wasn't moving. Who didn't seem to be conscious, didn't even seem to be breathing. Was she really Susan? She was built like Susan, had Susan's chin-length dark hair. But, in the moonlight, kicking and struggling to stay afloat, I couldn't be sure.

Treading water, I looked out at the dark surface, slowly focusing, taking in the shadowy lumps surrounding me. Oh my God. I was surrounded by them. Dead women, bobbing limply on the surface like so many dead fish. I looked behind me, saw more of them. Bodies were floating all around me, in every direction. I let out a howl, but my mouth was too low to the water, and all that came out was a bubbly gurgle. Oh, God, oh, God. This couldn't be real. Couldn't be happening. But a body floated by, catching an arm around my neck, trapping Susan and me in her armpit. I shoved her and kicked away, but the cool indifference of her flesh lingered on my fingertips. Get ahold of yourself, I thought. Don't panic. But my eyes darted from one corpse to another, and my back bumped drifting shoulders and thighs. How many were there? Six? Eight?

I wanted to swim away, escape. But I couldn't; I had Susan in my arms. If she actually was Susan. Was she? Oh, Lord. She still hadn't moved. Was she dead, too? Shivering, I let her go; the night sky revealed her blue, waterlogged features, her empty gaze. Her unfamiliar, bloated face. A noise rose from my belly, something between a moan and a bellow.

My stomach twisted and wrenched, threatened to fly out my throat. I had to get away from there. I thrust myself backward, crashed into the woman I'd just released and rebounded into the arms of the woman in the billowing dress. I was unable to think clearly or even to breathe. Oh, God. What was happening? I was caught in a swarm of dead bodies. What was I supposed to do? And, damn, where was Susan?

"Help," I managed to gurgle. "Somebody—help—" My voice was raw, clogged.

"Ugghh." Somebody whimpered softly, nothing more than a squeak. Had I heard or imagined it? The water slapped at sounds, distorting them, drowning them out.

"Susan?" I called.

"Unghh." Her voice was faint, and it came from the other side of the hull, near the bow.

"Susan—thank God," I breathed. She was alive. Her groan revived me, and I managed to crawl through the throng of bodies, shoving and swimming my way back to the boat. Susan clutched the bow, panting, staring and dazed.

"Uhnnnguh," she gulped, her gaze riveted to the water. She seemed stunned, unable to form words. I made my way to her, hand over hand, hanging on to the upside-down *Andelai.*

"Are you all right?" I asked. I touched her arm, her face. She remained frozen, unmoving.

"Unguhh," she wheezed, probably hyperventilating, her voice a clogged, frantic whisper. "Unghhud, unnghod."

We held on to our boat and each other, drifting under the stars, gaping at the scene before us. The clothing, the limbs. The faces. I stopped counting at thirteen. Dead women, their bodies floating down the river in an island of flesh.

THREE

The next minutes and hours passed in a blur. I remember the terror, the slow, sloppy confusion of righting our boat, and, shocked and shivering, the clumsy process of getting ourselves back into the *Andelai* without flipping it again. Time seemed stuck, as if it would never pass, never allow us to move on; our task seemed infinite, impossible. We were in an endless loop of effort and frustration, horror and exertion. I held the boat steady while Susan tried, for the fourth or fifth time, to climb into the bow, and I scanned the shoreline, peering into the darkness. Once, I thought I saw a human silhouette, a moving shadow. I even called out, hoping the person might help us. But as I focused on it, the image faded; I saw only streetlights and the outlines of trees. Alongside us, the flotilla of corpses slogged slowly downriver. Who were they? What had happened to them? How had they gotten into the water? Questions swam through my mind, and I tried not to dwell on the lingering sensations of the dead woman hanging in my arms or her hair floating into my mouth.

Somehow, we made it to the nearest dock at the Canoe Club, about two miles upriver from Boathouse Row, where a car on Kelly Drive stopped for two shivering, dripping-wet women who dashed in front of it, frantically waving and shouting for help. Before long, police cars, marine unit launches, ambulances, fire trucks and news media vans poured into the area. Spotlights beamed over the water, cameras flashed, commotion reigned, and the swarm of sodden corpses was dragged en masse, like a large catch of bluefish, to the dock. Susan and I were wrapped in blankets and ushered to a nearby bench where we sat shivering, only partly from the chill.

At some point, Nick appeared near the water, and, for a moment, I wondered who'd called him, how he'd known we were there. Then I realized he wasn't there for me; he was working. Nick was a homicide detective; he was there to take charge of the scene. As always, Nick was unflappable, in command, no matter how grisly the situation. I watched as if from a distance, as if the fifty yards between us were impassable.

But Nick must have sensed me staring at him. He looked our way; only his eyes registered surprise. "Susan? Zoe?" He gaped at us as if not sure the bundles in the blankets were really us, his eyes darting from me to Susan, Susan to me. "Oh, Christ." He slapped his forehead, figuring it out. "The two rowers? The women who found the bodies?"

We nodded, a pair of sopping-wet bobble heads.

"We rowed smack into them." Susan spoke for the first time since we'd flipped. She said nothing about who'd been in the bow, steering the boat. Not a word about who hadn't looked ahead as we'd sped into the darkness at full power.

"That water's maybe sixty degrees," he scolded. He put an arm around Susan, wrapped me in the other. Moist heat radiated from his body. I wanted to climb under his clothes and huddle there. "How long were you in it?"

How long? I shrugged. A few minutes? An hour? More? I had no idea. Nor, apparently, did Susan.

"You're hypothermic. You should go to the ER."

"Can't," Susan said. "Gotta get going." Her teeth were chattering.

I finally tried to speak, but my teeth were clenched together, my jaw locked shut. I couldn't make words.

Nick eyed us, one at a time. His hug warmed us, and he

whispered, asking again if I was okay, not noticing the silence of my reply.

"Did either of you see any boats on the water? Or anyone along the banks? Anything unusual?"

I looked at Susan; she'd been bow, able to look around. I'd had to keep my eyes ahead, had seen nothing but dark water until we'd hit.

Susan shook her head. "No. Nobody. Just us."

Suddenly, questions flew from the darkness and cameras flashed our way. The press had discovered us. Nick left to chase them away, and I huddled against Susan, aware of Nick's voice barking with authority somewhere in the dark. Someone handed us cups of hot coffee; my hand shook so much, I spilled it as I lifted it to my mouth. A detective held the cup for me while I sipped, then briefly took our statement. Susan, revitalized by the hot caffeine, spoke for us both. Finally, Nick came back and sat with us.

"We'll get details from you later. Now, you both need to get home and get warm." He called to an officer. "Officer Olsen, would you drive these ladies home—"

"No," Susan interrupted. "We have to go to back to Humberton. The kids are there."

I nodded, still mute, my jaws aching and stiff. I had no idea what time it was or how long the girls had been waiting there. Time hadn't seemed relevant until that moment.

Nick looked at me, surprised. "Molly's at Humberton?"

I nodded again. He frowned with half his face. Clearly, he didn't approve.

"It's okay. Julie and Emily are with her," Susan explained, but Nick still scowled. "And—oh, damn. The boat. We have to row it back."

"Forget it," Nick said.

"But we can't just leave it here." Susan was adamant, standing up, ready to get back in the boat.

I was trembling; under the streetlights, Susan looked blue, not a good color for skin.

"Forget the boat. Leave it here overnight," Nick said.

"We can't. Tony'll kill us. And Coach Everett needs it at six for his morning session."

Clearly, Susan couldn't process the gravity of what had happened, couldn't grasp that the flotilla of dead bodies in the river might minimize the importance of morning practice.

"You're in no condition to row, Susan." Nick's tone was final. "The boat stays here. Tony and Coach Everett will have to understand." He told an officer to drive us back to Humberton Barge, then home. "Go home and get warm." He stopped me as I turned to go, pulling me back, and held my face in his hands.

"You're sure you're okay?"

I nodded, still silent.

His arms encircled me and held me tight. "I'll be home as soon as I can."

I clung to him, soaking up his warmth, and when he released me the air felt raw and empty, even colder than before. I climbed into the car beside Susan. The police car pulled out of the parking lot, and I watched Nick turn back to the grisly scene at the river, where bodies were being lifted out of the water, bagged, loaded into the coroner's wagon. I followed Nick's gaze, saw a marine police officer carrying a watery corpse across the dock. He held her gently, gracefully, like a dancer in some gruesome ballet. His stance was strong and somber; her body arched swanlike and delicate, and her arm dangled from his grasp, slender and graceful, even in death.

FOUR

It was almost midnight when, stunned and exhausted, we got back to the boathouse. Humberton was old and reassuringly stuffy; even its name had to be dusted off when you wanted to say it. But that night, the boathouse seemed altered, almost sinister. Hollow and dimly lit, it hid corners with odd angles and cast shadows with unfamiliar shapes. I told myself to get a grip, that it wasn't the house that had become creepy; it was me. Still, I stayed close to Susan as we left Officer Olsen in the chandeliered foyer and climbed the winding stairs to the second floor.

We pulled open the old heavy doors to the members' lounge where two huge stone fireplaces grounded opposite sides of the room. A high beamed ceiling topped walls covered with Olympic oars, archival photographs and century-old regatta awards. The lounge was serene and old-fashioned, furnished with Oriental area rugs and clusters of heavy leather furniture. It offered members respite from competition and a break from the exercise equipment in the adjacent workout room.

We found the girls asleep, spread out on the oversized leather sofas near the doors to the deck. As we roused them, I mentally reviewed the explanation Susan and I had prepared about why we'd been gone so long. We were going to be as honest as possible, omitting the disturbing details. Molly woke up first, curls disheveled, eyes bleary with sleep, and I took a deep breath, ready to begin.

"Molls, I'm sorry we're so late—"

"Emily, Julie and me are in a fight," she scowled.

"—but we had a little problem." It took me a few heartbeats to stop talking; my reaction time was slow, my mind still dull, frozen by cold water. But as soon as her words registered, I aborted my speech, relieved to let Molly's crisis, whatever it was, take priority. "Why?" I finally managed. "What happened?"

Julie was awake, now, too. "She's a cheater, that's what—"

"I am not!"

"Julie," Susan sighed, "don't call names."

"She is a cheater, though—"

"I am *not*," Molly bounded off the sofa and stood in front of Julie, hands on hips. "You guys lost, that's all—you're a sore loser." All her front teeth had fallen out, and Molly's *s*'s sounded like *th*'s. In her rage, she sounded a bit like Sylvester the cat. "Besides, you're a tattletale."

Julie was twice Molly's size and almost twice her age. I probably should have intervened on Molly's behalf, but I watched, passive and numb, while Molly took Julie on, reminding me once again that my daughter had been adopted, that we shared no genetic material. When I was her age, if anyone had called me a cheater, I'd have dissolved into tears and run mortified out of the room, never ever to return. But Molly stood her ground without backing down, undaunted.

"Cheater, cheater, Molly is a cheater," Julie sang, but she sank into the cushions, backing away from Molly's small ferocious, mostly toothless face.

Wearily, Susan took Julie's arm. "Don't be mean, Julie. Let's get going. Just apologize."

"No—why should I?" Julie squirmed. "I'm telling the truth."

Molly's body stiffened, her fists clenched. "You're a sore loser." Molly glared at Julie with freezing contempt.

"Molls." My rhythm was off; my comment came a few beats too late. "Chill. Settle this later. Let's move." But Molly was sputtering mad, unlikely either to chill or to move.

Emily woke up then, yawning and stretching. She watched the spat mutely, without taking sides.

"All I said was you cheated." Julie pressed herself deeper into the back of the couch.

"Julie," Susan pleaded. "Drop it. Let's go."

"Not till she admits she broke the rules," Julie insisted.

"We never said the rules." Molly's hands were on her hips. "How could I break them if we didn't say them?"

"You knew them," Julie insisted.

"No, I didn't. Because if I did, I wouldn't've broken them."

With an exasperated sigh, Susan gave up, sprawling onto an easy chair beside Julie's sofa. She stared at the ceiling, rubbing her temples. I was cold and light-headed. I'd just been swimming with the dead and was desperate to go home.

"Girls, deal with this later. I mean it. We're leaving. Now." I tried to muster some authority.

"But Julie says I cheated—"

"Julie's a bitch," Emily finally spoke.

"Emily, don't use that language." Susan spoke on automatic, eyes still on the ceiling.

"I'm a bitch?" Julie fired back. "Well, you're an ugly stinky little piece of shit."

Susan's eyes didn't move from the beams. Her fingers continued their massage. "Girls—for the last time, don't curse."

"Why?" Julie countered. "You curse. You say 'shit' all the time. And 'bastard' and 'dammit' and—"

"*Shut up. Just for once shut the hell up!*" The roar was sudden, cutting off Julie's voice, exploding from Susan's belly, shaking the room.

Instantly, everyone was silent. Wide-eyed, Julie sat still. Emily went to Molly and hugged her; finally, Molly relaxed. Susan resumed rubbing her temples.

"I didn't cheat," Molly insisted. "I just didn't know we had to hide upstairs."

Wait, I thought. What was that? Suddenly I grasped the facts. "You mean you hid downstairs?"

Molly stared at the wall.

"Molly? You went down into the boat bays?" Alarmed, my brain jolted back into gear. "You know you're not supposed to go in there. It's dangerous."

"But we were playing hide-and-seek and I have a great hiding place—"

"Molly went in the boat racks," Julie tattled. "Way up high. How could we find her in the boat bays when we're not even allowed in there?"

"You climbed the racks?" I almost choked. The racks where the boats were stored were twenty feet high. And the floor below was bare concrete. "What were you thinking? You could have fallen and cracked your head—"

"Mom. Trust me. They're easier than the jungle gym. Julie's just mad because they couldn't find me and I won."

"You didn't win; you cheated. We thought you got kidnapped. We spent the whole night looking for you."

"Molly," I pressed on, "if Tony Boschetti'd seen you up there, he'd have our hides." The house manager was strict about boathouse safety.

"Our hides?" Molly asked.

"Hides-and-go-seek," Emily explained.

"You are simply not allowed in the boat bays unless you're with me. It's not safe. Understood?"

Molly nodded soberly.

"Good. Now, can we go?" I headed for the door.

Susan followed. The girls straggled behind. "Can we stop at Harry's for water ice? We've been waiting all night."

Harry, the unofficial mayor of Boathouse Row, was one of several vendors who sold balloons, sodas, candy and frozen treats from trucks under umbrellas in front of the boathouses. Harry knew everyone along the Row, and everyone knew him, especially kids.

"It's too late, Molls. Harry closed up a long time ago."

"Aw, that sucks," Julie said.

"Julie." Susan spoke reflexively. "Watch your language."

Molly took my hand. "Mom?" She squinted up at me. "What's in your hair?"

I touched my head, retrieved a skinny stem of a river vine.

"Wow. You're all wet—" She eyed me, head-to-toe, noticing me for the first time.

"What'd you do, flip?" Julie smirked, just then realizing that we were indeed damp.

Susan and I looked at each other, searching for a quick response. Nothing came to mind.

"You did?" Julie's eyes widened and her pout became a grin.

"You guys flipped? Emily—" Molly burst into giggles. "They flipped!"

Emily and Molly rolled with laughter. Apparently, the idea of us flipping was hilarious.

"What happened? Did you hit a bridge?" Julie went to Susan and began pulling tiny pieces of green stuff from her hair. "Yuck. Mom, you seriously need a shower."

"Let's go, kiddoes." Susan kept walking. "We're wet and tired. And it's late."

Finally, Susan and I herded the girls down the stairs to the door, where Officer Olsen waited. The girls asked endless questions. "How'd you flip? Did you crash? Is your boat hurt? Are you hurt? Why's that policeman here?"

Answers were tiresome, especially that last one. But Susan and I managed to avoid details, dodging questions with commands. "Watch where you're going," we said. Or, "Shh, you'll wake Tony."

Tony's attic apartment was on the top floor of the boathouse. As I mentioned his name, I glanced back up the stairs toward his door and saw a man, backlit by the hall light, at the railing. Wearing nothing but a towel, he stared down at us. Was it Tony? I couldn't see his face, but it had to be. Oh, damn, I thought. We must have awakened him. I didn't want to deal with Tony just then. Didn't want to explain what had happened or hear him rip us for rowing alone at night, flipping the boat, leaving it upriver, bringing the kids to the boathouse.

For a moment, he and I stared at each other in the dim light. Then, wordlessly, he turned and, towel flapping, headed up the hallway toward the attic stairs. Odd, I thought, that Tony hadn't said anything. Not one word. Maybe he wasn't as difficult as his reputation implied.

Susan hustled the girls out the door. Their tiff forgotten, they tittered with excitement when they found out they were going to ride in Officer Olsen's patrol car to the lot where Susan's car was parked.

Finally, we were going home.

FIVE

ll I wanted was a bath. A long hot soapy bath that would steam away the chill of the river, soak away the touch of dead flesh. I rushed Molly into bed; then, peeling off my damp socks and spandex unisuit, I turned on the hot water, poured in some bubbles, lit a few candles and switched off the overhead light. In the tub, I lay back, absorbing the heat, relaxing my muscles, my bones, letting the water rise around me, enclosing me. Suddenly, though, the moving water held me too tight, began to strangle me like a river. A hot river this time, but a river, nonetheless. Stop it, I told myself. You're being ridiculous. Just relax. Lie back. Focus on the heat, the comfort. I closed my eyes, letting my legs float. And slowly, surfacing in the darkness, I saw the pale, vacant face of a woman. My eyes opened and I sat up suddenly, splashing bubbly water over the side of the tub.

Okay, the bath wasn't working. Maybe I'd just wash off and relax with a glass of wine. I dunked under the bubbles, rinsing my hair, my ears, my nose. Sponging off all the places the river had flooded. Finally, the steam began to do its work, soothing my bruised and aching muscles, making them heavy and slow. I leaned back, resting, letting my limbs drift, closing my eyes. And heard someone moving in the room.

For a moment, I didn't dare open my eyes. I pretended I hadn't heard while I thought about what to do. Jump out of the bathtub screaming and streak out of the room? Throw a towel— or a shampoo bottle?

"Mom?"

Molly was perched on the toilet cover, the seat I often occupied while she bathed.

"Geez, Molly—I thought you were asleep," I breathed.

"I'm not tired. It's too hot to sleep."

I had no energy for a conversation. "You'll be tired in the morning."

She grinned slyly. "Too tired to go to school?"

"School's almost out. Another few days—"

"School's boring. All we do anymore is watch movies and have assemblies."

I breathed deeply, collecting myself, focusing on the moment. I waited a few seconds before speaking. Then, calmly but firmly, I said, "It's late, Molly. We'll talk about this tomorrow, okay? Go back to bed; I'll come tuck you in."

She didn't budge. For a while she poked at her gums, feeling for incoming teeth.

"I want to skip. Can you write a note and say I'm sick?"

"No. That would be lying."

"Please. They boss you. 'Watch this movie. Color this picture.' What if I don't feel like it?"

"Molls, just hang in. Next week you'll be done." If Molly hated kindergarten, what would she think of first grade? Or high school?

"It's hot in my class. There's only one fan, no AC. I don't want to go, Mom. I just want to hang out."

Hang out? There it was again, that teenage tone. "Molly, you've got to go."

"It sucks, Mom."

I didn't comment on her language. I was triaging our fights. "Sometimes you have to do things you don't like."

"Pleeeeze don't make me."

I was tired and I knew she could easily keep pestering me

all night. "Let's talk about this tomorrow, okay?" Damn. I'd weakened.

She sighed, giving up for now. "Were you scared?"

Scared of what? It took a moment to figure out what she meant. "When we flipped? Only a little. We can swim and the boat floats, so we just hung on and rolled it back over. Then we climbed in and rowed to shore."

"But then, why was the policeman there?"

Oh dear. What was that speech Susan and I had prepared? Why couldn't I remember it? "Oh, Molls. It's a long story and I'm way too tired to tell it now. Please, go back to bed."

"Was somebody killed? Is that why there was a policeman?"

I didn't want to answer, didn't want to tell the truth or to lie. "Sometimes there are accidents on the river. Once in a while, people drown."

"Somebody drowned? Really? Who?"

"I don't know exactly."

"You found a drowned person? A lady or a man?"

"A lady."

"Did she fall in the water? What happened?"

"We don't know yet. Nick was there. He'll try to find out."

She nodded, satisfied with the answer. Rubbing her eyes, she stifled a yawn.

Clearly, my bath was over. I grabbed a towel and stood, pulling the plug. "Come on," I said. "Let's tuck you in."

I pulled on my robe and together we blew out the candles. Holding hands, we walked to her room and she climbed into bed. Snug under her covers, eyelids drooping, though, Molly still fought sleep. She gripped my hand, not letting me leave.

"Mom." Her voice was sober. "What if you drowned when you flipped?"

"I didn't drown." I smoothed her curls with my free hand and smiled to reassure her. "And I won't."

She blinked a few times, not accepting that answer. "But if you did?"

"It won't happen," I said again, kissing her forehead.

"But what if it did? Who would I live with?"

"Nick would take care of you." I understood her anxiety. She was adopted, had already lost one set of parents. And I was a single mom. For all Molly's bravado, she was a little kid who needed to know she was safe. So I went on. "And not just Nick. Susan and Tim would take care of you. And Karen. And Davinder. And Ileana and . . ." I chanted on for a while, rhythmically listing our friends, people she knew who loved her. I was still going strong, naming Aunt Lanie in New York and our dozens of cousins in Chicago when I heard a soft snore and realized I could stop. Molly, thank God, was finally asleep.

SIX

And then, I was alone. Heavy with fatigue, I pulled on a nightgown and climbed into bed. And lay there, unable to sleep. Each time I began to drift, I felt myself tilting, spilling into the river, thrashing upside down in the water, choking, and I kicked myself awake. When I closed my eyes, I felt the gentle caress of hair against my face, the floating weight of a dead woman in my arms.

Who were those women? What had happened to them? How had so many bodies ended up in the river together? Memories and questions swirled through my mind. I rolled over. I rearranged the pillows. I turned the light on, then switched it off.

Finally I got up, wandered downstairs, poured myself a glass of wine and wandered into the living room of my small brownstone house, where I curled up under an afghan on my purple velvet sofa.

The sofa was, without contest, my favorite piece of furniture. Overstuffed and oversized, it swelled like a big purple cloud in the middle of an eclectic, usually cluttered, room. I sank into it, sipping cabernet, drawing comfort from the familiar and the personal. I gazed at the treasures crammed onto the built-in shelves. My great-grandmother Bella's weighty brass mortar and pestle; her porcelain soup tureen, bursting with dried flowers. A geisha doll my uncle Dave had sent my mother while serving in Japan after World War II. Books, photo albums. A painted clay sculpture Molly had made at school that looked sort of like a mongrel cat. And, on the bottom shelf, an enlarged framed picture of Nick, Molly and me, taken at Cape May in March. The ocean wind had been blowing Molly's curls against Nick's face, hiding part of the angry scar that crossed his cheek, almost blocking the paralysis that allowed only half his face to smile.

Paintings lined the living room walls, most of them by aspiring artists I knew. A bold abstract of yellows and umbers, a fat nude, a delicate etching of a farm beneath a crescent moon. One, the brooding profile of an olive-skinned woman, was new, painted just this spring. By me. I assessed it for the zillionth time. The eyebrow, a dark check mark, was the focal point of a face dabbed with purples and greens. Despite its flaws, I liked it. More important, I'd finished it. My first painting in years.

The room, as usual, was cluttered. Molly's red shorts and a lone sandal, a half-finished bead project, a worn stuffed bear, an empty glass and plate. Nick's library books stacked on the coffee table. In the far corner, my StairMaster, sulking with dust and disuse.

I sipped wine on soft cushions. Life, I assured myself, was pretty good. I liked my job at the Institute; being an art therapist was challenging and important, even though it hadn't been my ambition. Painting had been my dream. But I was beginning to paint again, gradually. And art therapy paid the bills.

And Nick, I thought, was also good. For the first time since my divorce, I was half of a couple again, and so far I hadn't messed up. I still had my issues, of course, but I'd gotten less protective of my turf. Less possessive of Molly. And, even if I hadn't completely torn down my protective walls, I'd let Nick pass through most of them. Sometimes I even managed to trust him. Nick, Molly and I were blending, feeling almost like a real family.

Yes, life was pretty much okay. I had close friends, a cozy home full of clutter. A job that was meaningful. A relationship that was relatively stable and a child I adored. Whatever had happened on the river had been an anomaly. I needed to relax and put the night into perspective, focus on the positives.

Still, I stayed awake, staring into the colored light of a stained-glass lamp, listening to sounds of the city at night. Distant sirens, screeching brakes. Occasional blasts of blaring music from a passing car. And, loudest of all, the impenetrable silence of empty air.

SEVEN

When Nick finally came home the sun was up, and so was I. I greeted him by leaning into his arms and staying there. We asked each other how we each were, and we both lied. Nick was pale and drawn, his blue eyes overly bright, as if haunted.

"What?" I asked. "Tell me."

"You sure you want to hear?"

"I have to. Nick, I was there."

He nodded, touching my cheek, kissing the top of my head.

"There were nineteen."

Nineteen dead women? "Lord." I tried to comprehend the number. "How could nineteen women drown at once? Couldn't any of them swim—Or call for help?"

He watched me gently, patiently. "I doubt they drowned, Zoe."

What? Oh. His answer began to sink in. The women had died before they'd hit the water. Someone must have put them there. I couldn't grasp it, even though I'd seen it. Nineteen bodies? How does somebody put nineteen bodies in the river?

"But then, how did they die?"

"We don't know yet. We're waiting on the autopsies."

Of course he'd say that. Nick never said more than he had to, didn't volunteer his theories.

"They were Asian."

Asian? "All of them?"

"Every one."

I hadn't noticed. Odd, I thought. I'd looked into a woman's face and hadn't even noticed her race.

Nick was telling me that he had to get back to work in a few hours. Had to get to bed. He slid an arm around my neck. "How about you join me?"

It was still early; Molly would sleep for a while. So, trying not to think, I lay beside Nick, huddling against him. I kept still, listening to him breathe, watching the rise and fall of his chest. For a few minutes, I pretended, as I suspect he did, to be asleep. Then he rolled over, burying his face in my neck, and whispered muffled words.

His whisper tickled. "What?" I hugged him with a reflexive giggle.

"No joke," he said. "I mean it."

"You mean what?" I had no idea what he was talking about.

He kissed my throat, then looked deep into my eyes. "Look, the timing is good, with Molly getting older. And, hell." He looked away, into the air. "You get to a point where you have to decide. Do you want to storm ahead or just drift? Grab on to life or let it slip past you?"

Nick sounded depressed. I didn't know what to say; I wasn't sure what he was getting at. And I wasn't in the most cheerful of moods, either.

"We love each other," he went on. "We're good together. So how about it?"

How about what? I waited, wondering, heart fluttering as it hit me—Nick must be asking me to marry him. I smiled, tears welling up in my eyes, about to give my answer.

Nick's pale eyes gazed into mine. "C'mon, Zoe," he whispered, enfolding me in his arms. "Let's make a baby."

EIGHT

Of course, I didn't take him literally. Actually, I was a little disappointed, having anticipated a marriage proposal. I thought "Let's make a baby" was just a sweet way of asking me to make love. But that morning, physically exhausted and emotionally drained, we found respite not in sleep but in each other. Nick held me more gently than ever before, and our bodies melted together with almost painful tenderness. Each kiss lingered, each touch connected. Somehow, we crossed the barriers of our skins, merging into parts of the same creature. I joined Nick, following his lead, not caring where he'd take me or how long we'd remain.

The next thing I knew, the phone was ringing. And Molly was tugging at my arm.

"Mom—I don't want to go—pleeeeze—"

I blinked, orienting myself. I'd slept heavily, dreamlessly. I had no idea what time it was. What day it was. What month or season. Go where? What was she talking about?

"You said maybe I might not have to. You said we'd talk about it today."

Oh. I began to remember. One by one, images floated through my mind. Black water. Dead women. Lights and sirens. And Molly complaining that she didn't want to go to school.

She was continuing the conversation of the night before as if seconds, not hours, had passed.

"Let me get up," I sat, my head protesting vehemently, and glanced at the clock. Ten after eight. I'd slept for maybe forty-five minutes. My brain began rattling back to life. Oh dear. The school bus would be here in minutes.

"Please, Mom," she whined.

"Stop whining, Molls. We've got to hustle." Memories stirred. I looked around, coming back to life. "Where's Nick? Did he get the phone?"

Nick had a small condo in Center City and a home in Chester County, but he often stayed with us, getting up before Molly and going downstairs so she wouldn't see us sharing a bed. The situation was neither honest nor ideal, but it had evolved wordlessly, and Molly accepted Nick's frequent presence naturally, without question.

"But Mom—" More whining.

Wait, I told myself. Listen to her; maybe she has good reasons for not wanting to go. I'd researched kindergartens carefully before selecting one; hers was rated one of the best in the Philadelphia area. But maybe something was really wrong there. Maybe there were bullies—or maybe the teacher was a child abuser.

"Molly, tell me. What's wrong? Why don't you want to go?"

"I already told you."

"Tell me again."

"It's everything."

"Like what?"

"It's stupid. We don't do anything."

"That's it? It's just boring?"

She cocked her head, realizing she had to come up with more. "And Mrs. Rutledge bosses you. She makes you stay in your seat."

I put my hand on her head, tossled her curls. "Well, it doesn't sound so bad. There're just a few days left."

"But Mom—"

"Molls, it's too late to skip today." I was on my feet, jumping into action mode. "The bus is already on the way. It'll be here in a couple of minutes. Are you ready?"

No. She wasn't. Molly was still in her pajamas.

"But you said . . ." she was whining.

"I said we'd talk about it. Look. You've only got four days left. Stick it out."

"Four days! No, Mom—that's so unfair—"

The phone was ringing again. Lord. Who was calling this early? I reached for it, but it stopped. Nick must have gotten it again. I picked it up anyway.

". . . from the *Daily News*." It was a man's voice. "Is Zoe Hayes there?"

"Mom," Molly nagged.

"Shh—" I gestured, telling her to wait. She stamped her foot, pouting.

"She's not available," Nick was saying. "Just like she wasn't when you called half an hour ago."

He'd called half an hour ago? Why hadn't I heard the phone?

"When can I speak to her? I'd need just a couple of—"

"I have no idea."

"Whom am I speaking with, if I may ask?"

Nick hung up, and so did I.

"Mom. That's so unfair," Molly continued where she'd left off. "I hate school. It's like jail—"

Jail? How would she know what jail was like? And how could a six-year-old argue so persistently and articulately? Molly was, as always, a bafflement to me.

"Three Corners School is not anything like jail, Molls."

"It is too. They tell you what to do and where to go. And what to wear—you have to wear their stupid skirts. And you have to eat their stupid slop for lunch."

"Molly, stop. The bus is coming. Go, get your clothes on." My head throbbed. I'd paid a hefty chunk for her to go to that "jail." Over three thousand dollars a semester for that private kindergarten near the Art Museum. The school had music, a library, art, drama, sports, hands-on math and science, computers—every sort of subject a child could possibly want. Hell, forget children— I'd have liked to go. I couldn't understand how anyone, Molly included, could be unhappy there.

"Mom, I can't believe you're making me go. It's torture."

Torture? "Get dressed, Molls."

"Mrs. Rutledge is a moron. If I have to go for a whole 'nother week, I'll die . . ."

"You'll die?" Nick walked in, scooping Molly into his arms. "We can't have that. What's the trouble?" He was playful, but his eyes were somber.

"She's going to be late for school," I said.

He set her down. "Then you better hurry," he told her.

Molly never argued with Nick. She was often coy or obviously manipulative, but she never argued with him. In some ways, I was jealous of her open adoration for him.

"Okay," she sighed. "I'll go. But only today. Only one more day." And she stomped off to get her things.

The phone began to ring again.

"Don't bother," Nick sighed. "It's probably the press again. They've been calling all morning."

All morning? "I only heard one call."

He smiled. "You slept right through them. There've been about six."

"Really?"

Grinning his half-grin, he hugged me. "You were snoring." He kissed me softly.

"Not possible. I don't snore. You dreamed it." I reached my arms around his neck and, as if on cue, the phone began again. We tried to ignore it, but the mood had shattered and we separated. I watched the phone, waiting for it to stop.

"Mom!" Molly yelled. "The phone! I'll get it—"

"No, Molls. Just let it ring."

"But Mom—" she yelled back. "Somebody's calling!"

Mercifully, the ringing stopped.

"I called Tony," Nick said. "He had the boat rowed back to Humberton. You and Susan don't have to worry about it."

Damn, I'd forgotten all about getting the boat. "Was Tony mad?"

"Didn't seem to be. He was mostly concerned about you and Susan. Wanted to hear all about it." Nick stepped into the shower. I followed him into the bathroom and looked in the mirror at an alarming woman with wild and tangled hair resembling jungle vines. Her eyes were hollowed out, and there was a fresh multicolored bruise on her left cheek. Disturbed, I looked away, squeezing cinnamon paste onto my toothbrush. It slithered out and wound around, clung snakelike to the bristles. Nothing seemed normal.

"Everyone in creation has called here this morning." Nick talked above the water. "Reporters. Cyrus Poole, that talk-radio guy. The *Good Morning Show*. And your friends. Let me see— Davinder, Karen, Marla. They read about you in the paper and were worried. And Dr. Arash and Amy Dennis from the Institute. And Susan's called about six times, frantic. The press is hounding her, too. The story's all over the news, Zoe. Headlines in the *Inquirer* and *Daily News*. And, not to alarm you, a couple of television trucks are setting up outside, ready to pounce."

"Oh, Lord." Patting my face dry, I stared at the mirror, feeling assaulted, examining an egg-sized scrape on my chin.

"You don't have to talk to them, Zoe. If I were you, I wouldn't."

"What do they want?"

"You know. Moans. Tears. Shock. Blood, if possible. The usual."

"I don't want to talk to them."

"Then don't."

Nick's cell phone rang. He reached for a towel while I handed him the phone, and he took the call running his hand through his hair, cursing. Frowning, he finally hung up and went into the bedroom, plopping down on the edge of the bed.

In general, Nick was a poker player, not revealing much, keeping his work separate from his personal life, refusing to discuss even the most general aspects of his cases. But this time I was personally involved. I had a right, I thought, to ask what was wrong. To my surprise, he answered.

"No surprise, really. The FBI and INS are yanking the case."

"Oh." I didn't say more. If I appeared too curious or asked too many questions, Nick would clam up and tell me nothing.

"The women were foreign nationals. There's really no way to trace them, but they were illegals. Maybe from Malaysia. Possibly Hong Kong."

"But how can they tell?" I didn't understand. Did an illegal immigrant look different from a legal one? An Asian different from an Asian American?

"There's an ongoing investigation into the business."

I wasn't following. "The business?"

"Trafficking." He rubbed his eyes.

I still didn't get it. The business of trafficking? But trafficking what? Women? As in slaves? Wait, that couldn't be right. "Are you serious?"

Nick stood and began to get dressed. "They bring women into the country, smuggle them or lure them here on false pretenses, promising them jobs or husbands and so on. Women come from Asia, Central America, Eastern Europe. All over. Then they get sold into prostitution, porno, factory labor, whatever. As slaves." He stepped into a pair of khakis but didn't zip them. "Murphy told me about a Park Avenue couple that got busted last month. They bought a Guatemalan woman to clean their apartment and baby-sit their kids. Apparently, they thought she was a good investment; they planned to sell up after they trained her. To make a profit."

I swallowed, trying to absorb what he was saying. Slavery. In America. In the twenty-first century. It made no sense. I checked Nick's face for traces of sick humor, but there were none. He was serious. And I'd seen the bodies myself—hell, I'd gone swimming with them. Still, I had trouble accepting what he'd said. "Why don't they run away? Or call for help?"

"I guess they don't speak much English." He pulled on a light blue sport shirt. "Plus they don't know their rights. Don't know they have any rights."

I still didn't quite get it. "But how does the FBI know that the women in the river are part of that?"

Nick was buttoning his shirt, tucking it into his pants. "There's evidence. Typical of the trade."

I waited, not daring to ask.

"Manacle marks on the wrists and ankles."

Manacle marks?

"And you saw their shoulders."

On its own, my hand rose to my shoulder. "What about them?"

"You didn't see?"

No. "See what?"

"Damn. I thought you'd seen them. Look, Zoe. This stuff isn't being released to the press. It can't leave this room."

I nodded. "Of course not."

Nick sat beside me, hesitating, measuring what he said. "The women had tattoos on their shoulders. Three small curved parallel lines." He traced the lines on my arm. "That's the logo of the cartel that sells them."

I shuddered, suddenly cold. The women had been branded? Labeled with logos, like cereal boxes? Like cans of soup?

"This cartel makes drug dealers look like teddy bears. They'd just as soon slaughter anyone who looks their way. Which is another reason you don't want to talk to the press. Keep a low profile on this."

I nodded. The women had been manacled, marked, murdered and dumped into the river.

"By the way, when you flipped, did you or Susan lose a Humberton hat?"

A hat? "No."

Nick frowned. "You're sure?"

"Of course I'm sure. Why?"

He tried to sound casual. "Just wondered."

"Nick, tell me. Was there a Humberton hat in the river?"

He watched me for a moment, then took a deep breath. "This is strictly confidential, Zoe. A Humberton hat was pulled out of the water with the women. Caught in their clothes. I thought it might be yours or Susan's."

"No." I pictured a floating floral skirt, a hat tangled in the hem. "It's not ours."

A Humberton hat? Was someone from Humberton Barge involved in the deaths? In the slave trade? No, I told myself. That was impossible. The hat had to be a coincidence. Probably the women had floated into someone's lost hat and carried it along with them as they drifted downriver. That had to be it.

"What I'm telling you stays here, Zoe. Not even Susan—"

"Of course." I nodded.

Nick had confided in me. I was flattered, amazed. But Nick frowned and stared into the air, eyes smoldering. Oh, God. Was there more? I almost didn't want to know.

"Nick?" He was scaring me. "Are you okay?"

He looked at me, surprised, almost as if he'd forgotten I was there. "Sorry. It's the damned FBI. I can't stop them from yanking the case, but until they do the paperwork, as far as I'm concerned the case is mine. There were nineteen homicides committed in this city and I won't give up on them. Not yet."

I didn't know what to say. Nick had just warned me about the slave cartel, how dangerous it was. Why couldn't he stay out of this mess and let the FBI do their job? I sat beside him, feeling hot anger radiate from his skin. No, Nick wouldn't let go. He couldn't. Not when nineteen dead women with tattoos and shackle marks had been found floating down the Schuylkill River.

A horn honked outside, and I realized it had been honking repeatedly for a while. Oh, Lord. I hadn't been paying attention. It was the bus from Three Corners School.

NINE

"Molly—" I called.

Molly didn't answer.

"Molls—" I called again, hurrying to her room, finding it empty. "Molly?"

Damn. She was ignoring me. Refusing to go. Being strong-willed and stubborn, hiding to avoid school. I ran downstairs, opened the front door to wave at the bus driver.

"Ms. Hayes—Zoe Hayes?" Someone shoved a microphone into my face.

I recoiled instinctively, shoving it away.

"Zoe, can we ask you about the events at the river—"

"Just one minute—she's coming!" I yelled to the driver, and slamming the door on the microphone, I raced through the house, calling Molly, reminding her that she'd agreed to go, pleading with her, threatening her, even bribing her, using every ploy I could think of to get her to come out. I searched the powder room, my studio, the living room, the coat and broom closets, the kitchen.

"Find her?" Nick called from upstairs.

I looked up at him and shook my head, eyes tearing. No, I hadn't found her. I was tired, aching, bruised, and suddenly overwhelmed. I'd survived a cold swim with nineteen dead women and was able to face a media frenzy, but an obstinate six-year-old was reducing me to tears.

"Molls," Nick called. "Yo. Hop to. The bus is waiting."

From out of nowhere, Molly bounced into the kitchen, all smiles and sunshine. Grabbing her backpack, she hugged Nick, then me. "See you later, Mom. 'Bye, Nick." And lightly kissing my cheek, she skipped out the door, bumping into the cameramen.

"Um—Mom?" She stopped on the steps, confused.

"Hi there," one of them began to interview her. "What's your name?"

"Ignore them." I pushed the door open and stepped onto the porch beside her. "Don't even talk to them—"

At the sight of me, reporters started calling, "Ms. Hayes? What were you doing on the river last night? Can you answer a few questions?"

Molly stood still, warily eyeing the news crews. Sheltering her with my arms, glaring fiercely, I forged a pathway through the squawking crowd, led Molly down the front steps and walked her to the bus. When she was safely on board and the bus had driven off, I turned back and faced the throng. And once again, having no choice, I closed my eyes and plunged, swimming blindly through a mass of bodies—hands, heads and arms—in order to get home.

TEN

The house was finally quiet, except for the ringing phone, which I'd begun to tune out. I sat on a stool at the kitchen counter and stared out at the street, watching traffic and pedestrians pass the lone television truck that was still parked outside. Nick had managed to convince most of the press to go away before he left for work, but a persistent young news reporter remained, recording her segment over and over again with my house as her background, doing take after take because the breeze blew her hair into her face. Or a truck grumbled too loudly up the street. Or horns honked and people hooted because they recognized her. I sipped coffee, ignoring the incessant ringing of the phone, hoping the news team would finally get it right and go away.

I moved to the sofa, my limbs weighing tons, my head pounding, my whole body wanting to crawl back to bed and hide under the comforter. But instead I picked up the phone and made a call.

"Thank God," Susan breathed. "Where've you been? I've been calling you all morning—"

"I didn't answer the phone. I thought it was the press—"

"Oh, God. It's been a damned circus here. All we needed were dancing elephants. The contractors couldn't get past all the cameras and trucks. And, right in front of the microphones, the bathroom guy tells me that our plumbing's so old, they're going to have to replace all the pipes with copper. It'll cost a fortune. And the deck guys are scurrying around carrying saws and lumber, so I'm waiting for someone to break a camera or a head, and—guess what—I'd be liable—"

"Susan, stop." I had no patience, couldn't listen to her tales of household repairs.

"Sorry, I'm going nuts." She raced, manic. "Tim's ballistic. You know how private he is. When he saw the press at our door, he started cursing and threatening to sue. His veins popped out like sausages. I thought he'd have a stroke."

I pictured stocky Tim with strings of purple hot dogs in his forehead.

"And the school bus couldn't get through. The kids got tired of making faces out the windows, so they went upstairs and—oh my God—Julie and Lisa threw water balloons at the TV crews."

"You're kidding." I couldn't help laughing. "Really? They hit anyone?"

"Dead-on. Some reporter from Channel 10 was drenched. So, I'm screaming at the kids, and Tim's screaming at the press, and the press is screaming at all of us—dear Lord, I can't imagine what they'll write about us—"

Headlines flooded my mind. "Press coverage all wet. Man's head explodes into kielbasa."

"If they air what went on here, we'll have to move."

"No, you won't, Susan. If they show it, their ratings will soar. And you'll probably get your own reality show."

"Not funny, Zoe. None of this is funny. And maybe we shouldn't discuss it on the phone."

Why not? Were our phones tapped? Who was listening in—the feds? INS? The slave traffickers?

"I'll meet you at the deli." She didn't offer an option. "Before we do anything, we've got to get the boat back—"

"No, it's done. Nick took care of it."

"Really? We don't have to row it back?"

"No. He got Tony to do it." Thank God. I couldn't imagine rowing again. Not yet. Not ever.

"Great. Then let's go eat."

I couldn't think about food, either. "You're hungry?"

"What does hungry have to do with it? Be ready. Ten minutes."

I looked at the clock. Almost nine thirty. As we hung up, the phone rang again. I picked it up reflexively, expecting Susan again, hoping for Nick, ready for a reporter.

"Hello?" I heard background noises, but nobody answered. "Hello?" I said again.

Nothing. Hanging up, I hurried to get dressed.

ELEVEN

Only a few people sat at booths in the deli; after nine, the place generally quieted down until lunch hour. Susan and I sat in the middle aisle near the back, away from the others.

Shadows circled Susan's dark eyes; her normally shiny dark hair was pulled back, tucked under a baseball cap. She wore tan baggy capris and a too-tight-under-the-arms-and-around-the-bust pale green T-shirt advertising Smokey's Bar-B-Q Ribs; probably, she'd thrown on some of her daughter Lisa's clothes. She'd picked me up in Tim's Lexus and hadn't stopped talking for a moment.

"So I was up all night," she continued as we slid into the booth. "Baked banana bread at four in the morning, washed the kitchen floor and the Venetian blinds. And then the phone started around six, with the press calling, and the phone woke up everyone but Tim, who can sleep through an earthquake. Worse than that, he can sleep through his own snoring. The kids got up, though, so it turned out good that I had the banana bread. And then the contractors started showing up. Pure chaos. And, sometime, I have to get to the office; I have to prepare depositions for the Jason White case." I had no idea who Jason White was, maybe a defense client, maybe a murder victim. Susan rattled on in an adrenaline rush until Gladys, our waitress, interrupted.

"What'll it be?" Gladys was usually glum, but that morning she actually smiled, revealing the stainless-steel star on her right front tooth, and offered a "How ya doing?" in my direction.

I ordered for us both; Gladys had a long-standing grudge against Susan and hadn't spoken to her for years. No one, probably not even Gladys, could remember why. But if Susan was to eat, I had to order her food.

"Bitch," Susan said when Gladys left. She always said "Bitch" when Gladys left. "Here—have you seen this?" She took the paper from her bag and shoved the front page at me. There were photos. The river lit by spotlights, body bags lined up on the dock. Headlines screaming, "Nineteen Bodies Floating in Schuylkill." And a subheadline, suggesting that the women, all Asian, had been intended sex slaves.

I scanned the article. Authorities estimated that a million people each year were sold into slavery. . . . Human trafficking was a thriving worldwide industry. Someone from INS said that the deceased women had probably been brought to the United States to be forced into prostitution. . . . Probably had been told that, if they went to the authorities, they or their families would be killed. Last night, nineteen women had been found. . . . And then I stopped reading. My eyes froze, staring at the newsprint, unable to go on.

"Zoe Hayes," it said. I gazed at the newsprint, blinking, seeing "Susan Cummings" in the same sentence. Oh dear. Our names were in the paper. In print. On the front page.

"We got ink." Susan clasped her hands together, her knuckles white. A criminal defense attorney, Susan generally saw publicity of any kind as a good thing. But today she seemed edgy, bothered by it. "People know who we are."

People? Did she mean traffickers? Gladys swooped by, dropping two mugs of coffee in the center of our table as she passed.

"So, tell me," Susan asked. "What did Nick say?"

I hedged, reaching for a mug. "Not much. You know Nick."

"But he must have said something." She poured sweetener and cream into her mug.

All I could think of were the things I'd promised not to mention. The hat from Humberton Barge. The tattoos on the women's shoulders. "Nick was pretty wiped when he got in. I mean, there were nineteen bodies to process." I shivered.

"Yeah, I know. But what about the slave thing?" She pointed to the front page. "They were being sold right here, in Philadelphia—didn't he even mention that?" Her voice was too loud. I didn't look around, but I could feel scattered stares.

"Of course." I kept my voice low. "But mostly, he was pissed that the FBI and INS are taking over the case. Because of the international stuff." I hated being in the middle, having to hide what I knew. "But honestly, I wasn't in shape to hear many details last night."

"So what do you think?" She lowered her voice. "How'd a bunch of Asian sex slaves end up in our river?"

I had no idea.

"Do you think they drowned? All together? That doesn't seem possible. I mean, they'd have made a racket kicking and splashing. They'd have screamed for help—unless . . ." She stopped to think, taking a sip of coffee.

"Unless?"

"Unless they were unconscious when they hit the water. Maybe drugged or something. But why? I don't get why they'd kill them. It'd be bad for business. You wouldn't throw a truckload of cattle into the water on the way to market."

My head was throbbing again. "Cattle?"

"From the trafficker's point of view, the women were just like cattle or cabbages. Or soda cans—"

"I get it." She was probably right. But my stomach was in a knot, twisting as she continued her list.

"—Or heating oil. They were just a product to be marketed. So, instead of selling them, why would they dump them and lose the profit?"

I rubbed my temples.

Susan wouldn't stop. "Unless—maybe they were damaged goods. Unsuitable for market. Maybe they all had AIDS—"

A gust of lilac announced Gladys's return. "French toast, bacon, OJ, toasted bagel with." Our plates clattered onto the table. "Anything else?"

"No, thank you, Gladys," Susan said.

Gladys ignored her and stared at me, waiting for my reply.

"We're fine, thanks," I managed.

Gladys winked at Susan. "Enjoy your meal." She smiled.

"What was that?" Susan asked. "Did you see that? She spoke to me!"

"Who knows. Maybe she spit in your food before she served it."

"Eeww. She wouldn't, would she?" She picked up a piece of bacon and turned it over, eyeing it closely.

"It's probably okay. Gladys's saliva can't be as toxic as the river water we swallowed."

"Yes, it can," she shuddered. "The woman's venomous. Speaking of river water, though"—Susan rotated a forkful of French toast, looking at it from all sides—"we can't let this defeat us. We need to get back on the horse. The longer we wait, the harder it'll get."

Oh, no. She wanted to row again. "We haven't waited all that long, Susan. It's been like fourteen hours."

"That's not the point. We should have gotten into the boat last night and rowed the damned thing back to Humberton."

I watched her chow down, knowing better than to argue. I recognized the signs. Normally, Susan was a powerhouse, capable of dictating legal briefs into a recorder while kneading pie dough, braiding Emily's hair and organizing repairmen while composing a closing argument. But, for all her routine energy, there were times when Susan had dramatic mood swings, flipping in a heartbeat from elated to glum, energized to enervated. She was probably a touch manic-depressive, and when she was at either extreme of up or down—which she seemed to be at the moment—reasoning with her was futile. She could be at once fragile and ferocious; it was best to let her mood run its course. I regarded my toasted bagel in silence without appetite and took a sip of coffee, its murkiness reminding me of another dark liquid, how it had immersed me, flooding my throat, my nose.

"Anyhow, we still have a date with Coach Everett tomorrow afternoon. Five o'clock."

"Oh, hell, we do?" No way. I couldn't face getting into a boat again. Or enduring Coach Everett's ego. "Can't we postpone it?"

"Come on, Zoe. You can't give up just because of one bad row."

Is that what it was? "Swimming with nineteen dead women was 'one bad row'?"

"That's the point. It wasn't our rowing that was the problem. It was the bodies. We're getting good. Remember how it felt right before we hit them?"

Of course I did. We'd been flying. Out of control.

Susan went on, pressing me to row. At five o'clock, she argued, it would still be bright daylight. And Coach Everett would be there in a launch in case of emergency. And besides, rowing was the only thing without calories that calmed her down.

"Really?" I shouldn't have asked. "What about sex?"

"It's fattening. Sex makes me hungry." She gulped coffee, washing down a mouthful of French toast. "Actually, Tim and I eat more after sex than any other time. Tim'll get out of bed and put away half a gallon of ice cream, seriously."

"Thanks for that, Susan." I pictured Tim standing naked at the freezer, spoon in hand. Lord. No wonder Tim had such a hefty paunch.

Luckily, Susan didn't pursue the topic; she went back to rowing. "If we don't go tomorrow, we're wimps. We'll never get over last night. We'll be stuck in that night."

I reached for the cream cheese, stalling, hoping to come up with an excuse. I smeared the stuff slowly, coming up with nothing. "I don't know," I finally managed. Great, I thought. How pathetic. Why couldn't I just say no?

"Zoe, we've got to get out there sooner or later. Sooner's better."

I sighed, took a bite of bagel, chewed it with a dry mouth.

Swallowed with difficulty. I had no escape. No excuse, except dread. And dread, I told myself, was no excuse. Don't be a wimp, I scolded. I pictured horseback riders falling and climbing back on. Skiers falling and getting back up. Rowers flipping, and cold black water rushing up my nose and into my ears. Stop, I told myself. Get over it. "Okay," I muttered. "Five o'clock."

"Good girl. I'll call and confirm." She chomped. "After all, the regatta's only a couple of weeks away."

Oh, Lord. The thought of the regatta knotted my stomach. I gulped lukewarm coffee and changed the subject. "How were your girls today? Still mad at Molly?"

"No, that's history. Lisa saw the headlines and—poof—I was a celebrity. And the press was calling and the TV vans outside. Believe me, they've moved on. How about Molly?"

"She figured out that somebody died in the river. Now she's afraid I'll drown. And she doesn't want to go to school anymore."

"Poor kid. She must be scared. She'll calm down after a few days. Once things get back—"

"All finished?" Gladys grinned in my direction, flashing her silver star. "Anything else?"

"No, thank you," Susan sat up straight as she answered. "Everything was delicious."

Ignoring her, Gladys caught sight of the newspaper folded on the table. She lost her grin, nodding at it. "What about that?" She frowned. "You two got yourselves in the paper. You'd best keep your heads down now. Nobody's safe anymore, not anywhere. Not in this world." She laid the check down with slender ring-covered fingers, displaying long acrylic-extended nails, and sashayed off, leaving us in a scented cloud.

"Ready to go?" I started to get up, but Susan didn't budge. Her eyes widened, aiming behind me, over my shoulder. I started to turn around, but before I could, someone landed on the booth beside me, blocking me in.

TWELVE

The woman was solid, her short brown hair held off her colorless face by heavy black-rimmed sunglasses, and she slid into the booth smoothly, looking smug.

"Ladies," she greeted us through lips that were thin and dry, devoid of lipstick. "You're not leaving, are you?" She reached over to Susan's plate, helped herself to a leftover piece of bacon.

"Who the hell are you?" Susan slid across the booth, starting to get up.

"Settle down, Mrs. Cummings. You don't want to draw attention to yourself." The woman cupped her meaty hand, revealing a badge and ID. "Special Agent Darlene Ellis, FBI."

Darlene Ellis wore a short-sleeved white shirt that revealed sturdy biceps and loose gray khakis that had been cut for a man; her hands and wrists were thick; her fingernails clipped short, coated with colorless nail polish. Agent Ellis was crisply ironed and smelled like Old Spice.

Susan sat still and said nothing. I mirrored her, doing exactly as she did. She was a lawyer, after all; she must know how to act around the FBI.

"You know why I'm here." It sounded like an accusation.

We did? I looked at Susan. Her face was blank. Neither of us spoke.

"Frankly, I read the so-called statements you gave the police, and you know what? I got the feeling you left some things out. There's nothing there. No beef. So, I'm thinking there's more. Stuff you remembered later."

Susan and I remained silent.

"Or stuff you held back."

We were motionless, mute. Two statues.

"Ladies." Agent Ellis lowered her voice to a husky whisper. "This case is bigger than either of you can possibly imagine. It's worse than your worst nightmare. You don't want to mess with the people involved in it. And, trust me, you don't want to impede an FBI investigation. Anything you know or remember, any thoughts you have, no matter how small, belong to me." She looked at Susan, then me. "Anything you want to share?"

We sat, blinking at her. No, there was nothing.

"Well, you think of anything, you call me. Report directly to me, and only to me." Her eyes narrowed. "If you don't, if you withhold a single fact or detail, you can be charged with obstructing a federal investigation." She smiled thinly, the face of a schoolyard bully. "Any questions?"

I shook my head. No, no questions at all.

"I have one." Susan's voice had a playful, lilting quality.

"Shoot."

"How did you find us here, Agent Ellis? Did you follow us?"

Agent Ellis leaned on her elbows and glared. Susan glared back. Oh, wonderful, I thought. Susan had started a staring contest with a testy FBI agent.

But Susan was undaunted. "Because we're just two private citizens out for breakfast here," she continued, her voice gaining power and momentum as she went on. "And the FBI has no business hindering our movements or badgering us. And I don't remember inviting you to join us. Did you invite her, Zoe?"

"Me? Uh-uh." I shook my head. "I assumed you had."

Agent Ellis glowered. "Your attitudes are unfortunate, ladies. Because you two should celebrate that I know where you are and that I'm watching you. You two stumbled into a nasty—I repeat—a very nasty arena. These people have seen your names in the paper. They know who you are and where you live, just like me. So, yes, I got my eye on you, and I'm betting they do, too. I'm watching who approaches you, who makes contact with you, who even looks at you. Because these people . . . they even imagine you know something about them? You're gone—poof. Just like that. You got it?"

She looked at Susan for a long moment. Susan stared back, eyes shining. Then Agent Ellis turned to me, her jaw extended, bullying.

"This case is FBI now. You hear or see or remember or even think you remember something, you call me, for your own sakes." She handed us each a card. "Someone contacts you, you call me. You even dream about the case, you call me. Understood?"

Agent Ellis nodded, first at Susan, then at me. "Mrs. Cummings. Ms. Hayes." When our eyes met, she winked. "Nice meeting you both." Then she slid off the booth and vanished into the rear of the restaurant.

THIRTEEN

There wasn't even the hint of a breeze, and the asphalt of the streets seemed to steam in the unnatural heat, sizzling almost as intensely as Susan. Dripping sweat, we stomped ahead without a destination.

"Why didn't you just deck her?" I asked. "Could you have been a little more belligerent?"

"Screw her." Susan was still mad. "I'm not going to be intimidated by some self-important female Eliot Ness wannabe."

"Susan, maybe you should pick your enemies. An FBI agent may not be someone you want to mess with."

"She was in my face. She thinks her badge is a license to bully people? Well, she picked the wrong victim."

Great. Susan was in her prizefighter mode. When she got upset, she started swinging; probably this reaction served her well as a criminal attorney. I wasn't sure, though, that it was an asset outside of the courtroom.

I looked over my shoulder to see if anyone was walking behind us, saw an elderly man, limping with a cane, about four steps back.

"What are you doing?"

"Looking around." I faced forward and spoke softly, trying not to move my lips. "To see if someone's following us."

"Nobody's following us, Zoe."

"Agent Ellis was. She followed us to the deli—"

"And she said what she had to say. Now she's done."

"How do you know?"

"The FBI can't keep a tail on every person who might or might not know some tiny detail about every single case they're investigating. They don't have enough people. So she made her point, and now she'll leave us alone."

We kept walking, and I kept looking behind us, ahead of us, across the street. Crossing Fourth Street, I looked to my left and right, straining my peripheral vision for anyone suspicious, anyone who might be stalking us. Didn't that man in the denim cutoffs look just a little too casual? Wasn't that woman's handbag way too large? And why was she looking at us? Why, when I spotted her, did she look away? By the time we got to Three Bears Park, I'd identified at least forty people who were probably on our tail.

"Let's sit a minute," Susan suggested. "I've got to get to work, but first I need to think."

"It's too hot to think," I said. "My brain's melted."

But the shade looked welcoming. We entered the park, passing the familiar concrete statue of *The Three Bears,* and settled on a shady bench behind the toddler swings. Probably, without being aware of it, we'd been heading to the park all along, like homing pigeons returning to a safe place.

We sat surrounded by the comforting shrieks of children at play, the commotion of little limbs running and climbing and chasing.

"So. Look around. See anyone suspicious?" Susan said.

"See anyone who isn't?"

"You mean, over the age of four?"

"Obviously. Under four, they're all suspicious."

A heavyset nanny pushing a little boy on the swings smiled at us. I eyed her suspiciously and looked away.

"Okay, be honest." Susan wiped her forehead. "Is it just me? Or was Agent Ellis really a butch belligerent bitch?"

I had to concede. "Both. Agent Ellis could use some work on her people skills. But it's just you who'd take her on."

"I don't get it," Susan said. "What does she think we know? What does she want from us?"

"I have no clue. But I'm calling Nick. Maybe he'll know what's going on." I took out my cell and punched his number on auto-dial.

Nick's voice mail invited me to leave a message, so I did. Then, hot and tired and not knowing what else to do, I sat in the shade beside Susan, watching a pair of determined toddlers climb the jungle gym where Molly and Emily had played only eye blinks ago. Now, Molly thought she was far too sophisticated for Three Bears, called it the "baby park." When had Molly stopped being a baby? How had time passed so quickly? I looked around at the young mothers with their small children, feeling as if I were watching my own past. How many hours had I spent in this park watching Molly, pushing her on the swings? Suddenly, all the clichés about time fleeting and kids growing up fast seemed painfully accurate and un-cliché-like. A priest walked by, smiling gently as if reading my thoughts.

"Well," Susan said. "Want to go?"

A hefty grandmotherly woman pushed a baby carriage over and planted herself on the bench right beside me, too close, especially in this heat. Odd, because there were plenty of vacant benches all over the park.

"Mind if I sit here, dear?" she asked after she sat.

"No problem. Actually, we're leaving." I began to stand.

"Wait. Don't go yet." The woman spoke softly, sweetly. "Just sit still, as if everything's fine."

The woman smiled and touched my arm with a surprisingly smooth, unfreckled hand. I looked at Susan, who looked back at me, baffled and a little alarmed. I tried to move my arm away, but the woman held on to it, as if to stop me. My cell phone was still in my free hand; I considered calling for help. But what would I say? Hello, 9-1-1? An old lady is touching my arm? I told myself that I was overreacting; the old lady might just be lonely, might be senile and not even realize that she was clutching me. Even so, I sat still, not calling 9-1-1, not turning around. Obeying a stranger.

"Lovely afternoon," the old lady mused, her hand beginning to feel like a bony vise. "But so hot. I think it's supposed to rain later in the week."

Susan was on her feet, ready to go.

"Sit down, dear," the woman told her. "Both of you. Sit with me awhile." Holding my arm with one hand, she reached inside the carriage with the other. I looked but saw no baby, only a lumpy bundle of blankets. Why was she pushing a carriage with no baby? Was she crazy? Or was she hiding something in the blankets? A gun? A bomb?

"Come on, Zoe. We're leaving." Susan took hold of my free arm and pulled. The old lady pulled back with surprising strength. It was tug-of-war, and I was the rope.

"Get up," Susan grunted.

"Sit down," the old woman insisted.

"Let me go," I groaned.

"Hush up," the hedge behind us commanded. "And Mrs. Cummings, sit down." The voice trembled, rumbling like thunder.

Nostrils flaring, Susan let go of my arm and sat on the edge of the bench, poised to take off. The old woman released the carriage, but not my arm. We sat in tense silence for a moment until the priest who'd walked by moments ago emerged from the dogwood hedges behind us. Elderly and stocky, he walked with a stride too limber for his age and girth, and he perched on the edge of a concrete planter beside our bench.

"Ms. Hayes. Mrs. Cummings." He called our names as if starting a meeting. As he spoke, the rest of the park seemed to fade away, leaving only the four of us under the shady limbs of an oak.

"Father Joseph Xavier," the priest introduced himself. "This is Sonia Vlosnick." The old woman nodded, smiling sweetly, her hand still on my arm.

"We had no intention of startling you. We merely wish to talk."

"Then tell Ms. Vlasic to let go of my friend."

"Vlosnick," Sonia corrected. "Vlasic's the pickles. But please, dear, call me Sonia."

"Let her go, Sonia."

"Let me go, Sonia." Susan and I spoke together, a fuming duet.

The priest said something to Sonia in a language I didn't recognize. Sonia released me, leaving an angry red handprint above my wrist.

"I'm so sorry if I hurt you, dear." She patted the red marks. "But I had to make sure you wouldn't run off before Father Joseph determined that we were safe here."

"Who the hell are you?" Susan was more than ready to run off anyway.

"Let me explain," the priest said. "I work unofficially with an immigration organization based in northeast Philadelphia. Sonia represents a coalition of citizens concerned with illegal immigrants."

"What organization? What coalition?" I tried to sound authoritative. Who were these people? The priest paused, gazing across the park.

"Actually, there are several. The Pennsylvania Immigration and Citizenship Coalition." The woman smiled. "And the Archdiocese and the Nationalities Service Center, and—"

"We've come about the young ladies," the priest interrupted. "The ones you found."

"We hope you can help us." Sonia's voice was high and birdlike. She began to roll the carriage back and forth as if rocking a baby to sleep. I rubbed my arm.

"It's terribly important that we learn everything we can about the women. What you saw. What condition the bodies were in. Who else was on the scene. And what was in the water with them."

Why? Who were these people that they should want to know about nineteen dead women? I leaned closer to Susan, jabbing her lightly with my elbow, hoping she'd take my cue and run with me screaming out of the park. But Susan didn't notice my jab. I leaned forward, trying to catch her eye, but she didn't look at me.

"We've already given statements to the police," she said. "We don't know anything else. There were a bunch of them and they were all dead; that's all we know."

"Not quite all, dear."

The priest looked over Sonia's shoulder, scanning trees and rooftops. His gaze never rested in one place. When he spoke, his voice was soft and gritty, like pouring sand. "Pardon my lack of eye contact. What Sonia and I do is quite dangerous. We have to be aware of who's around at all times."

Sonia nodded. "We're dressed this way to conceal our identities." She leaned close, whispering. "Father's mustache isn't real."

"Sonia—" The priest scowled and muttered foreign syllables.

"My bosom isn't either," Sonia continued undeterred. I looked at her more closely. A fine cloth seam peeked out along her hairline; her gray twisted bun was a wig. Oh, Lord. Who were these people? I clutched the phone, ready to speed-dial the police.

"Our work is risky, so we need to keep our relationship confidential—"

Relationship? We had a relationship?

"He's right, dears. You mustn't tell anyone about us." Sonia looked at me. "Even your policeman friend."

They knew about Nick? How? I examined their faces, wondering what about them, if anything, was real. Their noses? The color of their eyes? Would Susan or I be able to recognize them if we saw them again?

The priest turned and faced the park, looking around, smiling at the nanny by the swings. "My group is dedicated to rescuing the captives and destroying the traffickers. Sonia's assists those who've been rescued or who've managed to escape."

Susan squinted, suspicious and angry, maybe about to explode.

"Well, I don't see what we can do for you." I spoke so Susan wouldn't. "The women we found were beyond saving."

Father Joseph Xavier watched a little boy career down the

slide. "Let me clarify. The women you found were but a small part of a much larger shipment by a particular dealer. That dealer handles dozens of such deliveries each year. Philadelphia's a transit point for their northeast and mid-Atlantic regions."

The slave trade was divided into regions. Like soft-drink distribution and automobile dealerships. In this century. In America.

"And the authorities don't stop them, dears—"

"Sonia, be quiet. Let me finish." The priest spoke firmly, clasping his rough, unpriestlike hands. "The INS, the FBI, the police—all the authorities who are supposed to apprehend these criminals are completely inept. Useless. In fact, we know for certain that several of those agencies have been infiltrated by the cartels. Others—like the Archdiocese, the Farmworkers and so on—they try to help, but they're limited legally and financially. So, Sonia and I have come to represent a different group . . . less restrained than formal organizations. We conduct discreet rescue missions. We free captives and destroy traffickers by any means necessary, without regard to bureaucracy."

Oh dear. Sonia and Father Joseph looked elderly and harmless. Apparently, though, they were neither. Who were they? Who funded them? Who provided their information? Susan's brow was furrowed.

"But really, we don't know anything," I repeated.

"Just tell us exactly what you told the police," Sonia said.

"No. We're not telling them a damned thing, Zoe," Susan snapped. "Why should we? Who the hell are they? We're going to confide in strangers wearing disguises? Please. I'm not talking to some clown in a costume. This is bullshit."

Oh, excellent. Here we go, I thought. Susan was openly defying, even insulting them. Two disguised potential hit men with a possible bomb in their buggy had all but abducted us, and Susan was challenging their authority to ask us questions.

The priest's eyes darted around. "I advise you to keep your voice down, Mrs. Cummings."

"Look, dears. We have reason to believe that the cartel is in an uproar, and not just because of the loss of those poor women. Apparently, other materials were lost as well. Materials that contain critical information—"

The priest interrupted, blinking rapidly, urgent. "Just tell us one thing. Did you find anything—anything at all—in the water besides bodies?"

Susan and I exchanged silent glances.

"Do try to trust us, dears," Sonia cooed. When she reached into her diaper bag I thought she was going to pull out a gun. Instead, she took out two business cards and handed one to each of us. "This is the phone number where you can reach us. Day or night. Sometimes, the smallest detail can be important. Things they wore, like lockets or rings, can help us identify them. Or things they held on to, like photographs. Or things floating in the water with them—"

Like a Humberton hat? No, Sonia couldn't have known about that. Nick said nobody knew.

"Or marks on their bodies. Some of the larger cartels mark their people with logos."

I swallowed and said nothing, recalling what Nick had told me that three wavy lines had been tattooed on each woman's shoulder.

"They brand them," Sonia explained, "so, if one escapes, she'll be identified and returned to the cartel."

"We didn't see anything like that." Susan was adamant.

The priest took out his handkerchief and wiped sweat from his forehead. In the heat, his dark, collared costume must have been unbearable.

Sonia rocked the carriage back and forth. "Well, it gets quite grisly, dears. More so than you want to know."

"You're right. We don't know and we don't want to know—"

"How callous of you, Mrs. Cummings." The priest's voice was raspy and cold. "They were poor and helpless. Uneducated. Desperate. Risking everything to come here in hopes of jobs or marriage or just chances at survival. Instead, they were brutalized, taken into slavery. They lived in fear of the cartels and the INS. Fear that their families would be punished or killed. Fear of being deported home and imprisoned, tortured or killed. Fear ruled their lives, so they'd become quite docile."

Susan's eyes fired up and she shook her head. I knew she was girding for a debate. "It's hard for us to imagine," I blurted, swinging my leg and kicking Susan to shut her up.

"Ouch," Susan yelped.

"Shush," I whispered.

Sonia conferred with the priest in their tongue.

"Why'd you kick me?" Susan rubbed her leg, irked.

"So you'd be quiet."

"Really. Didn't it occur to you to say 'Be quiet'? Or did you see no alternative to breaking my leg?"

"Please, Susan. I didn't kick you that hard."

"I'll be limping for a week."

"Okay," Father Joseph said. "Since you apparently have trouble accepting what we're telling you, we're going to show you. If these women are seen talking to the police or the government, or trying to run away, they are tortured and disfigured, maybe killed. By the time they get here, they know this. They've seen what their captors will do." The priest's eyes had hardened to shining steel. He pulled an envelope out of his pocket and held it out to us. "Look. See for yourself."

Neither of us reached for the envelope, so he opened it and took out some photographs. I looked away, but not before seeing shiny globs of red and black. Oh, Lord. Charred flesh?

"You can see why it's important, dears," Sonia urged. "Tell us everything you saw. Even the FBI might not know what to make of the information, but we will. Tell us, for your own good." Sonia's voice was soft and melodic, but her words sounded chilling.

"We have nothing to tell you." Susan shoved the pictures back at the priest.

My cell phone began to ring. Maybe it was Nick calling back. Or Molly with a problem at school. Or the FBI agent warning that two psychos might ambush us in the park. I began to reach for it, but Sonia intervened, pushing my hand away, shaking her head, no. The priest was still talking, looking grave.

". . . And, in that case, you'll need our help."

In what case?

"This is an international multibillion-dollar, multitiered enterprise involving millions of women. Its tentacles reach everywhere—into governments, into law enforcement, into communities—"

"He's right, dears. And you can't count on the authorities; they may have been compromised. So don't talk to them—especially about us."

"Mrs. Cummings, Ms. Hayes." Father Joseph's eyes remained focused on the playground. "The people who run this operation . . . human life is nothing to them. They don't care if you really know anything about them or not. It's enough for them that you might. If they suspect that you might give a tidbit of information to the authorities or to us, they won't risk it. They'll eliminate you without hesitation."

"They're very violent, dears. You've seen just a few of their victims." She nodded at the photos in the priest's envelope. "We've dealt with many, many more. Believe me, by comparison, the young women you found were lucky."

"I think these people are trying to scare us, Zoe." Susan frowned. "Let's go." She started to stand.

"You should be scared." The priest blocked her way. "The local traffickers bungled their work. They not only lost a valuable cargo, but they also lost incriminating materials and exposed the slave trade to the public eye. Heads will roll for that. But, that aside, you and your friend found their property, and the traders don't know how much you saw or what you might have found or know—"

"So, even if we don't actually know anything, we're still in danger?" My mouth was dry; I had trouble forming the words.

"Ridiculous," Susan said. "All we did was bump into some floaters. We don't know a damned thing, and nobody in their right minds would think we did." She stood. My legs felt weak as I followed.

Sonia rearranged the empty baby blankets. "Nobody said

these people are in their right minds, dears. They might send someone to question you, to find out what you know. Or they might dispense with the questions and just omit the risk. You know, dears. Snuff you out."

"Okay, that's enough." Susan turned to go.

The priest put a hand on her shoulder. "We're not here just to ask questions, Mrs. Cummings." He looked away, scanning the trees at the edge of the park. "We're here to warn you about what you're dealing with. You've stumbled into a snake pit. Watch your steps."

"Well, thanks for your opinion," Susan said. "Guys, it's been fun, really. We're done here, Zoe." She began to walk.

Dazed, I managed to join her, with each step expecting bullets to rip our backs. But we passed kids on the jungle gym, nannies and young mothers chatting on a bench without getting shot.

"What the hell was that?" I whispered near the merry-go-round.

"Keep walking," she said.

We went on through the park, hearing the laughter of children as if it were miles away. When we'd made it to the exit gate, I looked back but saw no grandmother with a pram, no priest. The bench where we'd left them was empty. And they weren't anywhere nearby.

FOURTEEN

At the corner of Fifth and South, we stopped to breathe. Lord, it was hot. I kept looking around, searching for people who might be the priest or Sonia out of disguise. A pair of teenage girls strolled by in skimpy shorts and halter tops that exposed belly rings and shoulder tattoos. A young man with an aqua Mohawk, arm in arm with his magenta-haired girlfriend, both with rows of piercings in their eyebrows, nostrils and lips. A young woman with a ponytail in spandex jogging clothes.

"Christ Almighty." Susan fumed. Tiny beads of sweat coated her forehead. "Who the hell were they? How dare they—"

"Think about it, Susan. First the FBI agent. Then those two. Do you think you can try harder to piss people off?"

"Who cares about them? What about us? Everyone's accosting us."

"Susan, we don't know who those two were. They had us cornered. You could have cooled it a little."

"I don't think so, Zoe. No. Not in my own neighborhood. Not in my city. Hell, not in this country. I am not going to sit still and let some kooks playing dress-up besiege me and my friend and make threats—"

"—But Susan, what if they were for real?"

"Are you kidding? Nothing about them was real. Not the mustache, the wigs, the padding, the makeup—"

"I mean about the danger."

She exhaled, pushing hair behind her ears. "My God, Zoe. All we did was flip our boat, and now—poof—move over, Brittany and Madonna. Zoe Hayes and Susan Cummings are the most newsworthy, most followed, most threatened, most harassed women in the world."

The light changed; so did the motion around us. Cars stopped on South Street, started on Fifth. Pedestrians halted or walked. We stood at the corner, sweaty and indecisive.

A woman with an armload of packages bumped me as she hurried off the curb. A line of preschoolers from the Community Center walked past us two by two, holding hands like a human centipede with adults as its head and tail.

Without deciding to, we walked on. Susan blinked rapidly, head down, pounding pavement. "You know what?" She stopped suddenly, hands on hips as if she'd had a revelation. "It's all crap."

"What is?" We'd stopped in front of a condom store. Condom Nation, it was called.

"All of it. Pure bullshit. Think about it."

I wasn't sure what I was supposed to think about, but I was aware of the steady stream of people entering and leaving the condom store. Who'd have guessed they did that much business? And so early in the day—it wasn't even noon yet.

"Maybe I'm too suspicious." Susan stood close, whispering. "But think. What did those two tell us? One: They work independent of the authorities. Two: They want to know everything we told the police. And three: We shouldn't tell anyone about them. Not even the authorities, not even Nick. Think about that."

I thought about it. "So? What's your point?" I had no idea. I looked at the window display, waiting for her to explain. Condoms arranged like petals in a giant multicolored daisy. Some were patterned, others ribbed; some textured with curvy little bumps.

"The point is," she continued, "how do we know that Sonia Vlosnick and Father Joseph Xavier are who they claim to be?"

"They're not. They told us they were in disguise."

"No, I mean how do we know they're who they say they are? How do we know they represent the good guys? For all we know, they were sent by the traffickers to find out what we know. For all we know, they're traffickers themselves."

Sonia and the priest, slave traffickers? My head seemed to float, lighter than the humid air, and suddenly the condom arrangement in the window began to sway. Or no; it was me. I was swaying. Dizzy. I leaned against the glass to steady myself. Susan was right. Father Joseph had warned that the cartel might send people to question us; maybe he'd simply omitted that he and Sonia were those people. I pictured the two of them, a priest and an old lady. Not the image of killers and kidnappers who earned their livings selling women. But, underneath their disguises, maybe they were predators, there to find out what we knew, assess us as risks and, if necessary, eliminate us. Oh my. What if I'd have mentioned the Humberton hat? Or the tattoos? Would they have killed us right there in the park? Had there been a silenced pistol in the blankets of Sonia's pram?

The air was wet and sooty, weighing us down, but I shivered, oddly hot and chilled at once. Susan was on a roll, expanding her theory.

". . . And that would explain why they don't want us to tell the authorities about them. Or even Nick. The cartels want to be invisible. If they wanted to keep a low profile, they'd use disguises that would appear friendly and nonthreatening, outfits that would blend in and not arouse attention. Who could be less noticeable than two kindly old people? And who would we be more likely to chat with than those two?"

Susan was right. If the slave traders wanted to find out what we knew, they'd have a better chance sending a priest and a grandmother than, say, a pair of thugs.

"So what should we do? Tell the FBI? Call Agent Ellis?"

She shook her head. "I don't think so. They told us not to."

"But they wouldn't know."

"They might. The priest said they have people in the FBI."

Then whom could we trust? Not the FBI. Not the priest and

Sonia. Nick? Would he know? And, if he did, would he tell me? And, if he didn't, would I be endangering him by telling him?

I felt hot, frantic, unable to keep walking, unable to sit down. I wanted to go home. I wanted it to be yesterday, before we'd taken our moonlight row.

For a while, Susan and I stood side by side, staring vacantly into a condom-filled window. Her jaw was set, eyes gleaming.

"So what do you think?" I asked. "What should we do now?"

Susan shrugged. "You know what? I'm guessing we should do nothing. No matter who sent them, they were there to feel us out and find out if we know anything. They found out we know nada, zip. Nothing whatsoever. So they warned us to stay out of it and to keep quiet about their visit. If we do what they say, they'll back off and leave us alone."

"So that's it? They're done with us? That's what you said about the FBI agent, too."

"I did? Well, she might show up again, just to flex her muscles. But these two? I doubt we'll see them again."

Good, I thought. Except for one thing. "If we did, how would we know? For all we know, they're standing right next to us."

Synchronized, we turned to see who was standing beside us and faced a bony young couple dressed in heavy chains and black leather, their skin too white, eyeliner too thick, hair too black. Father Joseph Xavier and Sonia Vlosnick?

Susan and I looked from them to each other.

"You think?" Susan said.

"Doubt it." I shook my head.

"Yeah," she agreed. "Too obvious."

The couple eyed us coolly and walked into the condom store.

After that, we saw Sonia and the priest in every pair who passed. Acned adolescents, high-heeled hookers. Muscle-bound movers. Grungy garbage collectors. Tattooed bikers. Even two spry Afghan hounds. We amused ourselves that way for a while, until our nerves quieted.

"So, what now?" I asked. As if she'd know.

"Now, I'm going to the office for a couple of hours to work on Ollie Brown's appeal. Then I'm going home to fight with the deck guys. Go on with your life, Zoe. We can't change what happened to those poor dead women, but we'll be fine. Whoever Sonia and the priest were, we passed their test; they found out that we're ignorant, indifferent and harmless. They'll leave us alone and things will settle down."

I told myself that she was right. Life would calm down and be normal again. There was no reason for us to trek aimlessly up and down South Street in the miserable heat.

"I guess I'll head home," I said. Maybe I could even catch a nap before Molly got out of school.

Susan eyed the daisy display. "Good. I'll call you later."

We hugged and parted, and when I looked back, Susan was just stepping into the store.

The whole way home my head swirled with troubling thoughts. Human trafficking. Nineteen dead women. A sinister slave cartel. Sonia, the priest, Agent Ellis. But, absurdly, what disturbed me most was the single vivid, persistent image of Susan's husky husband Tim wearing only a neon-green condom. And a smile.

FIFTEEN

I took the crowded way home, avoiding the quaint cobble-stoned alleys and quiet flowered walkways that I usually favored. Instead, I stayed among people. I walked along South Street, the hub of the city's counterculture, passing funky boutiques, retro restaurants and bars, tacky tattoo parlors, antique shops. It was almost noon, and the street was just blinking awake. Shopkeepers hosed off the streets and swept up the stench of last night's parties, preparing for another unseasonably steamy day. The corner of Fourth and South was engulfed in the odor of frying onions from Jim's Steaks. Life was going on as usual. Cheese steaks were cooking; shops were opening. Cops double-parked their squad cars to run into the Wawa convenience store for coffee. I was surrounded by the familiar and the normal, and breathing evenly again. My shoulder muscles were unclenching. I turned down Fourth Street, approaching Queen Village. I was almost home.

My neighborhood, Queen Village, was a hodgepodge caught in a permanent process of gentrification. Ongoing renovations and new constructions stood alongside old houses in varying stages of decline. There was a high turnover among residents; I'd been there longer than almost anyone and didn't know most of my neighbors. Most were strangers, familiar faces that, at best, would smile or nod in passing. Young people who kept late hours. Couples who planned to stay only until their first child was born. A few elderly urbanites who kept to themselves, hanging on to sagging properties as long as they could. The neighbor I knew best was someone I almost never saw. Victor was an agoraphobic recluse who never left his home. We communicated by e-mail from time to time, and Molly and I sometimes left cookies at his door. Occasionally, I caught a glimpse of him peeking cautiously out his window, but to my knowledge, he'd ventured outside only once in all the years he'd lived there.

Even though my neighbors were mostly strangers and the area in flux, I loved my rehabilitated brownstone. I'd nurtured it from an empty shell into a home. And now, craving security and solitude, I hurried inside and locked the door, planning to cocoon myself in quiet for the rest of the day.

As I fastened the bolt, though, something alarmed me. A tingle began on my spine and rippled across my arms to the tips of my fingers. My hands lingered on the lock, and I hesitated, afraid to turn around.

Of course I did turn around. I even took a few steps and entered the kitchen. Then I stopped dead, staring.

It was only a ceramic mug, but it lay shattered on the floor in a puddle of spilled coffee. I stood frozen, watching it, disbelieving its existence. How had a coffee mug landed on the floor when no one had been home?

Maybe Nick had stopped by. Of course. He must have. And he'd knocked the mug off the counter, probably without even noticing. I kneeled down and picked up the biggest pieces, sponging up the coffee, ignoring the uh-oh feeling rumbling in my gut. I took out the broom and swept up the rest, then dumped it into the trash. Only when it was completely cleaned up did I venture farther into the house, back toward the living room.

It's okay, I assured myself. Nothing's wrong. But I kept my cell phone with me as I looked around, taking inventory. The dining table and chairs were as they'd been when I'd left. So were the paintings, the sofa and easy chair. The pillows, the woolen afghans. Molly's unfinished bead project was still spread over the floor, along with some books, a stray sandal, her worn-out, almost furless bear. Everything seemed untouched, in its usual disarray.

See? I told myself. It was nothing. Just a mug. But as I went upstairs to check out Molly's room, my pulse elevated. I stood at her door with my eyes closed for a moment before I looked inside, preparing for I didn't know what. Then I took a deep breath and looked. Nothing was unusual. The room was in its regular chaos. The bed was unmade, pillows on the carpet, blankets spilling onto the floor. Pajamas, T-shirts, bathing suits and socks lay everywhere, along with scattered puzzle pieces and loose cards, markers, crayons, Amelia Bedelia books, forty shades of Play-Doh, hundreds of Beanie Babies and a couple of dozen stuffed animals, mostly monkeys. Dresser drawers gaped, displaying more disarray. Shuffled shorts and underwear. A complete disaster.

I told myself that Molly's room always looked like that, that nothing had been disturbed. But hairs danced on the back of my neck as I continued down the hall toward my bedroom. At the door I stopped, unable to go in. Don't, I told myself. Go downstairs and get out while you can. What if the intruder's still in there? You could get killed. Go downstairs and call the police.

I pivoted, punching numbers into my cell phone. Then I stopped, realizing that I was being ridiculous. There was no intruder. No reason to call the police. Nothing had actually happened. There was a broken coffee mug in my kitchen; that was all. I was a jittery mess, letting my imagination run away with me, shaken up because of everything that had happened since last night. But now I was home. On my own turf. Safe. In reality, there was no evidence of a break-in, no proof of an intruder.

Even so, I was cautious as I stepped into the bedroom. I circled the room slowly, testing the carpet with each step, looking around, listening, making sure. Everything seemed as I'd left it. My robe still hung on the bathroom door. The dresser top was buried under piles of clean laundry, and my jewelry box looked undisturbed. I opened it, found my diamond studs, my great-grandmother's gold locket. My ruby and diamond rings, my Movado wristwatch. Everything was there, undisturbed.

Okay. Nothing had happened. I was imagining things. The air wasn't really unsettled, didn't carry the scent of a stranger. And the house wasn't unbalanced, its harmony disrupted by an alien presence. No, the place was fine. The only one unsettled and unbalanced was me.

I sat on the bed, collecting myself. My nerves were raw. I was exhausted, hadn't slept the night before. I needed to lie down, slow my pulse, breathe deeply, not think. Just close my eyes and take a nap. I'd rest for a little while, and when Molly got home, I'd talk to her, once again, about cleaning up her room. Then we'd make dinner in time for Nick to come home. I'd stick to routine. To simple tasks that felt normal and soothing. Good. I had a plan. I climbed under the comforter, and settling in, remembered the night before, how tender Nick had been. Nick. I wondered when he'd call back, where he'd been all day, and I opened my eyes to look at his picture on my nightstand.

I remember how the comforter tangled as I tried to throw it off, and how much time it seemed to take to bolt out of bed and run down the stairs. Cell phone in hand, I fumbled to unlock the door and race outside, punching numbers with trembling hands.

This time, when I called 911, I had something real to say.

SIXTEEN

It wasn't just the picture on the nightstand that had been vandalized. I hadn't noticed at first, but every picture of Nick in the house had been defaced. His head had been cut off in Molly's room. His face slashed to bits on my nightstand. In the picture of the three of us at the shore, Nick's face had been scribbled out and an awkward skull drawn over mine. Someone had taken time with the pictures, opening frames and maiming the photos, then replacing them on shelves. The intruder had even enjoyed a cup of coffee. Or half of it—until the mug had fallen or been dropped onto the kitchen floor.

I couldn't reach Nick. His voice mail still answered. And Susan hadn't gotten home yet. I redialed their numbers, one after another, reaching no one until the police arrived. Robert Bowman, the responding officer, looked like he might be sixteen, and his hat, too big for his head, slid down over his eyebrows, held up by his protruding ears. He took out a notebook and pen, firing questions faster than I could answer. "Who knew your schedule, ma'am?" he asked. "Who knew that you'd be out of the house this morning? Who has access to the property? How many people live here?"

I tried to remember the questions, to answer them in order. He wrote as I spoke, raising an eyebrow when I had trouble answering how many people lived there. Two. Sometimes three. But really two, just my daughter and I.

"You're not married?"

What did that have to do with a break-in? "No. Divorced."

"And your ex-husband and you . . . Do you get along?"

"Sure." Actually, I hadn't heard from Michael in months, not since his wedding.

Officer Bowman didn't look convinced. "Is your ex upset about your current relationship, ma'am?"

Finally, I understood; he thought Michael might have broken into my house and defaced Nick's pictures because he was jealous of Nick.

"A little. I mean, he knows there's somebody, and I'm sure he'd prefer it if there weren't. But he doesn't care all that much. He just got married."

Officer Bowman frowned. "Are there custody issues? Or child support?"

"No, nothing like that. Michael—my ex-husband—isn't my daughter's father." Lord. That didn't sound right. "Actually, I don't know who her father is. I mean, Molly's adopted. I adopted her after the divorce. I'm a single parent."

He rubbed his chin, as if categorizing me as a Single Parent. "Do you work?"

"Yes, at the Psychiatric Institute. I'm an art therapist."

"So, why were you home in the middle of the day?"

"Oh, I'm not working right now."

His eyebrow rose again, as if not working were grounds for suspicion. Again, I felt the need to explain. "I'm off for a few weeks. Vacation."

"So, you're some kind of a shrink?"

"Not exactly, but I work with the shrinks."

Officer Bowman puckered his lips, as if he couldn't think of anything else to say. He looked around the living room, his eyes drifting across furniture and artwork, landing on the damaged photograph, moving to the sliding doors.

"Did you see anything unusual? Or hear anything as you came in?"

"No, not that I remember." Just that electric tingling sensation.

"Are you sure? Because that broken coffee cup, ma'am," Officer Bowman explained. "It bothers me. It's possible you surprised the perp and he dropped it as he escaped out the back, through those sliding doors in the living room."

I swallowed, absorbing that possibility. I might have walked in on the intruder.

"Have you noticed anyone lingering in the area? Anyone observing your home as you leave? Anyone watching you or your family members?"

Automatically, I shook my head, no. Nobody had been watching us. Nobody except the media, Agent Ellis and her FBI team, Sonia and the priest and whoever they represented, and possibly members of a slave trafficking cartel. Lord, had anyone not been watching us? Should I tell him about all that? Something told me not to; something else insisted that I should.

"Well, the press was here this morning," I said. "About the nineteen bodies."

His eyes widened.

"The women in the river. My friend and I found them."

"That was you?"

"Yes. And my friend."

"Your name was all over the news this morning."

He nodded, as if making a connection between the press coverage and the break-in. But I couldn't see it. Media attention didn't explain why someone would come into the house only to defile some photographs.

"It could be some kook, somebody drawn to you by the news. Or it could be personal. Can you think of anyone who's angry with you? Or with your—I assume he's your boyfriend?" He pointed at the vandalized picture on my living room shelf.

I felt my face get hot, as if there were something embarrassing about being a forty-year-old woman with a boyfriend. "Nick and I are close. Actually, he's a homicide detective. Nick Stiles."

"Is he?"

"Yes. I thought you might know him?"

"No, ma'am. Never heard of him. But if he's a homicide detective like you say, that may be what's going on here. If you catch my drift."

I didn't. Not even a little.

"Look whose face is messed up in the pictures. His, not yours, ma'am. Off the record, I'd bet my boots this isn't about you. It's about him. The guy's in homicide? He puts bad guys away. So it follows that some of those bad guys must be very mad at your husb——" Officer Bowman's ears reddened at his mistake. "At your boyfriend. What cases had he been on lately?"

"I don't know. He doesn't tell me. But last night, he was with me down at the river."

"After you found the women?"

"Yes, but the FBI's taking over that case."

"And have you talked to your detective friend, ma'am? Is he aware of the break-in?"

No, and no. Where was Nick, anyway? Why hadn't he called back?

Officer Bowman finally finished writing. "Have you made a list of what's missing?" he asked.

"Nothing's missing."

Officer Bowman cleared his throat, as if asking how I could be sure. "When we're through here, be sure to go through the house and take an inventory of anything that's been damaged or taken. For insurance purposes. And you'll need the number of my incident report for your claim."

I nodded. What was wrong with him? Why didn't he understand the words "Nothing's missing"? Why was he insisting that I make a damned list? I sat on my purple sofa holding on to Molly's raggedy teddy bear, wondering why neither Nick nor Susan had called back. Where were they?

Officer Bowman wandered through the room, peeking at windows, examining the sliding doors. I had no idea why. I closed my eyes, picturing the seashore, trying to go there in my mind. It was a relaxation technique I used sometimes with patients, mentally visiting a happy place. I imagined myself there with Molly and Nick, walking along the water, feeling moist sand under my feet, hearing the ocean, smelling the sea, feeling the breezy salt air—

"Found it!" Officer Bowman yelled, and I jumped, startled, back to dry land. "Look at this, son of a blinkin' gun."

Officer Bowman was in my little studio/office, pointing his pen at the corner of a window. The pane had been cut along the frame. The glass had been removed and then replaced, concealing the break.

"That's how they got in, ma'am."

"Are there fingerprints? Do they need to dust for them?"

"Frankly, I don't see any fingerprints, ma'am." He sighed. "Fact is, for the department, this isn't what you'd call a high-priority case. We simply can't send a crime lab team out for every break-and-enter."

"Even though a homicide detective lives here?"

"He lives here?" There went his eyebrow again.

"Well, no. He's here a lot, though."

Officer Bowman sighed. "I'll be honest with you. According to you, nothing's been taken. Without even a theft, it's going to be tough to get them to dust for fingerprints. Now, if millions in valuables had been taken, or if someone had been assaulted or killed here, that'd be a different story. But just a break-in? Realistically, you're not going to see a crime scene team."

"But what if you're right and Detective Stiles is the target?"

"I'll turn it all in, ma'am. I'll do my best. I'm just trying to be real with you." Officer Bowman's eyes avoided mine; he looked at his shoes. They were well buffed and shiny.

"But maybe there are prints on the picture frames. Maybe they could identify the—"

"Like I said, ma'am. I'll do my best." His ears were the color of radishes, embarrassed at his lie.

"Don't you need to take the frames?"

"No, ma'am. You can keep them here. I've taken my report."

I knew he wasn't going to do anything. I'd watched enough crime shows to know that, for the evidence to be used in court, it had to be bagged, labeled and protected at the scene. Officer Bowman made no such move.

"But Officer. Maybe they'll come back. Maybe they were just here to check the place out—to see how to get in. Think about it. Who'd break into a house just to have a cup of coffee and attack some pictures? Why would anyone want to do that? They must be planning something bigger—"

"Ma'am, calm down. Don't try to figure out logical motives; these people don't think like you and I. Take it from me; if I've learned one thing in my four years on the job, it's never try to comprehend the criminal mind." Officer Bowman closed his notepad, handing me a carbon copy of a form he'd filled out. "Take my advice. Go over your belongings, double-check, and figure out what's been taken."

"I told you. Nothing."

"Ma'am. When there's a break-in, most people are too upset to notice at first. Eventually, after they have some time to think about it, they find that a lot of their valuables have gone missing. Cameras. Televisions. Jewelry. Heirlooms."

"Everything's here—"

"And so, for insurance purposes, they amend their original police reports. You can do that, too. If you catch my drift."

Oh. I finally did; he was telling me to lie so I could collect on my insurance policy. Officer Bowman stood to go. "Just come down to the precinct, anytime. Give them that form number and itemize what's gone." He headed down the hall, toward the front door.

"You're leaving? You're all done?" I followed him, not anxious to be left alone.

"I have all I need. If you think of anything else, you can always call."

I trailed after him, asking questions, stalling to keep him there. "Well, what happens next?"

"I'll file this. And keep your eyes open. You never know what can happen."

I stood at the door, watching him leave, feeling abandoned by a skinny guy with a bad complexion and an oversized, sagging uniform.

"Oh, there is one thing, ma'am." Officer Bowman called to me from the street. "You better call a repairman and fix that window."

I shut the door and bolted it, hoping nobody else had heard.

SEVENTEEN

I couldn't sit still when Officer Bowman left. I paced from room to room, calling Susan and Nick on their cell phones again and again, reaching nobody. I understood that Nick might be busy, but why wouldn't Susan pick up her cell phone? I called her home number and left a message there, too. I checked my voice mail, hoping to find a message, but heard only a dozen calls from friends and coworkers who'd seen my name in the paper and wanted to know how I was. Ileana, Davinder, Karen, Marla, Lanie. They were all concerned, each wanting to hear how I was, what had happened. But I couldn't talk about it again, not yet. Wasn't ready to go over everything that had happened, answer questions, revisit each moment. I felt unable to connect with friends, isolated from the life I'd had just two days before. Carrying my cell phone, waiting for it to ring, I went through the house, looking for things that weren't there, hoping I'd notice something missing, some stolen item that would explain the break-in. But I couldn't; everything I owned was there. The only things Nick kept at my house were clothes. Maybe something of his was gone. His sweatshirt from the Boston PD? I couldn't find it. But maybe it was in his condo. Or the trunk of his car. Besides, who would break into a house, leave diamond earrings and steal a sweatshirt?

I tried to ignore it, but the answer taunted me, obvious and inescapable. Maybe the intruder hadn't taken the diamonds because he hadn't been a thief. Maybe he'd been a slave trafficker. After all, the priest had warned that the cartel would try to find out what Susan and I knew. Maybe they'd sent someone to question me, but since I wasn't home, they'd broken in and left a warning. Destroying Nick's photographs was a threat, a way of telling me what they'd do if I talked to the police. Oh, God. What was I supposed to do?

Alone, distraught, I paced through the house, examining each room inch by inch, feeling invaded, defiled. My home had been contaminated, the intruder's presence coating it like a dense and rancid stench. I couldn't breathe without inhaling it. What had he touched? Where had he stepped or sat? I ran around opening the windows, every single one, letting fresh air into the house, expelling that through which the intruder had moved.

I'd have to find a glazier to seal the pane, repair the damage. Meantime, I duct-taped the glass into place. Then I set about removing every trace of the stranger from my home, expunging the vile oils and grime of his touch. I went into Molly's room and gathered up her scattered clothes, tossing them into the washer. I sponged her shelves with Lysol, then her headboard, bureau, nightstand. I stripped all the beds, changed the linens. While Molly's clothes spun in the dryer, a load of towels and sheets sudsed in the washer. I went downstairs and wiped down the treasures on my living-room shelves, one at a time. I scrubbed upholstery, furniture, anything—from knickknacks to nightgowns—that the intruder might have contacted. I sprayed Lysol everywhere, wanting to fumigate the entire house, clean the very space through which the stranger had moved, sterilize everything touched, even by his gaze. I mopped the floors to erase his footsteps. I swabbed the kitchen cabinets, throwing out all opened food packages—saltines, Oreos, cheese doodles, even coffee beans. I stood at the kitchen sink scraping the windowsills with steel wool, aware of the view outside. Was the intruder out there even now? Was it someone from the neighborhood? Were they watching? I looked out, saw a few passing cars, a couple of sweaty pedestrians. Not much traffic; there was even an open parking spot in front of Victor's house. Victor, who never came outside. I checked his windows but didn't see him there. Still, maybe Victor had been looking out earlier; maybe he'd seen the guy approaching my house. I'd ask him. But not now. First, I had to scrub the window over the sink, and the countertops, and the cabinets. By the end of the day, I'd almost finished emptying and sterilizing the refrigerator. Pine Sol, Lysol, Comet, Scrubbing Bubbles—I used them all, a mixture of chemicals lethal enough to exterminate any trace, if not any memory, of the break-in and, possibly, of the day.

"Hey, Zoe." Nick startled me. I hadn't heard him come in. "I just picked up your messages—" He stopped midsentence, staring at me, looking around the kitchen. "Zoe? What're you doing?"

But I was on automatic, too fired up to stop and chat. Running on pure adrenaline. I still had my office/studio and the spare bedroom to do. And I wanted to go over the living room, bathrooms and bedrooms again. I couldn't even slow down, didn't look up, kept tossing plastic containers and vegetables into the sink.

Nick put his arms around me and held me to make me stop. He was clammy with sweat, dressed in rowing clothes. I clutched a jar of spaghetti sauce, waiting for him to release me, determined to finish my work.

"Nick, please. I have to clean—"

"Zoe, the house smells like a chemical plant. Stop. What's going on?" He held on to me.

"I'm cleaning."

He blinked, confused. "I can see that. How about stopping for a minute. Take a break. Talk to me." He looked tired. Or maybe worried? "How about a drink? I'll make martinis. Or margaritas."

Margaritas? What was wrong with him? My house had been invaded. Did he think we should party? "Let go." I squirmed out of his arms. I was suddenly mad. Very mad.

"Honey, please. Come sit down."

Honey? How patronizing. Who did he think he was, calling me 'honey'? My blood pumped. I got even madder. "Sit down? Why should I?"

"So you can tell me what's happened."

"I tried to tell you. I called you all day. I left you messages."

"I called you back this morning. You didn't pick up—"

"Where were you all day? Rowing?" I glared at his unisuit. "Why didn't you answer your phone?"

"I just now got the other messages."

"Why is it you're there round the clock for the damned police department and for your rowing buddies, but when I need you, you're nowhere?" My voice slashed, quick and razor-sharp, surprising me. Apparently, it surprised Nick, too. His mouth dropped, eyes widened, and he folded his arms, protecting himself.

"I was on a case and had my phone turned off. Then I had to clear my head, so I went for a quick row. I didn't get my messages until now. Sorry. But I'm here. Tell me what's so important—"

"Oh, don't worry." I cut him off, aware that my phone had begun to ring. Probably Susan. "I'll tell you." But I didn't. I stared at him in silence, letting the phone go unanswered, fuming, not sure why I was mad at him.

"Okay, good." Nick's eyes studied me, twinkling. "I'm listening." He waited, arms still folded, muscles rippling in his spandex gear.

"You're listening."

"Yes."

I still didn't say anything. I wasn't sure where to start, which of the day's events to begin with. Mercifully, the phone stopped jangling; the voice mail finally picked up the call.

"Zoe, what is it you want to tell me? Because frankly, I'm tired and hungry and hot, and I've got to—"

"Someone broke into the house."

He unfolded his arms and blinked several times. Rapidly. "Go on." No emotion. No surprise. A cop's response.

"Why didn't your police colleagues reach you? I left messages. A crime happened at my house. And my boyfriend, who happens to be a cop, was nowhere to be found. He was on a case. Or busy rowing. So, see, I'm a tad upset."

"Was anything taken?"

"No!" I snapped. Obviously, he didn't get it. Whether or not anything was taken wasn't the point.

"You're sure?"

"Dammit, Nick. I said nothing was taken."

"Okay." He came closer. "You need to calm down, baby."

Baby? He reached out, trying to hug me. I resisted, clung to my jar of spaghetti sauce.

"Come on. Let me hold you."

"Not now. I'm cleaning."

"Well, stop cleaning. Talk to me."

I didn't plan them, but words flew out of my mouth. "Nick— oh, God, I think—the slave smugglers—they're watching us. Susan and me. I think that's who broke in here today. They think we found something or know something."

"Hey, wait, back up." He released me, examining my face. "What? Why would they break in here?"

"Maybe to scare me? Or to warn you to back off."

"Scare you why? Warn me why? About what?"

"Look around. They didn't take anything; they just ruined every single picture of you." I held up the one without a head. "They must have known you were on the case."

Nick's eyes narrowed. "Let me see that." He studied the picture. "What else did they do?"

"Every picture of you is like that. Destroyed. Even the one in Molly's room."

"Is that all they did? Ruin pictures of me?"

"Yes. Well, except for the mug. They spilled coffee."

He blinked. "Black? Or with milk?"

Not funny. "Don't be cute."

"Tell me," he said. "Was the coffee black?"

I pictured it. "No. With milk."

Nick closed his eyes, rubbed them and released a deep sigh.

"Okay." He seemed peculiarly unconcerned, as if the break-in were no big deal.

" 'Okay?' What does that mean? You know something? You do, don't you? Tell me." I was furious. Steam poured out of my ears. "Who did this? Was it the slave smugglers?"

"Zoe, settle down. You need to relax."

"Relax? Are you crazy? I woke up this morning with the news media on my doorstep. Then an FBI agent followed Susan and me to the deli—"

"An FBI agent? Who?"

"And then, two people in costumes cornered us in the park to tell us that the slave traffickers might come after us—"

"Wait, what? Slow down."

"They said they represented these underground organizations that were fighting the slave smugglers—"

"Zoe, stop." Nick pulled over a kitchen chair. "Sit down."

He seated me.

"Now, breathe. Go on. Take a deep breath." He tossed two ice cubes in a glass and poured in a finger of Scotch. "Drink this."

He sat facing me, and I realized I'd been ranting, hyperventilating. I sipped the Scotch.

"Start over. Slowly. From the beginning. What happened exactly?"

I told him, biting my lip, refusing to cry, sitting in my kitchen holding a Scotch on the rocks and a half-empty jar of spaghetti sauce. Why was I so certain that Nick knew something about what had happened? When would I trust this man? Nick watched with an expression of bemused concern until I stopped talking. Then he wrapped me in his arms.

"It's okay," he said. "Don't worry. Not about the break-in. Not about the slave smugglers. Frankly, I doubt they did this. Messing up pictures isn't what they do. If somebody gets in their way, they just kill them."

"Oh, good. That's reassuring." I moved out of his embrace.

"It should be. Because it means the burglars probably weren't the smugglers."

"But maybe they were, Nick. Maybe they don't want to kill

us because they need us for some reason. Maybe they think we have something of theirs, or—"

"Zoe, slow down." Half of Nick's face smirked and he touched my cheek. "Look, I'll talk to the FBI about Agent Ellis. I've been with the agents on the case most of the day, and she wasn't one of them."

"Then why was she following us?"

"I don't know. Her name wasn't mentioned today as part of the team. I want to know who she is, what her role is, why she was hounding you. I'd guess the feds will want to talk to you about the couple who confronted you, but other than that, you and Susan won't be bothered anymore. I'll see to it." He took my hand, the one with the spaghetti sauce in it.

"How, Nick? How are you going to see to it?" I looked up at him.

Nick's pale blue eyes were blank, revealing nothing. No emotion, no information whatsoever. He knew something.

"You know something. What? Do you know who did this?"

Nick said nothing, but his eyes shifted almost imperceptibly. Or did they? He wouldn't tell me, even if he knew. Furious, I pulled my hand from his, not wanting to succumb to his touch, but needing it badly.

Nick's voice was low, almost muffled. "Look, I don't know anything for sure. But it's possible that the break-in isn't about the slave traffickers. Maybe it's personal, against me. I've been a cop for a while. Maybe someone I sent away has gotten out and holds a grudge. It could be something like that. The traffickers may have nothing to do with it."

"So what are you saying? That it's just mere coincidence that the break-in happened today?"

"I don't know, Zoe. Maybe, maybe not. I'll find out. Either way, no matter who it is, don't worry. I'll take care of it." He let go of my hand, but nailed me with his eyes. "I promise. Nobody's going to hurt you."

"How can you say that? I've already been hurt. My home has been defiled."

"I know. But you're fine. And you're safe. Trust me."

Trust him? What was he talking about? Nick had kept secrets from the day we'd met. Not only about his work, but about himself. He'd told me only bits and pieces about his scar, his marriage, his past. He'd said that his face had been scarred when he'd been shot in a domestic dispute, omitting the detail that the dispute had been between himself and his wife. He'd told me that his wife was dead, but not that she'd been killed in that same incident. He'd also neglected to mention that he'd been suspected of murdering her and that the charges had been dropped not because he'd been cleared, but because there hadn't been sufficient evidence to try the case. No, Nick hadn't revealed much about himself. I'd found most of that out by chance, on my own. Trusting him wasn't easy.

"Nick, if not the traffickers, who do you think it was?"

"I can't discuss that. It's police business. You know I can't discuss ongoing—"

"The hell I do," I began. "This is my home. My life. I am not asking you to tell me; I'm insisting—"

"Mom?" The screen door flew open and Molly burst in, throwing her schoolbag onto the floor and peering out at the street. "Come here—quick."

"Hi, Molls." I bit my lip, trying to transition into immediate calm. I put down the Scotch and went to the door. Nick turned to greet her. We both wore smiles.

"Mom, hurry up! Look," she insisted, peeking outside. "See her? In the car. Right there, behind the truck—"

"Who?" Nick and I asked together.

"The woman," she squinted. "Oh, nuts. You're too late. She was in the blue car behind the bus. The whole way."

"What woman?"

"What whole way?"

"From school."

I didn't follow.

"She sat on a bench during recess, just watching. It was so creepy. And now, she was just here at our house. I swear. The lady in the blue car followed my bus all the way home."

EIGHTEEN

I don't see anyone, Molly." Nick stepped out the door onto the porch, looking up and down the street.

"Molly, wait. Are you saying that woman was watching you at school?"

"At recess. She was on the bench. When I looked at her, she pretended to be looking at something else, but I could tell."

My nerves were flashing red alerts. Oh my God, I thought. Was it the slave traders? The cartel? Had they followed Molly's bus to school that morning and sent the woman to watch her? First, a threat against Nick. Now, one against my daughter. What did they want from me?

Nick came back inside. "If she was there, she's gone now." Why was he so damned calm?

"She followed the bus here, all the way from school."

"Wait, Molly." Nick's voice was steady, rational. "Are you sure she doesn't work at school? Maybe she's a nurse or a secretary. Or somebody's mom."

Or an FBI agent. Or a slave trader.

"Have you told Mrs. Rutledge about her?" I asked.

"'Course not." Molly rolled her eyes. "Mrs. Rutledge is a butthead."

"Molly—"

"Well, she is a butthead."

I looked at Nick; his eyes leveled mine, bounced back to Molly. "What did the woman look like?" he asked.

Molly shrugged. "She has curly hair. Like mine. And she was wearing blue capri pants." That was it. A six-year-old's description.

"About how old was she?"

"She was old." Molly had no idea. "I think nineteen."

"Okay," Nick said. "Here's what I want you to do. If that woman shows up there again, tell your teacher. And don't go near her."

"But Mom said I didn't have to go to school anymore."

At the moment, I didn't want her to go back to school. I didn't want her to leave my sight. But I couldn't manage to verbalize that thought.

"School sucks." Lacking four front teeth, Molly declared emphatically that thkool thuckth.

"Language, Molly." I stifled my urge to smile; no matter how cute they sounded, her words were inappropriate.

"Well, it does suck." She turned to face me. "What's for dinner?"

Dinner? Oh, Lord. I hadn't even thought about it. Molly stepped into the kitchen, sniffing, stopping in her tracks.

"Eeeyuu," she scowled. "What's that smell? Bug-killer?"

The phone rang. I went to answer it, couldn't find the cordless. "It's ammonia."

"Eeeyuu. It burns my nose. It's disgusting." She looked around, wide-eyed. "Mom? Why's everything out of the refrigerator?"

"I'm cleaning." I followed the sound of the phone, searching behind the milk and orange juice, finally locating it under a bunch of tomatoes.

"Why are you cleaning?" Molly wailed. "It smells sickening!" She ran out of the room holding her nose.

"Okay, enough." Nick sighed, running his hands through his hair. "Go get changed. We're eating out."

"Hello?" I picked up the phone, expecting to hear from Susan. But I was too late; the caller had already hung up.

NINETEEN

Nick seemed preoccupied that night. At dinner, he was mostly silent, not bantering with Molly as usual. Not making leg or foot contact with me under the table. I told myself that it was my imagination. I was exhausted and vulnerable; he was tired and overworked. But when Molly was asleep and we'd stretched out on my bed, I knew for sure that it wasn't just my imagination. Nick was distracted. He went through the motions of kissing and holding, but he wasn't there. His body knew what to do and seemed willing to operate on its own, but his touches were hollow, automatic. I finally breathed that I was tired and hinted that we could stop and just go to sleep; he released me too readily, as if relieved. We lay silently, separately, and the phone began to ring.

"Damn," I said.

"Let the voice mail get it," he suggested.

But I'd already reached for the phone.

"Zoe . . ." Susan sounded half-dead. "Where've you been? I've been calling all afternoon."

"I've been calling you, too. Where've you been?"

"At the Roundhouse, filing police reports."

"I thought we were done with that."

"No, I wasn't there about the women. It was about today. After I left you, I got carjacked."

What? I sat bolt upright. "Oh, God. Are you okay?"

Nick lifted himself, resting on an elbow, curious.

"No, I'm not okay. I'm bruised in places I didn't know I had. This guy came up to me at the stoplight—"

"Where?" As if that mattered.

"Twelfth and Lombard. He stuck a gun in my face."

"A gun? Susan. My God. Nick—Susan got carjacked."

He sat up slowly, rubbing his eyes. "Is she okay?"

"So then he said, 'Move over, bitch.' I swear, I thought he was going to shoot me, but another guy was on the other side of the car and he just opened the door, pulled me out and threw me onto the street."

"In broad daylight?"

"In broad daylight. He threw me down and they took off, right through the red light, and there I was, lying on the pavement, blocking traffic like one of those orange cones."

"Gosh, Susan."

"What?" Nick asked.

"They threw her onto the street. She was just lying there."

"I'm okay, though. I got checked out at the hospital. And they took a description of the guys—"

"Was she hurt?" Nick asked. "Is she okay?"

I nodded, waving at him to be quiet.

"But I don't think it'll help. All I could remember was the gun."

"Damn, Susan."

"And I couldn't even call for help. My cell phone was in the car. In my purse. They got everything."

"Everything?" Absurdly, I thought of her newly purchased bag of condoms.

"Well, the car. My cash, my phone. My credit cards. I had to stop all of them and that took forever. And the police told me to pad the list of stuff in the car for insurance purposes."

Like Officer Bowman, I thought, telling me to think of extra items missing from my house.

"Maybe they'll get it back." I tried to be positive.

"Actually, I'm hoping they don't. I don't want to get in that car ever again, not after those creeps drove it."

I knew what she meant. I felt the same way about my house. "Yeah. That's why I'm dousing everything in cleaning fluids."

"Huh?"

I remembered then that Susan still didn't know about my break-in. As tired as I was, and even though Nick was lying there, I had to tell her. Her car had been stolen and my house had been burglarized the day after we found the bodies in the river. The traffickers had to be involved. And Susan had to be warned that her house could be next. I'd begun to tell her about my break-in when Nick sighed and got up, pulling on a pair of jeans.

"I'm getting a Coke. Want anything?" he asked. Without waiting for a reply, he walked out of the room.

TWENTY

aybe it's all just a bizarre coincidence."

"Your car is stolen, my house is broken into, Nick's pictures are defiled and Molly says a woman's following her, all the day after we found nineteen dead slaves in the river. That's all a coincidence?"

"Maybe."

"Susan, come on."

"Okay, say it isn't. What's the point? Are they trying to scare us? Fine. We're scared. What do they get out of our being scared?"

"What do they think we have or know? What would they be searching for in your car or my house?"

"Whatever it is, I hope they found it so they'll leave us alone."

"You said we wouldn't hear from them again, Susan. That they were satisfied we knew nothing."

"I said we wouldn't hear from those two again. I wasn't car-jacked by the priest and Sonia."

"How can you be sure?"

She hesitated. "Sonia wore a costume, but I doubt she's a wiry young man underneath."

"So, who took your car? The slave smugglers?"

"Maybe. We drove in it to the river that night; maybe they think we found something and put it in the car. They might have looked for it in your house, too. And since they didn't find anything, they'll probably try my house next. Thank God for all my contractors—nobody can get past them."

"But what are they looking for?"

Neither of us could think of anything. And we were both wiped out. So, reassuring each other that the next day would be less harrowing, we hung up. Nick still hadn't come back to the bedroom, so I went downstairs looking for him. The first floor was dark, reeking of cleaning fluids. The kitchen was as we'd left it before we'd gone to dinner: a mess. Stacks of dishes. Bottles and cans, unopened packages of food lay everywhere. Pots and pans, spice jars, dish towels and detergent covered the counters, waiting to be reshelved in newly sterilized cabinets. The sink overflowed with stuff to be thrown out. Looking at it, I shivered, realizing that, earlier in the day, I'd gone a bit berserk.

But where was Nick? Getting a Coke had taken a long time. I checked the living room, the dining room. He wasn't there. But the light was on in my studio.

"Nick?" I called. "You in here?"

I went to the door. Nick sat at my computer clicking away.

"What are you doing in here?" My tone was sharp. Nick was in my private space. The room I'd set aside just for myself.

"Just checking my e-mail." His fingers moved fast. Signing off in a hurry? Closing something he didn't want me to see? Stop it, I told myself. Give the man a break. Why can't you believe he's simply checking his e-mail?

"So, Susan okay?" he asked.

"Just peachy." I was surprisingly irritable. Bitchy, actually.

"As peachy as you?"

"She was carjacked. How would you expect her to be?"

"I don't know. Susan's pretty tough."

"If you think that, you don't know her. Susan's mush." I walked over to the desk.

"Okay, whatever." He pushed a button, minimizing the screen.

I glared at it, wondering what he didn't want me to see. "Why didn't you ask if you could use that?"

"The computer? Oh . . ." He shrugged. "I didn't think it would be a problem. Is it?"

"No. But it's mine. I don't use your things without asking." Actually, I didn't give a rat's behind if he used the computer. But he was hiding something; I could tell. My only chance of finding out what it was, was by pulling rank. Still, I sounded like a selfish six-year-old.

"Okay. I won't touch it again. Ever."

"Of course you can, Nick. I was just making a point—"

He folded his arms. A patient, patronizing pose. "Zoe, what's going on? Is this about me using your computer? Or is it about you trying to pick a fight?"

I didn't answer. I was feisty and cranky and I hated it that he understood.

"Because I think you're upset about what happened last night. And angry about what happened here today. And you can't do anything about those things, so you're taking your frustrations out on me. Which is understandable. Everybody needs a punching bag sometimes. So don't be shy. Don't stop halfway. Go for it. If you want to fight, let's fight."

In the lamplight, Nick's shoulders glowed golden and perfectly sculpted. His muscles bulged, casting soft shadows across the slopes of his skin. I stood in the doorway, tears flooding, unable to put my feelings into words. Anger? Confusion? Love? Fear? Rage? I couldn't separate one from the other, didn't know big from small, real from imagined. Maybe Nick was right. Maybe I was trying to start a fight to purge the turmoil inside me. I was definitely being picky and bitchy. Apologize, I told myself. It's not Nick's fault you're boiling inside.

"I don't want to fight, Nick. I'm just mad."

But Nick didn't back off. His pale eyes zeroed in on me, and his voice taunted. "Bullshit. You want to fight. Fine. Come on. Bring it on. I dare you."

He came closer, his arms reached out, grabbed my wrists.

His mouth brushed mine; his unshaven face scraped my cheek, my neck, my shoulder.

"Nick." I tried to push him away. "Come on. Stop it."

But he didn't. He held both my wrists with one hand, yanked at my T-shirt with the other, pulling me to the floor. "You want a fight?" His voice was a growl. "Okay. You got one."

For a long time, we stayed on the floor, rolling and twisting, grunting and grappling. Sweaty and panting, our bodies struggled in silence, slamming each other roughly, like animals. Afterward, breathless and spent, we went back upstairs and lay on the bed in each other's arms. I felt calm, tired, not as angry as before. I wasn't sure that what had happened had actually been a fight. But if it had been, I'd kind of liked it. And I didn't know, didn't care who'd won.

TWENTY-ONE

The next day, Molly absolutely refused to go to school. The good mother in me knew I should talk to her in depth, uncover the source of her resistance, help her work through whatever problems there were. But I was tired and overwhelmed, and I didn't do any of that. I simply accepted that Molly was Molly, making up her mind and not budging from her position. Even as a toddler, before she was two years old, she'd been strong-willed, rejecting food she didn't like, holding a bite of broiled salmon in her mouth for hours rather than swallowing it. Or climbing a tall kitchen stool onto the counter, scaling the highest cabinet shelves in order to reach a forbidden box of animal crackers. Now, with that same determination, she recited another litany of reasons why she should be allowed to skip school.

"They make you go to lunch even if you're not hungry. And you have to wait in line and hold hands with another kid."

"Molly," I reminded her. "You have just a few days left till summer vacation."

"That's just the point, Mom. I won't miss anything. I mean, seriously. What are they going to do in just three days? Besides, that lady's there. I don't like her following me around."

The lady was what convinced me. Maybe she wasn't actually following Molly, but I didn't want to take the chance. So I caved and made arrangements for Molly to spend the day with my friend Karen and her son Nicholas. Nicholas went to a Catholic school; he was already on summer break. If someone was hanging around the school watching for Molly, she'd be disappointed. Meantime, the kids would get hot and bored in the city, and I hoped that school, by comparison, would seem not so bad. But, as we were leaving, Karen called.

"Send a bathing suit," she said. "I'm taking the kids to the swim club."

Karen and her family belonged to Delancey Swim Club, a square-block urban haven of water slides, pools, restaurants and video games. Molly loved it there; it was where, in toddler classes, she'd learned to swim. By comparison, school wouldn't stand a chance.

Oh, well, I thought as we walked to Karen's. Maybe one day off school would refresh her; tomorrow, she might go willingly. But I knew better; once Molly made up her mind, she rarely changed it. Oh, Lord. I hoped she'd like day camp. If she didn't, what would we do all summer? I had to go back to work, couldn't entertain her. I could make occasional play dates, but most of Molly's friends went to camp. Hari. Emily. Nicholas—all of them. Scanning the street, looking for potential slave traders, I tried to figure out how many times I could miss work to go to the library or the zoo. Not many.

"What's wrong, Mom?" Molly grasped my hand.

"Nothing, Molls." I tried to sound cheerful.

"You look like something's wrong."

"Do I? I was just thinking."

"Can I ask a favor?"

"What?"

"Pleeeeze don't ever clean the house anymore? It smells sickening. My nose burns from it."

I smiled. "Okay."

"Promise."

"Promise that I'll never clean the house again?"

"Yes. Never ever. Not with that pneumonia stuff."

"Ammonia."

"It stinks."

"How's this. I won't clean with ammonia if you'll keep your room neat."

"That's not fair. I like my room the way it is."

There was no point arguing. I wouldn't win. I caved again, promising never to use ammonia again, ever, period. No conditions.

"What are you doing while I'm at Nicholas's?"

"I'm not sure."

"You're not rowing, are you?" She eyed me cautiously.

"Not until later. Why?"

"Don't row. Please?"

"Molly, I'll be fine."

Molly stopped walking. "Don't go, Mom."

"Why?"

Her brows furrowed. "Just don't."

"Nothing will happen, Molly. I promise."

She shook her head. "How do you know?"

"Well, Coach Everett will be with us. He won't let us flip again."

She thought for a moment. "When are you rowing?"

"Later. About five."

"Can I go with?"

I saw the worry on her face.

"Can I?" she repeated.

"Molls, what would you do? You can't stay all alone at the boathouse."

She pouted. "Maybe Emily can come. Like last time."

"I don't think so."

"Why not?"

Once again, I explained that the boathouse wasn't a place for children. That Tony, the manager, didn't want kids hanging around. But Molly had been acting strangely lately, unwilling to go to school, thinking some woman was following her. And who knew how the break-in at the house had affected her? Not to mention the terror of the night before on the river. Damn, how could I be so insensitive? Molly was just a little girl; how could I expect her to take all these traumatic events in stride? I stooped beside her and faced her eye to eye.

"Everything's okay, Molls."

She avoided my gaze.

"I promise. You don't need to worry. Okay?"

She set her jaw. "I want to go with, Mom. I won't bother anybody."

I thought of Tony, his aversion to children and pets. Still, Molly's feelings were more important than Tony's fussiness. "I don't want to leave you alone."

"So let's have Emily come."

As if two six-year-olds would be better than one?

"I'll talk to Susan. Maybe Julie or Lisa can stay with you."

Instantly, Molly's shoulders relaxed and her face brightened. "When you row, can I get water ice?"

"Sure." Why not? I hugged her and stood, amazed at how quickly her mood had reversed itself. If only the promise of syrup-flavored ice could affect everyone that way.

"From Harry," she went on. "Not the other guy. Harry's is better—he scoops it out fresh."

"You got it."

We walked along Pine Street and passed the quaint historic row houses of Society Hill, Molly waxing eloquent upon issues of water ice. The merits of fresh versus prepackaged, the assets of cherry versus mango or root beer. She continued her monologue all the way to Karen's, where Nicholas was waiting on the porch. As soon as he saw us, he ran down the steps.

"Finally." He grabbed her hand and pulled her to the door. "You took forever to get here."

"I had to pack my swimming stuff," Molly explained, but Nicholas had moved on, talking about the bicycle he was getting for his birthday, asking if she could come to his party, telling her about the magician who was going to entertain. The two, lacking front teeth, had matching lisps, and they were still exactly the same height, although Molly had slimmed down while Nicholas had grown sturdier and stockier. They'd met in a play group when they were ten months old and had been fast friends ever since.

"Come in and cool off." Karen hugged first Molly, then me. "Thank God for air-conditioning."

"Did you hear about my mom?" Molly sounded boastful.

"What, sweetie?" Karen hadn't heard the question.

"'Course we did." Nicholas was positive.

"My mom found a drowned person in the river."

Karen's mouth opened, then closed again.

"Molly," I began, "that's not something—"

"No, she didn't." Nicholas was loud, almost shouting. "She did not find a drowned person—"

"Nicholas." Karen frowned. "Remember? We agreed we were not going to talk about that."

But Molly's hands were on her hips, indignant. "Yes, she did. Ask her. Mom? Tell him you found a drowned—"

"Nicholas. Drop it." Karen spoke through her teeth.

"No, Molly," Nicholas interrupted. "You're wrong. Your mom didn't find a drowned person—"

"Yes, she—"

"She found nineteen. Nineteen drowned people. Everybody knows that."

"Nineteen? Uh-uh. You're making it up." Molly turned and gaped at me, stricken. "Tell him, Mom."

Karen watched with wide, tortured eyes.

"Molly," I fudged, "it was like I told you. Our boat flipped on one person." I'd made an omission, but that wasn't really a lie, was it? "But it turned out there were more people in the water with her."

She eyed me, wounded and suspicious. I recognized that look; I often wore it myself.

"You told me one person drowned."

"Molly, I never said how many."

"You lied." She was near tears.

"No, I didn't. I'd never lie to you." Oops—damn. Another lie. "We just never talked about how many people there were."

"There were nineteen," Nicholas announced again. "Look,

I'll show you. I have pictures from the newspaper." He ran into the living room. "Come look, Molly."

"Nicholas, wait—" Karen called, but he was gone.

Molly kept staring at me. And in her eyes, I saw them again—floating women, all dead. Someone's daughter. Someone's sister. Someone's lover or friend.

"Molls. When we talked about it, I didn't know yet that there were nineteen." Actually, I'd thought there were hundreds. "And it was awful that even one person died. I don't see why it's important how many there were."

"But Mom, it's important that you tell me the truth." Who was the child and who the parent? Not for the first time, Molly seemed older, more savvy than her years. "So, if you'd known how many there were, would you have told me nineteen?"

I closed my eyes and lied again. "Yes. Of course."

"Swear?" She pouted.

"Swear." I kissed her head, feeling awful. I hated lies, even small, friendly ones. Even lies meant to protect her, make her feel secure, keep the peace, explain the inexplicable. I tried always to be truthful with Molly, but one simple omission had led to a chain of lies, and now I couldn't seem to stop adding links. Hell, I was even lying about lying. "Now go and have fun at the pool. I'll see you later."

"Molly!" Nicholas called from the back of the house. "Come look at the pictures. Your mom's in the paper!"

"Coming." She pounded off after him. " 'Bye, Mom." She kissed me and ran off.

"How about some coffee?" Karen sighed, studying my face.

"Thanks, I can't. I've got to take off." I couldn't begin to explain why.

"How are you holding up? Have you recovered from the shock? It must have been awful."

"I'm fine."

She shook her head. "How could that happen here, in this country, in this century? All those women . . . Does anyone know who they are? Aren't their families searching for them at home? The press says they're all unidentified. I can't imagine."

I answered that I couldn't either, hiding behind glib answers and shrugs, not mentioning my break-in or Susan's car-jacking, not wanting to revisit the past day even in conversation. Instead, I steered Karen's attention to the new Spanish tiles in her kitchen, then to Nicholas's approaching birthday. And, as soon as I could without being rude I took off, alone, heading home.

TWENTY-TWO

I planned to stay inside for the rest of the day, alone, feeling sorry for myself, talking to no one. I collapsed onto my big purple sofa and sat curled up in a fetal position, sulking. I stayed there for a while, but moping was no help. My mind ricocheted from topic to topic, crashing into an idea and bouncing away. I should finish cleaning, I thought. I hadn't done the office yet, or the laundry room. Crash—zoom. I should call the glazier to fix the window from the break-in. Duct tape wouldn't provide much protection from a slave cartel, but then, glass hadn't either. Crash—zoom. What was going on with Nick? What had been going on with the computer? And was he ever going to ask me to marry him? Crash—zoom. Poor me. I'd worked hard, earned a master's degree, recovered from a divorce, adopted a child, created a home. And now my home had been invaded. My entire life—everything I'd struggled to build—was falling apart. Crash—zoom. I should relax. I shut my eyes and saw the blackness of the river, felt cold water swallow me and bumped slippery flesh. Trying to breathe, I gagged on a mouthful of wet hair. Crash—zoom.

Stop it, I told myself. You're just beating yourself up, making yourself miserable. Do something productive. Get off your butt and take charge of your life. Look forward. Be active, assertive. Make a plan. Okay, I thought. A plan. A plan was absolutely what I needed.

I got up, pacing, brainstorming randomly, and without even knowing what sort of plan I was trying to make, found myself in front of the bathroom mirror, silently talking to myself. You can do this, I told my face. You're tough. Independent. Strong. Pull yourself together and deal.

No, the face whimpered. I'm not strong, not tough. Not really. I've been faking. Pretending. Underneath, I'm a wimp, scared to death. A fraud and failure. I was a failure at marriage, so I got divorced. I couldn't make it as an artist, so I did art therapy. And I had no business adopting Molly; I don't know the first thing about raising a child. After all, look what I've gotten us into—trouble with some huge invisible international multibillion-dollar slave cartel? The face dissolved into tears, proving how weak and utterly pathetic it was.

I watched myself cry with a mixture of contempt and pity, feeling distant, regarding myself objectively. Crying, I decided, didn't go well with my face. It was aesthetically wrong. I was too old, had too many streaks of gray in my hair to be crying like a child. My cheekbones were prominent, bones too strong for weeping. And the smile lines around my eyes contradicted the tears. Physically, the face in the mirror was mixed up, full of incongruence. I pulled my hair back and dried my eyes, staring into them, seeking strength from my own gaze. Hazel eyes probed themselves, searching for a core, a source to connect to. Breathe deeply, I told myself. Stand up straight. Find your center.

"Zoe?"

I jumped, startled. I hadn't heard Nick come in. I checked the mirror for telltale smears or blotches of red.

"Nick. I wasn't expecting you." I stepped into the hall.

"I had a few minutes, so . . ." He touched my cheek. "I . . . well, I wanted to make sure you were okay. I mean, last night, you seemed . . . we were both . . . it was . . . kind of strange."

I hugged him, partly to hide the new wave of tears threatening to gush. I nodded. We'd been like beasts. "I'm okay. Are you?"

"I'm fine. If you are." He seemed tentative.

"I just spent an hour wallowing, so I'm better."

"Wallowing?" A hint of a smile brightened half his face; the scarred side remained ruggedly stoic.

"Yup." I rubbed my eyes, trying to erase any lingering puffiness.

He watched me closely; I felt like a specimen slide in biology class.

"Really, I'm okay."

He kept studying me, apparently unconvinced.

"I got sick of feeling sorry for myself, so I stopped. I'm fine now." I moved away, feeling exposed.

"Just like that?"

"Just like that. Never underestimate the value of a really good hard—"

"—Believe me, I would never."

"I was going to say 'a really good hard wallow.' "

"Yeah? I like mine better." Again the half-grin.

"Okay." I smiled. "That, too." I headed into the kitchen. There was chaos to clean up in there. "How long can you stay?"

"A few minutes only."

"Well then, for a few minutes you can help. Here." I handed him a pile of baking pans. "These go in the high shelf over the oven."

"Zoe," he complained. "Can't this wait?" But he put them where they belonged.

"Be careful with these." I handed him a stack of Aunt Edith's flower-patterned china plates and pointed to the top shelf in the corner. "They go up there."

He put the plates away. "I have some news about the case."

I froze, a blender in hands. "About the women? What?"

Nick reached for the soup bowls without being asked.

"Yeah. I thought you should know before it hits the news."

So he hadn't come home to see how I was; he'd really come to tell me some news. Why couldn't he just have said so? When would he just be honest? Angry, I shoved the blender into a cabinet and grabbed a colander. I was racing to put my kitchen in order, not wanting to know anything more about the women, not being able to resist finding out.

"The preliminary autopsy reports are in." Nick lifted the saucers onto the shelf. "They didn't drown. They were dead before they hit the water."

I held still, hugging myself, feeling chilled. "Then what happened? How'd they die?"

Laying a stack of soup bowls beside the saucers, he turned to look at me. "They fried."

The colander slipped from my fingers, clattering onto the floor. Fried? What was he talking about? Oh, God. I stooped to pick up my colander; Nick got to it first. I grabbed it from him and held it against my belly.

"You okay?"

"Sure." How could I be okay? Was he kidding? "Just clumsy."

"It looks like it was the heat. They literally baked to death. Probably locked in a closed compartment in the hot sun, most likely a truck or a van. It'll be on the news, so I'm giving you a heads-up." He put the cups away gently, two at a time.

They fried? My skin itched. I couldn't breathe. "Thanks. Thanks for telling me." Out the kitchen window, the sun beamed white heat. Vans were parked everywhere along the street. Construction vans. Delivery vans. Vans with unknown purposes. All were locked and closed up tight. I crossed my arms, trying not to imagine being left inside in the heat, what it would be like, dying that way.

"You ever use any of this stuff?"

Stuff? Nick was pointing at the china.

"Not really," I said. "It was my aunt's."

"We should use it." He held up a cup, examined the delicate roses on its side. "It's nice."

He put it back on the shelf, and after replacing canisters and stoneware, cutlery and cans, Nick promised to be back after work, kissed my cheek, and left. I stopped sorting silverware to call a glazier about the office window. But I got stuck, phone book in hand, and stood in my kitchen, looking out at the street, watching steam rise off sweltering parked vans.

TWENTY-THREE

Just before five o'clock, I picked Molly up at Karen's and drove Nick's car to the river where, as promised, I took Molly to Harry's water-ice stand. The sun was relentless and there wasn't a hint of a breeze. Harry's helium balloons hovered motionless over his truck like dabs of color in a still life.

"Cherry, please." Molly held up the dollar I'd given her. "Small." Harry's small dishes were the size of Molly's head.

"How are you, little lady? Nice to see you." The unofficial mayor of Boathouse Row, Harry tended to ramble. "It's sure been busy, with all this heat. Believe me, people can't get enough to drink. You don't want to get dehydrated. It's dangerous. You want to keep drinking. And if you have a pet, be sure to give him water. Don't leave him in the car. It's too hot. This early in the year . . . who'd have thought it would be so hot in June? What's August going to be like if this keeps up?"

Harry went on, maintaining a nonstop one-way conversation as he scooped out generous mounds of red slushy ice and handed the overflowing cup to Molly, whose eyes had widened with each scoop.

"Say," he addressed me. "Didn't I see your picture in the paper? What's your name again? Wait—I'll remember." He clapped his forehead, thinking. "Something different. Zoe?

That's it. Zoe Hayes, right? The lady who found all those floaters? Those dead women?"

I nodded, starting to usher Molly away.

"She is. That's her." Molly was bragging. "My mom thought there was just one, but really there were nineteen."

"Take care, Harry." I gave Molly a gentle shove forward. "Thanks."

"Wait—wait just a second." He grabbed my arm, reminding me of Sonia, and leaned toward me confidentially. "I gotta ask you something." He lowered his voice, as if to prevent Molly from hearing. "You know how it is; they call me the mayor of the Row because I'm supposed to know everything that goes on here. But honestly, this thing knocked me over, took me totally by surprise. Tell me, is it true what they're saying? That the floaters were slaves?"

I blinked, off-guard. How much did he know? And why was he cornering me? He held my arm, still talking. "What? Hadn't you heard that? Well, it's true. I'm serious. They say there's a slave ring operating right here in Philadelphia. On this river. Can you believe it? Have you heard anything about that?"

"No. Just what was in the papers." Thank God Molly was completely absorbed in digging out her water ice, not paying attention. Why was he talking about the slave trade in front of her? "I don't know anything." Again I started to move away.

"Well, between you and me"—he leaned closer, so close that I felt his breath on my face—"I'll tell you what I heard. I heard that those women got dumped in the river because the guy who was transporting them panicked. He messed up and let them die of the heat. In his damned truck. Now, how goddamn dumb was that? You wouldn't leave a dog locked up in a car in this heat. But this dumb ass left a bunch of women to bake to death."

I'd stopped breathing, recalling a lifeless face drifting in the water. How did Harry know so much? Had all of this been in the papers? I didn't know, had lost track of the coverage. But then Harry would know more than most people because he was Harry, unofficial mayor of the Row, aware of everything that went on there. To him, the story was just headlines and hot gossip. He wasn't deliberately harassing me by talking about it; he was just being Harry.

He watched me, waiting for a reply, but I didn't have one. I shrugged, lacking words. "Well, we have to go. See you, Harry."

But he kept on talking. "Seriously, think about it. Whoever that driver is, he's gotta be in some very deep shit. Unless he can make that delivery good somehow."

What was he talking about? Make it good? How? By bringing back the dead?

"Rumors are flying up and down the Row. And everyone asks me, 'Harry, what's going on?' They expect me to know. 'Harry knows everything,' they say. But this time, I got nothing to tell them. So, Zoe, maybe you can help me out." He met my eyes. "There must be something you can tell me."

Other than that he was being insensitive and pushy? "Sorry, nothing. Molly, it's time to go."

"Oh, come on. Do me a favor; think for a second. Anything. Like maybe there was something in the water with them? Some cash maybe? Or identification? Or—hey—maybe there was a survivor? Even one?"

I shook my head no, no, no and no. "There's nothing to tell. And I really don't want to discuss it, Harry. It was awful."

Harry winced, making a "tsk" sound. He looked bereft. "Okay, then."

"Look, I have a sculling lesson. I've got to go." I started to lead Molly away. Cherry syrup ran down her chin; I turned back to Harry's stand to grab a napkin.

"Enjoy your lesson, then, Zoe. Zoe Hayes. I'll remember it from now on. Which boathouse do you row out of again? Humberton?"

"Yes. Humberton."

"You must know Tony, then. He's house manager there."

"That's right."

"I know a ton of Humberton people. Larry Dumont. John Smith. George Plummer. Preston Everett—"

"Preston Everett's my coach."

"Everett? Really?" He sighed. "You know, he used to be

great. Great coach. Great rower, too, though you wouldn't know it to look at him now."

Coach Everett had developed a substantial paunch.

"He was a champ. Gold medal in the Olympics. Coached the Olympic team. Everyone thought he was destined for the stars. Who'd have thought he'd end up like this, coaching novices for a few bucks a pop? The guy doesn't even row anymore. It's a real shame, if you ask me."

A young man on Rollerblades skated up and asked for an iced tea and a soft pretzel.

"Hot today, isn't it?" Harry asked him, reaching inside the truck for a fresh pretzel.

As soon as his back was turned, I hurried Molly away. Her lips were dyed cherry-red.

Harry pointed at me. "See her?" he asked the skater. "That's the lady who found the floaters. Those nineteen dead women. You heard about that, right? You won't believe what she told me about them . . ."

I walked on, pretending not to hear. Molly turned and looked back.

"Mom, Harry's talking about you."

"Shh—I know," I whispered. "But I don't want to talk anymore."

Molly nodded. "Harry has good ice, but he talks too much. He's kind of nosy."

I tousled her hair, pleased at her insight. "I think so too, Molls." We walked on in silence, Molly slurping up her melting water ice, until we got to Humberton's front door.

TWENTY-FOUR

Emily couldn't come because of a piano lesson, but Lisa, Susan's eldest, was waiting when we arrived. I slipped her ten bucks for baby-sitting Molly and left them watching a rerun of *Seventh Heaven* on the television in the lounge. They weren't alone upstairs. A couple of rowers lingered at the juice bar; a few worked out on ergs in the adjacent exercise room. The girls would be fine for an hour while we rowed.

Downstairs, the boat bays were crowded with rowers. I stood at the bottom of the steps, trying to spot Susan.

"Hands on." A tanned woman with a platinum ponytail shouted commands; three other women obeyed, taking hold of a quad.

"Overheads," she yelled, and the four lifted the long white shell into the air, walked it out and across the dock, and set it gently into the water. Grabbing a pair of oars, I followed them outside, watching them work together with ease and familiarity. I wondered if I'd ever be as confident or graceful with the equipment.

A woman I'd never seen before walked past, carrying oars.

"Going out?" She smiled.

I nodded, yes.

"Looks great out there, doesn't it?"

"Sure does," I said, but she'd already moved on.

It was a busy time on the dock. Rowers of all ages and skill levels rushed to get their shells out, commenting lightly about the unseasonable heat and the calm conditions. They seemed friendly but preoccupied. Intense. Completely focused on the process of getting their equipment together and shoving off the dock. Not fazed or deterred by the deaths discovered in the water. I watched them, wondering what I was doing there. I was an outsider, a stranger. Not part of this tight community. I looked away, past the people to the river, watching small silver ripples tickle the surface. How quiet the water seemed now. How soothing. How unlike the choking black murk of the other night.

"Zoe—" Susan appeared from nowhere, frazzled. "You're five minutes late. You all right?" I hadn't seen her since before her car-jacking. The skin on her legs and arms had been scraped raw; plum-sized purple bruises covered her left side.

"Are you?" I eyed her wounds.

"I'm fine. Ready to go?" She held her oars awkwardly, almost bumping them into a tall young man walking by with a twenty-seven-foot-long single shell effortlessly balanced on his head.

"Oh, man." Susan seemed unaware of her near collision, but she froze, staring at his bottom. "Check out his stern."

I smiled at the nautical terminology. She was accurate, too; his stern was tight and meaty. And his spandex unisuit, rolled down to his waist, exposed a rippling back and shoulder muscles. I thought of Nick, the firmness of his thighs, the solid bulges revealed by his rowing clothes.

"What is he, twenty?" She sighed. "I could be his mother."

"So?" I shrugged. "Men date women twenty years younger all the time—they even marry them."

Her eyes remained fixed on the half-naked guy's butt. "Go ahead, Susan. Introduce yourself. Flirt with him."

"Are you kidding?" She frowned, appalled. "I could never."

"Oh? So flirting's okay for older men, but not older women?"

"Zoe, don't be ridiculous. It's not about my age. It's about my status. I'm a married woman. I can't go around flirting."

Even so, she kept staring, enthralled. "Look at him. What efficiency of movement. What confidence in his body."

"What drool on your chin."

"It's such a sad waste of stud muffins," she lamented. "Why didn't anyone tell me about this sport when I was younger?"

As her prey rowed away, two more young men came out of the boathouse, carrying a double. They were buffed and tanned, clad in tight spandex rowing shorts.

"Oh my." Susan stopped breathing.

"Whoa there, Nelly." I fanned her. "Settle down."

"Maybe I wouldn't be so distracted if Tim were here." She thought for a moment. "Hey—do you think we could persuade him to take up rowing?"

I tried not to imagine Tim in tight spandex rowing clothes; the picture was almost as disturbing as Tim in a green condom. I liked Tim, but if Susan wanted to see her round, middle-aged husband in formfitting, skin-clinging, shape-revealing shiny fabric, I hoped she'd do it in the privacy of her home.

"It wouldn't take him long to learn," she went on. "I mean, for a middle-aged guy, he's pretty athletic. And he'd look so cute in a unisuit."

I wasn't going to touch the subject. "Why bother Tim? These guys are doing a fine job of displaying the assets of men in spandex."

"Forget the spandex. I'll take just the ass sets."

"Cute. Very cute."

More rowers passed, carrying shells, shoving off for evening practices. "Heads up, ladies." Susan and I ducked, since "heads up" actually means heads down. An eight swung just inches over us as the women carrying it set it onto a set of slings on the dock.

Their coxswain eyed us as they whispered among themselves.

"Hey," the cox finally called. "Aren't you the new members? You found those dead women?"

Susan and I glanced at each other.

"For sure, it's them," said a tall brunette. "I saw their pictures on the news."

"How awful." They stepped closer in a slow swarm, like bees. "Especially for novices like you. We found a floater once—Remember, Paige? We were in the double."

"A guy jumped off a bridge." The one named Paige nodded, her pigtails bouncing. "Suicide."

"It happens now and then," said the cox. "But so many— nineteen? That's serious."

A pause while everyone agreed.

"It's amazing you two are rowing again." This came from a freckled woman in a polka-dot unisuit. She seemed covered head to toe with spots.

"If it were me and I were a complete novice like you guys, I'd never get in a boat again." That came from Paige.

"Of course you would." Susan bristled at being called a complete novice. "It's like falling off a horse. You have to get right back in the saddle."

"A horse? I thought that was a bike," said a blonde. "Is it horses, too?"

"Well, good for you." Paige ignored her. "That's a great attitude."

"Never let anything stop you," a thin woman with huge brown eyes advised.

"Anyway, welcome to Humberton."

"We're a close bunch here," the thin woman said.

"Just like a family," the blonde added.

"And every bit as dysfunctional." Polka Dots grinned. The others laughed a little too hard, too long.

"Anyhow, we just wanted to say hello—"

"—and if you ever want to talk—"

"—about anything—"

"—we're here—"

"—every night."

The women actually completed each other's sentences. They even nodded together, wearing identical expectant smiles.

The coxswain glanced at the boat. "Ladies, we've gotta shove."

"Nice meeting you," the blonde waved.

The women swarmed off to their boat.

"What was that?" Susan whispered.

Before I could answer, a thunderous voice roared at us. "Why are you two novices standing around yammering on the dock?" Coach Everett was about twelve feet away, but blaring at us through his megaphone. Everyone on the dock turned to look at us, including the women getting into the eight. I felt my face redden.

"Guess what, ladies. Singles today."

Singles? Was he joking? We'd rowed in singles only once before, briefly. They were twenty-five feet long and a butt's width wide, hard to balance, easy to flip. I remembered river water rushing into my nose, filling my mouth, pouring into my ears, and my heart plunged somewhere deep under my stomach, terrified.

"But in the regatta, we're going to race a double," Susan reasoned. "Shouldn't we practice in one?"

"Who's the coach here, Cummings?" Coach Everett barked into the megaphone. "I said, 'Singles.' Cummings, take the *John W. Smith*. Hayes, you're in the *Sexton*."

"But we've got the race—"

"Cummings. What part of the word 'singles' confuses you? Sin-gles. Don't stand there blithering—you have sixty seconds to get your boats out. Get your asses moving."

"This is absurd," I muttered.

"Let it go, Zoe," Susan begged, scurrying. "Just do what he says. He's the best coach on the river."

"Move it, Hayes. The clock's ticking."

Susan shoved me into the boathouse. "Don't let him get to you."

"He's an asshole."

"So? You're not married to him. The man knows rowing, and we're here to learn."

I glared outside. The eight was gliding away from the dock, strokes coordinated, timing exact.

"Come on." Susan pulled at me.

Our esteemed coach, Preston Everett, was waiting.

TWENTY-FIVE

Of course it took us much longer than sixty seconds. Susan and I struggled to get our two singles down to the end of the dock. The shells weren't heavy, but they were long and skinny and seemingly impossible to balance. Other rowers carried their boats to the water with graceful ease, but we battled with matter and gravity while Coach Everett criticized and scolded us at every tentative step. Somehow, we eventually managed to lift the boats off the racks and, dancing, juggling, tilting and bumping them against other boats and the ground, struggled to find the focal point from which to hold them steady. Dripping with sweat from heat and exertion, we finally made it to the water without dropping the boats or destroying any others. Susan was triumphant, but I was frustrated.

"He could have helped," I whispered. "Instead of just watching us screw up."

"Trust him, Zoe. He knows what he's doing."

"That was terrible, ladies. I've never seen a clumsier effort," Coach announced into his megaphone. Rowers on the dock of Vesper, the boathouse next door, turned to stare at us. "You two are the Laurel and Hardy of Humberton Barge."

The man was unbearable. Even though Susan urged me to ignore him, I couldn't. "Coach, what's with the megaphone?"

"Hayes, don't dawdle," he blared. "You have a boat on the dock."

"Zoe, cool it . . ." Susan begged.

"No. The man's standing right next to us. Why does he need to shout into a megaphone?"

"Ignore it," Susan pleaded. "Don't let him get to you."

"Ladies, if you would," Coach Everett taunted, "let's get into our goddamn boats. Please."

"That's it." I was ready to leave. "It's over. I can't listen to this."

"Please," Susan pleaded. "Wait . . . I'll talk to him."

She approached the coach, face-to-megaphone. Her voice was low, too quiet for me to hear. Coach waited for her to finish, looking bored. Then, loudly, he replied. "Tell me, Cummings. Who are you?"

Susan took a step back. "Sorry . . . what?"

He repeated the question, his tone condescending, sarcastic.

Susan was confused. Beginning to sputter. "Who am I? What do you mean?"

This time, he used the megaphone. "WHO ARE YOU?"

Now Susan was offended. "Who am I? Okay. I'll tell you. I'm a professional woman—successful. I'm a criminal defense attorney. And I'm the wife of a very successful businessman. And the mother of three healthy children—"

"No, no, Cummings. That's off the water, and frankly I don't give a rat's ass who you are off the water. You could be president of the United States for all I care. Here, on the river, I'll tell you who you are: Nobody. You're just a goddamn novice who knows nothing. And here's who I am. On the river, as far as you're concerned, I'm God. I am not just your coach; I'm your absolute master. Don't you dare question what I say or how I say it. But I'll tell you about the megaphone. I'm using it because I want my voice to burn into your brain. I want you to hear my voice every time you even think about rowing. Every time you get anywhere close to the water or even dream about it. Off the water, you can do or be whatever you want; down here, I rule your butt. Got it? Now shut your face up and get in the boat."

For an interminable moment, Susan didn't move. She stood still, bug-eyed and speechless. I thought she might go after him, pictured the two of them duking it out right on the dock. I even imagined joining in, the two of us tossing him into the river, his megaphone stuffed up an especially delicate orifice. But instead, Susan suddenly spun around and hurried to her boat.

"Fine," she said. And, without another word, she locked her oars on and wobbled precariously into the old Filippi single.

In hindsight, it seemed clear that we should have canceled the lesson right then. Just walked away, leaving Everett and his megaphone to put the boats away himself. But for some inexplicable reason, we didn't. I was already in my shell. The river was calm, beckoning. We both felt compelled to get out there and row, and, officially, novices couldn't row without a coach.

As Susan was climbing into her shell, the coach bellowed again. "Cummings," he blared. "Look at your boat. What have you done wrong?"

She stopped, staring at her boat. She walked alongside, gazing at it from bow to stern. "Nothing," she finally said. "Nothing's wrong."

"Nothing?" the voice boomed. "Think, Cummings. Think and look. And revise your answer."

Again Susan examined her shell. She crossed her arms. "I don't see anything," she said.

"You're sure?" His tone was condescending, sarcastic.

"What? Why don't you just tell me?"

"Look at your hatches, Cummings."

Susan looked. Red patches of embarrassment emerged on chest and throat as she realized her mistake. Each end of the hollow hull had a hatch to seal it watertight. In our very first lesson, we'd learned to close the hatches before launching. That way, if we flipped, the shell would float like a raft.

"Your hatches, Cummings. What's wrong with them?"

"They're open." Her voice was faint.

"What? I didn't hear that."

"They're open."

"Say again?"

"My hatches are open!" Susan shouted.

She was already on her knees, closing them. Coach Everett waited with exaggerated patience, and finally Susan and I each managed to push away from the dock without further incident.

TWENTY-SIX

From that point on, the lesson deteriorated. I was too busy trying to balance to watch how Susan was doing. The single shell was much lighter and less stable than the double. Every time I moved at all—whether lifting a hand, turning my head, shifting my legs—the boat tipped and wobbled. My shoulders tensed; my hands clutched the oars. Sweat soaked my body, dripping into my eyes, making my hands slippery. Slowly, dragging my oars in tiny strokes, I moved my boat across the river, waiting to overturn, listening for a splash.

Coach Everett followed in a motor launch, demanding that we row with squared oars. Squared oars meant that the blades had to remain perpendicular to the water. Normally, rowers feather or flatten their oars between strokes, holding the blades horizontal to the water, stabilizing the boat the way training wheels stabilize a bike. To row with squared oars required skill, balance and strong technique. None of which, as novices, Susan or I had.

As Coach Everett shouted scathing criticism from his launch, I struggled to stay afloat. My shell rocked and tilted, threatening to spill me out. I forgot to breathe. My entire body clenched, and I was sure I'd pass out from exertion or heat. The surface was calm and flat, but my blades kept catching on the water, tipping the boat. And when I stopped rowing to regain my balance, Everett hollered.

"Dammit, Hayes, did I tell you to stop? Is your brain up your butt? Slow your goddamn slide."

Don't let him shake you, I told myself. Ignore the insults. He's insufferable, but he knows how to row, so just do what he says. And gradually, a mantra began in my mind, with Coach Everett's voice chanting each part of the stroke. "Reach out, catch water. Push with your legs. Lean back. Arms back. Finish. Reach ahead, lean forward, slide up slowly, slowly, slowly. Reach out and catch water again."

Each slight movement, a roll of the fingers, a twist of the wrist, the position of my head, the stiffness of my shoulders made a difference in the stroke. There was so much to think about, so much room to make mistakes. The coach tore at me again and again. "No, not like that. Are you learning-impaired, Hayes? Go all the way up the slide. Onto your toes. More. More. Now, reach out. No—further out."

The farther I reached, the more off balance I felt. I suspected he wanted me to flip so he could humiliate me further, and I didn't want to give him the pleasure. In fact, I refused. So, with my shell teetering and body drenched with sweat, I concentrated not on the coach but on my rowing. On the sensations of being in the boat and on the water. And when he finally left me to torment Susan, I continued practicing, repeating his mantra, until, as I was beginning to tip and sway a little less, from somewhere beyond the roaring of the launch's motor and the coach's megaphone, I heard Susan shouting.

I stopped rowing to listen. Susan was screaming. "You goddamn son of a bitch," I heard. "You did that on purpose!"

I feathered my oars, stabilizing my boat on the water, and turned, scanning the water for Susan. Her boat was fifty feet downriver, overturned; Susan was beside it, treading water, shaking her fists at Everett.

"You sadistic egomaniac—you flipped me!"

Coach Everett sat calmly in his launch, talking through his

megaphone. "Cummings, you should try another sport. How about sumo wrestling. At least you have the physique."

Susan yelled back. "You buzzed me! You deliberately flipped me with your wake. You ought to be banned from coaching. From the entire river. I'll sue you. I'll file a complaint with the Schuylkill Navy—With U.S. Rowing—"

Coach Everett chuckled, watching Susan flail in the water. "Quiet down, Cummings. Save your energy. You still have to get back in your boat."

Cursing and sputtering, Susan lifted an oar and splashed around, trying to right her overturned boat. I rowed over, watching helplessly as she managed to roll the boat over and cross the oars. When she tried to lift herself in, though, she knocked the oars apart, flipped the shell again and fell back into the water. Cold memories tickled my neck; I could feel the river engulfing me, dead flesh embracing me, sodden hair floating into my mouth. I closed my eyes, told myself that no dead bodies were in the water today, that Susan would be fine. And the water would cool her off. The second time she tried, she almost made it.

"Be patient," I cheered her on. "You've almost got it. Take your time."

Head bobbing in the water, she scowled fiercely, eyes threatening violence if I didn't shut up.

Coach Everett commented on her every move, noting that she wasn't a bad swimmer and might have more success swimming back to the dock tugging the boat along with her. Finally, after a few more attempts, Susan hoisted herself up, successfully shimmied back into her seat and grabbed the handles of her oars.

"Are you all right?" I yelled.

She cursed and turned to Coach Everett. "You belong in jail," she shouted. "Or a mental hospital. You're insane. I swear, I am never ever under any circumstances going to row with you again."

Smiling, he saluted her. "Don't worry, Cummings. You won't have the opportunity. You're hopeless. You stink."

Without another word, feathering her oars, Susan rowed back toward the Humberton dock.

TWENTY-SEVEN

The lesson was over. I turned my shell around to follow Susan, and the coach slowly trailed me in the launch.

"Your friend's a hothead," he called through his megaphone. "Blaming me because she flipped her boat."

I didn't answer. I hadn't seen what had happened, but I had no doubt that he'd been at fault.

"I can see why she's so defensive, though," he continued. "She was the bow, after all. She was steering when your double flipped the other night. Nobody flips a double. You've really got to suck to do that."

I didn't want to engage in conversation, but I felt the need to stand up for my friend. "That wasn't her fault," I yelled. "Her oar got stuck on a corpse."

"No excuse. She should have avoided it. Nobody flips a double. Yo, Hayes—focus. Keep your hands down."

Drop dead, I thought. Still, I lowered my hands.

"Better. You actually seem to have some potential for this," he said. Wait. Had he said something nice? A compliment? Unbelievable. I felt myself blush. Stop it, I told myself. Don't listen to him; he's an asshole. Concentrate on your strokes. Push your legs and thighs, lean back. Lower your knees and hands.

The boat responded, gliding and bubbling smoothly beneath me, and I began to lose myself in the motions.

"So, what did you see?"

What was he talking about? "Sorry, what?" I lost the rhythm, stopped rowing.

"When you found the bodies," he called. "Was anyone else around? Was there anything else in the water?"

Wait. What was going on? Harry had just asked those same questions. Why? Weren't nineteen bodies enough? Why would anyone expect there to be anything else?

I shook my head, no, and began to row again.

"Slow down. Don't take your slide so fast. Let yourself take the ride," he called. Then he put down the megaphone and watched me row silently, without comment, all the way back to the dock.

TWENTY-EIGHT

When I pulled up, the Humberton dock was empty. Dozens of shoes and a few stray socks, towels and water bottles littered the deck, waiting for their owners to return and claim them, but nobody was around. Susan had already replaced her boat and apparently taken off, maybe gone upstairs to Lisa and Molly. I put away my oars and struggled to put my boat back on the racks; then, without waiting for the coach's postlesson critique, I rushed upstairs. As I climbed, I noticed how oddly quiet the boathouse was. No music blared from the exercise room; no chatter drifted from the juice bar. I entered the lounge, looking for Lisa and Molly, calling their names. No one answered.

I stopped, scanning the room, registering that no one was there. The leather sofa on which I'd left Molly was vacant. Her empty water-ice cup, her coloring stuff was there. Her bead kit was open; a bracelet lay half-finished on the sofa. But there was no Molly.

The locker room, I thought. Of course. That's where they must be. Lisa must have taken Molly to the bathroom. I went to the women's locker room, pulled the door open.

"Molly?" I yelled. "Lisa?"

Only silence answered. And the sound of running water.

Oh, Lord. My belly churned, my head felt light. After everything that had happened, how had I been so stupid as to leave Molly even for an hour? I stood shivering in the steamy heat, unable to figure out what to do.

"Molly?" I called again. "Lisa?"

No answer. Just the shower.

The shower. Someone was in there. Maybe she'd seen the girls. I hurried past the sinks and toilets into the shower room, found a closed curtain, peeked through the crack. Susan stood under the water, rinsing her hair.

"Susan," I called. "Have you seen Lisa and Molly?" Absurdly, I noticed that her nipples were large and surprisingly pink.

"They're in the lounge." She stuck her head out. "Can you believe Everett? That psycho jerk—"

"They're not in the lounge," I cut in. "I can't find them."

"Are you sure?" She turned off the water, grabbed a towel. "I was just in there."

"Then I don't know—" Susan emerged from the shower, shampoo still on her forehead. "Molly was in there, lying on the sofa when I came in. Lisa was getting a drink at the juice bar. And Tony was in the lounge, on the phone."

Tony? Oh, wonderful. He'd probably be ballistic that there was a kid in the boathouse. If he'd been in the lounge, he might have scared her away. But he also might have seen where she'd gone. I hurried out of the locker room, back to the members' lounge. No sign of Tony, so I rushed to the juice bar, looking for Lisa. No Lisa. I looked in the exercise room. No Tony, no Lisa. No Molly. Just a bald guy with a bunch of tattoos and a hairy sweat-drenched body lifting weights.

"Have you seen a little girl about this tall?"

He blinked rapidly, grunting under a barbell. "A little girl? No."

"Or Tony?"

"Tony's around. Try downstairs."

At the stairs, I ran smack into Lisa, who was coming up.

"Is Molly with you?" she wailed.

No. I shook my head. "She's not with you?"

"No, I don't know where she is. I looked everywhere."

My heart did a flip. "But . . . how . . . What happened?"

"Molly was lying down. So I went to the juice bar to get a root beer, and when I got back she was gone. I swear I was only gone two seconds . . ." Lisa was sweating, panting. Frantic.

"Go wait in the lounge, Lisa." I tried to sound calm. "She's got to be around. Don't worry."

Lisa nodded, tears in her eyes. "I'm sorry, Aunt Zoe. You know I'm a responsible person—"

"I know. Just go, though, in case she comes back."

Lisa bit her lip and headed for the lounge; I raced down the stairs. The boat bays were empty except for Coach Everett, who stood at the door to the dock, talking to someone outside. Was it Molly? No. Of course not. That was ridiculous—why would the coach be talking to Molly? Besides, it was a man's voice. I went closer, straining to hear.

"Look, man, you gotta give it to me." Tony, I thought. I recognized his voice, but I was too far away, couldn't hear much of what he said. ". . . . You have no idea what shit we're—"

"We? *We* aren't in any shit."

"Yes, we are. Both of us."

"Okay, look. You want it? No problem. Pay for it. You'll get it when I get some cash. Meet me at the usual—"

"You know I don't have that kind of money. I called to ask them for it, but they wanted to know why I needed it. Shit, man. If I tell them, no kidding, they'll skin us both—"

"Tch tch tch."

What was that? I looked around, saw no one, wasn't sure I'd heard it. Oh dear, I thought. Maybe it was a rat. Did rats make noise?

"—You want us both to get hammered?" Tony was frantic. "If they find out you've got—"

"I'm a reasonable man, Tony. You can pay over time, in installments. With interest, of course. But my terms are not negoti—" Coach Everett stopped midsyllable and wheeled around, eyes daggerlike. His expression quieted only slightly when he saw me. "Hayes, Jesusgod. Don't sneak up on people. You want something?"

"Is that Tony?" I stepped around him to look outside.

Tony pressed himself against the wall, looking unusually haggard. He needed sleep and a shave.

"Tony—have you seen my daughter? A little six-year-old? She was up in the lounge and someone said you were up there making a phone call. . . ." I braced myself to get yelled at. But Tony didn't yell.

"Sorry, what?" His eyes darted around, jumpy and unfocused.

"Weren't you just upstairs in the lounge?"

The question seemed to alarm him. "Why? Who wants to know?"

Lord, what was the matter with the man? "Did you see a little girl up there? Lying on the sofa?"

Tony's eyes darted from me to Coach Everett and back. "No. Nobody was there. I didn't see anybody."

"Are you sure?"

"Nobody was there." He was too loud. Too adamant.

Coach Everett glared at him. Tony shifted his weight, edgy. Secretive. Like a kid in the principal's office. What was going on? Obviously, I'd interrupted something private, maybe even embarrassing.

"Okay, well." I wasn't sure what to say. "If you see her, send her back to the lounge, okay?" I backed into the boat bays; Coach Everett stepped outside onto the dock. Tony seemed to shrink, almost cringing as Coach put his arm on his shoulder and escorted him to the water's edge.

TWENTY-NINE

The boat bays were long and silent, the sleek shells cupping each other in the dimming light, casting indifferent shadows over concrete floors. Oh, God. Where was Molly? Don't panic, I told myself. She's here, somewhere. But my heart was racing, adrenaline pumping as I headed back to the stairs. Maybe she'd returned to the lounge. Maybe she'd wandered into the kitchen, looking for a snack. Or outside on a balcony. Wherever she was, I'd find her. There was nothing to worry about. Molly was fine.

"Tch tch tch."

There it was again. That hissing sound. I stopped a few feet from the stairs, listening, wondering if my mind was slipping, imagining whispers. Wanting to hear Molly's.

"Psst . . ."

No. It wasn't my imagination. It was a definite hiss. Where was it coming from? I peered into the corners, saw only shadows.

"Mom?" The whisper was faint, but it came from above. Damn. The boat racks. She'd climbed them again.

"Molly?" I looked up. Molly was perched on a rack some fifteen feet above my head.

"Shh!" she warned.

"Molly Hayes, come down from there right now. You promised you wouldn't climb—"

"Mom. Hushh."

Footsteps stampeded down the stairs. "Zoe—have you found her? Lisa's a mess. She's crying." Susan leaned over the railing to see me. Craning her neck, she followed my gaze. "Oh, Christ," she said.

"Right this second, Molly." I was furious that she'd disobeyed, worried that she might get hurt. What had possessed her to go up there again? "Come down this second."

"Zoe, wait. I'll get a ladder—"

"No." Molly's voice sounded small and far away. "I don't need one."

"Be careful," I cautioned. I couldn't reach her, but I raised my arms anyway, ready to catch her if she fell. "Hold on tight."

"It's okay, Mom. It's easy." She scampered down quickly, monkeylike, and as soon as I could, I grabbed on to her.

Susan hovered. "What was she doing up there?"

"What were you doing up there?" I echoed, furious. As angry with her as I'd ever been. "You promised me that you wouldn't climb—"

"Don't be mad, Mom." Her eyes were wide and fearful, and I felt a pang, realizing that her fear was not of falling, but of me. Of my fury or, maybe worse, my disappointment.

"Why did you go up there?" I made myself calm down. "What happened?"

"What happened?" Susan stood beside me; now she was the echo.

"I got scared." Her small shoulders shrugged.

"Scared?" Susan and I chimed, a duet. "Of what?"

Molly stared blankly at the wall, maybe trying to form an answer. As we waited, Coach Everett stormed in from the dock, shoved past us and stomped up the stairs. Oh dear, I thought. We'd better go up, too; if Tony came in and saw Molly in the boat bays, he'd put me on probation, maybe even take away my Humberton membership.

Sure enough, when Tony came in he started toward us, eyeing Molly, who glommed on to me like an extra appendage. Susan took a step forward, ready to meet Tony head-on. I held on to Molly, trying to reassure her while bracing myself for battle. But there was no battle. Not even a skirmish. Tony didn't yell or scold. He didn't say a word. As he approached, his eyes flitted from Molly to me, on to Susan, back to Molly.

"So, you found her." His head seemed to twitch as he spoke.

"Yes—" I began.

But without waiting for a reply, without even chastising us, Tony walked on and started up the stairs.

Molly tightened her grasp on me, staring after him.

"What's wrong?" I asked.

"That man," she whispered.

"Tony? Is that who scared you?"

She squirmed, loosening her grip on my arm. "Can we go home now, Mom?"

"You don't have to be afraid of Tony," I assured her. "I told you. He's just the house manager. He's not used to kids, that's all." And he'd banned them from the boat bays, where we were standing.

Clutching my arm, Molly watched the empty stairs that Tony had just climbed and refused to move.

"Mom," she asked. "What's a gordo?"

THIRTY

A what?" Susan asked.

"A gordo."

"I don't know." I shrugged. "Where did you hear that?"

"From him. I heard him on the phone. He was mad that a gordo was coming."

"Maybe it's some kind of boat. Or maybe a launch."

"I don't know." Susan smirked. "Sounds like something from a grade-B horror flick. Some creature like Godzilla. 'Beware of the Gordo.'" She mimicked a monster, her hands like claws, making Molly giggle.

Molly continued to play Gordo monster as we went upstairs and found Lisa, reassured her that Molly was fine and that she'd done nothing wrong, gathered up Molly's stuff and, finally, walked Susan and Lisa to their car. All the way to their parking spot, Susan cursed out Coach Everett. He was unbearably rude. He was pathological. A pathetic has-been. A sociopath. A sadist. I only half listened, didn't bother to comment. I was too tired. Every one of my muscles ached from tension and exercise. The bruises on my arms and face hurt. And Molly's disappearance, even if brief, had shaken me. I wanted to go home and lock the doors, tuck her safely in bed and fall into mine.

Finally, Susan and Lisa drove off and Molly and I walked on in silence.

"It's not real, is it Mom?"

"What's not?"

"The Gordo."

"Of course not. It's pretend. Susan just made it up."

She held my hand tighter. "But that man was scared of it."

"You mean Tony?"

Of course she meant Tony. "I don't like him. He said the *F* word."

"Really?"

"On the phone." She mimicked Tony, lowering her voice, contorting her face. " 'No, no. Everything's fine here. There's no need for the Gordo. That'd just make it worse. No, no Gordo.' Then he said the *F* word."

Molly's impersonation was disturbingly good, but I had no idea what the conversation she'd overheard was about. "What else did Tony say? Did you hear?"

Molly shrugged. "I don't remember. I got scared."

"Is that why you hid in the boat racks?"

She nodded. "They're not dangerous, Mom. It's easy—"

"Molly, don't ever go up there again."

She pouted. "Are you mad?"

"You need to stay out of the boat bays, Molly. And you need to keep your promises."

"I didn't promise."

"But you agreed to stay upstairs. It's the same as a promise."

"I didn't pinky-swear."

"But I have to be able to count on what you say without pinky swears or promises. Just your word should be enough."

She thought about that. "Are you real mad?"

I was tired and aching. I was irritable and upset. But was I mad? At Molly? "No, not real mad."

She skipped, giggling with relief.

"For your information, Mom, I don't need a baby-sitter. Lisa didn't even stay with me. She was in the juice bar the whole time, flirting with some guys."

Lisa flirting? Probably with the very same guys Susan and I had been salivating over. My God, I was old. Hadn't it been just weeks ago that I'd been playing with Lisa's little piggies, making her giggle about the one that ran-ran-ran all the way home? Now, Susan moaned that Lisa was a thirteen-year-old with a D cup. An actual teenager. It was hard to grasp, but Lisa was old enough to want to flirt. No wonder she'd had no idea where to find Molly; her attentions had been elsewhere. On men. The idea rattled me.

Walking along the river, I held Molly's hand, trying to memorize the feel of her small, somewhat sticky fingers; in a blink, she'd be a teenager too, and the hand she'd want to hold wouldn't be mine. Damn, I was having one of those unpredictable sappy maternal moments. Time seemed to stop; the chaos of daily life screeched to a halt, letting me look at Molly and see not just a cherry-stained T-shirt or a scraped knee, but an actual person. How fleeting her childhood was, and how precious. Her curls bounced as she walked, and not for the first time I thought about how different we looked. The child was fair and dimpled, the mother olive and lean. A police siren wailed suddenly, ending the moment as abruptly as it had begun, leaving me reassuring myself that, even though Molly was adopted, I was still her mother. But was I? As much as Susan was Lisa's? As much as if I'd given birth to her? Not wanting to enter that spiral, I looked out onto the river. Shells were coming in, one after the other, silently sliding through the water, silhouettes in the setting sun.

"Why does Tony have to give the coach money?"

"What?" It took a minute to figure out what Molly was talking about. "He does?"

"Coach Everett said, 'I just want my money.'"

"Really? Are you sure?" Had Tony borrowed from him?

"Yes, Mom. I heard him from the racks."

"What else did he say?"

She shrugged. "Just stuff."

Great, I thought. Try to get details from a six-year-old.

"Why does Tony have to give him money?" she asked.

"I don't know, Molls. Maybe he borrowed it and has to give it back." But if Coach Everett was hassling him for money, no wonder Tony looked haggard.

"But what about the Gordo?" Molly asked again.

"I really have no idea. What did Tony say about it?"

"I told you. He doesn't want it to come here."

We'd parked in a small shaded lot beside the river, about a quarter mile from the boathouse just below the Museum of Art. The area was speckled with sculpture gardens and trimmed hedges, benches and bike paths. Earlier, the paths had been crowded with joggers and skaters; now, after sunset, they were empty. People had gone home. We were alone, or almost; a woman was sitting alone on a shadowy bench close to the parking lot. As we approached it, I recognized her short brown hair, her mannish slacks.

Oh, excellent, I thought. The day was getting better and better. What was Agent Ellis doing here? Was she still following us? Didn't she have anything better to do? Was she going to question me about the nineteen dead women right in front of Molly? I slowed, looking for a detour, hoping to avoid the encounter.

Molly pulled on my arm. "Come on, Mom." Her voice was loud, grating. Certainly loud and grating enough to attract Agent Ellis's attention. "Where are you going? The car's over there."

"Shh," I whispered. But Molly wouldn't.

"Why are you walking so slow?" She was almost shouting. If Agent Ellis hadn't noticed us until then, she would certainly now.

Well, so what. Maybe the best thing would be to face her head-on. I'd go over and ask what she was doing there. I had no reason to hide; the woman was out of line stalking me, and I had every right to tell her so. With Molly by my side, I marched right up to her.

Molly kept asking questions. "Where are we going, Mom? Who's that lady? Do you know her?"

I didn't answer. Instead, standing right beside the bench, I addressed Agent Ellis. "Nice evening, isn't it?"

Agent Ellis didn't answer. She didn't even move. She continued to stare into the street at passing traffic. Still gripping Molly's hand, I walked closer to Agent Ellis. She remained perfectly still, her eyes open and unblinking, her arms limp at her side.

"Mom, I think that lady's dead."

Oh my God, I thought—Molly. I had to take her away from there. But I also had to make sure that Darlene Ellis was beyond saving.

"Close your eyes, Molly," I said.

"What?"

"Go ahead, close them."

"Mom. Think it through. If you're afraid I'll see a dead person, I've already seen her."

She was right. I wasn't thinking clearly.

"Okay, just don't stare at her. Stand right here."

"What are you going to do?"

"Just stand here and don't move."

She stood there. And I went up to FBI Agent Darlene Ellis and put my hand on hers. Her skin was cool, but not very. I lifted her wrist to feel for a pulse, and she slumped over sideways. That's when I saw, in the fading light, the blood soaking her neck. And the three parallel curvy lines cut like waves into her cheek.

THIRTY-ONE

For the second time that week, lights flashed and sirens blared on Kelly Drive. And for the second time that week, I sat along the river unable to stop trembling. Molly watched, enthralled, as police cordoned off the area and fought off the media. While I gave my statement to one officer, another chatted with Molly to distract her from the grisly scene. When Nick arrived, though, she ran over to him, ignoring me when I called her to come back.

"Nick . . . guess what," she shouted. "Guess who found her! It was us—me and Mom. Mom's finding dead people everywhere."

The gaggle of reporters overheard her, and apparently figuring out who "Mom" was, dashed my way, hoping to grab the story of the woman who, so far this week, had found a total of twenty bodies at the normally tranquil Schuylkill River. I locked the car door and hunkered down, opening it only after some officers had cleared the area and Nick had personally escorted Molly back to the car.

"Can we go?" I greeted him. "I want to take Molly home." I was desperate to get out of there.

"You all right?" He held the door for Molly as she climbed back into the car, then came around to the driver's side to talk. When I opened the door, he took both my hands.

"You're shaking."

"Nick." I kept my voice low. "The dead woman—it's Agent Ellis. The one from the deli—"

"I know."

"You know? Oh, God. Was it the cartel? Did they kill her because she got too close? Did she find out who they are?"

Sighing, Nick released my hands. "Zoe, slow down. I just got here. Let me find out what's going on before the FBI shows up and takes over. Did you give anyone a statement?"

"A statement? Nothing formal. I talked to that cop—"

"That's fine." He glanced around, eyeing the scene, then his eyes returned to me. "Don't worry about this. I'll take care of everything. Are you okay to drive?"

I nodded yes, I was.

"Then go home. Put Molly to bed. We'll talk later."

I started the engine; Nick closed the door and waved as we drove off. Molly stared out the window at the lights until they faded from view. She seemed thoughtful, and I wondered how she'd been affected by finding a murder victim, how badly she'd been traumatized.

"Molls," I said. "Don't worry. There are some bad people in the world, but Nick's there, and he'll catch whoever did that. We're fine now. Everything will be okay."

She nodded quietly. Then, still pensive, she added, "Mom, do you think we'll be in the newspaper? Or maybe on TV? That would be so cool—Nicholas would see me. And Emily . . ."

She went on listing friends who might see her face on the six-o'clock news, fantasizing about the glories of fame, and gradually, wondering at the ability of a six-year-old to take life—whatever it brought—in stride, I tuned her out, hearing her voice only as bizarrely cheerful background music for an otherwise horrible day.

THIRTY-TWO

By the time we got home, Molly had fallen asleep. She snored softly, her body completely relaxed. I pulled into the parking spot behind our brownstone and, without waking her, gently undid her seat belt and lifted her out of the car, surprised as always that a person as powerful and energetic as Molly could weigh so little. She was still, in many ways, a baby. Her skin was soft and pale, almost transparent; her bones slight. I tucked her into bed, brushing a golden curl off her face, once again struck by our differences. As a child, I'd been big for my age, awkward, gangly, never agile and athletic like Molly. I'd been shy, cautious, obedient, eager to please; Molly was self-assured, outspoken, even boisterous. She made friends easily but was confident enough, even at six, to stand up for herself, no matter what others thought. In many ways she was a mystery to me, and I could rarely predict or even understand her reactions. At the boathouse she'd been so afraid of Tony that she'd hidden in the racks, but she hadn't even flinched at finding a corpse in the park. I watched her sleep, wondering for the millionth time who she was, feeling amazed again that she called me Mom, hoping I'd be worthy of the name. I kissed her forehead, listening to her steady, trusting breath.

"You're safe now," I whispered. "I'll take care of you, and you'll be all right. We both will. I promise."

And then, feeling like a liar, I went downstairs.

The house was too quiet. Still gleaming cleanly, unnaturally, still smelling of disinfectant. Still disturbed. I wandered from room to room, agitated, not able to focus on any one issue, mind bouncing from one jarring event to another. Agent Ellis had been killed. Nineteen women were dead. My house had been broken into, and Susan had been carjacked. Coach Everett and Tony were involved in something shady, and Molly had seen and heard too much. And then there was Nick. Nick knew more than he was telling me. Nick kept secrets.

At some point, my mind spinning, I opened the liquor cabinet and took out the Scotch. Get drunk, I told myself. Pour a tall glass, straight up. Quiet your brain. Go ahead. Molly's safe in bed, and you don't have to drive or do anything at all. If ever anyone had reasons to drink, you do. So, go for it. Chug-a-lug.

I took out a glass and opened the bottle. I was pouring a glass when the phone rang. Don't answer, I told myself. Don't talk to anyone. Just drink and numb your brain and get blotto so you don't have to think anymore. But the phone kept ringing, so I set the bottle down and went looking for it. Damn cordless phones; they were like socks. Always disappearing. I found it on the kitchen counter, and as I answered, I thought, Damn; I bet it's going to be a hang-up. And, sure enough, as I was saying hello, there was a click.

I cursed. For a moment, I considered calling star-sixty-nine to get the number and find out who'd hung up on me. But I didn't want to bother. I didn't want to do anything. I told myself it was just a telemarketer whose automatic dialer had run amok. Or maybe the FBI. Or a slave trafficker. But what did I care who was calling; there was a bottle of Scotch waiting for me. I was on my way back to it when the phone rang again. I hesitated, but answered.

"Did you hear?" Susan's voice was shrill, upset. "They just found Agent Ellis. She's dead."

Oh, Lord. I hadn't told her. I'd called 9-1-1, and I'd called

Nick. But I hadn't called Susan, hadn't even thought of it. I'd been shaken, not thinking clearly. And if I admitted finding the body, Susan would be furious that I hadn't called her instantly.

"Yes, I know." I omitted the details of how I'd found out.

"This is bad," she said. "If they'll kill FBI, they'll kill anyone."

Great. "Anyone," I assumed, included us. Agent Ellis had warned us; so had Sonia and the priest. "So, what are you saying?"

"What do you think I'm saying? Your house was broken into, I was carjacked, and the FBI agent who approached us was murdered. And that's not even all of it. Get this: I called the Archdiocese. They do have people working on human trafficking, but not anyone called Father Joseph Xavier."

"Of course not. That was an alias. They said they were undercover. In disguise—"

"I also called the Pennsylvania Immigration and Citizenship Coalition. Not only have they never heard of Sonia Vlosnick, they insist that they have no undercover agents. None. Same for the Nationalities Service Center. They gave me the names of the other organizations that help trafficking victims. I went down the list, calling them. Nobody, not one, had any idea what I was talking about. None of them have undercover workers. Not a single one."

"Then who were Sonia and Father Joseph? Why would they pretend to be with those agencies? What would be the point?"

As soon as I asked the question, I knew the answer. Sonia had told us herself: "The cartel might send someone to question you." She ought to know; she'd been the one they'd sent. In the guise of warning us, to find out what we knew, she'd even told us what the traffickers would do if they thought we knew too much. "They'd omit the risk. You know, dears. Snuff you out."

Oh, Lord. Had grandmotherly Sonia and scholarly Father Joseph Xavier been actual hit men, working for the cartel? Had their knowledge of the slaves' suffering come not from rescuing them, but from committing the maiming and torture—even photographing their deeds themselves? I shivered thinking about them. Realizing what would have happened if they'd decided we knew anything of substance.

But we didn't. And obviously they must have known that, since they hadn't killed us. So maybe we were out of trouble?

"Zoe, we're in trouble." Susan canceled my thought. "Big trouble."

I groaned. "But you said they'd leave us alone!"

"And you took that as what? A guarantee? What the hell do I know? Nothing. Except that these are ruthless sons of bitches with no scruples—"

"Stop it, Susan. I know all about it." I closed my eyes, saw the three logo lines carved in Agent Ellis's face. "But maybe it's not so bad. I mean, if they were going to kill us, they'd have done it right there, wouldn't they?"

"Maybe. Maybe not. I don't think they're done with us. I think they want something. Look what's happened in the last twenty-four hours. Break-in? Carjack? And if not for the horde of contractors here, I'm sure my house would have been ransacked, too. And now there's a dead agent." She was in high gear. Panicked.

"But what are we supposed to do? We don't know anything."

"But Nick does. You can find out from him—"

"Nick's not on the case, Susan. The FBI took over."

"No, not entirely."

What was she talking about?

"I talked to Ed." Ed was one of Susan's cop friends. Her link to the grapevine. "He told me something fascinating. Even with the feds in charge, the local police still have a hand in the investigation. And guess who's the liaison?"

She didn't have to tell me. My heart knew instantly; it smoldered, searing my ribs. Damn Nick. Why hadn't he told me? Would he ever be open with me? Could I ever trust him? Suddenly I was exhausted. Wiped out. I took the phone into the living room, sank into the purple sofa.

"Hasn't he told you anything?"

Not a damned word, except about the Humberton hat and the tattoos on the women's shoulders. "You know Nick. He doesn't discuss his cases." I tried to make light of it. But I knew better. This case was different. I was involved in this one. Why hadn't Nick told me he was working on it with the FBI?

"That's absurd, Zoe. This case is huge. Nick has to talk to you about it. It's not right for him to keep you in the dark; you're in it whether he wants you to be or not. Especially now that Agent Ellis has been offed and we know for sure that Sonia and Father Joe are fake. This slavery thing—trafficking women? Ed says they sell over a million women each year, plus at least as many children. It's a growing international multimillion-dollar business. Maybe multibillion. This case is as big as they get, and as nasty."

My chest raw, I stared at the bottle of Scotch, at how warmly the amber liquid glowed in the lamplight. I was silent for a moment, thinking of nineteen hapless women, wishing them peace. And of Nick, wishing him a fat lip.

"But on the other hand"—Susan sounded more chipper—"if Nick can help crack this one, it'll be a career maker."

I didn't say anything. It wasn't enough that I might be in danger from the cartel; Nick was, too. I picked up a throw pillow and held it to my belly.

"I'm serious," she rolled on. "He's already got a high profile for somebody who's only been in Philadelphia—what—not two years yet? Nick's a rising star."

"Susan, he's making enemies in a multibillion-dollar international crime ring. How is that a good thing? Look what happened to Agent Ellis."

"Are you kidding? He's not out on the front lines; the feds are. But he's the local guy in the arena, going after bad guys— Big ones. Playing hardball with the big leagues. It's like a lawyer arguing before the Supreme Court. Or an actor doing Broadway, or a violinist playing in Carnegie—"

"But lawyers and actors and musicians don't get killed."

"Zoe, Nick's a cop. You know the deal. He's at risk no matter what case he's on. Do you want him to rise to the top of his field? He could be commissioner someday—"

"Dammit, Susan. If it was Tim, you wouldn't be so cavalier."

"Tim's in airplanes every other day. Do you think I don't worry? I worry every time he leaves the house."

There was no point arguing. Susan raved on, a volcano

spewing words and energy, and not for the first time that week I suspected that she was more than a tiny bit bipolar.

"I gotta go," I begged off. "I'm wiped. I'll call you tomorrow." And then, with a desperate determination, I made a beeline for the Scotch.

THIRTY-THREE

I took it to the kitchen, shivering. My hands trembled as I took out a juice glass decorated with panda bears. They trembled as I opened the bottle. And they trembled as I poured, threatening to spill precious Johnnie Walker Black all over the counter.

"Bottoms up," I toasted myself, and I finished off the entire glass in two gulps, as if it were medicine. Then steadying myself at the kitchen window, I poured another, letting the booze rush through my body. Absorbing it, and the news. Nick was the liaison on the slave-smuggling case. Nick hadn't told me. I gazed out the window, unfocused, letting the streetlights blur into globs of hazy ghostlike white. Eventually I realized that I was staring at Victor's house, and that Victor himself was silhouetted at his window. Oh my. A genuine Victor sighting. Was he watching me? Did he think I was watching him? Had I unwittingly entered a staring contest with my shut-in neighbor?

I looked away, embarrassed, but remembered that I'd never asked him about the break-in, whether he'd seen anyone hanging around that day. Was it too late to call? Of course it was. It was almost eleven. But, hell, I could see him; he was awake, sitting at the window. Still, Victor wouldn't want to know I'd seen him. The very idea that he was visible to the outside world might send him into an agoraphobic spin. No, I shouldn't call. But I could e-mail him. And I'd do it now, before I could get interrupted again.

It was good to have a purpose, something active to do. So, carrying Johnnie and my glass, I went to my study and sat at the computer. As soon as I touched the keyboard the screen came alive. I blinked, startled. Why was the computer on? Then I remembered. Nick had been using it the night before. I'd interrupted him, and then we'd rolled around on the carpet like a pair of rutting hyenas. He'd apparently never logged off. I began to sign him off, then stopped, staring at the screen. The computer was still connected to his e-mail. If I wanted to see it, all I had to do was click.

Of course I had no business looking at Nick's e-mail. That would be an invasion of his privacy. A breach of his trust. It wouldn't be right. I should have felt bad even considering it, but I didn't. I was too busy reading, and too immersed in what I saw.

THIRTY-FOUR

There were about twenty messages from someone named Kiddo2. Randomly I opened one. "Look behind you, Nick. I'm here for you, finally. Can you find me?" I read it again. And again. Someone was threatening Nick. What had Nick said? That the break-in might not have been the slave smugglers. That it might have been someone from his past. An old case. Someone with a grudge. I closed my eyes, saw the vandalized photographs, Nick's face obliterated in each. Oh, God. I opened another message.

"You did what you did; now it's my turn. Want to dance, Nicky? How about a two-step?"

A two-step? Was Kiddo2 a woman? Maybe she was someone from Nick's past. Not an old police case, but an old romantic one. Someone he'd broken up with. I read on, looking for clues to the writer's identity, finding nothing but anger. Veiled threats, one after another, indirect and chilling. And they'd been sent over a period of weeks. Which meant that Nick had known about them long before the break-in. And of course he'd said nothing. Not a word.

Sipping Johnnie Walker, I read them all, one after another. A few rambled on for paragraphs of long run-on sentences, making no point, spewing spirals of rage. "Where am I, Nick? On the street corner, waiting for you to pass? In the doughnut shop? Outside your Chester County bungalow or your boat club? Inside your car? At your ladyfriend's door? You have no clue, do you? Okay, then. I'll tell you where I am. I'm in your shadow, Nick. I'm right here. Behind you."

Another read: "Ignoring me doesn't help, Nick. You thought you could just walk away, but think again. See, now, because of you, I have nothing left to lose. Send me back to jail, lock me up again. I know the drill. I'll be good and obedient and get out again. And if it takes ten years or twenty, or the rest of my life, I'll be back. It isn't over, I promise. She was my damn sister." Her sister? Who was her damn sister? I kept reading, finding out nothing, until I read the final e-mail. "Nice house, Nick. Nice photos. Is the kid yours?"

The kid? Molly—oh, God. Ice washed through my body. The maniac who called herself Kiddo2 knew where Molly lived, what she looked like. That she was connected to Nick. Was she threatening Molly too? Was Kiddo2 the woman Molly had said was following her? Oh, Lord. She had to be.

Stop it, I told myself. Nick knew about this person, whoever she was. Nick was secretive, but that was because he was protective. He didn't want me to be upset. But he wouldn't let anything happen to Molly. He had the situation under control. Of course he did.

I scanned the list of e-mails, saw one dated a few weeks ago from someone named Bosscop. "Heads up, buddy," it said. "You no doubt know that Heather's parole came through. She's out. And I'll bet my pension she's still got it in for you. Family reunion time, pal. Watch your back."

Family reunion? Was Kiddo2 related to Nick? In one of her e-mails, she'd written Nick about her sister. Facts swirled around my mind, falling into jumbled heaps. And then, with a jolt, I finally began to understand. "Family reunion time" meshed with "She was my damn sister." Was Kiddo2 Nick's sister-in-law? Nick's wife might have had a sister. Was her name Heather? Was she Kiddo2?

I remembered Nick's spotty account of his wife's death, how

difficult it had been for me to find out what happened. At first he'd let me think that she'd shot herself when she'd found out he was leaving her. Later I'd learned on my own that there had been an investigation, that he'd been suspected, briefly, of shooting her. Apparently, Kiddo2 still believed that he had.

Well, one thing was clear. Nick had been right about the break-in; it had not been by the cartel, but by someone from his past. From "an old case." But he'd known all along that it was his sister-in-law. And he had deliberately hidden that fact from me, even though it affected not just his life, but my child's and my own.

I swallowed what was left in the panda glass, poured another. There was no point anymore in e-mailing Victor. I knew who'd been in my house. Who'd damaged my photos. Probably, who'd been following Molly, too. Everything began to make sense, merging together in a hazy but somewhat coherent blur. Wandering away from the computer, I listened to the quiet of the house, and observing that the Johnnie Walker bottle was much emptier than when I'd opened it, drank more, bolstered with the confidence that even if it couldn't fix life, it could blur it for a while.

THIRTY-FIVE

Sometime in the dark, a man's voice drifted through the haze, insisting that I open my eyes and go with him. The voice was soft and gravelly, and I liked its persistent urging, its presence, but I didn't like what it was saying. My eyes were happy being closed, and I was comfortable. I was fine. But the voice continued, and I realized that I wasn't actually all that comfortable after all. The mattress had become hard, and I had no pillow. And now someone was touching me, pushing a hand under my back, lifting me up.

"Come on," the voice urged. "Let's get you to bed."

To bed? If I wasn't in bed, where was I? I managed to open an eye, and it managed to look around. Oh. The light was dim, only the stained-glass lamps were lit, but I was in my living room. Definitely the living room.

The man kept talking, asking questions. "How much did you have? Since when do you drink?" His lips brushed my forehead. "Come on, Zoe. You can do it. Lean on me, just like that."

I had no choice, actually. I had to lean on him; the room was rotating, and so was my stomach. I needed to steady myself when I lifted my head; my temples throbbed and my pulse was a base drum.

"You know," he snickered, "you're going to have a hell of a headache tomorrow."

A headache? Oh, damn. Reality washed over me. And so did nausea. I forced myself up and dashed to the bathroom. When I took my head out of the toilet, Nick was waiting, eyebrows furrowed, with a cool damp washcloth. Gently, he wiped my face, my eyelids, my throat.

"Feel better?" he asked.

I nodded, yes, but knew otherwise. Shards of memory began to float through my mind, teasing, staying close enough to bother me, but too far away to grab.

He sat beside me on the powder room floor and rubbed his eyes, tired. "Well? Want to talk?"

I shook my head no, but knew I had to. "Okay," I said. "Sure." The toilet seat seemed almost as good as a pillow, offered itself to me as a place to rest my head, but I leaned against the wall, drifting.

"Okay." Nick smiled with half his face, the other half immobile, paralyzed and scarred. He knelt beside me and touched my cheek, a tender gesture. I studied his crooked features, imagining how handsome he must have been before he'd been shot, and I reached up and touched his scar. Lord, I loved this man. Or, wait. No. Did I? Did I even know this man?

"Okay," I agreed, not remembering anymore what I was agreeing to.

"Okay. So, tell me. What's driven you to drink, my sweet? What?" He waited, his pale eyes patient but tired. And something else.

Good question. What had made me drink so damned much? Even the thought, the memory of drinking made my stomach churn. I didn't want to talk about it. I didn't want to talk at all.

"Zoe, let's just put you to bed." Nick put an arm around my back, starting to get up.

But when he reached for me, I recoiled, remembering the e-mails, the threats. Nick's secrets. I pushed him away.

"What?" He looked wounded. "What's wrong?"

Go on, I told myself. Tell him. Don't play games. "It's everything." Why had I said that? It was not everything. It was one thing. It was him.

"Everything?" he repeated.

I nodded. Not a good idea. My brain sloshed in my skull, sending the room into a dizzying swing.

"Well, that's a long list. How about we take things one at a time?"

Tell him, I thought. Tell him what you found, about the e-mails. About Kiddo2. I took a deep breath, tasted recycled Scotch. "Okay," I agreed. "One at a time."

"Okay, I'll start. Here's the first thing."

I blinked, waiting for him to explain himself.

"You're beautiful."

I smelled like puke and my legs were rubber, but Nick had chosen this moment to admire my appearance? How endearingly sweet. Or was it? I struggled to figure out why it felt wrong, then grabbed on to my drifting memory: the e-mails. Nick's secrets and lies. The reasons I'd been drinking. I leaned my head back against the wall, wishing the powder room would stop spinning.

Meantime, Nick had moved on. "Are you sober enough to hear the next item? It might reassure you. It's about Agent Ellis."

Agent Ellis? Oh, God. How had I forgotten? She was dead. I saw her again, propped up and lifeless on the bench. Three lines, the logo of the slave cartel, carved into her face. "What about her?" I turned my head too fast. Damn. The walls whirled.

"I don't think she was killed by the cartel."

Suddenly my vision popped into focus. The walls stopped spinning. Johnnie Walker lost his protective haze. "What are you saying?" I didn't follow, didn't want to try.

"She was one of them. Or, at least, working for them."

I shut my eyes, trying to focus, realizing that what he was telling me was important. "She was working for them?" My tongue felt wooden, unwilling to move.

Nick nodded. "She was dirty. Officially, Ellis wasn't sup-posed to question you. She was working on transport—another aspect of the case. So when she approached you on her own, she gave herself away."

I blinked, struggling to make sense of what Nick was saying, focusing on the straight thin lines of grout between the floor tiles, using them to clear my mind.

"Darlene Ellis was an informant for the cartel."

A cartel informant? Inside the FBI? Was nobody safe?

"She kept the traffickers updated on the FBI investigation, and she led the feds offtrack whenever she could. She was a valuable resource to the traffickers. There's no way they'd want her dead."

That made sense. Almost. Suddenly, I had a coherent, sober thought. "But you said that she gave herself away. So the FBI had found out she was an informer. That meant she'd be useless to the traffickers. Even a liability. So that would be why they eliminated her."

"But the traffickers don't know she blew her cover."

"How do you know that?"

"Because, except for you and Susan, I'm the only one who knew she'd talked to you."

Wait, what? Nick hadn't told the FBI? Why would Nick keep information from federal investigators? Oh, Lord. How could I even ask that—Nick kept information from everyone. My head was reeling; I held the washcloth against my eyes, recalling again what had led me to drink. The e-mails. The secrets. The lies. I tried to make sense of all that had happened. Darlene Ellis hadn't been representing the FBI. And according to Susan, Father Joseph Xavier and Sonia Vlosnick hadn't been working to help cartel victims. It seemed that nobody was who they claimed to be. Maybe not even Nick.

But he was still talking. I tried to follow, wondering if I could believe anything he said.

". . . So you don't have to worry that slave smugglers are going around killing people. They aren't. It's simply not happening. Agent Ellis wasn't killed by the cartel."

And my break-in hadn't been by the cartel, either. I knew that and Nick knew it, too. But Nick didn't say that. Instead, he watched me, as if expecting a happy grin of relief. As if, even now, he weren't withholding important facts. As if he'd just given me good news. But how was it good news? Even if it hadn't been the cartel, someone had killed Agent Ellis and carved their logo onto her face. Who? I leaned against the wall, feeling green.

"Then who killed her?" I managed.

"Don't know yet. But it's not the traffickers. Come on." He stood up, offering me an arm. "Let's get you up to bed."

My head throbbed, limbs weighed tons. But somehow Nick helped me upstairs to bed. He mixed up a fizzy, awful-tasting concoction that he promised would prevent a morning hangover, and I swallowed it, not certain either that it would stay down or that I'd survive until morning to find out if it worked. Finally, I lay back against the pillows, trying to muster the energy to confront Nick. I had to. I couldn't go another night, another minute without telling him. I felt too ill to speak, too angry not to. How should I begin? Should I start small, asking why he hadn't mentioned that he was working as liaison to the FBI? Or should I jump right into the deep end, asking, for example, why he hadn't told me about Kiddo2?

I lay with my eyes closed and the cool washcloth on my forehead, planning my speech as Nick undressed and climbed in bed beside me. I'd almost decided on my opening line when I felt him staring and opened my eyes. His face was right beside mine, not an inch away. He lifted the washcloth and planted a gentle kiss on my forehead.

"Let's get married."

I blinked, deciding I must have passed out or, at least, misunderstood. Obviously, he hadn't said that.

"We're a family—you, Molly and me. I want to be your husband. And a real dad to Molly." He half-smiled. "And maybe to a few other kids." He looked away, suddenly sheepish. Sheepish looked all wrong on Nick, like grandmother's flannel nightgown on the fairy-tale wolf. "Don't answer now; you're smashed. But think about it."

Was I dreaming? Had Nick just asked me to marry him? What had inspired him? Why now, when I'd just been doubting that I could ever trust him? When we'd just been discussing murder and slave trafficking? I couldn't think, wasn't altogether positive that I hadn't imagined his entire speech. Dazed, still half-blitzed, I blinked at him. His pale eyes glowed softly, and he still wore his half-grin. Lord, he had wonderful teeth. Perfectly aligned. Again, I thought of the wolf.

"You're in no condition to talk now." His voice was cushioned and husky. "Sleep on it. We'll talk tomorrow." He kissed me with lips like butterfly wings, and lay back on his pillow. In a moment his breathing became heavy, deepened into a snore.

And I stayed awake in the dark, replaying his words. "Let's get married." I played them again and again in my head. Had he really said that? I tried on the title: Mrs. Nick Stiles. Or, no, maybe I'd hyphenate: Mrs. Nick Hayes-Stiles. Zoe Hayes-Stiles. I tried the various combinations. Mr. and Mrs., or Ms.; Nick and Zoe Stiles and Hayes or both. But wait—what was I thinking? How was I even considering marriage to Nick? How could I let him be Molly's stepfather when I didn't really know how his first wife had died? Had it been an accident or suicide? Or had he murdered her? Why was his former sister-in-law convinced of his guilt? And why hadn't he told me about her, that she wanted to kill him, that she'd invaded my home? What other myriad of secrets was Nick keeping? What about openness or honesty or trust?

I couldn't absorb any of it, and I lay in bed exhausted, mind spinning, watching Nick sleep until I couldn't stand it anymore. I had to deal with the truth and, drunk or sober, I couldn't wait. I put a hand on each of his shoulders and shook.

"Hunnhh." Nick's eyes popped open. In a heartbeat he sat up, braced for an attack. Looking around, seeing no one but me, he began to relax. "What?" He rubbed his face, trying to wake up.

"Tell me the truth," I said. "I just need to know. Did you kill your wife?"

He blinked a few times, still half asleep. "Did I what?" Then, as if to help himself understand my question, he repeated it. Finally, its meaning must have registered; Nick threw off his covers and stormed out of bed.

THIRTY-SIX

The argument was not pretty. I don't know how it escalated so quickly, how we evolved from an affectionate, loving couple to a pair of predators, jabbing at each other's most vulnerable parts. But somehow the discussion became heated and grew hotter until it finally exploded.

For my part, I threw coal on the flames, firing questions at Nick. Before he could answer one, I asked another, jumping randomly from topic to topic, voicing all the unmentionable unasked questions that had been festering in my mind, preventing me from trusting him, holding us apart. How come you didn't tell me you were liaison to the FBI? Why didn't you tell the FBI that Agent Ellis had questioned me or that she was working for the cartel? Why haven't you told me the whole story about your wife's death? Why didn't you tell me that the person who'd broken into my house was your wife's sister? Who is Kiddo2, anyhow?

Until the questions about Kiddo2, Nick did a convincing job of defending himself. He told me again his version of how his wife had died. When she found out that he was leaving her, she'd shot him in the face, then killed herself. I asked him to explain what I'd read in old newspapers about the case. I asked why his wife, a left-handed woman, had shot herself in the right side of her head. Why they'd found gunfire residue on his hands. I asked him, once and for all, to deal with that.

Nick's face hardened as he spoke. His eyes became steel and his jaw clenched. But he answered me. He said they'd struggled. The gun had gone off during the struggle. His hands had been on the gun when she'd shot him in the face. After that, he'd been unconscious, had no idea what had happened.

Did I believe him? Could I? I wasn't sure. I didn't stop, though. I was on a roll, asking questions, demanding answers. He explained why he hadn't mentioned the liaison position; he simply hadn't thought it was all that important. It hadn't been a secret, but with everything else that had been going on, it hadn't seemed worth talking about. As for Agent Ellis, he suspected that the FBI had been compromised, that possibly more agents were being paid off by the trafficking cartel. He wasn't sure Ellis was the only one, so he wasn't sharing his thoughts with anyone yet. He had answers for everything, but his patience was waning. Nick wasn't accustomed to being on the receiving end of an interrogation. Clearly, he didn't like it, especially in the middle of the night by a half-drunk woman he'd just asked to marry him.

When I asked about the break-in, about Kiddo2, he became quiet. Instead of answering, Nick sat silent, muscles tensed, no longer interested in defending himself. I could smell his anger rising, smoldering like burned flesh. But I was relentless, waiting for an answer.

Finally, he spoke. "How do you know about Kiddo2?"

Oh, God, I realized. I had to admit I'd read his e-mail. Oh, well. It had been right there on my computer screen. "I saw the e-mail."

"What did you do, hack into my password?"

Was he crazy? "Nick, you left your mail up when you used my computer."

The memory registered on his face. "So? Does that mean you can read my mail? What about privacy, Zoe? What would happen if you found me reading your e-mail?"

"That's entirely different—"

He laughed out loud, an ugly bark. "I don't know, Zoe. Clearly you've been harboring some doubts about me. Digging up old newspaper articles about my wife's death. Now you're reading my e-mail. Why? To check up on me? What about trust? What about respecting my privacy?"

From there, it all went south. Nick became belligerent. His eyes narrowed. Half his face contorted; he didn't even look like himself.

"Okay." His voice was clipped, razor-sharp. "You want to know about Kiddo2? Okay. I'll tell you. Kiddo2 is Heather. My wife's younger sister. She had a crush on me, mistook my fondness for her as . . . encouragement. So, when my wife . . . after the suicide, Heather came on to me. She wanted . . . a romantic relationship. I was frankly dumbfounded. I wasn't particularly gentle about it, either. I rejected her pretty bluntly. She couldn't take that. She became obsessed. Came after me. Stalking, calling night and day and hanging up, e-mailing. Blaming me for her sister's death. Swearing to get even. Finally, she broke into my apartment and waited until I came home, then jumped me with a meat cleaver. She's been away for the past five years, attempted murder. But she's out. And the first thing she's done is come after me again."

"So you knew—"

"I knew. It was Heather who broke into your house. It was Heather who messed up the photos. It wasn't the slave traffickers. It was Heather." His eyes met mine but his gaze was guarded. Still hiding something?

"If I hadn't insisted, you'd never have told me."

"That's not true."

"Isn't it? I don't believe you, Nick." My voice was venomous. "I don't know what you hold back, what you don't tell me, whether to trust you—"

"How is that my fault? You had trouble trusting people long before I was around. As I recall, you yourself told me you have trouble letting down your guard and that trust is a problem for you."

Wham. I'd been blindsided, symbolically punched in the gut. Nick had used my weakness, something I'd confided to him, as ammunition. He was turning the tables. Hitting below the belt. Making it my fault, not his, that I didn't trust him. No, I wasn't going to let him. This confrontation was mine; I'd do the steering. I shook my head, clearing my thoughts.

"My problems aren't the issue here, Nick. Why didn't you warn me about Heather? The woman came after you with a meat cleaver. How could you not tell me? How could you put me and Molly at risk?"

"Dammit, Zoe. Heather isn't going to hurt you or Molly. The only one she wants to hurt is me."

"Really?" I was sputtering. "What if we happen to be there?"

"She won't mess with you. With either of you."

"How can you be sure of that?"

"You'll just have to trust me." Half his face smirked sarcastic.

"Give me one reason to trust you. Just one. An hour ago, you asked me to marry you. Are you kidding? How am I supposed to even consider marrying you? A man who can't be open? Who doesn't tell the truth? Who conceals his past and keeps the present secret? Who doesn't tell me even the smallest details, like, 'Oh, by the way, dear, my former sister-in-law's a psycho-maniac stalker who's been breaking into your home and may appear any second with a meat cleaver to kill me'?"

I finished, flushed and breathless, not even sure of what I'd said. The words had flown out of my mouth. Nick sat still, not saying anything. Then he pulled on a pair of jeans, a T-shirt. The silence crystallized, dense as ice.

"Where are you going?" My voice cracked.

He was out the bedroom door. "I can't do this, Zoe."

I followed. Maybe I'd been too harsh. Said too much without thinking. "Why—what do you mean?

He was halfway down the stairs, didn't stop. "I mean, I can't do this. I need some air."

I stood at the top of the stairs, watching as he stepped into his flip-flops and opened the door. Before he left, he turned and looked up at me. Our eyes met, but he didn't say a word.

Neither did I.

THIRTY-SEVEN

It was just after midnight when he left. For a while I sat on the stairs, looking down at the door, half expecting it to open and bring Nick back. I replayed bits and pieces of the argument, trying to justify my position, rewriting my words, reinterpreting Nick's. "I can't do this." What had he meant? He couldn't fight? He couldn't explain himself? He couldn't do our relationship?

I waited, expecting that he'd walk around the block and come back, cooled off, and we'd talk. We'd make up. I'd apologize and he'd explain. We'd both promise to be more patient, more open with each other. To work harder on our relationship, become closer. To find Heather and send her back to jail. I was at least half at fault. I hadn't been open with Nick, either, letting suspicions and problems simmer so long before talking to him about them. Maybe we'd be better now, both of us learning from the fight. Maybe, if he'd ask me again, I'd accept his proposal.

I sat on the steps until my back ached, then went back to the bedroom. Twelve fifty-seven. I sat on the bed but couldn't lie down, not without Nick. His pillow was dented where he'd slept, the sheets on his side lay disgruntled, tossed aside as he'd stood to get dressed. My head and body ached, probably the be-

ginnings of a hangover, and phrases from our fight began to ric-
ochet against the walls.

I couldn't stay there. I put on a robe and went down to the
living room. Then into the kitchen for some headache pills.
Then back to the sofa. Then back to the kitchen for a strong cup
of coffee. I watched the clock, listened for the door. At one
thirty, I decided to be an adult. Why fight? What good was
pride or winning or losing? Wherever he was, Nick was probably stewing just as I was. But where was he? Nick and I had
never fought before, not like this. Not where he'd walked out. I
had no idea how our fight would affect him, what he'd do to
calm down. I called his cell phone. No answer. Lord, I thought.
Was he too angry even to pick up his phone? Too angry to
speak to me?

It didn't seem like Nick to shut me out entirely. Maybe he'd
turned his phone off. Maybe he'd left it in his car. Maybe he'd
be back any minute. I waited. I watched out the window. I replayed the fight, again and again, trying to make excuses for his
words and mine. Trying to end it differently in my mind. Why
had he walked out? Were we finished? I didn't want to be finished. I loved Nick. I didn't trust him, but I couldn't think about
him without my entire chest cavity fluttering. I thought of his
eyes, so pale they looked more silver than blue. His rugged,
craggy face, made vulnerable by the scar carved across his
cheek. The way he fit into our lives, Molly's and mine, and
made us feel like a family. His banana pancakes and pasta
sauces. His love of the outdoors. And of rowing.

Rowing. I thought of Susan and Coach Everett, our awful lesson, and I remembered the darkness of the water when we found
the nineteen women. And the spirals began. My head swam with
images of Sonia and the priest. Agent Ellis, dead on the bench.

Lifeless, floating women. And I closed my eyes, giving in,
letting the headache rage, riding waves of emotions I didn't want
to name. Breathe deeply, I told myself. Relax. And I lay on the
purple sofa, too sad to be tense, listening for the door to unlock,
hearing only the silence of the air-conditioned summer night.

THIRTY-EIGHT

At three that morning, Nick was still gone. and he wasn't answering his phone. It had been three hours. Where could he be? Bars were closed. If he'd gone to the office, he'd have answered his cell phone, if only to tell me to stop calling him. In fact, no matter where he was, he should have picked up his phone by now, just to stop it from ringing. Unless he couldn't. I pictured Heather coming at him with a cleaver. Had she been stalking him? Waiting in the shadows outside, following him on his walk? Ambushing him in some dark alley? Oh, God.

I told myself that Heather had nothing to do with Nick's absence. Nick was fine. But I got up and paced, thinking. If I were Nick and upset, where would I go? And instantly I knew. Of course. Nick was at the river. He was rowing. Rowing was what he did to work off stress; I should have known all along. But he'd been gone for hours. Rowing usually took him an hour, maximum two. He should have been back by now. Or at least picked up his damned phone.

Worrying, I continued to pace. I sat down, stood up. Poured another cup of coffee, dumped it down the drain. No matter what I did or told myself, I couldn't settle down. Something was wrong, and it wasn't just our fight. I didn't know what it was, but I felt it; Nick was in trouble. And I had to find him.

And so, at three fifteen in the morning, I pulled on a T-shirt and a pair of shorts and went into Molly's room to shake her gently awake.

THIRTY-NINE

Except for a dim night-light in the boat bays, Humberton barge was completely dark. I unlocked the heavy carved wood front doors, and Molly and I stepped into the foyer. Molly stood quietly while I felt the walls for the light switch. Then, under the faceted light of the crystal chandelier, she waited, holding my hand. She hadn't said a word since I'd pulled her out of bed; she'd simply held my hand and floated along with me, somewhat dazed, not fully awake. How cruel of me, taking her from her sleep. But I'd had no choice. I had to find Nick. Holding Molly's hand, I stood at the steps, looking for signs that he'd been there. Upstairs, the hallways were black and silent, the door to the lounge closed. Downstairs, the boat bays were shadowy and still. No one was around. What was I doing here? Maybe Nick had gone home while we'd been on the way to the boathouse—maybe I should try calling him one more time. I took my cell phone out and punched Nick's buttons. Nothing.

"Mom," Molly finally spoke. Her voice was husky with sleep. "Are you going to row?"

"No, Molls. We're looking for Nick."

She seemed to accept the answer as if it made sense. As if we did this sort of thing regularly.

In the bays, a single lightbulb lit each row of shells. Long and sleek hulls lay on the racks, one over the other, wall-to-wall and floor-to-ceiling, the darkness slicing thinly between them. From the doorway I scanned the room for signs of Nick, but there were none. The room was empty, silent. Humid. Undisturbed. No, wait; it wasn't silent—not quite. I listened, heard a rustling. An undertone of movement. The scuttle of little feet? Oh, God. River rats?

My knees felt weak; my toes curled. Rats infested most buildings along the river. Everyone knew that, but I hadn't encountered any until now, in the middle of the night. They could be everywhere. Surrounding us. Eyeing the floor, looking for red rodent eyes or long hairless tails, I clutched Molly's hand and turned, ready to run. Nick wasn't there; we could go. But at the door, I stopped. Wait, I told myself. Slow down. You haven't even checked the sign-out log. Every boathouse had a log; for safety purposes, rowers signed the book each time they went out on the river and each time they came in.

Humberton's log was on an antique secretary's desk at the bottom of the boat-bay steps. Cautiously, stomping loudly to scare away small creatures, I led Molly down. In the dim light, I scanned the entries. The last name on the list was Nick Stiles. He'd signed out at twelve twenty. And so far, at three thirty, he still hadn't signed in.

FORTY

Maybe he'd forgotten. Maybe he'd been tired or mad and had just come in, put his boat away, and left without signing in. In fact, he was probably home in his condo now, not answering his phone because he was sleeping too deeply or snoring too loud.

Or maybe, my gut told me, he was still out. Maybe he'd had boat trouble. Maybe he was hurt.

Images of cold dark water and clammy bodies flooded my mind. Stop it, I told myself. Don't imagine disaster. Just go check. Go see if his boat's here. If it's on its rack, he's back.

Good plan, I told myself. Members who had their own boats rented rack space. Each boat had an assigned spot; it made sense to check Nick's. So, taking a deep breath, bracing myself to walk through a swarm of scurrying vermin, I picked Molly up and carried her like a toddler.

"Mom?" She didn't resist. She leaned her head on my shoulder, the way she had as a baby. "Why are you carrying me?"

I kissed her forehead and kept moving, not looking down, weaving my way through row after row of smooth, torpedolike shells, coming to the singles rack, looking up and down, searching for Nick's boat, finding only one empty space. Nick's.

FORTY-ONE

I stood there, holding Molly, staring at the empty rack. Nick had signed his boat out almost three hours ago. And he still wasn't back. Even if he'd rowed the normal course of the river twice, he should have been back by now. Where was he? What had happened? Images flooded my mind, thoughts of floating corpses, overturned boats.

Oh, God. The air became fuzzy, too thick to breathe. I had to think. Figure out what to do, how to find him. At this hour, no one was around except Tony, and Tony lived up in the attic apartment. Tony wouldn't appreciate being awakened, but too bad. He was the house manager; it was his job to attend to emergencies, and I had one. Still carrying Molly, I sped up dark stairs through the heat and humidity to his apartment.

Molly seemed to gain weight with each step, but I didn't put her down. I held on to her as I ascended stairs out of the boat bays up to the lounge, then up to the locker rooms, finally up the attic stairs to Tony's door. Panting, I knocked rapidly, loudly. I knocked, waited a beat, and getting no answer, knocked harder. Then, setting Molly down, I banged both my fists on his door. Tony didn't respond. I shouted his name. Still nothing. Molly gaped at me in alarm, but I kept pounding and shouting. And getting no reply. Maybe Tony was deliberately ignoring me. Or maybe he was sleeping somewhere else. Either way, he wasn't opening the door. I was on my own. Oh, God. Desperate, unwilling to accept that, I tried the knob; the door was locked.

"Mom," Molly said gently. "Stop. He's not answering."

She was right. It was useless. But I had to do something. Maybe I should call the police, get the authorities to search the river for Nick. I pictured them arriving, taking my statement, setting up spotlights, assembling rescue vehicles. I recalled the media circuses of recent nights. And I realized that by the time the responding cops got authority to call out the river police with a search launch, it would be dawn. If Nick was in trouble, it might be too late to help him. More likely, though, Nick would have rowed his boat in to face cameras and lights. I'd look like an idiot. And Nick would not be amused that the entire police force and the news media had been alerted just because he'd gone for a late-night row.

No, no police. Not yet. I led Molly down the stairs, trying to figure out what to do. I had to hurry, had to go find Nick, but what about Molly? I couldn't take her with me, but I couldn't leave her behind. There wasn't time to take her to Susan's, not enough time to wait for Susan to get out of bed and come to us. I was in an impossible situation. Nick was missing. He might have had boat trouble, might be hurt or stranded. Or suffering from hypothermia. Minutes, even seconds might make a difference. But I couldn't endanger my daughter, either. Heather was prowling around somewhere. And so was whoever had killed Agent Ellis. And the entire slave cartel.

"Mom, tell me again? What are we doing here?" Molly was waking up, beginning to think.

"We're looking for Nick." I tried to sound casual. I didn't want to frighten her.

"Why? Is he lost?"

"Not exactly. I just don't know where he is."

She seemed unimpressed. "Did you call him?"

"He's not answering his phone."

Molly sighed deeply. "Mom. Did you ever think that maybe he doesn't want you to know where he is?"

Oh, Lord. Had she heard us fighting? "Why wouldn't he?"

"I don't know." She shrugged. "Sometimes people just need to not be found. You know, to go hide."

I blinked. Once again, Molly had startled me with her six-year-old insight. As we headed down the stairs into the boat bays, I held her hand, knowing what I had to do.

FORTY-TWO

H'lo?" Susan answered on the fourth ring, sounding unconscious.

"Wake up," I told her. "I need you to come get Molly at the boathouse."

She didn't grasp what I was saying the first few times. I had to repeat it again and again. By the time Susan understood the situation and realized that her protests were futile, Molly and I had gone down into the racks.

"Why's Susan coming to get me, Mom? What are you going to do? You're not going rowing, are you?"

I didn't want to lie, so I changed the subject.

"Molly," I began. "I might be out awhile looking for Nick. So you might as well go to Susan's and get some sleep."

"Mom. Why don't we just go home and sleep? We can look for Nick in the morning."

Molly was, as ever, sensible. "Good idea. But I really want to find him tonight. I'm going to look for him one more time in one more place."

"Where? Nick's a policeman. He could be anywhere. Chasing criminals." She shook her head as if her mother were beyond hope. "So what am I supposed to do until Susan comes? Wait here?"

Yes. That was what she was supposed to do. All alone. I told myself that it wasn't so bad. Susan was already on her way. She'd be there in less than fifteen minutes. The doors were safely locked, and no one could get in but Humberton members, and the earliest of them wouldn't show up for at least another hour. Molly would be fine. But she looked so small and pale, her eyes glazed with sleepiness. How could I leave her there? I couldn't. Except that I had no choice.

"Molls. This is a tough situation. I don't want to leave you alone for even a second. But Susan will be here soon. Meantime, here's what I want you to do."

FORTY-THREE

S he looked at me like I was crazy. "Are you serious?"

I nodded.

"But wait. You told me never never ever to—"

"I know. But this is different. Just this once is okay. It's a special case."

She eyed me cautiously, as if wondering when exactly her mother had lost her mind.

"Look, Molls. It's just until Susan gets here. A few minutes."

"But I can wait in the lounge—"

"I'd feel better if you stayed where nobody but Susan could find you."

Her eyes were grave. She got it. I hadn't told her there might be danger, but she understood. She didn't cry or seem afraid. She simply nodded.

"I'll leave the cell phone with you. In case you need to call Susan while you're waiting."

She nodded again, looking like a small adult as she pocketed the phone. "It's okay, Mom. I get it. This is an emergency." She made it sound so simple.

"You're sure you'll be okay?"

"Positive. Don't worry."

"You'll stay right there until Susan comes? You won't move?"

She stiffened her arms and legs, imitating a statue, and answered without moving her lips. "I won't move."

How was she so brave? Why wasn't she the least bit upset at being left alone? I kissed her head, gave her a quick hug.

"Okay, then. The sooner I go, the sooner I'll get back." I didn't say where I was going. Or how I'd get there. But she knew without my telling her.

At the bottom of the boat-bay stairs, I knelt to give Molly a hug.

"Don't drown, Mom," she said.

"I won't, Molls."

"Promise."

"I promise."

"Pinkie swear."

Soberly, we linked pinkies. "I swear," I told her. "I won't drown."

Molly studied my eyes. I dodged her gaze by hugging her again, aware of the bonds between love and deception.

"I love you, Molls." I kissed the curls on top of her head.

"I know, Mom. Love you, too." And then, as I watched, she scampered up the racks and disappeared into the shadows.

FORTY-FOUR

I told myself again that I had no choice. After all, it was my fault Nick had gone rowing; if we hadn't fought, he'd be home safe in bed. And there was no question that something was wrong; his boat had been gone way too long. I had to go find him. Molly would be safe until Susan got there. She'd have to be.

But without Molly by my side, the boat bays looked even darker. The shadows were harsher, more menacing. Just keep moving, I ordered myself. I opened the door to the dock, grabbed a pair of oars, lugged them outside, and came back in for a boat.

The shell I'd rowed the day before was about twenty-five feet long, weighed about thirty-five pounds. But it felt heavier, bulkier, longer and wider as I strained to lift it off the rack. It's a lever, I told myself. You're the fulcrum. Stand at its center and balance it like scales. But I couldn't find the boat's center, couldn't get it to balance. It tipped like a seesaw, too far to stern, then too far to bow. I bumped its nose against other boats, its tail against metal riggers. Thunk. Scrape. Thwap.

"Mom?" Molly called from somewhere near the ceiling. "You okay?"

"Fine."

But Coach Everett screamed in my mind, blasting me for clumsiness, blaring out commands. "Correct your grip." I heard him bark. Resting the bow gently on the floor, I moved my hands toward the center of the boat and lifted again. Better balanced, but still unsteady, I concentrated on where I was heading, aiming the stern carefully through the narrow aisle, slamming it only six or seven times into shells resting on the racks.

Oh, God. What was I doing? I couldn't even carry the thing down to the dock; how was I going to row it? I had no idea, but also no choice. I kept going, tipping the shell at impossible angles, squeezing my torso between its hull and the metal riggers that were supposed to hold oars but instead contained my twisted, contorted body.

Slowly, the shell and I sidestepped along, proceeding in tiny increments to the dock where, sweating and panting, I paused to steady myself and let my eyes adjust to the moonlight. Then I continued, step by step, toward the water, assuring myself that the boat was not getting heavier, that I was not going to drop it, that I could manage one more step, then another. Finally, miraculously, the boat and I made it to the water's edge where, without proper form or grace, I ducked out from under the rigger and let the boat splash into black water where it bobbed awkwardly, eventually righting itself.

My lungs felt heavy with dense night air, and I smeared sweat across my forehead with equally sweaty arms. The oars, I thought. Get the oars. In moments, my oars were locked onto the boat and I stood on the dock, ready to shove. I glanced back at the boathouse, trying to catch a glimpse of Molly, wondering if Susan had arrived yet. I considered going back in to check, but didn't. Because if I did, I might not have the nerve to come back out.

FORTY-FIVE

The moon was almost full, almost the same shape it had been a few nights before when Susan and I had rowed. And the dark water glittered the same way, alive with slivers of reflected silver light that slapped gently, teasingly at the dock.

Balancing carefully, I stepped barefoot into the boat and lowered myself onto the seat, fastened the clammy Velcro shoes and shoved, letting the current carry me. For a moment I sat in the dark, watching the dock float out of reach. I gripped my oars and held my body rigid, not daring to breathe.

Oh, God. What was I doing? I was alone on the river in the middle of the night. A novice without a coach's supervision. Using a Humberton shell without permission. Leaving my child alone not just in the boathouse, but up in the racks. I was breaking every rule there was. And not thinking clearly, either—I'd rowed a single only a couple of times before during lessons, and then I'd almost flipped. What was I going to do if I flipped again? I felt Molly's pinkie gripping mine, heard myself swear that I wouldn't drown.

Stop it, I told myself. There's no sense thinking about flipping. You're here, on the water. Just settle down and row. Go look for Nick's boat. That's what you're here for. I took a tentative stroke, then another. The boat wobbled, tilted dramatically, first to port, then to starboard. Steady, I told myself. Breathe. Keep your hands level. Relax your shoulders. Push with your legs. Gradually, my body began to remember the drill, moving the way it had the day before. The mantra of Coach Everett. Push with your thighs and legs. Lean back. Finish.

I looked over my shoulder to see what was ahead, saw nothing but black space, shimmering surface, silhouettes of trees along the banks. No other boats. Nothing. Just quiet, undisturbed water. Even the expressway along the river was deserted. The only sounds were my oars clunking in their locks and the water gurgling under the boat, and I kept moving, scanning the surface for Nick's single shell. But there was no sign of it. Or Nick.

The night air felt dense, clammy. Moisture clung to my skin, as if the river were oozing upward, trying to engulf me even in my boat. Keep moving, I told myself. Lean forward, slide up, reach out. Pull. The mantra. Keep repeating the mantra.

With each stroke I held my breath, afraid that my oar would catch something other than water, that I'd feel the tug of a body dragging on my blade. I waited for the boat to lurch or tip, and I recalled the helplessness of falling into murky liquid, swallowing it. Pulling a woman out of the water and feeling the limp, slippery indifference of her skin. Oh, God. I rowed on, expecting that a hand might at any moment reach out of the water and grab my oars. Or a head pop up and grin with blind, glowing eyes. Stop it, I told myself. Concentrate on what you're doing. Think about your stroke. Reach out and catch the water. Push with your legs and thighs.

Somehow, after a few minutes, I passed under the Girard Avenue Bridge and headed upriver past the statues of three angels. My eyes had grown accustomed to the night. The darkness glowed black beams; the river seemed a negative of its daytime self. I peered into the darkness but saw no boats, no Nick. Nothing but shadows in varying shades of darkness. No movement. I rowed on, losing track of time. Had I been rowing for five minutes? An hour? I kept looking around, ignoring grisly memories, focusing on balance. My technique was sloppy but I was moving. And as I approached the Columbia Bridge, I told myself that, for a novice, I wasn't rowing badly. My boat was not as wobbly as before; its glide was steadier. I was getting into a rhythm, and the boat was responding. I felt almost confident that, despite the darkness and the dangers it might conceal, I'd be able keep rowing as long as I had to. Until I could find Nick.

FORTY-SIX

A bove Peters Island was where Susan's oar had gotten caught on a woman's dress. It was where we'd flipped among the bodies. As I neared it, my skin prickled with memories, my muscles tightened involuntarily. Stop it, I told myself. No one's floating in the water. But my body reacted on its own, on alert.

The island itself was no more than a mound of craggy rocks overgrown with wild shrubs and trees. Maybe three hundred yards long and thirty-five wide, it sat in the middle of the Schuylkill River about a hundred yards above the Columbia Bridge, and although a jagged stairway was carved into the rocks on one side, a weathered sign, almost hidden by vines and branches, declared: KEEP OFF: NO ENTRY.

People were not welcome on Peters Island; its only inhabitants were geese, turtles, ducks, occasional egrets. Wildlife. So when I saw Nick's shell and a coaching launch banked at the top of the island, I froze. What I saw made no sense. Nick's boat and a launch? At Peters Island? In the middle of the night? Why? I sat in the middle of the river, gaping, unable to comprehend what I saw.

But there they were. A motorboat and, with its distinctive red markings, Nick's brand-new WinTech racing shell. The launch was tied to a tree trunk; the shell had been dragged partway out of the water onto the rocks so it wouldn't float away. Its oars were crossed, and it rested, partially submerged, against the island's steep incline. I sat for a moment staring into the dim woods, listening for I didn't know what sounds. But all I heard was the water lapping softly, indifferently against my hull. Everything else, even the air, even my breathing, was still.

Inside my head, though, nothing was still. Questions ricocheted—What was Nick doing here? Whose launch was that? Why would they abandon their boats on the rocks of Peters Island? Had there been an accident? Had someone been hurt? Or, I wondered, had something more sinister happened? Something to do with nineteen floating dead bodies?

The boat swayed gently, rocking me, and I had the sense that none of this was real. I wasn't alone in the middle of the river on a dark, humid night. I wasn't staring at Peters Island searching for Nick. I was home in bed, dreaming. On my sofa, wrapped in an afghan. But my skin tingled, alert, and my eyes insisted that I stop resisting and accept the shadowy images before me.

Get moving, I told myself. It was clear what I had to do. I rowed as close as I could to the spot where Nick had left his boat, but no matter how I steered, either my oars or the length of the boat kept me ten feet or so from the shore. There was only one way to get onto the island; I had to get wet.

The water shimmered in the moonlight, trying to look innocent and calm. Feathering my oars to steady the boat, I took my feet out of the shoes, centered my weight and slowly stood. There must be a better way to do this, I thought. But, not knowing what it was, I simply held my nose, let go of my oars and, before I could fall, jumped into the river. I closed my eyes, waiting for chilled, dark water to swallow me. But the river didn't swallow me. It splashed my chin and neck, but when it settled, the water came barely to my waist and my feet hit bottom, sinking into swampy, knee-deep, toe-swallowing muck.

Don't stop, I told myself. Go find Nick. Each step was a challenge; river mud sucked me down, clutching my ankles. Struggling, I grabbed my boat and, crossing the oars, lifted its stern onto the rocks, resting it beside Nick's. Then, squishing and soggy, disentangling myself from river plants, slipping on slimy rocks, I splashed out of the mud and pulled myself up onto the veiled darkness of Peters Island.

FORTY-SEVEN

My arrival hadn't gone unnoticed. Geese, aroused from their sleep by my splashing, began honking and hollering, alerting every creature on the island. Shrieks, hoots, quacks and howls assaulted me from all directions, and the night came suddenly alive with rattling leaves and cracking branches. I stood at the edge of the island balancing on a boulder, waiting for the pandemonium to settle, telling myself to keep going, hoping the geese wouldn't attack.

There was no bank, as such. No gradual incline out of the water. The rocks were steep, but grabbing onto branches and stepping into sticky mounds of what smelled like goose poop, I made my way up to the dark carved stone steps that led into the island. At the top I stopped, my path blocked by a dense growth of trees and bushes. The squawking had grown deafening; even the turtles had to be screaming. I hugged myself, surrounded by unseen creatures and impenetrable panic.

Great, I thought. Now what are you going to do? There was no path, no light. My eyes had grown accustomed to the darkness on the water, but I was in a forest now, surrounded by shadows, commotion and cries. The glow of the night sky was blocked out by treetops. Still, Nick was there, somewhere, and I had to find him.

"Nick?" I called. My voice was lost among the others. "Nick? Are you here?" I tried again, louder. Still, the only answers came from creatures screeching in alarm. I groped through vines and bushes, aware of scratching branches and biting insects. Stepping gingerly, I felt with my toes for the sting of brambles, the slither of snakes. Oh, God. Were there snakes on the island? What if I stepped into a nest? What if one was in the trees, dangling over my head? Hunched and bent, I hurried ahead, afraid of what might be at my back. Was that the nip of night air or a spider biting my neck? Was that a sharp rock or fangs jabbing my bare foot? Was an outraged goose chasing me, her strong wings outstretched like blades? I pressed on blindly, feeling my way, wondering where I was headed, how long it would take. The island had seemed tiny from the water, but it was almost impenetrable, and my progress was slow. More than once, island creatures careened past me, swooping or flapping in warning or alarm, and, too often, I tripped, stubbing toes or scraping limbs. Cursing and moaning, I told myself to keep going. To find Nick. And, clearing my way with frantic arms, squinting futilely into darkness, I stumbled on the habitats of turtles and disrupted the peace of geese until, suddenly, I was flat on my face.

It took a moment to realize what had happened. I'd fallen. I must have, although I couldn't remember it. I lay still, stunned, absorbing the shock. And then, slowly climbing onto my hands and knees, I realized what I'd tripped on. What lay under me wasn't a rock or a bush. Not even a snake. No. It was human. The body of a man.

FORTY-EIGHT

Oh, God. oh, God. My hands were shaking, slapping at him.

"Nick . . . Nick." I kept calling his name, trying to revive him. I felt his mouth for breath, his chest for a heartbeat. Nothing. But his shirt was soaked and sticky, drenched in what felt like blood. Oh, God. A wail rose on the island, penetrating the night as I pounded on his chest, performing CPR. And then, breathing into his mouth in pitch-darkness, it hit me that the mouth didn't feel right. The lips were too thin. The nose was too sharp. The smell wasn't familiar.

The body wasn't Nick's.

Then who the hell was it? And where was Nick? I stopped CPR, felt again for a pulse. Finding none, I felt the face of the dead man, trying to recognize his features by touch. Dimpled chin. Thin lips, pointed nose. Bushy eyebrows. Thick belly. Oh, God. I knew this man. What had happened here? Coach Everett was dead.

FORTY-NINE

N ick?" I screamed his name, and my voice blended into the other maddened screams of the night. "Where are you?"

I thrashed around in the bushes, crawled in circles, feeling rocks and dirt, dreading what I might find. I clawed through the undergrowth, feeling for something softer than rock, warmer than plant life. I pushed my way through clods of earth and clusters of weeds, searching, moaning Nick's name.

I found his hand first. My fingers came upon it as they clawed through roots and soil. Nick's hand. I followed it to his arm, his arm to the rest of him. He lay on his back, and I smelled the metallic odor of clotting blood, felt the syrupy texture of his shirt. Caressing his face, I kissed his mouth, recognized the shape of his lips, repeated his name.

"Nick. Wake up. Please." But he didn't wake up. He just lay there, limbs heavy and unmoving. Oh, God. Was he dead, too? I sat holding his hand, rocking his arm, moaning.

Then the island went silent, and I heard a single voice. "Stop dawdling," the coach growled, giving orders even in death. "Quit whining and move your butt. Help the man." Damn. He was right. I had to get a grip. I took a breath, and trying not to tremble, felt Nick's wrist for a pulse. There it was, faint but steady. But wait—Was that Nick's pulse or mine? I rested my head on his chest, listening, and stayed there for a few of his shallow breaths, rejoicing in the weak but reassuring throbs of Nick's heart.

Oh, Lord. What the hell had happened? Had Coach Everett stabbed Nick? Or had Nick stabbed the coach? For God's sakes why? I had no idea, couldn't stop to think about it, had to help Nick. Gently I lifted his shirt, let my fingers wander his chest, searching for a wound. A few inches under his left nipple, I found it. Small and round, the shape of a bullet, oozing warm blood. Instinctively, I pulled off my T-shirt and pressed it against the wound. But I couldn't stay and hold it; Nick had to get to a hospital. My free hand reached around, searching, finding a large flat rock. I lifted it, placed it over my blood-soaked T-shirt, hoping it would continue the pressure. I had no idea if the rock was a smart idea or not. Pressure could help stop bleeding, but too much pressure might weigh down Nick's chest, preventing him from breathing. I knelt beside him just long enough to make sure he was drawing breath. And then, cursing myself for leaving the cell phone with Molly, I explained to his unconscious body that I loved him and was going for help.

Reversing my steps, I tore through branches, over roots, around boulders, past indignant hoots and threatening screeches. Running too fast either to fall or be caught, I flew across the pitch-dark island back to the slimy steps where I could see the moonlight glimmering on the water. My boat leaned against the rocky bank, waiting beside Nick's. Trying not to slip, I descended into waist-deep water and waded through river weeds across the swampy bottom to my shell. And struggled to hop, shimmy, twist and lift my body back in.

FIFTY

I wobbled and swayed, but managed to get my feet into the shoes, my boat away from the shore. I headed upriver, toward the Canoe Club, where I could get help. I rowed along the island madly, sloppily, inefficiently, stroking too quickly, losing my breath. The splashing of water and the piercing cries of wildlife obscured other sounds. So it wasn't until I'd almost reached the end of the island that I heard the buzzing. It was faint at first, but getting louder. I turned and saw a launch coming around the island, headed my way.

The launch! I'd forgotten about it—it had been there when I'd arrived at the island, but not when I'd come back for my boat. Which meant someone else had been on the island. But who? And why hadn't he answered when I yelled for help? Had he seen Nick and Coach Everett? Their fight? Was he going for help? Whoever was in the motorboat would be able to get help far more quickly than I would. Thank God.

The launch was moving fast, coming closer. I looked over my shoulder, taking slower strokes, waiting for it to come within shouting distance. It gained speed as it approached, its engine accelerating from a buzz to a roar. I clutched my oars, expecting it to slow as it neared me. By the time I realized it wasn't going to, that, in fact, it was going to ram right into me, it was too late.

FIFTY-ONE

When I hit water, the motor muted instantly, hushed by bubbles. For the second time in a week, I drank undiluted river. It rushed into my mouth and nose, flooded my ears as I flew headfirst into shallow water; the mush at the bottom cushioned my fall. Plants coiled around my arms and legs as I rolled under the surface, hiding, holding my breath, waiting for the launch to pass. My hair floated in my face, reminding me of the other night, my mouthful of a dead woman's hair. Oh, God. I held myself down, swimming underwater, and my foot bumped an oar from my overturned boat. Damn. I was too close to the surface, had to get down where he couldn't see me. But I needed air. Had to breathe. Had to come up for just a second, just for one breath.

Quickly, before the driver could see me, I let my head come up, inhaled dark air and did a fast surface dive straight down to the bottom, which wasn't very far. I tried to swim away from the spot where I'd heard the launch idling overhead, but the water was dense with stems and slimy plant life, difficult to swim through. Still, I closed my eyes and, trying to stay submerged, worked my way forward, holding my breath until my lungs ached. When I couldn't stand it anymore, I let myself come up again to grab some air.

I surfaced and filled my lungs. And noticed how quiet it was. Tentatively, I stayed above water, listening for the motor, hearing only the twittering of the island, the lapping of disturbed water against the rocks. No engine blaring. No sound whatever of the launch. Had it roared away? Was it gone? Was it safe to look? The water still rolled from the launch's wake, and I floated in it, bobbing some twenty yards from my abandoned, overturned boat. Careful not to splash or make a sound, I rotated, looking first to the side, then behind me. And I had just enough time to dunk as the oar came flying at my face, grazing my head.

I fumbled for a moment, then went down to the bottom, and kicking like a frog, swam through murky water, tearing ferociously at slippery tangled things that grabbed me as I passed. What the hell was going on? He hadn't been gone; he'd been sitting in the launch, engine off, waiting. An oar's length away. Watching for me to surface so he could bash my head in. But who was it? Who'd rammed my boat? Who'd been on the island with Nick and the coach?

Pumping adrenaline, I pulled my way through the river toward the spot where my upside-down boat drifted, guessing the distance. And then, hoping I was out of batting range, I came up for a fast breath and look. Damn, I'd gone too far. My boat was behind me. I aimed again and slipped under the surface, coming up under the single's hull, head above water in the hollow space between the seat and the shoes. Breathing the pocket of air trapped inside the boat, wiping blood and water from my face, I stayed there, hidden from sight and protected from blows. And I thought about Nick, who was lying under a heavy rock bleeding to death.

FIFTY-TWO

I stayed beneath my boat, blood pouring from my forehead. Head wounds bleed a lot, I reminded myself. Even superficial ones. It might not be as serious as it seemed. Shivering, blinking away scarlet streams, I breathed slowly, hoping the man in the launch would assume that he'd knocked me unconscious. After a while, I heard his engine start up again. The sound was muffled, but I could almost feel it idling, vibrating the water. Probably, he'd wait just long enough to be certain that I wouldn't surface again, that I'd drowned. And then he'd leave.

But how long would that be? How long did it take for a person to drown? I had no idea. Three minutes? Two? In certain circumstances, ten? How long had I been there? I had no idea. Time had distorted, taken on lethal dimensions, become significant only in that it took time to suffocate. To freeze in chilly water. To bleed to death.

Again I pictured Nick outstretched on the island. Was he still alive? Had the pressure of the rock stopped the bleeding? Every second that passed gave him less of a chance. I waited, counting heartbeats, gradually realizing that the sound of the motor had faded. I listened, held my breath, heard only the slaps of water until, unable to wait any longer, I slipped out from under the hull and quietly spun around, scanning the water first on one side of the boat, then, crossing under the boat, on the other. The launch was gone.

My body was numb and shivering, head still bleeding as I turned the boat upright. Chilled and shaking, I worked my way back in, strapped my feet into sodden shoes and began to row. For what seemed like hours, I rowed. My oars weighed tons. My head pulsed with pain and dizziness. The half mile to the Canoe Club became elastic, stretched like rubber. I'd never get there. I wouldn't make it. Nick would die. Maybe both of us would. But I kept going, taking a stroke. One more. Another. Long after I'd given up hope, I was still rowing. Muscles burning, head searing, I finally felt the impact of a crash, turned and saw the planks of a dock. Thank God, I whispered, and crawling out of the boat, I began to yell for help. For the police. For anyone. I saw myself crawling as if from above, as if I were watching from the sky. Then I was standing, running up the dock to the Canoe Club, pounding on the doors to the Police Marine Unit, hurling myself into the road, waving at cars along East River Drive.

At some point, I realized I wasn't using actual words anymore. I was merely making noise. Waving my arms, screaming.

FIFTY-THREE

The cops already knew me. For the third time in a week, I'd summoned them to a violent crime scene. Officer Olsen was there, and I told him about Nick, Coach Everett, the man in the launch. Wrapped in blankets, gauze around my head, I refused to go the hospital, even though Officer Olsen advised it and the EMT said I'd need stitches. But no, I wouldn't go, wouldn't move until rescuers had reached the island and brought Nick off on a stretcher. I stayed where I was until I saw for myself that Nick was still alive. He was limp and unconscious, covered with bloodstains and bandages. But my boulder, it turned out, may have helped; he hadn't bled to death. I pestered the EMTs, asking questions they couldn't answer. Would he be all right? Had he lost too much blood? Would he survive surgery? Could he hear me if I talked to him?

Only when the ambulance had taken off with sirens blaring did I agree to leave the scene. And even then, I wouldn't go get stitches; I had to go get Molly.

Officer Olsen sighed, eyeing me, and offered me a ride. He called ahead to Susan's to say we were on the way, and hesitated, when he hung up, to tell me that Tim had said Susan wasn't home yet. Neither she nor Molly was there.

I must have looked deathly, face smeared with blood, head

bandaged, body scratched and bruised, hair disheveled, sports bra torn and soaked. Officer Olsen hadn't wanted to upset me further. But I was on my feet, not waiting for him to help. By the time he'd finished his sentence, I was already telling him to try Molly on my cell phone as I was climbing into his car.

FIFTY-FOUR

I rushed into Humberton calling Molly's name. My voice reverberated under the hollow dome of Humberton's foyer, rattling the walls, the chandelier. And, when she didn't answer immediately, my bones.

Officer Olsen followed me down into the boat bays. "Molly?" I shouted. "Molly, come out."

Head throbbing, holding on to beams for balance, craning my neck, I scanned the shadowy racks for the form of a little girl, finding only long gleaming boats. And two empty spaces, one for Nick's single; the other for the shell I'd left at the Canoe Club.

"Molly? Molls? Susan? Where are you?" My teeth chattered, even in the heat, and trembling, I scoured the bays, examined the spaces between racks. I told myself that Molly was fine, just hiding. Any second, she'd pop out, smiling at her game. But she didn't.

"Ma'am, are you sure she's down here?" Officer Olsen looked doubtful. "Wouldn't she be waiting upstairs where it's more comfortable?"

Yes. Of course. Molly wouldn't still be in the racks; Susan would have taken her upstairs to the lounge. They'd probably fallen asleep on one of the oversized leather sofas. Slowly, shivering, I followed Officer Olsen to the stairs. I told myself to calm down; wherever they were, Molly and Susan were safe. Nothing could have happened to them at Humberton Barge. But in a corner of my brain, Nick's question bellowed: "Did you or Susan lose a Humberton hat?"

A Humberton hat had been found floating among the bodies. Was a Humberton member involved with the slave smugglers? Could that member have accosted Susan as she arrived in the night? No. Ridiculous. Besides, what would a slave smuggler want with Molly, a little six-year-old girl? Oh, God, what an awful question. I couldn't imagine, didn't want to.

Officer Olsen began climbing the boat-bay steps, but I hesitated, looking around one last time, and noticed that the doors to the dock were still open. I'd forgotten to shut them when I went out after Nick. Gazing outside at the water, I saw, at the water's edge, the dim shapes of two figures, huddling together.

"Molly?" My throat was raw as, running to the doors, I called her name. "Molly . . . Molly." Thank God.

"Mom?" The figures jumped to their feet, and the small one came flying, arms outstretched. "Mom . . . you're back! How'd you get here? We were waiting for you—where's Nick?" She looked over my shoulder into the boathouse. "Did you find him?"

I hugged her tight, avoiding having to answer.

Susan was right behind her, looking confused. "How did you get in without us seeing you? Where's your boat?"

I wasn't ready to answer her either. "Dammit, Susan," I breathed. "What are you doing here? I called your house and Tim said you hadn't come home, and I was scared to death. We've been looking everywhere for you. Didn't you hear us shouting your names?"

"No. I guess we couldn't hear you from out there."

She was right. Of course they couldn't. But I was still mad. "But what were you doing out there?"

"We told you. Watching. Waiting for you to get back."

"But you agreed you'd take Molly home. To your house."

"She wouldn't go. Zoe, she was worried to leave without you. And, frankly, so was I. So we were waiting on the dock—".

"You've been here all this time?"

"For a while, why?"

"Did you see anybody dock? A launch?"

"Mom, guess what." Molly pulled on my arm.

I ignored her, repeated my question.

"One went by maybe ten minutes ago. It docked down at Vesper or maybe Malta." Susan pointed toward the other boathouses.

"Did you see who was in it?"

"Zoe, no. It's dark out." Susan shook her head. "Why? Was I supposed to?"

"Mom, listen. Guess what." Molly grabbed my hand, jabbering. "The Gordo was here. I saw him."

I blinked at her, then at Susan, still annoyed, not ready for the change of subject.

Susan nodded. "She's been talking about the Gordo ever since I got here."

"Because he was here. Looking for Tony."

The Gordo? It took a second for me to cool off and remember. The Gordo had been the imaginary creature Molly had been talking about just before we found Agent Ellis. Oh, Lord. What was Molly talking about? She must have imagined him again, must have been more afraid to stay alone than I'd realized. Damn. Well, who could blame the girl? First her mom finds bodies in the river, then there's a break-in at her home. Now, she's left all alone to hide in a dark boathouse in the middle of the night. No wonder Molly was imagining monsters. I felt dizzy. Nick was in the hospital fighting for his life. My head had been slapped and slammed; my body was raw with scratches and angry bites. I hurt from head to toe, inside and out. And now I was finding out that my daughter was plagued by terrors, might even be delusional. I lifted her hand with both of mine and kissed her gritty fingers.

"You're okay, now, Molls."

"Anyway, Molly refused to leave until you got back," Susan defended herself. "And frankly, I was glad. I wanted to stay to make sure everything was okay. So? What happened?" She was frowning at the gauze wad on my head.

"Mom, why isn't Nick with you?" Molly looked pale. "Did you find him?"

"I did, Molls. I found him." I pulled her close, inhaling the scent of warm, overtired child.

But Molly pushed me away, grimacing. "Eeww, Mom. You're all wet. You flipped again, didn't you? That's why your boat's not here? And that's why the policeman had to drive you back? I knew it—I knew you'd flip. What happened? Did you bump into more bodies?"

"No, Molls—"

"But you hurt your head." She eyed me. "Mom, why are you just in your sports bra? Where's your T-shirt?"

I didn't have the energy to explain, but it didn't matter because Molly wasn't listening; she was too busy talking. Her pitch rose as her questions came faster and faster. "Why were you gone so long? Where's Nick? If you found him, why isn't he here?"

I pictured Nick on the stretcher, limp and blood-soaked, tubes in his arms, oxygen mask over his face. I was speechless, drained, and I closed my eyes, refusing tears.

But Molly grabbed my arm, persistent, demanding answers. "Mom, tell me." Her eyes were as somber as her tone. "What happened to your head? And where's Nick?"

FIFTY-FIVE

olly almost never cried, but when she found out that Nick had been hurt and was in the hospital, her chin wobbled and tears flowed. Susan wanted to know details, but I didn't want Molly to hear them, and besides, had no energy to give them. While Officer Olsen waited we sat together, the three of us on a leather sofa in the lounge, and I explained briefly that doctors were taking care of Nick and that we'd visit him soon. I told Molly that I'd cut my head while I was looking for Nick, that I needed a few stitches, and that she would stay at Susan's while I got them.

"Stitches?" Molly was mystified. "Like with a needle and thread?"

I nodded, feeling queasy.

"They're going to sew up your head? Like the way you sewed my yellow shorts?"

"Just like that."

She frowned. "Do you get to choose the color thread? Can you get purple?"

"Molly," Susan interrupted, "why don't we get going? When Emily wakes up, we can make waffles."

Molly drew a few shaky deep breaths and stoically stood to go. But as she did, Officer Olsen stepped over and stooped be-

side her. "Can I ask you a question befo
heard you talking before. Tell me about the

She was quiet for a moment, assessing hir
me for permission, and I nodded. Even if he wa
her imagination, it might do her some good to talk
"The Gordo's scary. And real mean." Her voice was sn
she looked away.

I stroked her cheek, studied her guileless face, her gold
curls. Molly looked delicate, but she was strong-willed and
mischievous, generally not fearful. She'd seemed fine when I
left her, hadn't protested or seemed the least uneasy about staying alone for a few minutes. Now she was telling a cop that
she'd been terrified. Next, she'd tell him I made her hide up in
the racks. Great. In a minute, Officer Olsen would be calling
Child Protective Services. I closed my eyes, feeling faint.

"Scary and mean. How do you know that, Molly?"

I relaxed. Officer Olsen didn't seem concerned about my
parenting, only in what Molly had thought she'd seen.

"Because I could tell." She answered with furrowed brows
and deadly seriousness.

Officer Olsen waited for Molly to go on. When she didn't, he
came up with another question. "What's the Gordo look like?"

Molly bit her lip. "Like . . . maybe a gorilla."

No surprise. Probably he was a shadow in the dark.

"Is the Gordo a man?"

Molly paused, thinking. "I'm not sure. I mean, he's hairy
like a man, but he's got a long ponytail and bracelets and earrings and necklaces like a girl."

That was a lot of detail for an imaginary creature. I held on
to her hand, began to feel cold.

"Have you ever seen the Gordo before tonight?"

"Uh-uh, but I've heard about him."

"You heard about him? From whom?"

Molly shrugged. "Some people. Grown-ups."

"Do you know their names?"

She looked at me. "You know, Mom. You heard them, too.
Tony."

? What was Molly saying?

o continue. "Tony. And who

...san blurted.

remembered them talking—

y. I'd been looking for Molly,

...'d seen her.

on the dock. Tony goes, 'The Gordo is coming.' ... 'It's not just me. It's you, too.' And the coach got mad and said, the Gordo wasn't his problem, but Tony goes, 'Yes, it is." And he said the *F* word."

Susan and I looked at each other, mute.

"And that's all you heard?" Officer Olsen asked.

"Yes, but tonight, after my mom left? The Gordo came here, just like Tony said he would. He came looking for them. I heard him come in the door. He went, 'Tony? It's the Gordo.'" Molly imitated a raspy voice.. "'Tony? Yo, Tony. You up there? Come on out. I just wanna talk.' Then the floor creaked and he was banging on the door. Then he came downstairs to the boat bays and came down the steps and looked around, so I hid until he left, even after the outside door slammed, and I kept hiding until Susan got here."

We were all quiet, rapt.

I pulled her close and stroked her forehead. "You're safe now, Molls. No more Gordo. Nobody's going to hurt you."

I looked at Susan, then at Officer Olsen, wondering what they thought of her story. I recalled the exchange between Tony and the coach on the dock the other evening. I remembered the coach wanting money, but not any mention of a Gordo. True, Molly had been there longer and had heard more. Maybe she'd misunderstood. Maybe something she'd heard had sounded like "Gordo." But what? Nothing sounded like Gordo. The Bordeaux? The porthole? Thug oar dough? I had no idea.

Officer Olsen gently put his hand on Molly's shoulder. "Well, Molly. In my opinion, you're very brave. And, on behalf of the police force, I want to thank you. You've done your duty and alerted us. Because of you, the police will be on the lookout for the Gordo. So you don't have to be scared anymore. Okay?"

Molly looked singularly unconvinced. Officer Olsen seemed to have dismissed her fears as the products of a child's overactive imagination.

But I hadn't. I'd changed my mind. I'd become convinced that, to the best of her abilities, Molly was telling the truth. I watched Molly and Susan drive off as the sun began to rise, certain that someone had been at the boathouse that night, looking for Tony. And that the Gordo—whether or not that was his actual name—was real.

FIFTY-SIX

W hen Molly left, so did my energy. Suddenly I had no strength, no balance. As we started out of the boathouse, I staggered and swayed, and if Officer Olsen hadn't caught me, I'd have collapsed right there. Planting me in the foyer at the bottom of the steps, he called for an ambulance and went outside to wave it down.

Woozy, I leaned my head against the wall and let my eyelids drop, thinking about Nick. About our fight. If not for that, we'd both be home asleep. Cuddled up. And engaged to be married. Oh, God, why couldn't I have kept quiet about his e-mail? Why had I even read it to begin with? If only I'd simply have trusted him, I wouldn't know about Kiddo2 aka Heather, wouldn't have wondered again about his past. I'd have been blissfully ignorant and he wouldn't have been out rowing, much less left to die on Peters Island, his blood seeping from a bullet hole.

I hugged myself, feeling chilled, then realized that a shadow had passed over me. I opened my eyes to see Tony leaning against the railing on the steps above me. He was bare-chested, wearing nothing but a towel, and he didn't seem to notice me sitting beneath him. Slowly, cautiously, he proceeded down the steps.

"Yo." He peered into the foyer. "Somebody down there?"

Spotting me propped against the wall, he jumped. His eyes popped, jaw dropped. I must have been a sight, blood smeared all over, gauze on my forehead, damp hair clumped, hanging in my face. But he didn't ask what had happened; he simply cursed. "Fuck me," he said. Then he said it again.

He continued down the stairs, holding on to his towel. Tony seemed paler, jumpier, more gaunt than he had been even a few hours ago, and the circles under his bloodshot eyes were deeper. Maybe he was on drugs. Maybe Coach Everett had found his stash and that's what their fight had been about. Maybe Coach wanted Tony to pay him to get his drugs back. Maybe the Gordo was Tony's dealer.

Tony came to stand beside me, his hair dripping wet, probably fresh from the shower. He was nude except for his towel; a thick stripe of black curls poked out of the terry cloth and ran up his belly. Why was he standing so close? Hadn't he heard of personal space? My head thundered with pain and worry about Nick. Couldn't Tony just go away? He stared down at me with haunted rodent eyes, as if I were a slice of moldy cheese. Too weak to stand, too exhausted to talk, I looked away, began to study scuff marks on the hardwood floor.

"Okay. Okay. So now what? What's the deal?" Tony bent over me, whispering. His red eyes narrowed. "You win. I give up. So tell me the deal."

I'd won? What deal? "Officer Olsen brought me." For some reason, it seemed important to mention the police presence. To let Tony know I wasn't alone.

Tony couldn't stand still. He circled the foyer, breathing shallowly, quickly, looking through the window at the policeman in the street.

"So, okay. What do you want?" he asked. Was he talking to me? I wasn't sure. His free hand ran through his wet hair, his fingers carving tracks. "You tell me. What now?"

"What now?"

"Yeah. What now?" He rotated, forming questions. "What's with the cop? What's the deal?"

I didn't have the strength to answer him, didn't know how.

Sirens blared outside and Tony watched the window, cursing, until the front door bust open and EMTs rushed in with a stretcher and gear. Strangers began working on my body, flashing lights into my eyes, probing, questioning, pressing, jabbing.

When Officer Olsen came in, Tony had almost disappeared up the steps. But not quite. Officer Olsen called him back down, then took his time, circling Tony, assessing him in his towel. I heard him ask Tony's name, then use it repeatedly, taunting him with every sentence. "So, you live here, Tony? Where were you earlier tonight, Tony?" He walked up to Tony and stood face-to-face, stood belly-to-belly.

"I been here. Sleeping." Tony's eye twitched. "I just woke up now, with all the noise down here."

I strained to follow their conversation while the long gloved fingers of the dark-skinned EMT unwrapped my throbbing skull.

Officer Olsen rubbed his chin. "You were here, sleeping, Tony? All night?"

"Yeah. Since . . . I don't know . . . midnight? Maybe one."

But wait, I thought. Tony hadn't answered when I'd banged on his door. I tried to remember what time that had been. Around three? I heard the scrape of Velcro. A pair of hands wrapped my arm and took blood pressure; another pair repackaged my head. Someone mentioned running a bag. Running a bag?

Officer Olsen pushed his belly forward; Tony took a step back. "Ever hear of the Gordo, Tony?" Wait, why was he asking about the Gordo? Did he believe Molly's story, after all?

Tony's eye twitched again. His mouth began to open, then snapped shut. He blinked rapidly. "The what?"

"The Gordo. We have a little girl says she saw the Gordo here tonight."

"A little girl?" Tony smirked, shaking his head. "Here? Not possible. Nobody was here tonight, least of all a kid."

"Tony, I'm afraid you're mistaken. Because there was."

"A kid? Here? No fucking way. Oh, shit . . ." He looked at me, putting pieces together. "Your kid? She was here again?"

Oh, damn. Why had Officer Olsen mentioned Molly? Tony didn't need to know she'd been there. He'd be furious, and I'd be on probation—or worse—for leaving her there. But then it hit me how ridiculous I was being. Who cared about probation or Tony or rowing or Humberton? None of that mattered anymore; nothing did, except for Nick. I saw him again lying on the stretcher, and I let my eyes roll, pretending to be half-unconscious. Wishing I were.

"The kid says this Gordo character was looking for you."

Tony's eyes bounced from Officer Olsen to me, and back again.

I felt a jab in my arm. An EMT was hooking me up to an IV.

"Well, the kid's wrong," Tony insisted. "Nobody's been looking for me, cuz, if they were, they'd've found me. And nobody did. So what's going on?"

"There's been a homicide." Officer Olsen stared into Tony's eyes; his belly pressed Tony against the staircase. "And a police detective's been shot."

"A homicide?" Tony's hand tightened on his towel. "Who got killed?" He didn't ask about the detective. My heart twisted. Nick.

"You'll read about it in tomorrow's paper, anyway, Tony. So I might as well tell you. The dead guy's Preston Everett. A coach. Friend of yours?"

"Shit. Preston Everett?" Tony echoed, sounding hollow. His legs seemed to cave. I hoped his towel wouldn't fall. "For real? No shit. He's dead?"

Four arms reached behind and under me.

"On three," the redhead said.

"Oh, yes. He's dead. But luckily, the other victim survived." Officer Olsen moved to the window, frowning, his face flashing red and yellow, reflecting ambulance lights. "It'll be interesting to hear what he has to say."

"One, two—three."

Suddenly, I was airborne. Arms lifted, then deposited me flat onto a wheeled stretcher. Hands busied themselves strapping me on.

"Okay, I guess that's it for now, Tony. But let's keep in touch. And, whatever you do, don't leave town."

Tony forced a grin. "Oh, blow me. Real cops don't say that."

Olsen leaned into Tony's face, and I saw his eye twitch. "This cop does."

Lying flat on my back, I watched the dome of the boathouse foyer, then the branches of trees, then the night sky being washed away by the pink hue of dawn as EMTs rolled me to the ambulance. I waved good-bye to Officer Olsen and let myself drift.

FIFTY-SEVEN

Nick was in surgery forever, and, slipping in and out of wakefulness, I waited for word of his condition for what seemed like days. Finally, long after my gash had been closed and other wounds tended to, eons after I'd showered and changed into a donated pair of hospital scrubs, Nick's gurney rolled out of Recovery and I followed it to his room in Intensive Care. He was hooked up head-to-toe, oxygen tubes in his nostrils and an IV tube in his arm. Another tube carried urine from his bladder. Wires connected to a monitor measured the beats of his heart. Gauze peeked out of his hospital gown, covering the wound on his chest, and his skin was stained orange with antiseptic. All in all, he looked gorgeous. Alive. Sometimes, his blue eyes opened and floated around aimlessly. Settling on me, they focused for a moment, then slipped back into their haze and closed again.

I held Nick's hand, stroking it as I talked to him. I told him he'd be okay. The doctors hadn't said so; in fact, they'd called his condition "critical," but I told him anyway. A thousand times I told him I loved him. And I made a thousand promises. I'd never argue with him again, never give him a hard time. I'd trust him, even if I thought he was lying. I'd never interfere with his work or pry into his past or doubt his intentions. And I'd marry him. He'd be Molly's official dad. And we could have more kids, too. Babies, as many as he wanted—two, three, a dozen. All he had to do was hang on and get better.

I talked nonstop, partly to cover the labored sounds of Nick's breathing and the whirring and beeping of his machines. Partly to keep myself awake. Partly to hear my own assurances, to convince myself that, despite the doctors' reservations, Nick would survive. Other people came by during those first, hazy hours. Most of them were cops, keeping a vigil outside Nick's room around the clock. A few were FBI. Some asked questions, probing my memory for details of finding Nick. What had I heard? What had I seen? Why had I gone there? How had I found him? I answered the questions, but I wouldn't let anyone get close to Nick. Everyone, even cops, had to stay outside the room and pay their respects from the window. I sat beside him, fierce as a guard dog, even when nurses came to change a bag or dress his wound. I held his hand even while I dozed in the fake leather armchair, refusing offers of relief and suggestions of rest, skipping meals, unable to eat. And I obsessed, reliving the darkness of the island, the awful, isolated helplessness of finding Nick there in the night. Again and again I replayed the scene in my mind, watching myself stumble off the island and row for help, wondering who'd been in the launch, whether he'd thought I'd seen him and could recognize him. What he'd do when he found out I'd survived.

Tony's face popped suddenly to mind, the way he'd jumped when he saw me. Why had he been so startled? Was it because he'd thought I was dead? Had Tony been the man in the launch, swinging an oar at my head? I considered it. As boathouse manager, Tony had access to the launches. And Molly and I had heard him arguing with Coach Everett; now the coach was dead. Was Tony a killer? No. I couldn't believe that. Tony was crude, but he was too nervous to be a killer. He was just a rough-edged young guy who liked to row. He'd argued with the coach, and he'd been stressed out, but that didn't make him a murderer. No, I told myself. It couldn't have been Tony. But a fragmented thought shuffled in my brain, trying to fit itself together. Something was bothering me.

Resting my battered head against the back of the chair, clasping Nick's fingers, I let that thought rebound through my mind until, too tired to fight anymore, I gave in to fatigue. Dozing, I saw Tony again in the foyer of the boathouse being questioned by Officer Olsen. And suddenly, even in my dream, I knew what had been bothering me: If Tony had been upstairs sleeping as he'd claimed, why had his hair been wet?

FIFTY-EIGHT

Someone was there. In the room. Creeping around. Sneaking up on me. Oh, God. Kicking and slapping—smack—I made contact—

"Jeez—dammit, Zoe!"

I opened my eyes, trying to orient myself, and saw someone in motion, fluttering. Susan? And then, beside me, I saw Nick's tube-covered, sleeping face. I felt a stab, remembering where we were. Already, his suntan had turned sallow, gave him a sickly, jaundiced look.

"Here, take this." Susan was annoyed. She held out a steaming cup in one hand, wiped at her aqua sundress with a napkin in the other. "You spilled soup all over me."

"What?" She wasn't making sense.

"You almost knocked the cup out of my hands."

"Susan. I was asleep—"

"Well, I tried to wake you gently."

"You startled me."

"I said your name about forty times but you didn't move. Finally, I touched your shoulder, lightly, like this, and you flew at me like a Tanzanian devil."

"Sorry." I wasn't, but it seemed as if she wanted me to be.

"Drink the soup. We have to talk."

Oh, Lord. I took the cup, but I didn't want any soup. The very thought of food was sickening. The smell of chicken soup made me choke, but I didn't say so. Susan believed that food cured anything, apparently even a gash on the head and a comatose boyfriend.

"How's Molly?"

"Fine."

"She's 'fine'?" What did 'fine' mean? Susan was exasperating. She knew I was worried about Molly; why was she being so vague?

"Yes, she's fine. Don't worry about Molly. I can manage Molly."

"And Nick? I was sleeping . . . Is there anything new?"

Susan put a hand on my shoulder. "He's stable, Zoe. He's going to be fine."

"Really? You swear?"

"Swear."

I closed my eyes, thanking God.

Susan's eyes were teary. "Now, you need to go home and rest. You're not in great shape yourself. You're all banged up. Look at you. Your skin's purple, yellow and green and scary shades of gray. You look terrible."

"Come on, Susan." I smoothed my hair. "Don't dress it up; I can take the truth."

"Sorry, but somebody has to be honest. You need to go home."

It was no surprise that I looked like hell; I felt like it, too. My neck and back were cramped from sleeping in the chair; the gash on my head throbbed, and my body was tender all over with bruises and scrapes. I felt weak and dizzy, and my legs were going numb from sitting. But no way was I going home; I was not going to leave, not until Nick woke up.

"Drink the damned soup," Susan ordered. "I made it myself and brought it all the way over here. The least you can do is swallow it."

I looked into the cup, at a sloshy yellow liquid, felt its steam coating my face. I wanted to puke.

"Go on, Zoe. Drink it. You need your strength or you'll be

no good to anyone. I bet you haven't eaten all day."

What did she know? I'd forced down a package of crackers and half a plastic container of vanilla pudding. But I knew Susan; she wouldn't quit until I obeyed. I closed my eyes and put the cup to my lips, faking it. I forced a swallow, pretending to have actual soup in my mouth. She watched, waiting for a reaction.

"Thanks," I said. "It's delicious." When I spoke, a few drops trickled through my lips onto my tongue; they tasted rich and salty. Soothing. Not so bad. Not sickening. I lifted the cup again and took a small sip. Warmth ran down my throat, reminding me that my stomach was empty. I drank again. And one of Nick's machines began to beep.

Technically, patients in Intensive Care had extremely limited visiting hours. Because Nick was a cop in critical condition, the rules had been bent for us. Even so, when the nurse came in to respond to the beeps, she scowled.

"You'd be more comfortable in the waiting area, ladies." Meaning, of course, that she'd be more comfortable with us in the waiting area. "I have to change his IV bags. Why don't you two step out for a few?"

My legs were stiff and wobbly, but Susan hustled me out of the room.

"Come on, Zoe. Let's go for a walk. You need to move around. And I have stuff to tell you."

We stepped into a waiting room furnished with upholstered love seats and easy chairs, one of which held an elderly man who was snoring. Paintings of flowers and the seashore hung on the walls. There was a nighttime baseball game going on the television, but the sound was off. We sat.

Susan smoothed her dress, examining the soup stain.

"What do we have to talk about?"

She looked around as if to make sure no one was listening. "A few things." She leaned toward me, lowering her voice. "First, I spoke to Ed. The cops combed Peters Island all day, looking for evidence." I leaned closer; I could hardly hear her.

"And?"

"And they didn't find a damned thing. No clear footprints. No weapons—"

"Wait, no weapons? Then how did they shoot each other?"

Susan watched me, waiting for the facts to sink in. Gradually, they did. If there were no weapons, Nick hadn't shot Preston Everett, and Coach Everett hadn't shot Nick. If they'd shot each other, their weapons would still be with them. Obviously, they'd both been shot by someone else, a third person who'd been on the island with them. The man in the launch. Who might have been Tony.

But even that didn't make sense. "Susan, the guy who came after me didn't have a gun," I began. "If he had, he wouldn't have hit me with an oar. He'd have shot me—"

"His gun's probably at the bottom of the river. He must have chucked it after he shot them."

It made sense. I pictured a gun flying off the island, the plop it would have made hitting the water. The bubbles as it sank. Who had thrown it? Had Nick seen him? Would he come after Nick again? Or me?

"Zoe, there's more."

I swallowed. "Okay."

"Are you sure you can handle it?"

"Susan, tell me. What is it?"

"It's on the news—you'll find out anyway. Maybe it's better if you hear it from me. So . . ."

She stopped jabbering and fingered her rings. Damn, Susan could be maddening. Did I have to beg? Or smack her?

Okay, I'd beg. "Susan, tell me."

Still she hesitated.

"Please don't make me hurt you. What did they find?"

She folded her hands and looked at her grease-blotted lap. "It wasn't a 'what.' It was a 'who.' They found two more bodies." I stiffened, felt my heart rate kick up.

"They were way down below the dam, near the South Street Bridge. And, guess what. There were three curvy lines carved into their cheeks, just like Agent Ellis had." Oh, no. Two more murder victims. I pictured Agent Ellis, the carvings on her face. The logo of the cartel.

"So who were they? More slaves?"

She shook her head. No. Not slaves.

"FBI?"

No again.

"But the cartel killed them?" I breathed. After all, the three lines were their trademark. Who else would use it?

"It looks that way."

But Nick had said the slave smugglers weren't killing people. Had he been wrong? My mind was racing. Why would the cartel label the bodies with their logo, announcing their responsibility for the crimes? Until now, the traffickers had kept a low, even invisible, profile. Why were they now advertising their presence, staying in the headlines day after day, attracting attention? The nineteen women apparently had died accidentally, resulting in unavoidable but unwanted press. But Agent Ellis's death had been deliberately public, right in the park. And now there were two more?

"So, who were they?" If they weren't FBI, maybe they were the bungling deliverymen. The guys who messed up and let the nineteen women die.

Susan watched me for a moment, pressing her lips together. Then she spoke slowly, as if to a child.

"I'm not sure who they really were, Zoe. They had no identification on them. And they were disguised. One wore the wig of an old lady, and the other was dressed like a priest."

FIFTY-NINE

Their throats had been slit, and they'd been in the water, dead, for about two days. Sonia and the priest had approached us in the park three days ago. Which meant that, not long after our encounter, they had been killed. Why? What did it mean?

I pictured the two of them in the park, Father Joseph scanning the playground, Sonia rocking an empty baby carriage. And now they were dead. Oh, God. First Agent Ellis. Now, Sonia and the priest. All murdered.

"Susan." I felt faint. "What's going on? Who killed them?"

"I told you they were fakes. They weren't who they said they were."

"But who were they? Why would someone kill them?"

"I don't know. I'm clueless. I thought they worked for the slave traffickers. But if they did, why would the traffickers kill them?"

Good question. "Maybe they messed up somehow. The traffickers seem to be killing anyone who ticks them off." I thought of Nick, his role as FBI liaison. Maybe it was good that he'd be out on sick leave for a while.

"Or maybe there's a power struggle going on among the traffickers. Or rival smugglers fighting for turf?"

Maybe.

"Or maybe Sonia and the priest were FBI informants, working both sides, like Agent Ellis. Maybe the traffickers found out."

I nodded, felt my brain slog inside my skull. Probably Susan was right. Whatever the reason they'd been killed, their deaths probably had nothing to do with us. Or Nick. It was bad guys killing bad guys, fighting bad-guy battles. But I wondered. Who were Sonia and the priest really? Whose side had they been on? Had they actually been working for the traffickers?

I heard Sonia's sweet, syrupy voice. "Be careful, dear," she'd warned. I pictured the gaping slash in the folds of her throat, the bloated features of the priest's face as he drifted in the Schuylkill. I stood up too fast, trying to escape my thoughts.

Susan reached out to steady me and helped me back onto the love seat. The old man in the easy chair stirred at the commotion. Opening his eyes, he stared our way, and I had the sense that he hadn't been asleep at all. That he'd been listening to us the whole time.

SIXTY

Nick's nurse impressed on me that he was weak and exhausted. That he needed to rest undisturbed, that he wouldn't be ready for company—even mine—for at least the next twenty-four hours. So reluctantly, assured that various police would remain round-the-clock at his door, I went home with Susan and crashed with Molly at her house.

I slept fourteen hours and woke up on a fresh-smelling down pillow under a floral comforter, starving. When I woke up, Molly was sitting beside me, staring at me. I reached for her and she lay down, cuddling, and for a blessed few moments we lay dreamily, snug in a four-poster bed, minds blank and drowsy, free of memories. But as I rolled over to face her, the aching stiffness of my body, the sharp pressure in my head kicked my memory awake. Oh dear. I had to get up. Had to call the hospital and check on Nick. Had to go see him.

"Mom, I've been thinking." Molly touched my face, her fingers gentle and breezy.

Damn. Of course she had. Probably about the nineteen bodies. Or finding Agent Ellis, my injuries or Nick's. The poor child must have been thinking quite a bit. "Tell me, Molls. What about?"

She frowned intensely. "Everything."

"Everything." I held her hand. "Like what's been happening?"

She nodded. "And about Nick."

"He's going to be okay, Molls. Really."

She nodded, watching the blanket. "Mom. I don't know how to tell you this, so I'm just going to come out and tell you."

"Okay." I tried to sit up to listen better. A moan escaped my throat as I pulled my aching parts, forcing them to defy gravity, to bend and move. Molly watched, waiting, until I'd settled against the headboard.

"So, tell me."

She took a deep breath. "It's just . . . today's the last day of school."

Oh, God—it was? I tried to remember what day it was, but I knew she was right. Molly was missing the last day of kindergarten. I looked for a clock—maybe she could still get there.

"It's okay, Mom. I didn't want to go anyway. But the truth is, you need to do better."

I blinked, knowing I'd messed up. She was right. "Okay. Tell me what's on your mind."

"You can't just go out and get in trouble every night. You're a grown-up. You have a child to take care of. It's not fair to me to have to worry about you all the time." Her chin wobbled. "I just want to go home with you and Nick and for things to be normal again. Like before."

Oh, God, so did I. I held her close, cradled her the way I had when she was a baby, promised that we'd all go home, that life would get back to normal soon. My bumps and bruises would heal. Nick would get better. We'd be a regular family. Plus, summer vacation was starting. We'd go to the pool, the shore. We'd put burgers on the grill and watch fireworks at the Art Museum. Gradually she relaxed, even began to smile through teary eyes. When she finally barreled out of the room to find Emily, I sat still, considering what I'd just said. Would life ever seem normal again? Would the slave traffickers ever leave us alone? Or did they consider Nick, Susan and me to be troublesome loose ends like Sonia, the priest and Agent Ellis? And maybe Coach Everett? Had he been killed by the slave trade, too? Why?

I leaned back against Susan's pillows, closing my eyes, trying to make sense of the cyclone that had sucked up my life when I heard a sudden stampede and felt an earthquake erupt on the mattress.

Emily and Molly had arrived, and Molly's mood had obviously escalated. "Mom. Come on. Get up."

"I am up." I would have gotten out of bed, but Molly was sitting on my legs.

"How come you're not in school, Emily?"

"I'm back already. It was just go get your report card and come home."

Oh. I'd slept late.

"Molly said you got stitches." Emily eyed my forehead.

"Can we see, Mom? Show us."

"I got stitches once," Emily boasted.

Molly's eyes widened. "For real?"

"I stepped on broken glass when I was little." Emily held her foot up, displaying a faint pink scar on the ball of her foot. "See?"

Molly examined Emily's foot, and I nodded, tried a smile. "It's impressive, Em. Where's your mom?"

"Outside with her flowerpots."

"She's not working today?"

"Nope. She doesn't work Fridays."

She didn't? I had no idea. I hadn't even realized it was Friday. I seemed to be losing my hold on all aspects of normal life. Things like knowing what time it was, or what day. Even Molly seemed out of reach. I had no idea what time she'd gone to bed. Or when she'd eaten last. Or even when I had. I'd have to remember how to manage all that. How to make sure that Molly's life became normal again. And secure.

But first, I had to get out of bed.

I showed the girls my stitches and answered their questions until they ran off to play outside. Then I moved slowly, painfully, out of bed. Borrowing a pair of too-loose shorts and a

T-shirt from Susan and assuring her that I was all right, I grabbed a doughnut from her kitchen and made sure Molly was okay about staying there awhile longer.

Then, brutally aware that nothing about the morning or my aching body felt the least bit secure or normal, I took a cab to the hospital to see Nick.

SIXTY-ONE

As I entered the room, Nick half-opened his eyes. Half his mouth slid into a smile, as if nothing were wrong. As if this were a regular morning, and nothing unusual had happened. He motioned for me to come closer. He seemed urgent, needing to tell me something. He'd been near death, must have some poignant insight to share; I leaned forward, eager to hear.

"Hi." I waited, but he said nothing else. Just "hi." And, having stated that, he lay there grinning dopily. Morphine, I thought. They must have given him drugs.

I took his hand and bent down to kiss him; he lifted his non-IVed arm to pull me in. He was surprisingly strong, or maybe I was just off balance. But he held on to me, his lips pressed to mine, sucking on them, as if he were dying and I were life itself. When I pulled away long enough to catch a breath, he smiled again. Then his eyelids dropped. And he was asleep.

When he woke up, he was a little more alert. He noticed the bandage on my head, the sores and bruises all over my limbs. His cop friends had told him that I'd saved his life, but not that I'd been hurt. It amazed him, not so much that I'd figured out he'd been rowing and come after him, but that I'd done so in a single. Sculling all by myself.

His breath was short and his skin was an awful avocado shade. I didn't want to exhaust him. I told myself not to push him too hard. But, on their own, questions flew from my mouth.

"Who shot you?" I heard myself ask. "What were you doing on Peters Island? Why were you with Coach Everett? Who else was there?"

And slowly, as well as he could, Nick explained. He hadn't shot the coach; he hadn't taken a gun with him. He'd been rowing to work off the heat of our argument. But as he approached the island, he heard the place going wild, birds squawking and shrieking. He'd seen a launch tied up on the rocks, so he rowed closer to see what was going on. Above the honks of angry geese, he'd heard someone shouting for help. So, grabbing his night-light, Nick had hopped into the water, laid his shell against the rocks, and climbed onto the island.

He wasn't sure what happened next, whether he'd heard the shot or called out, offering help. But he definitely heard a shot as he started up through the trees, flashing his light. He hadn't seen Coach Everett or anyone else. He didn't know who'd shot either of them. The next thing he knew, he was lying in the hospital, too tired to open his eyes, hearing some woman promise that she would never again argue with him, never question him about his work. He half-smiled, letting me know that he'd heard.

Oh, man. He'd heard me? All of it? The part where I said we could get married? The part about having babies? Nick's blue eyes drooped, veiled and drowsy, not revealing what they knew. He was, as ever, withholding facts, keeping secrets. Maybe he was being a gentleman, not holding me to promises I'd made under duress. Or maybe he'd reconsidered his offer.

Nick didn't say. Talking had wiped him out. He reached for the remote control, turned on the television and, staring briefly at the screen, fell asleep. The Three Stooges, dressed as surgeons, bonked each other in the eyes, whopped each other on the head. How appropriate, I thought. I sat staring at them, digesting what I'd heard. Nick didn't really know anything, not

who'd shot him or the coach. Not what the coach had been doing on the island. Not who had been in the launch. Apparently,
the clearest memory he had of the entire event was of my promise never to argue with him again.

SIXTY-TWO

All day people—cops, rowers, Nick's new buddies from the FBI— dropped in. Flowers, cards, baskets of fruit, boxes of candy, books and magazines cluttered the dresser, the nightstand, any spare surface in the room. And before long, Susan arrived, carrying fresh hoagies and coffee.

"Eat." She sat and watched me, making sure I obeyed. I chewed and swallowed tuna with provolone; she paced and hovered. She rearranged the water pitcher, washcloths, tissue box and paper cups on Nick's bedside table. She stood beside him, staring, straightening his blanket, disturbing him as he slept.

"Susan, stop. You're making me crazy." I couldn't stand it.

"Why? What am I doing?"

"You're fidgeting."

"I am not." She fidgeted with the flowers and organized the books and candy on the dresser. "I'm just trying to help."

"You have helped. You've watched Molly for me. You took care of me last night and you brought me this hoagie."

"I brought you something else, too. For later." She sat on the tan faux leather chair beside me and pulled a brown paper bag out of her purse. I took it and set it down beside my purse, figuring it was more food; Susan wanted to be sure I was eating.

"Tim says I should stay out of it and leave things to the authorities. He says there's nothing we can do. But you know me. I'm not good at passive."

No, she wasn't. "But Tim's right. There really isn't anything we can do. And you said yourself we don't want to mess with these people—"

"No, but at least we should protect ourselves. Look, Zoe. Face it. Every single person we've met who's been connected to the slave traffickers has been either shot or killed—"

"Wait, hold on." She was jumping to conclusions. I told her what Nick had said. That he'd been rowing and heard someone on Peters Island calling for help. "Nick's shooting wasn't because of slaves or traffickers. He got shot because he interrupted somebody killing Coach Everett." I pictured Tony. Tony on the dock, nerves frayed, arguing with the coach. Tony in the foyer of the boathouse, hair wet, wearing only a towel.

Susan frowned, fiddling with her rings. "But who would want to kill Coach Everett?"

She had a point; Tony wasn't the only one. "Are you serious? Who wouldn't? Susan, even you make a decent suspect after the way you cursed him out. Probably anyone he's ever coached would want to—" I stopped midsentence, picturing Coach Everett in his launch, always wearing a Humberton hat. Just like the one found floating with the dead women. Could that hat have belonged to the coach? Had the coach been involved with the slave smugglers, too? Is that why he'd been shot?

Stop it, I told myself. The hat didn't have to belong to the coach; there were hundreds of Humberton hats around and as many ways for one to end up in the river.

"I don't know, Zoe. There are too many coincidences. The fact remains that, of all the people we know who were directly connected to the slave case, we're the only ones still walking. And I'll be honest. That worries me."

"Susan. According to you, everyone's involved with the slave smugglers. That just can't be true." But I wondered. Coach Everett had been acting pretty shady when he'd been fighting with Tony. For all I knew, that fight could have been about slave trafficking.

Susan looked grave. "I have no idea who's working with anybody, Zoe. All I know is we need to be careful. I think these people are methodically wiping out anyone who knows or even suspects anything about them—"

"Stop it, Susan." I didn't want to hear it.

"No. You need to hear this."

"Well, fine. I heard. You can stop now."

"No, because you still don't get it."

"Yes, I do. We've run into some very nasty people and we need to be careful."

"But not just us, Zoe." She leaned forward, lowering her voice. "Who knows what happened last night? Who was that Gordo guy that Molly saw? What was he doing in the boathouse in the middle of the night?"

"No. Stop it." I wasn't going to hear her tell me that Molly was in danger, too, even though I knew.

"Showing up just coincidentally about the time that Nick was getting shot? Don't you think that if he knows Molly saw him—"

"Susan, stop!" My voice was too loud; Nick's eyelids fluttered, and he thrashed around in his morphine haze. When he settled down, I continued quietly. "Molly's fine. Even if she saw him, he didn't see her. She's safe. She's with Tim and the girls." I wasn't willing to consider any other possibility. "If there even is a guy named Gordo, he was probably just some guy looking for Tony—"

"Really. And how did he get into the boathouse?"

I stopped. "What?"

"The doors were locked. How did he get in?"

I shrugged. "Maybe he's a member and has a key."

"But Tony said he doesn't know him. If he were a member, Tony would know him."

"So? What are you suggesting?"

"I'm not sure. Maybe Tony's lying. Tony knows who this Gordo person is but he's pretending not to."

"Why would he do that?"

"Maybe he's scared. Because maybe the Gordo is somebody Tony doesn't want to see. Maybe the Gordo is the bad guy."

The bad guy? My eyes ached. My body hurt. Nick lay oblivious and asleep, only half alive. And Susan was trying to tell me that Molly was in danger, too. I couldn't listen anymore.

"I think it's far-fetched, Susan." At least I hoped it was.

"Maybe. But, just in case, be careful. Especially with Nick laid up. Let Tim get you a gun—"

"No. No gun. No weapons."

Brows furrowed, she stared at me. "Then at least use what I gave you. Keep it with you, in a pocket or your purse."

She sat back in her chair, waiting for me to look. I reached for the brown paper bag and looked inside, saw a small but serious can of pepper spray.

"Be careful with it." Susan showed me how to hold the thing. "You want to grip it right; otherwise, in the panic of the moment, you might shoot yourself in the face. Sort of defeating the purpose."

Wonderful. If I ever tried to use it, I'd probably end up blinding myself. Or Molly. I put the can of spray back in the bag, laid the bag beside a potted chrysanthemum.

"It's small, so you can carry it with you all the time." Susan meant well, but I wanted nothing to do with her miniature chemical weapon. Molly might see it and think it was hairspray or cologne, might aim it at herself. It made me nervous. So, as soon as she left, I tossed it into the trash.

SIXTY-THREE

It was getting dark, but I insisted to the cops and the hospital staff that I was fine walking home alone. It was only a few blocks and I desperately needed the air. But as I left the hospital I felt enervated, sorry I'd turned down offers for rides. I stood at the cabstand amazed that the heat hadn't broken even with sunset, hoping my wait wouldn't be long, going over Susan's comments yet another time. Were we in danger? Were slave traffickers really eliminating everyone even remotely connected to the nineteen deaths? If so, did that include us?

For the zillionth time, I told myself it couldn't. We didn't know anything. At least, we didn't know that we knew anything. Which was just as good.

Exhausted, I waited in front of the hospital for a cab. And I kept thinking about Tony. Every day, he'd looked more haunted, more stressed. What had he and the coach been arguing about that day? I tried to remember. What had I heard? Tony warning the coach that they could both get hammered. Hammered? How? By whom? For what? And the coach had wanted money. Why? Had he been selling Tony something? Or blackmailing him? I replayed what I'd heard of their fight. "You want it?" the coach had said. "Pay for it."

I was stumped. What could "it" have been? Again I remembered the night Nick got shot, how Tony had come downstairs wet, smelling of soap, wearing only a towel. It had been after five in the morning, and he'd just showered. Why? Was it because he'd just come back from Peters Island, grimy and sweaty, maybe even bloody from shooting Nick and the coach?

I shuddered, recalling Nick's blood-soaked chest, the screaming and flapping of maddened geese. The rocks and branches ripping at my skin as I ran through the blackness back to the boat. Had Tony been the man in the launch? The man who'd smacked my head with an oar?

I had to know, kept going back over snippets of the argument. But all I remembered was Tony's panic and Coach Everett's flat demands for money. "Pay for it," he'd insisted. For what? What did the coach have that Tony needed? My head throbbed; my brain felt swollen and overloaded, unable to think.

"Lady, you want a cab or not?" Sweat dripped over his bushy eyebrows as the driver leaned out the window.

Climbing in, my skin stuck to the hot leather seat. I closed the door, cursing my luck; probably every other cab in the city had its air-conditioning on.

"Where to?"

I started to give Susan's address, but stopped halfway. No, it wasn't time yet to get Molly and go home. I was too wound up; I had to try to find out what had happened, even though I wasn't sure how. Molly had been at Susan's all day; she could stay a little longer. I leaned back on the hot worn-out seats, trying to get comfortable.

"Boathouse Row," I told the driver. "Humberton Barge."

SIXTY-FOUR

It was dark when I got there; most evening rowers had already come off the water. Just a few pairs of shoes littered the dock; a couple of people moved around the bays, putting away boats and oars. I looked around, feeling conspicuous, but nobody noticed me climbing the stairs to Tony's attic apartment. And nobody answered when I knocked on his door. I stood there motionless, listening, half expecting the door to fly open and arms to grab me, but nothing happened. Slowly, silently, I tried the knob. It wouldn't budge. The door was locked. No surprise. But I wasn't about to give up. There had to be a way to get in. If not through the door, then how? A window? I leaned out the window outside Tony's door and saw another window, just a yard away. The window of Tony's apartment was open wide. Not stopping to consider dangers or legalities, I climbed out onto the ledge, clutched the drainpipe for support, and swung first one, then the other leg over Tony's windowsill. Before I had time to think about what I was doing, I'd slid under the raised sash and, with a graceless thunk, I was in.

The room stank of sweaty sheets and stale man. And of something sour. Fear? The air hung motionless, festering, and I felt faint, almost unable to breathe. Looking for a light switch, stumbling over scattered clothes, I turned on a lamp, saw upheaval. An unmade bed, towels strewn over crumpled, graying sheets. An empty pizza box. Empty bottles from water and beer. A cluttered desk, a laptop computer, a dresser. A closet. I hurried, searching, not knowing for what. Not knowing where Tony was or when he'd return. Quickly, listening for feet on the steps, afraid to get caught, I opened drawers, sifted through clumps of socks and underwear, finding nothing hidden among them. In the closet, I found empty luggage, a sport coat and slacks. On the desk, scattered bills for his cell phone, his credit cards. Receipts for pizza, for Chinese food. A handful of loose change. Nothing else. Maybe there was something important in the computer. But if there was, I'd never find it. As far as I could tell, Tony was guilty of nothing except being a slob.

And then, breathing the stifling claustrophobia of Tony's room, it hit me: Of course there was nothing here. I was looking in the wrong place. Turning out the light, peeking into the hallway, I crept out of Tony's attic apartment and down the stairs. I knocked on the door to the men's locker room, listened for running showers or male voices. When I was sure no one was inside, I opened the door and went in, heading for the lockers, the argument between Tony and the coach echoing in my mind. "You want it?" the coach repeated. "Pay for it."

Tony didn't have what I was looking for. Whatever it was, the person who had it was Coach Everett.

SIXTY-FIVE

The first thing I noticed was how nice the locker room was. Much nicer than the women's. Not only was it larger, there was also a lavish sauna/steam room. Towels were stacked neatly, ready for use. The showers were individual, with cream-colored tile walls separating each from the others. Women had to shower around a cluster of nozzles spraying from the center of a large single stall. Not only that. Forget urinals. Each toilet had not only its own stall, but its own entire room. The main room was lined with sinks, supplied with shaving cream, disposable razors, aftershave, deodorant—the place was a veritable spa compared to the paltry little space designated to women. Even the lockers were better; the men's were wooden, their doors carved, each with a bronze plate naming the member assigned to it. It was outrageous. Women paid the same dues as men; we should receive at least similar amenities. But what was I thinking of? Who cared about saunas or wooden doors? I was there to search. Poised to dash into a private toilet if anyone came in, I scanned the names on the lockers. Found Nick's. And Tony's. Finally, near the door to the sauna room, I found the one belonging to Preston Everett.

Of course I didn't have a key. I tried, knowing it would be futile, to pry the door open with my nails. Then I looked around, trying to find something that could help me get into the locker. Think, I told myself. This is a boathouse. It's full of tools. There would be wrenches and screwdrivers downstairs in the boat bays. I'd run down and look. I started for the door, passing the sinks. And I saw what I needed lying on a countertop among Q-tips and mouthwash. It wasn't as good as a hairpin might have been, but the nail file worked perfectly, popping the lock on the very first try.

Coach Everett's locker was jam-packed with gear for all seasons. A dozen pairs of sweats and underwear, twice as many hats. A yellow rain suit. A tool kit. Night-lights. Energy snack bars. Batteries. A few copies of *Rowing News,* a clipboard with various workout regimens. A megaphone. His shaving kit was in there, as well as a couple of polo shirts and a pair of khakis. What couldn't be hung was folded or stacked neatly, but every inch of the locker was filled. And nothing seemed out of the ordinary.

So what had he been selling to Tony? And, if it wasn't in his locker, where could it be? Maybe I was wasting my time. Whatever it was might be anywhere. Stashed at his house. Or in a safe-deposit box somewhere. I closed the locker, disappointed; I'd been so sure, almost certain that I'd find a clue to what Coach Everett had been up to. But if not in his locker, where?

Slowly, quietly, I peeked out the men's locker-room door, and seeing no one, hurried into the hall and down the steps to the lounge. Think, I told myself. If you were Coach Everett and you wanted to hide something, where would you hide it? What places did the coach have access to? I began listing them, realizing how many potential hiding places Humberton had; Molly had already demonstrated that, hiding all over the boat racks. But the racks were just one possibility. The boathouse was huge, a compilation of dark corners and shadowy nooks. There might be floorboards that lifted, wall panels that came loose. Something could be tucked into a cabinet or alcove, or stuffed inside a sofa cushion or slid beneath the carpet in the lounge. Or taped under a drawer in the kitchen. Or hidden right out in the open, maybe among boat parts piled under the boat-bay stairs—invisible amid seats, shoes, oarlocks, even oars. And then there was the gasoline shed where launch fuel was kept. And inside the launches themselves.

Okay, I was wasting my time. If Coach Everett had wanted to hide something, Humberton Barge offered endless possibilities. I wandered downstairs into the now abandoned boat bays, replaying over and over the lines of his argument with Tony.

"You want it? Pay for it."

What was "it"? And where? In the dim light, I stood among the rows of shells, hearing Tony's frantic warning: "You want us both to get hammered?" Or was it "skinned alive?" Or both? I wandered to the dock door where they'd stood as they fought, but nothing more came back to me. It was useless. Time to give up and go.

Leaving, I turned once more to scan the empty bays. And halfway up the steps, I stopped, came back downstairs and looked again. Right beside the boat-bay steps, at about eye level, was a rack labeled PRESTON EVERETT. Which meant that the rack was reserved for Coach Everett's own personal single shell. I stood beside his dusty old Filippi, a remnant of his glory years. Eyeing it, I wondered why he kept it; everyone knew he hadn't rowed in years, that he'd become way too stocky to start again. And rack space was precious; Nick had complained about the price more than once.

Before I knew it I was standing among boat riggers, reaching up and under, feeling inside and behind and under the shoes for I-didn't-know-what. I stuck my hand into the hole under the seat where the tracks can be adjusted. Nothing was there, not even a spiderweb. Nothing. Whatever the coach had hidden, it wasn't there. I'd never find it. Giving up, I started to leave again. In fact, I'd made it all the way up the steps before I realized what was wrong. I remembered our lessons, heard him yelling at Susan. "What have you forgotten, Cummings?"

The hatches. Coach Everett was always reminding us about them. When you took a boat out, you closed the hatches so the hull would be airtight. But when you put it away, you had to leave them open to let air in and keep the interior dry.

But I was sure: Coach Everett's shell's hatches had both been closed. Of all people, Coach Everett would have been a stickler for boat maintenance. I ran back down to his single, opened the forward hatch and reached inside. And felt nothing but air. Okay. I'd been wrong. Even so, I tried the stern hatch. The lid was stuck at first, but, grunting and turning, I finally managed to twist it off.

Slowly, standing in the shadows, I reached inside and pulled out a zipped plastic bag filled with papers and a bunch of little booklets that looked like bankbooks, or maybe passports.

SIXTY-SIX

I scanned the papers, found coded lists. Nicknames of people and places with dates. "Trashcan, Cherry Tree, 1, 18." "Skipper, Swamp, 13, 20." "Tamale, Towers, 17, 16."

When the door to the boat bays opened, I knew it was Tony before I saw him; the evening rowers had gone home. Nobody but Tony would be in the boathouse this late. Shoving the papers back into the bag with the booklets, I spun around, looking for a place to hide, realizing too late that I had no reason to do so. I was a member of Humberton Barge, had a right to be in the boathouse, whatever the hour. I didn't need to hide; I needed to act relaxed. Normal. But Tony had already sensed my panic and zeroed in on it, like a predator on prey.

"Tony," I greeted him, trying to look innocent, as if the plastic bag were a purse. Or a bag of pepper spray.

Tony wore a pair of baggy shorts and flip-flops, nothing else. His chest seemed hungry; I could see his ribs and the curly black hair striping his abdomen. He took a step down. Keep going, I told myself. Go up the stairs casually. Pass him. Tell him to have a nice night. But Tony took another step down, eyeing both me and the bag, and I didn't go up the stairs. I backed away from him, still wearing a stupid, silent smile. We continued that way, Tony descending the stairs, me walking backward, until I'd made it almost to the dock door.

"What are you doing down here?" He glanced at the bag in my hand.

I couldn't think of anything to say. "I was just . . . looking for something." I kept backing up slowly, stalling.

"You find it?" His eyes glowed, overly alert. Feverish?

"Yes." I smiled lightly, holding on to the bag. "It was right where I dropped it."

He stepped toward me. "Yeah? What is it?" He eyed the bag.

"This? Oh. Nothing. Just some papers and stuff. Bills, mostly."

"Really. No shit." He looked at the plastic bag.

Keep moving, I thought. Get out of here. "I'm always losing things." I sounded idiotic, but I kept talking, didn't seem able to stop. "Luckily, most of the time I find what I lose. But while I'm looking for one thing—like my keys, I lose something else—like my credit cards. It never ends." I giggled stupidly.

Tony ignored my chatter. He kept coming, matching my steps with longer ones; unlike me, though, he was moving forward, able to see where he was going. Soon, he'd be within arm's reach. And I'd be up against the wall. Or the door to the dock.

"Let's see that." Tony reached out for the bag, and I dodged, hopping awkwardly across the aisle, bumping noisily into the riggers of a quad.

He watched me recover, apparently in no hurry.

I backed up, clutching the bag, glancing over my shoulder. I was almost at the dock door, near the button that opened the automatic door. Just a few more steps.

"That's my bag." Sweat dripped down his forehead, onto his eyebrows. "It belongs to me. Shit, where'd you find it?"

I didn't answer, didn't move. He looked around to where I'd been standing when he came in, saw Coach Everett's boat on the rack. He blinked at it, then rolled his eyes. "Are you shitting me? His Filippi? It was in his stinking boat?" Tony slapped his head, decrying his own stupidity. "Oh, fuck me—it was in his fucking boat!" He rotated, his eyes wide, grasping the idea. His eyes narrowed, menacing.

I didn't say anything. I just kept moving back, back, step by step. And Tony moved forward. He was mere inches away when I got to the dock door. With nowhere to go, I reached out and slapped the "open" button, and the door began its slow, groaning roll-up. The noise distracted Tony for just an eye blink, but I used it, dashing around the boat racks into another aisle and, clutching the bag, running as fast as I could across the boat-bay floor.

SIXTY-SEVEN

Shedding his flip-flops, Tony took off after me. I could hear his bare feet punching the concrete, feel air whirring close behind me. I sped ahead, aware that there really was no escape; the boat bays ended in a wall just yards ahead. My only chance was to zigzag around and over the boats at the end of the aisle. But Tony was too close; he'd catch me before I could get there. So, suddenly, I bent forward and literally took a dive between two stacked boats to my left. Arms outstretched, I flew headfirst over one double and under another and, breaking all the rules of boat care, I shoved the one above me hard so that it lifted off the rack and tottered, slipping off the rack, apparently landing right on Tony.

For once, Tony wasn't concerned about proper care of Humberton equipment. Instead of catching the boat and reracking it, he let it clatter to the floor and, cursing, climbed through the racks after me. But the falling boat gave me a few seconds; I hurried over another boat rack and darted to the steps. I saw him as I climbed, tearing his way through closely stacked boats, seeming to slather at the mouth, and I flew ahead, scarcely making contact with the stairs as I climbed. At the top, I reached over and flipped off the light switch, sending the boat bays into complete darkness. And, as the door swung shut behind me, I heard a serious thud, then Tony's distraught curses and a series of nonmusical crescendos from percussion instruments of fiberglass, concrete and metal.

SIXTY-EIGHT

A few falling boats didn't stop him. I'd crossed the foyer and opened the front door but hadn't quite made it out of the boathouse when Tony burst from the boat bays. He staggered a bit, but he kept after me.

"Hayes—" He was breathless, panting. "You got to give me those. I swear, I'll—"

I didn't slow down. I ran. Boathouse Row was quiet after dark; I saw no runners or bike riders, no skaters. Once again I found myself running toward Center City, searching for police, trying to flag down a passing car. It was becoming routine. I had no idea what I was carrying, but whatever it was, I knew it would explain Coach Everett's murder and Nick's shooting. I was certain now that the coach had been blackmailing Tony, that Tony had killed him for whatever was in the bag. I ran past boathouses, hoping to see a rower who'd hung around, lingering over a few beers, or a coach who'd stayed late, working on equipment. But nobody was around. I glanced behind me; Tony was lagging, probably injured, but not giving up. Adrenaline flooded my veins, giving me an edge, but I didn't know how long I could keep it up—my mouth tasted coppery like blood. My wounded head pounded; my entire body was spent.

Don't stop, I told myself. Go on. You have no choice. Somehow, I kept going. But so did Tony.

I headed to the parking lot behind the Art Museum where I'd found Agent Ellis, hoping that police would be cruising the area. Ducking through the shrubs, across the grass, between parked cars, I saw a familiar face. Oh, thank God. Harry was there. Harry, the mayor of Boathouse Row. The water-ice man, standing behind his water-ice van. Harry, my salvation. Finished for the day, he'd pulled his van into the lot to pack up, getting ready to go home.

"Harry—" I gasped, breathless. "Harry—"

I looked back; Tony was twenty yards behind me, sprinting. I bolted ahead, shouting.

"Harry—Harry, help—"

Harry looked up, trying to make sense of what was coming at him, a frazzled gasping forty-year-old woman chased by a mostly naked, rabid, barefoot young man.

I barreled into him, grabbed on to him, tried to take cover behind him. Gasping, with no time to explain, I pointed to Tony, who'd suddenly slowed his pace to a jog, then a walk. What was he doing, trying to act nonchalant? If so, it wasn't working. His eyes were too desperate, his body too taut.

"Harry—" I panted, holding the bag to my chest.

"What's all this?" He looked from me to Tony, Tony to me, frowning. "What's the trouble?"

"Harry—Tony—I think he killed Coach Everett." I swallowed air, pointed at Tony. "He shot Nick—"

"What . . . what are you talking about? That's Tony. From Humberton."

I nodded, grabbing his arm, panting. "He shot Coach Everett. It was him."

Harry's gaze bounced from me to Tony, back again. "Settle down, miss. It's Zoe Hayes, right? See, I told you I'd remember your name." He smiled, proud of himself. Not grasping the situation.

"Harry, please. Tony killed the coach."

"Him? This guy? You got to be kidding. I know this guy."

Harry raised an eyebrow as he regarded Tony. Oh, Lord. Didn't he believe me? "What the hell, Tony? What's she talking about?"

Tony stopped just yards away and waited, assessing the situation, uncertain what to do. Harry wasn't young or big, but he was street-smart. And tough. As he regarded Tony, his expression darkened. Maybe he was beginning to believe me. Harry turned to me, saw the plastic bag I was clutching.

"What's that?"

I held it out. "I'm not sure. It's papers. I think it's some kind of code. Coach had it hidden and I think it's why Tony killed him."

"Jesus." Harry scowled at Tony. He took the bag from me. "Coach Everett had this?"

Tony lunged for the bag. "Give me that—"

"Back off, Tony." Harry pivoted away and took a few papers from the bag. "Let's see what we have here."

"Tony. Mercy. 'Cowboy,' " he read. " 'Rob Roy, seven fourteen. Widower Ebony six twelve.' What the hell is this, Tony?"

Tony stammered, shifted his weight, ready to take off.

"I'm just guessing," Harry said. "But it looks like a bunch of code names. And these numbers—what are they? Dates? Are these sales slips? Shipping orders? Looks like some kind of merchandise lists. And—oh my—look what else is here. Passports?" He opened one, another, looking at the photos. "Shit. Yes, sir. That's what these are. Passports. Of Asian women."

Oh, God. The slaves. "Harry, the dead women," I began. "The ones in the river—those must be their papers." But Harry wasn't listening. He was glaring at Tony.

"What the hell is this, Tony?"

Thank God. Harry was beginning to understand.

"How did Coach Everett get ahold of this stuff?"

Tony stammered. "I don't know. He stole it from me."

"So you killed him? Why? To get it back?" Harry scratched his head, confused. "Then how'd she get it?" He gestured my way.

What difference did it make how I got it? "Harry," I urged. "We need to call the police." But Harry wasn't listening; he focused on Tony.

Tony didn't answer. "Give it, Harry. You don't want to mess with me." He tried to sound firm but managed only a sickly whine.

"Let me understand. What happened? Everett stole this stuff. Then, what'd you do? Tell Everett you'd pay for this? That you had money stashed on the island and you'd pay him there?"

Tony glowered. Why was Harry asking so many questions? Why didn't he just call the police?

"No shit. And Everett believed you? He met you on the island? Geniuses, both of you." Harry definitely did not seem alarmed. Oh, God. Why wasn't he?

"For your information," Tony sneered, "Everett thought he was helping me rescue an injured woman."

Harry shook his head "An injured woman. That's good."

"Harry. Give me the bag."

"Or else what? You're going to off me, too? How many people you gonna kill? Why bother? Don't you know it's too late? Everybody you work with already knows you fucked up. First you lose a load. Then you lose these papers and kill Everett and shoot a cop. Now you go assaulting this young lady, who happens to be the cop's girlfriend. Seems to me you're a real problem for your organization. You know, I'm betting you're a dead man already."

"Me? I'm a dead man?" Tony was growling, baring his teeth. "How about the fucker who left the shipment at the wrong goddamn location?"

"How about you get going while you still can? I was you, I'd run for it."

I hunkered behind Harry, trying to follow their conversation, disturbed that Harry had grasped the situation so quickly. I told myself that Harry was familiar with what Tony had been up to; after all, he knew everything that went on. That's why they called him the mayor of Boathouse Row. Harry stood in front of me protectively and opened the back door of his van.

"Listen." He spoke softly. "I got a gun in there—for protection. It's in the pocket behind the driver's seat. Hop in and get it for me?"

I released a breath, relieved. Harry was finally going to help me. Tony—the man who'd shot Nick—had been caught. Harry and I had him.

When I turned to climb into the van, Harry was gripping the plastic bag, and Tony stood poised for combat, wearing his twisted, desperate grin, refusing to back off. After that, all I remembered was landing flat on my face and how hard I'd been shoved.

SIXTY-NINE

The first coherent thought I had was that I was locked in. The van had become a cage. A closed, walled-up cage with light shining through only a ribbon of window at one end. Then I realized that I couldn't move. My hands and feet were cuffed, and the cuffs were chained to a wall. And it was hot. Stuffy, without ventilation. The air was close and thick, hard to breathe.

I lay still for a while, too woozy to sit up, my head swirling with pain where I'd banged it yet again. Oh, God. I lifted my wrists as far as the chains would permit, felt my head, the place where stitches throbbed. Oh, Lord. Tony had tackled me and wrestled me, held me down and locked me up. But if he'd been able to attack me, he had to get past Harry. How had he done that so quickly? What had he done to Harry? I didn't know. All I knew was that I was chained up inside Harry's water-ice van and I had to get out.

But wait, I thought. This couldn't be Harry's van. Harry's didn't have chains inside; it had tubs of frozen sugar water. I closed my eyes again, wishing for a cup of it, any flavor. I was thirsty and sweaty. Struggling to inhale. I gazed at the light gleaming through the sliver of window, wondering how long it would be until morning. And, in this stifling airless box, how I would survive the night.

I didn't want to find out. Yelling, screaming for help, I pulled at my chains, twisting and yanking, tugging until, depleted and panting, I fell back against the wall. I sat there laboring on each breath, realizing that help might not come. Nobody would know where to look for me. I might die there, choking, suffocating, alone and in chains. I thought of Molly, of Nick. Of never seeing them again. And, panicking, I pulled at my chains some more, screaming until my voice was gone.

Finally I fell back and stared at the thin beam of light streaming through the crack of exposed window. I focused on it, watching tiny dust particles float through the rainbowlike ray. Don't give up, I scolded myself. Think. Find a way to get out of here. I boosted myself up onto my elbows and squinted, peering through stifling darkness. And I saw the other chains.

Mine weren't the only ones. Chains were everywhere. Lining the floor, hanging from the walls, connecting to dozens of handcuffs. Big handcuffs, not shiny and chic like the ones cops used. No, these were like the ones on me—thick, heavy ugly ones, the kinds slaves wore.

Oh, God. Slave chains. I stared at my wrists, the chains, the closed compartment, finally absorbing all of it. This wasn't just an airless van; it was a slave trafficker's vehicle. In the shadows I counted ten pairs of handcuffs, ten pairs of ankle cuffs along each wall. Space enough for twenty prisoners. Twenty slaves. Nineteen women had baked to death, locked in the hot, unventilated van. Had they been afraid? Comforted each other? Or had they passed out, unaware, too weak to think? Oh, Lord. Nineteen had died. I was one of them. I would be the twentieth.

I drew a deep breath, felt my chest ache with the effort. There was no air, and it would get much hotter once the sun came up. As the day went on, the heat would intensify, become sweltering. In the next few hours, I was going to fry. Again, I shouted for help through raw lungs. I pulled at the chains, strained at the cuffs until my wrists bled. I jerked and twisted, bit the links, rattled them, and finally, head throbbing, drenched with sweat, fell back against the wall, panting, gasping for air. Spent.

Fading, I studied the walls around me. Soundproofed, insulated. Seamless. No wonder no one had heard my shouts. I lay shackled. Baking. Slowly dying. Could death, I wondered, be this understated? So quiet? There was something, I knew, that I should be doing, but I wasn't sure, couldn't remember what it was. And what should I feel? Sorrow? Rage? Something? Fading, I pictured Molly and Nick, wondered if they'd be okay. But I didn't worry. I lacked the clarity and strength.

SEVENTY

The floor shook, destroying the peace. Someone, a slender figure bathed in light, was shaking me, making shrill guttural sounds. Moving my arms, messing with my legs. She lifted my head, jabbering, holding a bottle of water to my lips. Oh. Now I understood. She was—had to be—an angel. A beautiful angel with a bright halo, wearing a tank top and running shorts. She kept tugging on my arms, yammering, speaking gibberish. Didn't they speak English in heaven? Shouldn't they be less aggressive? I reached for the water again, and she handed it back to me, letting me drink. I swallowed too fast, poured water into my throat, coughing, choking. That's when I noticed that the angel was Asian. And that she had three curved parallel lines tattooed on her arm, just below her shoulder.

I sat up too fast, but she caught me as I fell, and she stroked my sore head, urgently telling me something that I couldn't remotely understand. With a cool damp cloth, she washed blood from my raw wrists. Wait—my wrists? Where were the chains? They were off. Gone. I saw them, then, lying on the floor beside me, the handcuffs open, the key still in the lock. Who was this woman? She had the tattoo of the slave cartel, but clearly she was free. How had she found me? Where had she gotten the key?

"Who are you?" My voice was raw from yelling, sounded like a frog. "How did you find me?"

She chattered on, urgent and animated, gesturing as if to help me understand. And as she moved her arms, I noticed raw marks like those on my own wrists, the sores I'd gotten fighting with the handcuffs. Crouching beside me, she pointed to the chains, talking about each set of handcuffs, one by one, motioning by clasping her wrist that she had been once captive herself, just like me. She pointed to a pair of handcuffs, to chains along the wall. Was she saying she had sat there? That she had worn those cuffs? She sat silent for a moment, her eyes closed as if in prayer. Or remembrance.

I sat up to comfort her, but she wouldn't allow it. Kneeling beside me, she took both my hands firmly in hers and looked into my eyes. She was young, I thought. Maybe twenty. But her eyes were tunnels, endlessly dark. She struggled to speak carefully and slowly, to be sure I'd understand.

"Yo kay now. Yo unstad?" She handed me the bottle of water. "Yo kay. Me go. Yo no say 'Shu Li.'"

"What?" I no say Shoe Lee?

"Shu Li naw fished," she went on. "Yo unstad?" She pointed to the chains. "Awda peepow die. Ma sestah die."

Her sister? Her sister died? Oh, God. Her sister had been locked up in here. Had ended up in the river. I pictured the bodies floating, remembered holding one of them in my arms. Had that been her sister?

The woman tapped my arm, bringing me back. "Shu Li no die. In wodda. Wake up." She moved her arms in pantomime, doggy-paddling in the air.

"You swam?" Instantly, I understood. "You didn't die. You woke up in the water and swam away. You escaped." She'd been one of them. The twentieth slave.

Of course. Nineteen bodies had been found, but the van had chains for twenty. The traffickers wouldn't have left an empty set of shackles; the van would have been filled to capacity. All twenty were dumped in the river, but one got away. She was a miracle. I stared at her, jubilant; if I'd had the strength, I'd have hugged her.

"Me, yes." She nodded. "Swam." She gazed at the empty chains.

Slowly, my mind creaked into gear, and the thrill I felt at her survival fizzled, surged again as fear. This woman was considered cartel property. And she knew far too much about the traffickers. She was in major danger. I thought of Agent Ellis. Sonia and the priest. I had to help her.

"Muss go. Me go fish." She turned to the door.

"Wait," I began. "Don't leave—"

"Yo kay now. No say Shu Li." She placed a finger gently on my lips, as if to silence me, her eyes connecting a final time. Then she opened the compartment door and jumped out.

"No . . . wait. Please don't leave," I yelped.

Clumsy and stiff, I scrambled after her, scooting crablike to the door, lowering my legs, sliding unsteadily to the pavement, free. But she was gone. And my legs gave way, unsteady, unable to support me. I grabbed on to the door of the dungeon on wheels, taking deep breaths and looking into the blinding morning light, trying to figure out where I was. And that took no time. I was right where I'd been the night before. In the parking lot behind the Art Museum. In a van marked HARRY'S WATER ICE.

SEVENTY-ONE

Wobbly, I tried to grasp what had happened, couldn't quite believe it. Harry was a slave trafficker. I saw him scooping out Molly's water ice, chatting with rowers, gossiping, selling sodas to joggers and skaters. But that same Harry had a van full of horror and chains. And, oh, God, I'd gone to him for help, run right into his arms. It made no sense. Normally, Harry's van was stocked full of candy and pretzels, sodas and barrels of water ice. Where was all that now? And then it hit me. Harry had a second van, painted like the other one with his name and cheery logo.

But this second van was no mobile concession stand; it was a prison on wheels with room for twenty captives. It was unimaginable, but there it was. And I had to get away—Harry could be anywhere, might show up any second. I tried to run, but I was still off balance, legs rubbery and stiff. I leaned against the van, steadying myself, telling myself not to linger, to keep moving. Harry might be anywhere. Or Tony. He was in the cartel, too. Both of them were. And who else? I spun around, looking, seeing no one nearby. Some joggers along Kelly Drive. Someone walking his dog across the park, too far away to hear me yell. It had to be early, too early for rush-hour traffic, even for police cruisers. But the sun was up; it wouldn't be too early for rowers. If I could get myself to the boathouses, I could get help there.

Take a deep breath, I told myself. Get your equilibrium. It wasn't that far to Lloyd Hall, the start of Boathouse Row. But even getting around the van seemed monumental. I stumbled with each step, but continued, slowly making my way toward the sidewalk, keeping one hand on the van for support. Go on, I told myself. Keep going. You might meet a cop or a jogger on the path. Someone to lean on. Just take one step at a time.

Coaching myself, I moved forward, tottering and catching myself, taking a step, then another. What was wrong with me? Why couldn't I walk normally? I didn't know, couldn't think, just kept edging forward, hoping that Tony wouldn't spring at me, that Harry wouldn't grab me. I stepped forward, thinking of the woman who'd rescued me, assuring myself that she wouldn't have abandoned me if I weren't safe. That Tony wasn't around, and neither was Harry.

But I was wrong. As I came around to the front of the van, I stopped, frozen. Harry was right there, sitting in the driver's seat, and Tony was beside him. I crouched, afraid they'd seen me. But they sat still, oblivious, facing the windshield. I watched, waiting for them to talk or scratch or yawn or shift their weight, slowly understanding why they weren't and wouldn't.

No longer afraid, I moved to the front of the van and looked through the window. Three curved parallel lines had been cut into both men's faces. Tony slumped as if gazing at his lap. And Harry stared straight ahead, looking surprised.

SEVENTY-TWO

The next few hours were a jumble of commotion. More police. More sirens. Officer Olsen wasn't on duty; the policeman who showed up urged me to go to a hospital. I absolutely refused. I'd had enough of hospitals. And no way was I going to get back inside a van, even one marked AMBULANCE.

Besides, I had to go get Molly. She and Susan must be mad with worry about me. I explained all this to the officer. I said that I had to call them. And I told him about the danger—the slave cartel, the traffickers. I said that Tony and Harry had been involved with the cartel, that they'd transported the nineteen dead women, and I began to describe the woman who'd rescued me, but stopped. "No say Shu Li," she'd told me. So I didn't. I left out her identity, made no mention of the twentieth slave or her survival. I pretended not to know anything about my rescuer, not even that she must have killed Harry and Tony. The officer took a few notes, but didn't seem alarmed, at least not as alarmed as I thought he should be.

An EMT wrapped the blood pressure cuff on my arm. I told her I didn't need to go to the hospital, I'd be fine, but I needed to call my friend. She nodded patronizingly, assuring me everything would be all right, but she didn't get me a phone. I sat beside the van, wondering why no one would listen to me. Were they all idiots? Why didn't the EMT or the policeman react to what I was telling them? For an awful moment I thought they were all cartel members like Harry and Tony, just pretending to be police and EMTs. But if they were, there was nothing I could do. I was just one person, and I had been hit on the head too often, was dehydrated, had no strength. Weaving in and out of an exhausted haze, I kept losing focus. I had to remind myself again and again that I was safe in the open sunlight on Kelly Drive, no longer hidden away in chains. That the woman beside me was an EMT, not an escaped slave. That the lines engraved on her face represented years of smiling, not the logo of a slave cartel.

And that, despite my adamant refusals, she and her coworkers had no sinister reasons for strapping me onto a gurney and taking me into a van.

SEVENTY-THREE

S ome time passed before Susan showed up, looking frantic and haggard.

"Zoe?" She rushed through the curtain separating me from the rest of the Emergency Room. "Zoe—thank God. You're conscious."

"Where's Molly?"

"With Tim. You didn't think I'd bring her here, did you? Here. Drink some water."

Water? Why? I had an IV in my arm, rehydrating me. Still I obeyed, sipping from a cup she shoved at me.

"Don't worry. Molly's fine. Tim took her and Emily to the pool. Molly wants to have a party there, by the way. But I haven't told her anything about you or what happened. When you didn't show up, she was worried something had happened to Nick, so I lied and said you'd called to say she could sleep over."

Oh, Lord—Nick. "How's Nick?"

"Better. His room's nice. Big, full of flowers, view of South Philly. I looked in on him before, when they wouldn't let me see you. He insists he'll be out tomorrow, but the nurse says it'll be several days."

Thank God. Nick was okay. "Did you tell him . . . does he know I'm here?"

"I told him you couldn't come by because you have a fever and don't want to expose him. You better call him later and pretend you have a cold."

A cold? She told him I had a cold? Another lie. I hated lying; trust was the issue Nick and I had been fighting about before he'd gotten shot. Still, I couldn't be angry with Susan; her lies had been kinder than the truth. Molly needed to feel safe and Nick needed to rest. Still, her lies made me uncomfortable, made me wonder if she was hiding disturbing truths from me as well.

"You're sure they're okay? Molly and Nick?"

"Yes, positive. Now, tell me what happened. Everything."

I closed my eyes, not ready yet.

Susan yawned, rubbing her forehead. "What a night. When you didn't show up for Molly, I called the police and waited up. I baked a poppy-seed cake and washed the floors in the kitchen and bathrooms. Then finally, about six, Ed called and said they'd found you and brought you here, so I came right over— I'm dead, Zoe. I haven't slept in like thirty-six hours."

"Go home," I told her. "Sleep."

"Are you serious? I can't sleep until you tell me what the hell happened. All I know is somehow you got locked in Harry's van with a ton of handcuffs and chains, and oh—by the way— Harry's and Tony's dead bodies. What were you doing there? Who killed them? How did you get out?"

"Oh, God. Susan." I grabbed her arm. She didn't know; nobody did. But I had to tell her. She deserved to know. "Swear you won't tell anyone. Nobody. Not even Tim."

"What?"

"Swear."

She eyed me doubtfully. "Okay. I swear."

"I'm serious. You have to keep this completely between us."

"Fine. Tell me."

I lowered my voice, eyeing the crack of open space between white curtains that wouldn't quite close. "There weren't just nineteen. There were twenty."

"Say again?"

"Women."

"Women?" She'd become an echo.

"The van," I enunciated carefully. "Harry's van had twenty sets of handcuffs, room for twenty women."

"Twenty?"

"Yes. One lived. One got away."

"A floater? What are you saying? One escaped?" Susan's voice was way too loud.

"Shh." I scowled. "One got away. The twentieth woman is alive."

"My God." Susan gaped, absorbing the concept. "But . . . how do you know? Oh, shit. That's how you got out? You saw her?"

I nodded, explained that she'd been dumped in the river with the others and now seemed to be going after the slave traffickers, killing them one by one, marking them with three parallel lines, the trademark of the cartel. First Agent Ellis, the crooked FBI agent. Then the people disguised as Sonia and the priest. Now Harry and Tony. She'd killed them and set me free.

Susan tilted her head, confused. "But that doesn't make sense. I don't think she killed Harry and Tony."

"She had to—they were just like the others. They had three lines cut into their faces—"

"If she killed them, Zoe, why'd she leave you in the van all night?"

"She got me out as soon as she—"

"Zoe, you were in the van until morning. Harry and Tony were killed last night."

What? "Uh-uh, couldn't be—"

"Zoe. They were strangled last night."

"Strangled?" How could that tiny little woman have strangled two strong men?

"Yes. That's what the preliminary coroner's report showed. And it said they'd been dead for more than six hours."

"But they couldn't have been."

"If she killed them the night before, why didn't she let you out right away? Why would she leave you locked in the van all night?"

Susan was right. She wouldn't have. Harry's keys had been right there in plain sight; the woman had used them to let me out. If she'd been there the night before, she'd have unlocked the van then, freeing me right away.

And there was more that wasn't right. The woman was killing deliberately, following a pattern, leaving a consistent signature. Even if she could have, she wouldn't have strangled Harry and Tony; she'd have killed them the way she had her other victims. I pictured Agent Ellis's blood-drenched body, remembered the newspaper articles about Sonia and the priest. All of them had had their throats cut. None had died by strangulation. No, the woman who'd rescued me hadn't killed Harry and Tony. Someone else had.

SEVENTY-FOUR

I spent the next hours telling my story to the police. I explained how either Harry or Tony or both of them had shoved me into the van and chained me up. How I had no idea who'd killed them. How a young woman had released me in the morning. The detective taking my statement seemed uncomfortable, maybe overtired. Maybe his hemorrhoids were bothering him. He shifted his substantial weight repeatedly, constantly running his hands over his crew cut.

When he took a break to refill his coffee I closed my eyes, trying to piece facts together. What was it Tony had said? "How about the fucker who left the shipment at the wrong location?" He'd aimed that barb at Harry. Harry's water-ice van had doubled as a transport vehicle for human cargo, but apparently Harry had messed up; he'd let nineteen people die inside and dumped them into the river.

What, then, had been Tony's role? He and Harry must have both been small change in the cartel, not too high up in the hierarchy. Maybe Tony was the one who was supposed to pick the women up and deliver them to buyers. Lord. What jobs were involved in slave trafficking? Did they have titles like ordinary businesses? Were there drivers and deliverymen? Dispatchers? Salespeople? Regional managers? Bookkeepers?

And what had Tony been? A hit man, maybe? I doubted it; he was too jumpy, not nearly steely enough. Still, he'd killed Coach Everett, shot Nick and tried to murder me. He'd been working for the cartel in some capacity. The papers were the key, had to be. What exactly were all those encoded names and dates? The buyers' names? Delivery deadlines? When the detective returned, I asked him if they'd gone over the papers yet, if they'd figured out what they meant.

"Papers?" He leaned forward and looked up at me, his elbows resting on his knees. "What papers?"

"In the plastic bag. The papers I found in the hatch of Coach Everett's boat."

"Oh." He relaxed. "You mean the passports."

Yes. I nodded. There had been passports there, too.

"We found them in the van, a plastic bag full of fake passports."

"But wait," I told him. "There were other papers there, too. Lists. Names and numbers. Like Rob Roy Cowboy seven fourteen. Or Widower, Ebony six twelve. They sounded like codes, maybe of orders and shipping dates—for the slave cartel."

He eyed me askance. "I don't know about that. All we found were the passports." He took out sheets of photos. "Recognize anybody here?"

Twenty Asian women stared out from the pages, the faces of the dead. I searched their eyes for shadows of doom, for awareness of what was to come. But their expressions, blank or falsely hopeful, nervous or grave, told me nothing about what they knew. They were young and some were beautiful; all I could tell about them was that they had died too awfully, too soon. Except, of course, for one.

Even in her photograph, she looked petite. But her eyes burned intensely. Fiercely.

"Shu Li" was the name on her passport. But the passports were fake; had that been her real name? I remembered her touching my lips, insisting, "No say Shu Li."

And so, deliberately, trying to look sincere, I shook my head. "No," I told him. "Nobody."

He accepted my answer without question or surprise.

"Maybe"—I changed the subject—"whoever killed Tony and Harry took the other papers."

He shrugged. "I don't know anything about any other papers." Again he rubbed his hand over the bristles on his head. Then he stood, lifting his bulk off the faux leather chair. He thanked me for my time and input and reminded me to call if I thought of anything else. And then, wishing me well, he left.

I sat there, sore and increasingly weepy, bones aching with fatigue. I was alive and safe, but the sense of impending danger hadn't left me. I longed to reconnect with my daughter, my life, and, as if it were a lifeline, I picked up the phone and dialed Nick's room.

When he said my name, his affection warmed me, massaged my nerves. He said he was getting stronger, and he sounded sturdy, almost normal. Thank God. Nick was going to be okay. He asked how I was feeling, and suddenly I fell apart. Unexpected tears ran down my cheeks. Letting them flow, I sniffed and blew my nose, so that, in the end, I didn't have to lie to him. I sounded nasal and drippy, just as if I'd had a cold.

SEVENTY-FIVE

That night, Molly and I dined on canned tomato soup and grilled cheese sandwiches. We snuggled and watched a DVD of *The Lion King*. We colored a get-well card for Nick and cuddled up and read Amelia Bedelia books until she fell asleep on my bed, and I let her stay there all night, comforted by her steady, trusting breath.

By the next morning I'd talked myself into a better mood. Despite everything that had happened, I had to keep a perspective. I was lucky; my life was basically fine. I had a good career, close friends like Susan and Karen, a home, and my health, a few bumps on the head notwithstanding. Best of all, I had Molly and Nick. And Nick had asked me to marry him. With Tony and Harry dead, the local branch of the slave cartel seemed to have wiped itself out; it would probably not surface again, at least for a while. When I closed my eyes, I tried not to feel the coldness of chains or to recall chill bodies in black water; I shifted my thoughts to wedding bouquets and ivory lace. And as soon as I had dropped Molly off to play with Emily, I rushed to see Nick.

"You come to take me home?" he greeted me grumpily, his mouth full of graham crackers. "How's your cold, better?" He swallowed, frowning. "I told them I was hungry, and this is what I got. Cardboard wrapped in cellophane."

"Ask the nurse for Jell-O," I suggested. "They always have Jell-O."

He grumbled. "I'm never eating Jell-O again. It's not food, it's water. Until this morning, all they gave me was forty different flavors of water. Jell-O, broth, water ice, tea. Now, it's all bran. You should have seen breakfast. Branflakes, bran muffin, bran pancakes. I swear they're trying to kill me here."

Obviously, Nick was much improved. He complained that the nurses had refused to let him go home, or even to detach his IV. I took his hand and kissed it sympathetically, then bent over and kissed his mouth. His lips were warm, familiar, vulnerable and needy, and I lingered there, delivering mouth-to-mouth, feeling his tensions ease, his muscles relax.

"If you'd convince them to let me out of here, we could do a lot more of that." He stroked my cheek.

"In good time." I straightened up too quickly and, suddenly dizzy, bent over again to get my balance.

"You all right?" He'd noticed. "You seem a little wobbly."

"Just clumsy." I sat beside him on the bed, looking him over, realizing how pale he was. It was my fault that he'd been shot. "Nick, about our fight—"

"What fight?" He half-smiled. "We never fight."

"I'm serious. If not for our fight, you wouldn't have been shot."

"Zoe, don't even think about woulda-coulda-shouldas. Besides, you saved my life. You rescued me."

"But if I hadn't read your e-mail, we wouldn't have fought, and if we hadn't fought you wouldn't have gone out in the middle of the night, and if you hadn't gone out, you wouldn't have seen the launch or gotten shot."

He started to sit up, then stopped, grimacing with pain. "Damn. Goddamn." He caught his breath and took my hand. "Zoe, I need to take a little break, okay? Just forget about it. We were both out of line that night. Let it go."

I sat beside him as he pressed the button that released his

painkiller, watched him as he settled back, staring glassy-eyed at the television. As he dozed off, even as he slept, I held his hand, assuring myself that we were and would be okay, that the nightmare that had almost killed us both had passed.

SEVENTY-SIX

I spent the early afternoon greeting his visitors, playing hostess to cops and rowers, listening to stories about Nick. Nick as a sculler; Nick as a cop. Stories of his taking dares and derring-dos, of his audacity and ingenuity. I heard about sides of Nick I didn't know, saw admiration and fondness in the eyes of people who knew him. And gradually I began to feel optimistic. Nick was healing fast. People cared about and supported him. He—we—would be all right. And I was determined to make us be.

When I went to get Molly, I thanked Susan for taking care of Molly all weekend and being there for us, but I turned down her invitation to dinner. I didn't want to impose anymore, and couldn't bear to hear any more theories about slave traders or assassins. It was time to be independent again, to take control of my life. My wounds were still prominent, but they were mending, and I needed to put the slave cartel behind us. I focused on the future. My daughter. My engagement to Nick.

Besides, Molly had just finished kindergarten. Her graduation was in two days; we had a major occasion to celebrate. Maybe I was in denial or experiencing a manic high. I wasn't sure, but I rode a surge of something like happiness. Molly and I went out for an early dinner, just the two of us. I wasn't supposed to drive yet, but Chinatown was only a few miles away; I could manage that. We took Nick's Volvo to Chinatown, and Molly and I went to Tsi Wang's, our favorite restaurant, and ordered too much food. Wonton soup, spareribs, dumplings, spring rolls, Moo Shu Pork and General Tso's Chicken, lychee nuts and ice cream. Molly dipped noodles into duck sauce and chattered as I sat across from her in wonder, relieved to be out among people, feeling like a normal family—or part of one again.

As Molly took the cherry from her Shirley Temple, I told her that Nick was getting better. She kept eating without comment, reluctant to talk about Nick. Of course she was. She'd been terrified that he'd been shot, must be too upset to talk about it.

"He asked about you, Molls."

"Uh-huh."

"He misses you."

She nodded. "I miss him, too." But the comment was casual, reflexive. "Can we have a party for my graduation, Mom?"

Okay, she was avoiding the topic of Nick and the shooting. That was normal. They were disturbing and scary.

"I don't know, Molls. It's definitely an occasion for a party, but parties take time to plan. And I've been at the hospital all day—"

"The zoo would be fun. We could take my friends to the zoo."

I had no idea what to say. I couldn't begin to plan a party, but I didn't want to disappoint her. "Maybe," I said. "After Nick gets home."

She pouted, and I thought she was going to complain. Instead she asked, "When's that?"

"In a few days, I think."

"You think? You don't know?" Her eyebrows furrowed.

I reached across the table and squeezed her hand. "I know it'll be a few days, just not exactly how many. Nick's going to be fine. You can come visit him tomorrow."

"I can?" Her face brightened. "Is there TV in his room?"

"Yes."

"Can we bring him a present? Maybe candy. Or balloons. Or maybe a Good-Luck Bear. Can we?"

Luckily, the waiter interrupted, bringing our appetizers; Molly reached for a sparerib and began to chew.

"So," I approached the subject gently. "What would you think about having Nick live with us?"

"You mean, for good?"

I nodded.

She shrugged. "It's already like he lives there."

"Well, this would be different."

She stopped chewing. Her eyes widened with understanding. "Wait . . . Are you getting married? Oh, man. Can I be flower girl?"

The family at the table beside us turned to look.

"Molly, slow down. I'm just asking—"

"So, wait. Would Nick be my dad, then?"

I smiled. "Would you like that?"

She thought so, she said. But her eyes were guarded. Molly had never had a dad; it had always been just us. I wondered what the word "father" meant to her, couldn't imagine.

"So will you guys have babies?"

Babies? She was way ahead of me. I was, after all, fortyish. "I don't know. Would you want us to?"

"I'd like a baby brother."

"Really. Why a brother?"

"Brothers are more fun. Girls are so . . . , you know . . . girlie. Can I get one?"

Oh dear. We'd have to discuss the birds and the bees soon. "It's not entirely up to me, Molls."

"Nick wouldn't mind." She was quiet, chewing the rib. "Ask him. If he really wants a girl, I guess it would be okay."

Barbecue sauce covered her mouth, and she was so earnest, I wanted to squeeze her. "Molls, we wouldn't really get to choose. Some babies are boys; some are girls. You get what you get."

She frowned. "But you chose a girl when you got me."

"Well, yes. I chose you because I wanted to be your mom. But you'd already been born. And your birth mother didn't get to choose what you'd be; you just happened to be a girl. And this baby ... I mean, if we ever have it ... wouldn't be adopted. I'll be his or her birth mother."

Oh, Lord. What had I done? Somehow, I'd opened a barrel of confusing definitions and major issues, and I'd gotten tangled up in them. How would Molly react if I had a baby? As an adoptee, how would she feel about a sibling her mom had given birth to? Would she be jealous? Resentful? Insecure? Would she feel less loved or less part of the family?

Molly took a long drink of Shirley Temple. "Can we name the baby Oliver, Mom?" She grinned devilishly. "I love that name."

Maybe I'd been thinking too much, creating problems where none existed. I grinned. "Let's wait and see, Molls. Oliver wouldn't be all that great for a sister."

Molly laughed and attacked her spring roll. By the time the entrees came, she was full. She leaned on her elbows, staring at her Moo Shu. I offered to show her how to use chopsticks. When we had Chinese food, I always offered; she always refused. This time, she opened the packet of chopsticks and speared a piece of General Tso's Chicken, lifted it to her mouth. It wasn't the way most people used them, but it worked.

We finished dinner and read our fortune cookies. Molly's advised that real wealth lay in friendship; mine cautioned that financial decisions should be carefully considered. On the way to the car, Molly and I held hands. The night had become breezy, and thick clouds covered the sky. The air smelled of an approaching storm. Good. The heat wave that had smothered the city might finally break. At Nick's car, I helped Molly fasten her seat belt and tousled her hair, telling myself that even the weather was about to get back to normal.

As I pulled out of the parking spot, the first drops hit the windshield. In a matter of seconds the skies opened up; we were inundated by torrents of rain. Molly seemed mesmerized, staring at the wipers rushing to clear the glass. And as I drove through the blinding deluge I felt myself relax, as if the dams had broken and now the water was free to cleanse the city of its recent crime wave, washing away the last of its lingering stains.

SEVENTY-SEVEN

The rain was so heavy, though, that I had to stop driving. At the intersection of Eighth and Market I veered into a bus zone along the curb. We sat quietly watching the rain, hearing it pound the roof of the car. Lightning whitened the streets for a moment and Molly counted three beats until thunder cracked.

"It's three miles away, Mom," she said.

"What is?"

"The lightning. You count after it flashes and as high as you get until the thunder is how many miles away the lightning is. Emily said so."

Well, then I guess it had to be true. Under a streetlight, I watched Molly's face reflect the streaming rain. Her eyes were so open, full of energy, her features still soft and undeveloped. Again I was smitten with her self-assured, centered presence. Who was this small girl who called me Mom? Who would she become?

"Mom, what if you knew something you weren't supposed to?"

"Like what?"

"Like something important, but nobody would believe you."

Oh dear. "Is this about the woman in the blue car? Because it isn't that we didn't believe she was following you—"

"No. It's not about her."

"Then what? Tell me."

She squinted, thinking for a moment. Then she turned to face me. "I know who shot Nick, Mom."

I opened my mouth, but didn't know what to say.

"It was the Gordo—it had to be."

Oh, the Gordo. Molly was still afraid of him. And she didn't know about Tony. "Molls, no, it wasn't." I took her hand. "The police know who shot Nick. It was Tony. The man from the boathouse."

"Tony?" Under the streetlight, her face looked as if it were being washed with giant tears. "I don't think so, Mom. The Gordo wanted to shoot Tony—"

"The Gordo had a gun?"

Molly nodded.

"Why didn't you tell that to Officer Olsen?"

She looked worried and fragile. "Was I supposed to?"

Oh dear. Molly was just six, didn't see things from an adult perspective. But clearly she believed what she was saying. "So wait. Tell me again. When the Gordo came looking for Tony, he was carrying a gun?"

"Yup."

"What did he look like again?"

She shrugged. "I couldn't see his face, Mom. I was up in the racks."

"So what did you see?"

"Well, I saw him from on top." Molly's face flashed white, reflecting a lightning strike.

I was having trouble following her. "Did he see you?"

"Mom. Think about it. I was hiding." Thunderclaps rattled the car, two beats after the lightning. "Mom, but wait—what if he did see me? Is the Gordo going to come after me?"

"No, of course not." Lord, I hoped not. "He didn't see you, and anyway, he doesn't even know who you are."

"Are you sure?"

"Positive." Liar. "So what do you remember about him?"

"I already told you. He was scary."

Good. That helped. "Scary, how?" I thought it would help her to talk about it; I didn't really expect details from a six-year-old.

"He was all hairy, and he had a ponytail except the top of his head was bald." She cringed, remembering. "And he had big muscle arms with tattoos all over and lots of jewelry. Earrings and bracelets."

"Tattoos?" Hairy body. Balding and tattooed. Hadn't I seen someone like that at Humberton? I wasn't sure. Still, it was good information. Usable. More detailed than what she'd told the police.

"I think the Gordo shot Nick, Mom."

"I told you, Molls. Tony shot Nick. The Gordo was in the boathouse with you when Nick got shot. No matter how scary he looked, even the Gordo couldn't be two places at once. It was Tony."

Molly bit her lip, thinking.

I reminded myself that Tony had admitted the shooting; nobody named Gordo had anything to do with it. But then who was the Gordo? And where? Was he part of the cartel? I didn't want to think about him, didn't want to accept that even a single slave trader might still be around. Or the remote chance that he might have seen Molly.

"It's good you told me, Molly. But don't worry anymore. The Gordo's gone, and Tony is, too."

"Are you sure? How do you know for sure?"

"The police took Tony away." I wanted to protect her, so I omitted the part about Tony being dead. I saw him again, lifeless beside Harry in the front of the van, remembered the look in Harry's eyes. And now I had an idea who'd killed them. The Gordo was no doubt strong enough to strangle them. Suddenly the streets looked darker and more menacing.

"How about we go home?" I reached for the steering wheel, determined to make it home no matter how dense the rain.

Molly was quiet for a while. "Mom." She sounded urgent. "I

had an idea. Do you think Officer Olsen would come to my graduation party?"

I smiled, glad for the length of her attention span. "Maybe. *If* you have a party." I turned onto Fourth Street, splashing through hidden potholes, maneuvering through the storm.

"Listen who else I want to invite. Serena and Hari. And Emily and Nicholas . . ."

Molly planned her party all the way home. I squinted through driving rain at the blue car following too closely. I told myself that the driver was not the woman Molly had seen at school. Not everyone was plotting against us. Some things were merely coincidences. They had to be.

SEVENTY-EIGHT

I t was still raining the next evening when the glazier finally came to replace the cut-out windowpane in my office. While he worked, Molly and I sat in the kitchen making a grocery list. We were seriously low on food, particularly because I'd thrown out everything in the refrigerator after the break-in. When the phone rang Molly was trying to decide what kind of cereal she wanted. Nothing with cinnamon. Maybe something Sponge Bob or Shrek.

"Zoe." Nick's voice was thin, reedy. "Come get me."

"In a few days, Nick. Be patient." The doctor had said it would be a while until his release. "But we'll stop by this afternoon."

"It's Nick?" Molly brightened.

"No, come now. I'm out of here. Bring a pair of jeans and a sport shirt. Not a T; one with buttons."

"What? Now? You're not serious."

"Mom . . . can I talk?" Molly hung on me, grabbing for the phone.

"Yes, now. I'm serious."

"Mom, let me talk—"

"But"—I pushed Molly's hands away—"the doctors told me you'd need to stay until—"

"I reasoned with them. I explained that I'd heal better at

home where I can actually get some sleep. The nurses here wake you up every three minutes to mess with you, and all day people come by to visit. I haven't slept since I got here. And the food frankly sucks. I want to go home and rest uninterrupted. And eat real food. I want pizza, not liquefied brussels sprouts."

"So they're releasing you?" I still couldn't believe it.

"Nick's coming home?" Molly squealed, tugging on my arm. Jubilant.

"I've already showered. I'm ready. Just bring my stuff."

I hung up and began racing around, looking for Nick's flip-flops, underwear, cutoff jeans. Molly helped, choosing a bold blue short-sleeved shirt with bright green and orange stripes, singing, "Nick is coming home" over and over to a tune that vaguely resembled "Jingle Bells."

By the time the glazier had finished and brought me his bill, the sun was setting and we were ready to go. I thanked him, handed him a check, and we all walked out together into the pelting rain.

"You know, ma'am," he said. "You might want me to come back and fit some iron bars over that window. It's so close to the ground. You don't want another break-in."

I thanked him and told him I'd get back to him about it. Then I took Molly's hand and together we bolted through the puddles and raindrops and hopped into the car. Unbelievably, unexpectedly, Nick was coming home.

SEVENTY-NINE

The blue of his eyes was flat and dull, his skin ashen, face unshaved, but he sat up on the bed as soon as we came in, determined to leave. He greeted us shakily, hugged us carefully, then asked Molly to wait outside the curtained area so I could help him into his clothes. Awkwardly I knelt to hold his pants while he struggled to lift each leg and slide it in. I wrapped his shirt around his back, understanding why he'd said no T-shirt; he still couldn't lift his arms high enough to slip them into the sleeves. I dressed Nick, saw the muscles of his back and shoulders hanging shapeless and limp, watched him tremble with exertion just buttoning his shirt, and I realized again how close to death he'd come. But he's going to be all right, I told myself. It would take time, but he'd get his strength back again.

Finally, he was clothed. Ready to go. The daily gaggle of cops had come to visit, and when they saw that Nick was being released, they wanted to party. They offered to escort us out, even to take Nick home, to join us for coffee and Danish at home. Nick thanked them, but a little too curtly sent them on their way. He wanted to be left alone. So, leaving all his flowers and candy with the nursing staff, thanking them profusely, as soon as the orderly brought the wheelchair we were on our way. Molly skipped alongside Nick's chair to the elevator, and at the ground floor the orderly helped us to the car, an umbrella over Nick.

The air had cooled with the storm, but the steady rain showed no sign of letting up. The evening was dark, brooding, as if reflecting my thoughts. As glad as I was that Nick was coming home, I was equally concerned that he wasn't ready. He said nothing as we drove; just sitting up seemed to drain all his energy. Molly chattered at first; then, realizing that Nick wasn't responding, she sat in the backseat silently. I watched her in the rearview mirror, somberly studying the back of his head.

When we got to the house, I double-parked and ran through the downpour to unlock the door. Molly scampered inside, and I went back for Nick. He leaned on me heavily as I helped him out of the car, and we progressed slowly from the street to the sidewalk, up the steps, into the house. We were dripping wet, and Nick seemed barely able to stand.

The house still smelled faintly of ammonia, but the odor wasn't as pungent as before, didn't sear our nostrils, and it was masked by other scents, like brewing coffee and the summer storm. Molly stood beside Nick, still watching him, holding his hand.

"It's good to be home." Nick kissed me on the forehead and tousled Molly's curls.

"Where should we plant you?" I asked. "The sofa?"

"I just want to go to bed. Would you ladies mind tucking me in for a nap?"

Nick panted as we led him upstairs. He peeled off his wet shirt and fell into bed, asleep almost before I pulled the comforter over him. Outside, horns blared fiercely. I glanced out the window and saw Nick's Volvo blocking traffic. Damn. I'd forgotten that I'd double-parked.

Molly stood at the bedroom door, looking worried.

"I'll be right back, Molls," I said, and touching her cheek, I hurried outside to move the car.

EIGHTY

It took forever to find a parking spot, and when I finally found one, it was almost three blocks away. When I came in, I was drenched.

"Molly?" I called quietly, not wanting to awaken Nick. Although, I realized, probably snare drums wouldn't awaken him. "I'm back."

I stopped to pick up the mail that had piled up all week beneath the slot. I glanced at bills and ads, plopped them onto the kitchen counter and, drying my hair with a dish towel, I began to check my phone messages.

"Mom?" Molly called from upstairs.

"Come on down, Molls. Let Nick rest."

It had been days since I'd opened a bill or answered a call, and now that Nick was home, I was determined to get back to normal, to be responsible for my life again. Deleting a dozen calls from telemarketers, I listened to messages from friends wanting to hear from me, wanting to know if we were all right. Karen and Davinder had called. Ileana had called four times. And Gretchen. And Victor. Victor? I played his message over again.

"This is Victor Delaney, your neighbor from across the street." As if I wouldn't know who Victor Delaney was. "I wonder if you could call me at your earliest convenience." He gave his phone number, then repeated it. How odd. I wondered what had happened; Victor almost never made direct contact. He never went outside, hid behind his window shades, cracked his door open only to admit grocery deliveries. Whenever Molly and I left tins of cookies on his front step, he thanked us by e-mail. I couldn't remember Victor ever actually calling before. It had to be important; I'd better call him back.

Lightning flared and thunder shook the house almost immediately; according to Molly, the storm must be centered right over us. Half expecting her to come flying down the stairs in terror, I dialed Victor's number. But Molly didn't appear; she must be braver than I thought. Another lightning flash cast blue light through the rain-drenched kitchen windows. I waited for my call to connect, listening to the pounding of the storm and watching the lights flicker, hoping the electricity wouldn't go out.

That's when I noticed that my coffeepot was on. And that it was full. I stared at it, frozen, holding the phone. The coffeepot couldn't be on, I decided. Couldn't be full. I hadn't eaten breakfast at home in the last two days, hadn't made coffee in at least as many. Besides, if I had turned it on, I would have also turned it off. Wouldn't I?

I gaped at the brewing coffee, remembering the break-in, the broken mug, the spilled coffee on my kitchen floor. Nick asking, "Was it black or with cream?" Because he'd suspected who'd spilled it, how she liked her coffee—

Heather? Oh, God. She was here? In the house?

"Molly . . . Nick?" I ran up the steps, the phone still in my hand. "Molly, where are you?" My mouth was dry, my throat like sandpaper. Oh, God. Had Heather found them? Were they okay? "Answer me—"

I sped to her room, panting, sweating. "Molly—where are you?" Clutching the cordless phone like a weapon, watching shadows, I recalled the decapitated photos, the jagged scissor cuts, and I flew through the door, ready to swing.

Molly sat on her bed, watching the door. "I'm in here," she said. Her voice sounded small. Maybe tired. Maybe she hadn't answered until now because she'd fallen asleep and hadn't heard me. Maybe she was fine.

Stepping in, I turned on a lamp. Molly was a mess, still in her wet T-shirt and shorts. Her damp curls were matted, her eyes wide. Thank God. She was all right. Thunder rattled outside.

"Molls." I spoke softly. "Come have a bubble bath. Let me just check on Nick."

She didn't move. She just watched me. And I noticed that she seemed to stare at the wall behind me.

"Come on, Molls. Let's go."

"Mom . . ." Molly began. But she didn't go on. Her eyes didn't leave the doorway, even as I started across the room to get her, and, too late, I realized why.

EIGHTY-ONE

I'd walked right past her. Heather stood against the wall, beside the door; I'd been so focused on Molly that I hadn't seen anything else. Not Heather. Not her gun.

"Mom!" Molly dashed for me and I caught her, wrapped her in my arms. Instinct kicked in; I felt no fear. Only outrage.

"I know who you are, Heather. I'm not afraid of you. Leave us alone. Get out of my house."

"Mom." words spilled from Molly's mouth. "When you left, she got in and started tying up Nick. I ran out but she chased me—"

Nick. "Is Nick okay?"

"She tied him up. I don't know. I ran away." She looked guilty.

"I'll go check." Ignoring Heather, I started out of the room.

"I don't think so." The bullet whizzed past my head before I even heard the shot. I stopped cold and turned slowly. Heather studied me, her gun aimed at my chest. "So you know who I am. Interesting. I want to hear about that."

Heather was tall, about twenty pounds heavier than she should have been, in jeans that were too tight. Her features were symmetrical, even pretty, but her skin was pasty, washed out.

Locks of damp mousy hair had come loose, falling from her ponytail. She smiled, revealing a gap between her front teeth.

She pointed the way with the gun. "Let's go downstairs. I need coffee. We'll chat."

Molly clung to me so tightly I couldn't move. "Heather," I said. "There's a child here. How about you lose the gun?"

Molly dug her face into my belly; her arms strangled my hips.

"No, I don't think so. But I'll take the phone, thank you."

I hadn't realized I was still holding it. I handed it to her, and her lips curled unpleasantly, more a grimace than a smile. "Let's go. Now."

Apparently Molly and I didn't move fast enough; the crack of gunfire convinced us to hurry. There were two bullet holes now in Molly's bedroom wall, right above my head. Molly and I walked, two bodies curled into one four-legged creature, into the hall and toward the stairs.

I looked back, saw Heather's gun aimed at us, its barrel a hollow, indifferent eye leveled at my back. Or maybe at Molly's head. Would she actually shoot us? What had we done? I knew why she'd stalked Nick; she believed he'd murdered her sister, his wife—and she wanted revenge. She'd already gone to jail once for assaulting him. But what did that have to do with us? We hadn't even known her sister.

Think, I told myself. Don't try to figure her out rationally; clearly, she's not rational. She's obsessed with Nick and getting even. You're a therapist. An expert. You've dealt with psychos before. Psych her out. Be professional. I tried to remember what I knew, anything that might apply. My mind went instantly blank, completely void of any knowledge. I recalled not a single theory or pertinent principle. As I descended the stairs all I could think of was that, if she liked us, she wouldn't hurt us. I might even be able to convince her that Nick was innocent. So I set about building rapport, making Heather our friend.

"Okay, Heather." I tried to sound warm and cordial as I said her name. Then I said ours, making us seem like people rather than objects. "How about we introduce ourselves? I'm Zoe Hayes and this is my daughter, Molly—"

"Shut up." She shoved the gun into my spine.

Molly and I stumbled down the steps, Heather right behind us. At the bottom of the stairs she stepped over to the window and looked out at the rain.

"It's supposed to go on all night," I tried again. "There are flood warnings."

"Stay right there. Don't move." She stepped into the kitchen, and holding the gun with one hand, poured herself a cup of coffee with the other. She opened the refrigerator, took out the milk and poured it into the mug.

"You're almost out of milk," she complained. "By the way, kids shouldn't drink skim. They need the fat. Two percent's better. Even one percent. Not skim. Skim sucks."

Heather was chatting. Good. Keep it up. Make her your friend, I coached myself. "Really? That's good to know. I'll remember that."

She eyed me as if to say that I might not need to. That I might not be shopping anymore.

Thunder rolled overhead, long and low, and the lights flickered. For a moment we stood in the hall beside my kitchen, lit only by the blue of the lightning flash. Without saying a word, Heather motioned us to the living room.

"Sit," she commanded.

We sat on my purple sofa, Molly a wide-eyed appendage on my hip. Heather sat in a wingback chair, gulping French roast, her eyes darting around the room.

"So, you know who I am." She swallowed coffee. "He told you about me?"

I nodded.

"Was he expecting me?"

I shrugged. "I don't know."

"He should have been after he stood me up the other day. We had a date. Son of a bitch didn't show up."

Nick had a date with her? "Well, he probably couldn't get there. He got shot. He was in the hospital."

"Bullshit, don't make excuses for him," she said. "Do you think I'm stupid? Do you think I don't read the papers? I know he got shot, and I know when. He was supposed to meet me before that. I told him when and where. Did he show? No."

I didn't know what to say, said nothing.

"So what did he tell you about me?" She smirked, exposing her gap. "Did he say I'm crazy?"

"No, of course not."

"Then what? That I want to kill him? I bet he told you some load of crap. Like I was coming after him because I was jealous of my sister. Or like I was in love with him but he married her, instead. Is that what he told you?"

I shook my head. No. Nick hadn't said anything like that.

"Because I know his ego, I know what he thinks. He thinks I never got over my teenage crush on him. He thinks I was jealous of Annie."

"I don't know. He never said that."

Molly whispered, "Who is she, Mom?" I squeezed her tighter, signaling her to keep still.

Heather scoffed. "Did he tell you how Annie died? I mean the truth."

I didn't answer, didn't know what to say. Molly squirmed, whispering something I couldn't hear.

"Answer me. Did he tell you how she died?"

I held Molly close. "He said it was suicide."

"Shit. That's the bullshit story they gave the press. I mean the truth. Did he tell you how she really died?"

Oh, God. Was she going to say that Nick had killed her?

"I guess not." She laughed at that, shaking her head. "Of course not. Why would Nick tell the truth? Suicide, huh. Yeah, he would say that."

She lifted the coffee mug again, slurping when she drank. Molly pressed against me, whispering again. "Who is she? Who died?"

I kissed her head, whispered, "Later."

"Well, trust me. It wasn't suicide. My sister didn't shoot herself." Heather shook her head. "Annie liked herself way too much for that. Way too much."

So, if she thought it wasn't suicide, Heather must believe

that it was murder. That Nick killed her sister. Apparently she was here to take her revenge. "Heather," I used her name again. "Nick was never even charged—"

"Of course he wasn't. I knew he wouldn't be. Cops don't get sent to jail. But, trust me, my sister didn't kill herself. It wasn't suicide."

"But how can you be sure? You weren't there. Nick's the only one who really knows what happened."

"Nick? Nick only thinks he knows." Chugging coffee, she tilted her head and studied me, examining my face. "You look like her, you know. A lot like her."

I'd seen pictures of Nick's wife. She was right; we had a resemblance.

"Did you ever think maybe that's why he's with you? You ought to consider that. Because maybe he's trying to replace her. You know, make you into her. And that would be worrisome, wouldn't it. Because what happened to her could happen to you."

"What's she talking about, Mom?" Molly squirmed.

"Heather," I used her name again. "Molly doesn't know anything about this. She's just a little girl. Why don't we let her go upstairs—" Molly's grip tightened on my arm.

"What? You think I'm going to let the kid leave the room so she can dial 9-1-1? Do I look that stupid? Forget it. The kid stays here."

"My name's Molly, not 'the kid.'"

Heather looked at her then, as if for the first time. Molly, sensing a challenge, looked directly back. Loosening her hold on me, she sat up straight, meeting Heather's gaze. Great. Molly was taking her on, eye to eye.

"Molls, cool it," I whispered, but she wasn't listening.

"Guns suck." Molly glared.

Still eyeing her, Heather gulped more coffee. "Keep your kid quiet."

"Not 'kid.'" Molly corrected. "Molly."

"Shut up, you little toad."

"You. You're the toad."

"Molly—" I began. What was she doing scrapping with an armed, unbalanced psycho?

Heather stood, her shadow crossing the room ahead of her.

I jumped to my feet, stepping between them, breaking their eye contact, ending the contest. "Molly, be quiet!" I scolded. Then I turned to Heather. "Back off, Heather. Molly's got nothing to do with you. What do you want?"

Her attention shifted away from Molly back to me. "What do I want? Are you kidding? I want Nick, my beloved brother-in-law. I want to be done, that's what I want. But first I have to deal with you two."

Oh, God. "Heather, think about it. You really haven't done anything wrong yet. If you leave now, we can forget all about this. You don't want to go back to jail, do you?"

"Jail?" She laughed, a hoarse, raspy sound. "Don't worry. I'm not going back there." Heather watched us while she finished her coffee; then she played with the gun, aiming at my face. "It's creepy how much you really do look like her."

Heather rambled on about her sister, how I didn't measure up to her, how Annie was much more striking. How Nick had been infatuated with her, but not really in love. Molly stayed beside me, clinging to my waist.

We sat that way until once, as lightning flared and thunder crashed, the lights dipped and didn't come back on. In a flash of lightning, I saw stark violet shadows and Molly's small form dashing out of the room. In a heartbeat, I ran after her.

EIGHTY-TWO

I didn't see her anywhere. Which way had she gone? I flew through the hall toward the front of the house. Should I go after her or try to get outside for help? I had no time to decide.

"Molly—" I yelled. "Hide!"

Heather cursed, crashing through the darkness into the coffee table, and I heard the crack of breaking pottery as she dropped her coffee mug. But she kept coming. I felt her behind me, her frantic breath on my back and, expecting a gunshot to tear through me, I veered left into my studio, hoping she'd follow me and forget about Molly and Nick.

And she did. I plunged down, ducking behind my drawing table, tossing the stool into Heather's path. As she tripped over it, her gun went off, the bullet lodging somewhere in my hardwood floor. I crouched between the desk and the storage cabinet, trying to figure out an escape route or a place to hide, finding none. Except the window. Damn. Heather would probably blast me away before I could slide it up. But I had no choice. I tossed a pencil across the room, creating a diverting noise in the opposite corner. When Heather turned that way, I scooted around the cabinet to grab the window frame. And saw that the pane was gone. She'd taken it out again. Damn. I'd just had the thing fixed.

Water puddled beneath the glassless window where Heather had once again broken in. Rain spattering my face, I leaned out, crawled over the sill. A gun fired and wood splinters jabbed my hindquarters; Heather had spotted me. I plunged forward, landing on my already battered head in the muddy patch of shrubs along the brownstone, curling and rolling as my legs fell and, tottering upright again, I huddled against the brick wall, hoping I was too close to the building for Heather to take aim. Bruising raindrops pummeled me, resoaking my clothes, blurring my vision as I inched my way between hedges and brick toward the street. Nick, I told myself, would be okay as long as Heather was in sight. And Molly would be hiding. She was great at hiding, an Olympian; she'd be safe long enough for me to get to the street. Crouching, peering into the darkness, I moved to the front corner of the house, ready to spring across the sidewalk into the street, stoop between parked cars, dash to Victor's. Victor would be home; he always was home. Victor would call 9-1-1.

I wiped rain from my eyes, ready to sprint ahead, and peeked around the corner of the house. Heather stood at the front steps, waiting for me, her gun aimed at my head.

When she fired, it surprised me. Heather's earlier shots had been meant to scare, not wound. But this time, she'd aimed carefully. I felt the heat of the bullet too close to my cheek, blasting through the rain. I ducked back behind the brick as her next shot flew by, and I looked out cautiously, just long enough to see her take a step forward. Coming after me. I wheeled around and ran; maybe I could make it to the gate behind the house—Or leap back inside through the window, get a broom or frying pan, slam her from behind—

A yowl pierced the night, drowning out even the storm. A soul-searing, wild cry of pain and despair, and it seemed to come from the front of my house. I froze. Heather? I looked behind me; she wasn't there; she hadn't pursued me. Why? What had happened? Water poured down my face, into my eyes as I rushed back to the front of the house, stuck my head out, peering around the corner.

Molly rode Heather like a wild, bucking pony. Well, not exactly. She would never have pressed her fingers into a pony's eyes. Or sunk her few remaining teeth deep into its neck, breaking skin.

EIGHTY-THREE

I found the gun where Heather had dropped it in the mud; only then did I get Molly off her. Heather moaned, cursing, holding her wound. How bad could the bite be? I thought. Molly was six—her front teeth were all missing. Maybe Heather was faking, trying to throw me off-guard. But even in the dark I could see Molly's lips drip, vampirish, with dark blood, and I watched it wash pink by the rain.

"Go inside," I told Molly. "Call the police."

"I can't find the phone. I looked already."

Right. I'd been on the phone when I saw Heather. Heather had taken it from me. "Get a flashlight from the kitchen. Use the one in my office."

Molly was wiping her mouth, wincing from the taste of blood.

"Know what? You're the toad," she shouted to Heather. Then she headed into the house.

As soon as she was gone, Heather turned to face me, her neck dripping blood. She lowered her head, bent her knees. I stood alone, pointing the gun at her, aware of its awkward heaviness. I'd never held a gun before. It was cold, slippery in the rain. We stood facing each other, silent. Then Heather charged. She came running at me, head down, like a football tackle in a slow-motion replay. I didn't know what to do, couldn't believe that Heather was actually barreling straight for me. Did she think I wouldn't shoot her? Was she right? Go on, I told myself. Shoot, dammit. Pull the trigger. Heather's head was inches away; if I fired, I couldn't miss. And when she sprang, grabbing my arm, wrestling for the gun, I was still telling myself to shoot.

EIGHTY-FOUR

I held on to the gun, stiffening my muscles, resisting her grip. She strangled my wrist, twisted my arm, trying to point the muzzle at my head. Together, we fell to the sloshy ground in the relentless storm. Heather outsized and outweighed me, but I was in shape from rowing, and I fought back, using my body as a lever, sliding out from under her, kicking her shins, pressing my knees into her sopping stomach, all the time gripping the gun, trying to keep it turned away from my body while Heather twisted, squeezed and scratched at my arm.

We wrestled, splashing around on cement and in mud, even as sirens began to blare, even as lights flashed over us, even as police yelled for us to drop the gun and release our holds on each other, even as Molly yelled to me from the doorstep. I didn't dare, and Heather wouldn't let go. My limbs burned, muscles on fire with pain, and I knew I couldn't resist much longer. But we were caught in a death grip, each unwilling or unable to be the first to give way.

Police yelled again, flashing lights on us, ordering us to drop the weapon.

Panting, strength fading, I gasped, "Heather, please. Let's stop."

And she answered, "Fine." She stopped struggling, retaining only her grip on my wrist. "It's over."

I believed her; I shouldn't have, but I wanted to, needed to, couldn't fight anymore. So I eased up, relaxing my muscles, except those holding the gun.

"Do me a favor," Heather panted, "tell Nick. Tell him I wish I'd let Annie kill him."

What?

She smirked, let out a gruesome laugh. "Bastard. He never even noticed me. Not even after what I did for him. I mean, Annie was my big sister. My own sister." She smirked then, bitterly. "Think she's forgiven me? Well, I guess I'll find out . . ."

She stopped midsentence, and we lay face-to-face, nose-to-nose, her hands gripping mine. I couldn't process what she was saying. Had Heather stopped Annie from killing Nick? How? I'd almost figured out an explanation, almost formed a thought when Heather began heaving. I winced, thought she was going to be sick.

"Tell Nick. Tell him I'll see him in hell," she panted. Her smile was twisted, showing the space between her front teeth.

And before I could react, she yanked my wrist and pressed my finger. And shot herself in the eye.

Even in the rain, I felt the warm splash of tissue and blood. Even over the sirens I heard Molly scream, "Mom!" Her voice came to me muffled, muted by the deafening report of the gun. Images, sensations seemed to occur one by one, as if lined up in single file, and I took them in separately, each in its own time. Nothing blended or merged with the rest. Even my own cries.

EIGHTY-FIVE

I rolled away, twitching and kicking. I remember the cops like through a scarlet haze, as though the rain itself had turned to blood; and I remember searching for Molly, for Nick, desperate to find my family.

Someone held an umbrella over me, assuring me that Molly and Nick were in the house, safe and dry, away from the grisly scene. And someone else led me away from the body, took me inside, gave me a blanket to cover my watery bloodstained clothes. The hallway glared blinding and bright; my eyes had become accustomed to the dark, and at some point while I was outside, the electricity had come back on. I blinked, squinting, searching for Molly, and she ran to me before I could find her. I grabbed her, kneeling beside her, covering her rain-soaked head with kisses.

"I am so proud of you," I told her. "You're my hero."

She beamed proudly, then frowned. "Who was she, Mom?"

"Somebody from Nick's past. From an old case." It was true, mostly.

"She's dead, right, Mom?"

I nodded. "She won't bother us anymore." Holding her hand, I started upstairs to find Nick.

"I bit her—eww—she was bleeding right in my mouth. My whole mouth tastes disgusting—"

"You were brave, Molls. And smart. You stopped Heather from shooting me. And you called the police."

She tilted her head. "No, uh-uh. I didn't call them. I told you. I couldn't find the phone—"

"But there's one in my office."

"But she was shooting at you, Mom. I didn't have time. I had to come back outside."

Molly hadn't called? Then who had?

Nick, I thought. He must have managed to untie himself and called from his cell.

I rushed upstairs to the bedroom. Two cops were with Nick, arguing with him, trying to get him to lie down. When he saw us he relaxed, almost collapsing onto the bed. Still soaking, we ran to him and hugged him too tightly. "Thank God," he said; it sounded like a moan.

The police had found Nick lying on the bedroom floor. His arms and ankles tightly bound, he'd thrust himself out of bed and had been trying to roll to the steps, coming after us. Weak and depleted, he could barely speak; his skin was damp and transparent, colorless. Clearly, Nick had not been able to call for help. Not Molly, not Nick.

Molly and I sat beside him as he faded off to sleep. Sitting on the bed, gazing out the window at the rain, I looked at the houses across the street. Victor's bedroom light was on, and there was a shadow behind the shades.

EIGHTY-SIX

Molly eyed my blood- and mud-stained clothing, the clots still in my hair. "Are you all right, Mom?" She was mothering me, reversing roles as if she had to take care of me, not the other way around. I had to reassure her. Make her feel secure, that she could count on me.

I smiled. "I'm fine, Molls."

"You look gross."

"I could use a bath. How about you? Are you all right?" I touched her chin, studied her eyes.

"I'm disgusting." Her hair was matted and drenched, and red dirt streaked her pale skin.

"Let's fix that. We have to talk to the policemen. But first, why don't we get rid of the yucky taste in your mouth?"

While Nick slept and police scurried in and out of the house, I fixed Molly a huge dish of strawberry ice cream topped with chocolate syrup, gobs of whipped cream and a cherry. I watched her spoon it up, wondering at her stamina. Was she really as okay as she seemed? Not even a little traumatized? She'd seen so much the last week, and now a stranger had held her at gunpoint, tried to kill her mother, and shot herself. Hadn't that affected Molly at all? Molly wolfed down pink ice cream as if it were a normal summer night, as if there were nothing odd about police wandering through the kitchen or a dead body outside the front door. I wondered if Molly was employing psychological defenses, walling off her emotions to protect herself from unbearable reality. I wondered if she'd need counseling. Stop it, I told myself. Don't play therapist with your own child. Besides, it was too soon to see how she'd be affected long-term; I'd have to wait and see. For now, she seemed all right. At least her appetite was strong.

While Molly polished off her sundae, Officer Bowman came in to chat. He remembered the first break-in, the cut-out windowpane. And I recognized his too-large hat, the way it rested low on his ears. He was the first to question us, but certainly not the last. Detectives asked the same questions we'd already answered. Nick would give his account later. For now, first Molly, then I gave our impressions of what had happened. How Heather had broken in while I was out moving the car. Who Heather was. How she was connected to us and to Nick. Why she might have wanted to harm us, or him.

Crime-lab people took samples of the crud under my fingernails and the blood smudges on our skin. It was all evidence, as were my fingerprints on the gun, the blood clotted in our hair and on our clothes. They wanted to know anything that Heather had taken or touched, even my coffeepot, even her mug.

The detectives tried to be kind to me, probably out of courtesy to Nick, and they seemed to believe that I hadn't deliberately shot Heather, that she'd forced my finger to pull the trigger. Still, they needed to complete their reports in thorough and accurate detail. They seemed as tired as I was as they reviewed events of the night, and I couldn't even offer them coffee; my pot was out of service for the night.

After a while Molly began yawning. I was drained, had trouble focusing on the questions, let alone my answers. Words seemed hazy and slurred, memories blurry. All I knew for certain was that I needed to go back and pick up where I'd left off hours ago, to finish what I'd started to do before Heather interrupted us. Answer phone calls. Give Molly a bubble bath. I had to wash her hair, wrap her in a fluffy towel, read her a story and put her to bed.

Apparently, the detectives saw my plan as symptoms of shock and denial. They wanted us to go to the hospital. I refused, insisting that we'd been there too much already, that now we needed to rest and be alone together as a family. Unfortunately, they didn't agree. To them, our house was part of a crime scene where criminologists had to collect evidence, and statements had to be made. It seemed endless, the asking and answering, the waiting, but finally we had permission to go upstairs, where Nick snored hungrily.

While Molly got undressed, I ripped off my bloody clothes. Then I threw all of them—hers and mine—into a trash can. If the cops wanted them, fine. But neither of us would ever want to see, let alone wear, those outfits again. I pulled one of Nick's shirts out of the laundry basket and put it on. Then, wrapped in his scent, I poured rose bubbles into steaming water and sat on the edge of the tub washing traces of mud and God-knew-what off Molly's back, out of her hair.

I clung to routine that night like a drunk to a wine bottle. I did what seemed regular. Normal. After her bath, we fixed her hair and read a chapter of *Winnie the Pooh*. Then I lay down beside her, cuddling her until her eyes began to close. I told her that we would be fine. Nick would feel stronger every day. And she could relax because Heather wouldn't be following her anymore.

Her eyes opened, sleepy but confused. "What?"

"Heather's gone now, Molls. She won't follow you anymore."

"Mom, what are you talking about?" Molly frowned. "Heather's not the lady who follows me."

She had to be. "Are you sure?" I told myself that Molly was mistaken; she simply hadn't recognized Heather. It had been dark, after all. And we'd been taken by surprise.

"I never saw that Heather lady until tonight, Mom. She's not the same person. Not even close."

"Okay." I didn't argue. The woman who'd been following Molly, I reminded myself, might not actually exist. She might be invisible to others. A figment of Molly's imagination, the embodiment of her fears.

Molly turned, snuggling into her pillow, and I stayed until

her breathing became steady and slow. When I came into my bedroom moments later, I tried not to disturb Nick, but he was sleeping so deeply that nothing—not retreating thunder or police sirens, not even a woman desperately kissing his face—could wake him up.

EIGHTY-SEVEN

I turned on the shower and waited until the room became a steamy cloud too dense to see through, and then I stepped in and closed my eyes, letting hot water stream through my hair, over my face, down my back. I kept my eyes closed as I lathered up, afraid to see the suds, pink with the last traces of Heather, wash down the drain. I scrubbed every inch of my body, then scrubbed it again. I was bruised from my scalp to the soles of my feet, and my hand ached from Heather's grip, my whole body from her assault. I couldn't wash her touch from my skin, her words from my mind.

"Tell him I'll see him in hell." Then, *bang!* I could still feel her twisting my hand, pressing my finger against the trigger. The woman had been mad, obsessed with Nick. Suicidal. Blaming Nick for her sister's death, for her own demons. Well, it was over. Tony was dead; the slave traders were gone. And Heather was, too. Nobody would break into our house again; Heather wouldn't harass or threaten Nick. Now, once Nick got well, life would be ducky.

But what had Heather said before she shot herself? That she'd stopped Annie from killing Nick? That she hoped Annie had forgiven her? For what?

And as water poured over my eyes, I knew. I saw it. Heather

had been there. She had witnessed her sister's death. Oh my God. That was it, had to be—Heather had seen what happened, had seen Annie die. Oh, Lord. Had Nick actually killed his wife?

Is that why Heather was so angry? Because he had never acknowledged her silence, much less returned her love? She'd said it. "Bastard . . . never even looked at me."

Don't think about it, I told myself. Nick hadn't killed Annie, at least not deliberately. It had been self-defense. These were the ravings of an obsessed woman, referring to events that, if they had any connection to reality at all, had happened long years before I'd even met Nick. Besides, what she said wasn't entirely coherent; it was choppy, distorted by unrequited emotions and warped perceptions. Not to mention by time—she'd spent years in prison for attacking Nick.

I turned off the shower and wrapped myself in a fresh towel, went into my bedroom and put on my robe. Then I went downstairs and waited for everyone to finish up. The rain had lightened to a drizzle before all the detectives and the body were gone. I watched the last of them pull away. Then, just before dawn, unable even to think of sleep, I went into my office and sat at the computer. I needed to put my mind at rest. Had to review the old newspaper reports again, even though I already knew what they'd say.

EIGHTY-EIGHT

As soon as I sat down, the phone rang. What now? I thought. It was just five in the morning—who could be calling? Oh, God. The press? I almost didn't answer, but I did.

"Zoe? Are you all right? I've been sitting here all night watching, beside myself, wondering . . ."

It took a moment to recognize the voice.

"Victor?" I sighed with relief. "Thank you. We're fine."

"I called earlier. I suppose I should have called the police right away. But I wasn't sure. Didn't want to be a nosy neighbor, you know. But I saw her lurking around in the rain, so I thought she might have been a friend or family member. I didn't want to . . . you know . . . interfere."

"You saw her?"

"Yes. That's why I phoned earlier. They've been hanging around for days. I guess they've been . . . you know . . . casing the joint—"

"Wait—'they'? Are you saying there are more than one?" Oh, God. Was someone else stalking us?

"Oh. No. I don't know."

"Then why did you say 'they'?"

"I thought there were two, but actually, maybe there weren't.

The one tonight was alone. Maybe she just wore a wig some-times. But, Zoe, she's been loitering. Passing your house oh-so-casually, as if she's just strolling down the block, but then turning back around. Then tonight, out in the rain, I saw this woman on your front porch, looking in the mail slot, and walk-ing around back. Very suspicious. And I knew about your break-in the other day; I listen to the police radio. Ever since those murders last year, I like to be informed about what's hap-pening out there. So I called you to let you know. Just in case."

"Victor. Thank you so much—"

"But thank God you called me back. I picked up, and you never said hello, but you must have been holding the phone be-cause I could hear your whole conversation. When you asked her to put away the gun? Zoe, swear to God, I just about choked. And then, when there was an actual gunshot, I had a complete heart attack. But right away I got on my fax line to call 9-1-1."

So it had been Victor who'd called the police. He'd an-swered my phone call, heard what was happening. And called for help.

Now he rambled on about how frightened he'd been. How he'd been sick to his stomach with worry. How he missed the old days, when he'd known everyone in the neighborhood and could have called a dozen people for help. How he didn't know anyone now. Not a soul besides Molly and me. But now Victor's curiosity had been aroused.

"Who was she? I saw the coroner's wagon—is she dead? How'd she die? Is little Molly all right? She must have been ter-rified, poor little thing . . ."

Victor, normally reclusive and shy, couldn't settle down. Adrenaline rushed through his veins, and he kept spouting ques-tions until he couldn't think of anything more to ask, until I'd answered everything to his satisfaction, until long after the sun had come up and the silhouette at his bedroom curtains had faded in the light.

EIGHTY-NINE

When we finally got off the phone, the calls immediately began. The press never slept. I left the office phone off the hook and snuggled up against Nick around six, when the rest of the city was about to wake up, but, tired as I was, I couldn't sleep. I dozed, disturbed and restless, drifting to a place where dreams muddled with reality, where, in an endless hospital filled with curtains, dazed wet women wandered, eyeless people drank coffee from barrels, and blindfolded children played catch. A doctor with a carving knife operated on a corpse on a carpeted floor, and, finished, he took his mask off to reveal that he had no face, only flattened skin marked with scars.

When I woke up, Molly stood at our bedside, proudly holding a tray. She'd made breakfast. The juice hadn't entirely spilled, and the toast, slathered with butter and jam, wasn't completely burned. Nick was already awake, munching toast, and I sat, hammers slamming my skull. The three of us ate and chatted as if we were a regular little family on a regular morning in June. If Molly was surprised to see Nick and me sharing my bed, she didn't let on.

"Are you going to be my dad?" Molly asked.

Nick eyed me over his teacup, sipping apple juice. "If you'll have me." He half-smiled. And he took her hand. "Molly," he asked, "may I be your dad?"

She blushed and looked down at her fingers. "'Course," she said. "If I can be your kid."

The storm had broken the heat spell, and the rain had washed away the blood outside. After breakfast I returned phone calls and paid bills, and Molly and I finally went to the grocery store, buying ingredients for chicken soup and brownies. The entire day, as if by some tacit pact, we did not discuss shootings or stabbings, slavery or death. Nobody mentioned Heather. We were all, apparently, insisting on the same happy dream.

Our day focused on the future. On ourselves, on healing. On becoming a family. On Molly's desire for a brother rather than a sister. Molly wasn't interested in arranging play dates or getting ready for summer camp, just in doting on her daddy-to-be. I was in my own daze, trying to recover and move on, secretly scanning the newspaper for lingering signs of the cartel.

Days passed and we fell into a routine. Nick wasn't back at work yet, but Molly began day camp. Susan and I resumed practicing for the upcoming regatta, which she insisted upon racing. "We've worked too hard to back out," she said. "We don't have to win; all we have to do is race."

Life went on calmly, at least on the surface. Underneath, I remained unsettled, off-balance. I lay beside Nick at night listening to him breathe. I watched the line of his jaw, the slope of his nose, and wondered about what I was about to do. Marriage? I'd already been divorced once, didn't want to mess up again. Maybe I was jittery because marriage was so daunting. What did a good marriage require? Was love enough? Maybe love was a liability, not an asset; maybe love obscured the truth, distorted a couple's impressions of each other. Maybe a good marriage wasn't about love but about accepting each other totally, seeing each other clearly, flaws and all. Maybe I didn't know Nick well enough to marry him. Could I entrust Molly to him, give him full membership in our little family? Who was he, after all? What were his weaknesses, his faults? I knew one, of course; he wasn't big on sharing his secrets. How many had he kept so far?

Again and again, Heather appeared in my head, growling, "Tell him I'll see him in hell" before her face exploded. What had she witnessed that made her hate Nick so? Could she have seen her sister die?

At night I often lay watching Nick sleep, his mouth hanging slack, completely relaxed, his scar almost invisible in the darkness, his features boyish and symmetrical. Lord, I adored that face. But it was too appealing; it was a face that could conceal anything. People wanted to like it, didn't challenge it. Had he done it? I wondered. Had he killed his wife? I heard Heather saying that I looked like Annie. That what happened to her might happen to me. That Nick was with me to replace Annie. Absurd. Nonsense.

Still, as days passed, I became more unsettled. My stomach was perpetually upset; dizziness was my normal state. At night, as Nick slept, I often wandered down to the computer, looking up the old newspaper articles about Annie's death and Nick's acquittal, reading them over and over, memorizing each one, assuring myself that Nick had been a victim, innocent in her death.

One night I studied one of the articles that insisted Nick had to be guilty. The angle of Annie's bullet wound was wrong for a suicide. And it had been on the wrong side of the body. Why would right-handed Annie twist the gun to the left side of her body before firing?

"So what do you think?"

I jumped, startled, trying to cover the screen, push a button, close the window all at the same time. "Nick . . . you scared me."

"What are you doing?"

He looked wounded. Or worried. Oh, damn. What could I say? I searched for an excuse, couldn't find one.

"They acquitted me, you know."

I nodded. "Of course they did."

"So why are you down here in the middle of the night reading about it?"

I dodged his eyes. They were too blue, confusing me.

"If you want to know something about Annie or what happened, why don't you just ask?" There was an edge to his voice.

I nodded again. "I didn't want to bring it up."

"Zoe, every night you've been getting out of bed and sneaking downstairs. Is this why? What for? What are you trying to find?"

"Heather said some stuff. It's stupid. I should just let it go."

He sat. "Heather talked to you?"

We'd tried to spare Nick the grisly details because he'd been so weak. He knew only that Heather had been killed as we were struggling over her gun.

"She said it wasn't a suicide."

He blinked rapidly.

"Tell me. What else did she say?"

I told him everything. What she'd said. How she'd shot herself. He sat head in hands. "Goddamn," he said. "Goddamn."

I watched him, waiting, not sure what to do. He pulled a chair over, sat beside me, took my hand.

"Zoe—you and Molly—I'm sorry this came home to you. This had nothing to do with you." He touched my cheek. "But, believe me. Heather . . . Heather was jealous of her sister. All her life. And she had a crush on me. It got out of control. After Annie died, she stalked me. I guess, in her fantasy, with Annie dead, I'd marry her or . . ."

"Or?"

"Oh, Jesus." He slapped his forehead and slumped onto the desk.

"What?"

"Oh, man."

"Nick?"

"She must have been there. She had to have been there."

I'd thought so. "Tell me, Nick."

"Shit. Heather had to have been in the house. I never saw it until now. I swear—I don't really know what happened. It's like I told you and like I told the investigators. Annie and I fought over the gun. She shot me. I passed out, so I don't know how she died. But if Heather was there, she'd have seen Annie shoot me and—oh, shit. Maybe Annie didn't shoot herself after all."

Blue eyes the color of ice met mine, waiting while the information filtered through my brain and formed a coherent thought. Slowly, I began to understand why Annie's fatal wound had been at an odd angle on the wrong side of her body. And how Heather had known her sister's death hadn't been suicide.

NINETY

The day of the regatta arrived before Susan or I were ready. Susan had spent the morning arguing with electricians; she arrived at the boathouse in full fighting mode. Rowers crossed the dock, carrying oars and boats and bow numbers for their races, wishing each other good luck. A few who recognized me asked how I was, but the slave cartel, Harry and Tony and the circumstances of their deaths weren't the topics of the day. People were there to race, and their attention was on the water conditions, the weather, the level of competition in their events. Despite the recent death of the head coach, the water-ice man, and the house manager, rowers maintained their priorities; it was race day. Energy was focused.

"You scared?" Susan asked as she pulled a pair of oars off the rack. "You look green."

As usual lately, I felt green. Not just nervous. Sick to my stomach. "Scared? Me?"

"It's not fear," Susan explained. "It's adrenaline. Your body is prepping for a challenge, so you feel an adrenaline rush. It feels like butterflies in the stomach, but it's really strength. You're gearing up."

She went on as we carried our oars onto the dock. She was,

after all, the bow. "Just remember to relax your shoulders and square at the catch and we'll be fine."

I watched a quad of men shove off the dock, their heads wrapped in bandannas, their oars moving in perfect synchrony.

"We're not ready for this, Susan. I still have a bump on my head and bruises all over."

"Just remember to swing your body and push with your quadriceps."

My quadriceps?

"Zoe. Relax. It's our first regatta; all we want to do is finish upright."

"Great."

"Nick and Molly will be cheering us on with Tim and the girls. They are all excited to watch the race."

That only made me more nervous.

"Zoe. We'll be on the water for maybe an hour. The race will take less than five minutes. No big deal. What's the worst that could happen?"

I blinked at her, but she saw no irony in her comment. Together we went to the boat bay and lifted the *Andelai* off its rack, then walked it down to the water. While Susan gave me a nonstop last-minute course on how to row, we locked our oars in, adjusted our shoes, stepped into the boat, sat and shoved off the dock.

We were on the way to our first race. The whole way up to the starting line, Susan chattered. We were good enough to do well, she said. We'd worked hard. We'd practiced. We knew what to do. I told myself I shouldn't be nervous. Compared to being shot at or hit on the head and chained into an unventilated overheated van, racing a shell down the river was nothing. I was a mature woman. A mother. A professional and almost a wife. In the scope of life, an event as insignificant as a thousand-meter sculling race shouldn't affect me, shouldn't make me blink. It wasn't an event; it was too minor to be an event. It was a nonevent.

At the top of the river we turned and approached the starting line. Susan had stopped yammering; she sat at attention, uncharacteristically quiet.

"You okay?" I asked.

"Look," she said. "The other boats."

I turned and looked around the river. An official's launch and several other doubles—five, in all—floated above Strawberry Mansion Bridge, waiting to be called to line up at the start. Women wearing matching unisuits sat in their doubles, looking large and intimidating. Muscular. Beastlike.

I looked off to the shore, focusing on a row of happy turtles lined up on a log, telling myself that the race was only a few minutes of our lives, shorter than a commercial break, shorter even than many a bowel movement, less important than either. When the official in the launch yelled for our race to move to the start, I made myself take deep breaths and willed myself not to faint. We can do this, I told myself.

At the starting line, the officials yelled for one boat to move up three feet, another to move back half a stroke, trying to even us out. I sat with my oars squared in the water, ready to take off.

The official called, "Attention."

I sat ready, and when he yelled, "Go," I pushed my legs down, pulled my oars up, feeling the rush on either side of us as boats shot out of peripheral vision. I took a second desperate stroke, a third. Our shell shuddered but went nowhere. Susan sat frozen, her oars not moving.

An official yelled at us from a launch, and I kept stroking, forgetting about technique, frantically pushing my legs and pulling on my oars, tugging us away from the starting line, barely managing to shout, "Row, dammit!"

Susan finally sprang to life. I heard her grunt as her oars slapped the water behind me, and soon afterward, realizing that I was going to faint, I remembered to breathe.

After that, I was out of my body, watching from the clouds as our boat plowed ahead. Somehow, cold water was splashing even in the clouds, and voices were yelling, "Go, Mom!" Susan and I each assumed that we were the moms being cheered for, so we rowed even harder, beyond exhaustion, beyond pain. At some point, my lungs began to throb, and my mouth to taste coppery like blood. At some point I prayed to God that, if only he'd let me survive this race, I'd never ever get into or even close to a boat again. At some point I thought of death, how merciful it would be never enduring another agonizing stroke or searing breath.

"Pick it up!" Susan yelled.

"Go, Humberton," someone called from the shore. I kept my eyes ahead and rowed, hoping my heart would finally explode so I could stop.

"Power twenty," Susan coughed.

Somehow, the thousand meters had extended into an endless loop, but, muscles screaming, I pulled my oars, accepting that I was in hell and that it was always going to be this way. There would be no end, no relief.

At some point in the maze of experience we think of as time, the race ended. From eons away came the toot of the finish as we crossed the line, and Susan and I were both alive, still in the boat, still above water. I remember leaning over the side and donating my lunch to the fish as Susan began shrieking, jubilant and surprised. And then, recovering, wiping sweat out of my eyes, I looked to the shore to see Nick and Molly near the grandstand with Tim and Susan's girls, waving and cheering. Dimly, I heard another toot as another boat crossed the line.

Not only had we survived the race; we hadn't come in last.

NINETY-ONE

S uddenly, it was summer. Molly liked day camp, especially swimming. She'd stopped worrying that the Gordo was chasing her, no longer seemed concerned that a woman was following her. Nick was almost ready to start work again, and so was I. My two-week so-called vacation had extended to four-plus, and it was time to go back.

Life was moving on. Susan's deck was finished, but her bathrooms were still not complete. She was packing up Lisa and Julie for six weeks of camp in Maine while defending a man accused of suffocating his invalid mother, so she hadn't had time to row since the regatta. That was fine with me. I wasn't feeling well, and I doubted I'd be rowing for a while.

We went on, trying to continue life as before, but of course that was futile. I could never again look at a windowless van or truck without wondering what—or who—was inside. And I couldn't make coffee without seeing Heather slurping from a mug. Still, we had to recover. We made changes, adapting. Instead of brewing coffee, I walked each morning to the Pink Rose to get takeout with fresh scones. Instead of battling bad memories, I avoided them, starting new routines, focusing on the future. I made arrangements to have Molly's belated graduation party at the zoo, began to plan our wedding, thought about taking a year's leave from work.

In truth, the horror wasn't over. The world remained dangerous, and people were not always who they seemed. The smugglers we'd run into were gone, but others were out there somewhere, still trafficking human cargo. Foreign governments, even our own FBI, didn't seem able to stop them. From time to time I thought of Shu Li, wondered where she was, even if she was still alive.

On the last day in June, after breakfast, as I was fixing Molly's lunch, I felt queasy from the smell of her peanut butter sandwich and wondered if I were going to heave. Taking a deep breath, I looked out the kitchen window and saw the bus for day camp at our curb. It was early, waiting out front.

I ran to the door to wave to the driver and yell that she was on the way. Molly came running, stuffing her bathing suit into her camp bag, dragging a towel. Nick tossed an orange and a drink into her lunch, passed the bag to me, and I thrust it at Molly as she flew out the door and down the steps. I blew her a kiss from the doorway as the bus grumbled off, noticing only vaguely the woman in the blue car idling behind it.

No, I didn't think much about her that day. I might have, but after Molly left I sat down to read the newspaper, and my attention was diverted by the report of a murder in northeast Philadelphia. I almost overlooked it, turning the page. But some detail nagged at me, made me look again. His picture was there. A bald man with a ponytail, heavily tattooed, wearing earrings. I stared at it, recalling Molly's description of the Gordo. Bald on top. With a ponytail. And jewelry. And tattoos. No, I thought. Couldn't be. But there he was; tattoos ran all the way up the dead man's neck. And my eyes caught on his name. Gordon. Gordon Terrell.

I scanned the story, hoping to find out that he'd died in a lover's quarrel. Or that he dealt drugs and owed some kingpin millions of dollars. Instead, I read that his throat had been slit and that his face had been cut three times, in curved parallel lines. I closed my eyes and saw the small Asian woman unlocking my chains, saving me. Shu Li, I thought. She was still alive, still avenging the dead, still chasing down cartel members.

Shu Li, the twentieth slave, had found the Gordo.

NINETY-TWO

Almost every evening detectives still dropped in to see Nick and keep him in the loop during his recovery. The night after Terrell's murder was no exception. Three of them were visiting in the living room when I came downstairs after tucking Molly in. I meant to get them some pretzels, but I didn't make it to the kitchen. I stopped in the hall, eavesdropping, when I realized what they were talking about.

"So Terrell was a slave trafficker?"

"Had to be. Why else would the perp go after him?"

"Maybe it wasn't the same perp. With all the press, it could be a copycat."

"No way. I saw those cuts. It was the same perp, no question. The slices on his face weren't just similar. They were a hundred percent identical. Same curves as the guys in the van. Same as Ellis and the others. Nobody would know how to do that except the perp. It's a signature, unique."

"Well, that's it for us then," Nick said. "If you're right and Terrell was in the cartel, the FBI'll grab the case just like the others."

"Which means it'll go nowhere just like the others."

"Maybe not. This one was different." The detective named

Al lowered his voice. "Between us, right?" He paused. "This time, there was a witness."

A witness? I held my breath, straining to hear.

"No shit."

"Terrell's girlfriend was hiding in the bathroom. She says she saw the whole thing."

"So who did it?"

"An Asian woman. So small, in fact, she thought it was a kid at first."

Oh, God. No question. The killer was Shu Li. I pictured her tiny form unlocking my handcuffs in the van, freeing me. And the lifeless eyes of Harry and Tony, the carvings on their faces. Shu Li was executing cartel members one at a time.

The men were still talking. "I'll be damned," somebody said.

"It's got to be the missing slave, what's her name—"

"Shu Li was the name on her passport." Al was way ahead of them. "So we put the passport photo in a book, and guess what. The girlfriend ID'd her. Shu Li's our doer."

I bit my lip. Now not just the slave cartel, but the cops and the FBI would be hunting for Shu Li.

One of the detectives sighed. "Well, try to convict. Eyewitness identification is shabby."

"Kiss my ass, Pete. She picked her out of three dozen faces." Al was miffed.

"Still. It's shabby."

"Yeah? Well, it's a hell of a lot more than we've had so far."

"Not necessarily," Pete insisted. "What about the vigilantes? It could be one of them; there might be a hundred of them who are small, female and Asian—"

"That's just a theory," Nick interrupted. "The FBI didn't say anything definite."

"Whatever," Al growled. "Whether it's just Shu Li alone or an entire vigilante group of escaped slaves, somebody's having a lot better luck catching the traffickers than law enforcement— Local or federal."

"Of course they are," Nick reasoned. "They're not held to the same standards. They don't need to follow procedure. Forget about warrants or evidence or law—"

"So that's the future of law enforcement? Police are so bound up in legalities and bureaucratic paperwork that effective justice is left to vigilantes? That's what we're coming to. Soon cops'll be ineffective and obsolete."

"In that case, Al, you're ahead of the game—you're already ineffective and obsolete."

More jabs almost drowned out Al's "Fuck you."

There was a silence then. I imagined heads shaking, sighs. Then one of them must have stood up.

"Anyone want another brew? Nick? Anyone else?"

He was looking back at the others, so he didn't see me standing in the hall until he'd almost stumbled into me. "Jeepers!"

Jeepers? "Oops, sorry." I fumbled for an explanation. "I—I was just coming in to see what you guys want. More beer? Something to eat?"

"Thanks. A couple more beers would be great." He was fair-skinned, reddening. Feeling oafish.

I hurried to the kitchen, trying to piece together what I'd just heard. Was there a vigilante group fighting back against the slave cartel? Did that mean Shu Li wasn't acting alone? I hoped so. I didn't like to think of her all by herself. But what was I thinking? Shu Li was a killer. She'd murdered repeatedly, methodically. Would her crimes be less serious if she was part of a whole group of murderers? I got the beers and put them on a tray with a bunch of crackers and a lump of cheddar, so engrossed in my thoughts that I almost didn't hear the soft, persistent knocking at the door. And when I did, I assumed it was more cops, so I opened the door with beers in my hands, ready to hand them out. But the person knocking wasn't a policeman. It was Shu Li.

NINETY-THREE

S he was dressed in black, so all I saw in the dark was her face. She scampered inside before I could react, and looking out into the street, clutched my arm.

"Yo hep," she whispered. "Shu Li know. Yo hep."

I rushed her into the kitchen. Oh, Lord. How had she found out where I lived? The newspapers, I thought. They'd shown my residence, mentioned where I lived. Or the phone book. But Shu Li didn't read English, did she? Had someone helped her? What did she want? Why was she here? The police and the FBI were looking for her. And at the moment a large portion of the police force was sitting in my living room.

"Peepow." She pointed to the street. "Come fo Shu Li."

"What people?"

"Yo hide Shu Li."

"Wait, no. You can't stay here," I whispered. "The police are here." I pointed to the living room. "They know who you are. They're looking for you—"

"Shu Li wait heeh." She was adamant. "Peepow come heeh soohn."

What people? Who? The cartel? Were they coming after her? At my house? I spoke slowly, softly. "Who is coming? The cartel?"

She blinked at me.

"The slave traffickers?"

She shook her head. No. "Ma peepow. Yo hep Shu Li."

"Shu Li," I began again. "You killed a man. Gordon Terrell." I mimed a big man with a ponytail. "Somebody—a woman—saw you. The police know who did it. They want to arrest you."

"No. Poreese no fine Shu Li. I wait heeh. Okay. Ma peepow come fo Shu Li. Soohn."

Her people? Who were they? Was she talking about vigilantes?

"Who's coming for you? How do they know where you are?"

She shook her head and looked up, as if trying to form words I could understand. "Some peepow . . . hep Shu Li. Like seestahs. Wook togeddah."

Vigilantes.

"Yo, Zoe—What's with the brews?"

Oh, God. The beers. Any second, Al or Pete or that other one would come into the kitchen and find Shu Li.

"On the way," I yelled. "Just a second." Then, grabbing the tray, telling Shu Li to wait there, I went into the living room and served Nick's guests, trying to smile as if I had not a single care. As if no one, certainly not a fugitive multiple murderer, were hiding in my kitchen.

NINETY-FOUR

M oments later, I rushed back to find Shu Li chomping on a banana, raiding the refrigerator.

"You're hungry." I reached for a package of turkey breast I'd bought for Molly's lunch. "I'll fix you a sandwich—"

But Shu Li had found a blackberry yogurt. She poured it down her throat and grabbed an orange, began peeling it.

"Okay," she assured me. "Yo no woolly. Shu Li okay." She found a slice of wheat bread, wadded it up and stuffed it into her mouth.

"But there are police here, Shu Li. You can't stay. They'll find you."

She shook her head. "No. Yo hep. I know yo hep. Yo Shu Li seestah." She touched her heart, met my gaze, and instantly I was back in the van, chained, half-dead, beyond hope, looking up to see those same dark, glowing eyes. Shu Li had rescued me. She'd saved my life. We were connected, and I couldn't turn her away.

"Shu Li," I tried to explain. "You killed people. Agent Ellis. And a man dressed like a priest—"

She nodded. "I kiw, yes. I kiw aw dem. Find dem. Kiw dem."

She seemed to be bragging about it. I thought of Harry and Tony. "But you didn't kill the men in the truck?"

"Shu Li save yo, but men dead awready. I cut faces."

The Gordo had gotten to them first.

Shu Li grabbed my arm. "See. Ma seestah. Ma peepow kiwd. Yo know. Yo ahmost kiwd, too. Shu Li hep yo. Now, yo hep Shu Li."

"But there are laws. You can't just kill people, even if they're bad." Why was I even trying to reason with her? She barely understood what I was saying, and besides, the subject was moot. She'd already killed half a dozen people. Nothing could change that.

"Shu Li stay heeh." She swallowed a chunk of orange. "Ma peepow come by in tomow mownee." She looked at me without a trace of doubt, completely confident that I would help her until the morning. Oblivious to the untenable position she was putting me in.

But I was acutely aware of it. I was on the line. I had to choose between aiding and abetting a killer and informing on her. Shu Li had put herself above the law, and in doing so had become as much a criminal as those in the cartel. Hadn't she? And, oh, Lord, if I hid her, wasn't I condoning her crimes? Participating in vigilante justice? Becoming part of it? Legally, I could be prosecuted for helping her. Sent to jail. I pictured bars, a narrow cot, a tiny window. Oh, God.

I watched her finish off the orange and dig into a pint of Chubby Hubby ice cream, amazed that this petite creature could pack away so much food so quickly. I wondered when she'd last eaten. And what I was going to do with her. Hiding her from the police was bad enough. But I'd also have to hide her from Molly and Nick. And I was the one always pressing for openness and honesty. Stressing the importance of trust. How hypocritical it would be to keep Shu Li secret. But I couldn't tell Nick about her; Shu Li would be arrested, found guilty of multiple murders, maybe sentenced to death. What was more important, upholding the law and being honest with Nick or protecting someone who'd saved my life?

Male laughter rumbled in the living room, barreled along

the hall, past the office where Shu Li was hiding. It sounded like the men were wrapping up their visit. I listened closely, heard the one named Pete promise to buy Nick a cheese steak when he came back to work. Then Al told Nick not to count on it; Pete would never pay for a cheese steak. He was too cheap even to put an occasional dollar in the office coffee pool. The guys bantered, insulting one another as partners do. And on their way out they stopped to thank me for my hospitality.

"You're doing a great job looking after this son of a bitch." Al grinned, pointing at Nick. "Pardon my French." His breath smelled of Budweiser.

"Yeah, he's almost back to his old obnoxious self," Pete ribbed. "And we have you to thank for that."

Nick smiled. "Yes, you do. Zoe takes good care of me."

"What do you see in this guy?" The third one—I still didn't know his name—frowned and put a boozy arm around me. "You're way too good for him, sugar. When you figure that out, give me a call. I'm still available."

"Back off, Walt." Nick stepped in. "Zoe'll never be that desperate."

Walking them to the door, I laughed at their sorry barbs and hugged each good-bye, thanking them for dropping by. Then, as soon as Nick went up to bed, I hurried to my office and opened the door. Shu Li was huddled on my old reclining chair, already sound asleep.

NINETY-FIVE

I lay awake all night worrying. Imagining what-ifs. What if Molly were to see her? What if Nick were to find her? What if her vigilante friends were seen coming into the house? What if they didn't show up? What if the cartel came looking for her? Or the FBI?

I thought of calling Susan, but couldn't involve her. She was a lawyer, could lose her license if she helped hide a criminal. Besides, Susan had no ties to Shu Li. I was the one who owed her. The problem was mine alone.

All night, images haunted me. Countless dead women floated past me in the river. Slave chains cut into my ankles and wrists. The faces of Shu Li's victims stared vacantly into the beyond. And Nick turned his back as prison bars slammed in my face. But by seven, when Molly's clock radio blared the morning traffic report, I'd figured out what I had to do.

I got up quietly, letting Nick sleep. I looked in on Molly, gave her a good-morning kiss, helped her pick out which shorts to wear. I packed her camp bag with a bathing suit and towel, made her lunch, put out cereal and milk for her breakfast. Waited with her for the camp bus.

"What's in my lunch?" she wanted to know.

"Turkey sandwich."

"What else?"

"Granola bar and an apple."

"But I want an orange."

"We don't have any oranges." Shu Li had eaten them.

"Yes, we do—"

"No. Sorry. I ate the last one last night." Now I was lying not just to the cops and Nick, but also to Molly.

"Mom, why? You know I like oranges in my lunch."

"Sorry. I had a craving." Another lie.

"A what?"

"I was just hungry for an orange."

Molly complained tirelessly, unable to accept our fruit situation. When the bus finally came, I was relieved to hug her good-bye; for a while anyway, I could stop lying. I brought in the newspaper, and listening to make sure Nick was still asleep, prepared a breakfast tray of coffee, eggs, juice and toast. Silently, I carried the tray to my office and opened the door, ready to talk to Shu Li.

Except that I couldn't talk to her. Shu Li was gone. The reclining chair was empty, the window opened wide. Her people, whoever they were, had already come for her. I stood at the door holding the tray, feeling oddly lost. Then, fighting tears, I carried the food upstairs to Nick, letting him believe that I'd fixed him breakfast in bed. Another lie.

NINETY-SIX

My mind was on Shu Li, so I forgot all about the woman in the blue car until I saw her twice in one day. Once, on Saturday morning, she was walking slowly along our street. She looked familiar, and I thought she must be a new neighbor. But then, when I dropped Molly off at Nicholas's birthday party, I saw her again.

She sat in her blue car pretending not to watch Molly kiss me good-bye. I pretended not to notice her. But as soon as Molly was safely inside, I looped around to the back of her car, ready to confront her. This was the stranger, had to be the woman who'd been following Molly for weeks. I was sure now that Molly hadn't made her up. The woman gazed at Nicholas's front door, didn't see me storming up to her window from the rear, my blood surging, poised to attack. Whatever she was—a kidnapper, a child molester—I'd have her arrested and jailed. After I tore her hair out. She'd be sorry she'd ever laid eyes on Molly Hayes.

"Hey!" I shouted at her, an arm's length from her door. "You. What do you think you're—"

She turned to face me, lips parting, stunned. And I froze, gaping. She was young, more girl than woman, really. I knew her face, the strawberry curls, the fair skin, the round eyes widening in surprise.

"Oh, gosh," she said. "I'm sorry. I'm sorry." She reached for the ignition, trying to start the car.

I was speechless, stunned. She was almost gone by the time I shouted, "No . . . wait."

She stopped, though. And for a few intense and awkward minutes, she stayed to talk.

NINETY-SEVEN

er name was Rose. "I was only fifteen," She explained. Her eyes darted away, beginning to fill up. "Too young to keep her."

She said she hadn't wanted to bother us, had meant us no harm. She hadn't realized she'd been seen. She'd only wanted to know that Molly was happy. That she was okay. Rose was about to get married and move to Colorado, but she said she hadn't been able to leave without finding out about Molly, so she'd searched and managed to learn where we lived, intending to come see Molly only once. But then she couldn't help herself. Once she'd seen her, she had to see her again. And again. She couldn't stop herself. She drove past the house at odd hours, watched her in the playground at school, at the pool in camp. Now, looking at me through Molly's eyes, speaking with Molly's pouty lips, Rose apologized for worrying me, thanked me tearfully for taking good care of Molly. She didn't call her Molly, though. She called her Katrina, the name she'd given her at birth.

I should have found out more about Rose. I should have invited her for coffee, or at least asked her last name, learned whom she was marrying, who Molly's birth father was. But the contact began and ended so quickly I had no time to figure out how to handle it, let alone what to say. By the time I'd thought of half the things I wanted to ask her, she was gone, almost as if she'd never been there. Except that she had been. I'd wondered about her for almost six years—who she was, if she'd make an appearance, how I'd react. Now I knew. I'd recognized Rose's undeniable resemblance to Molly and watched the unmistakable pain in her eyes. I'd sensed her desperation, her need to glimpse her child, even from afar. Rose was no longer a concept; she was real now, and I worried that, however subtly, my awareness of her would change my relationship with Molly.

But Molly seemed not to notice anything different. She bounced through early summer, sprouting new front teeth, losing others, learning to swim and ride a bike, shooting basketballs, making new friends, growing taller. She was apparently comfortable being Molly, unconcerned with either of her mothers, more interested in playing Capture the Flag.

Days passed. And although Rose had stopped following Molly, she was still with us, gradually integrating herself into my thoughts, becoming a constant, even endearing, presence. I hadn't told anyone about her; I'd kept her to myself, thinking of her occasionally throughout the day at odd times, when Molly's lips puckered in a certain way, when she shook her curls. Rose seemed to be invisibly, permanently with me, and somehow, amazingly, that felt okay.

NINETY-EIGHT

The next Sunday, I thought of Rose as I rehearsed my little speech, but no matter how I phrased it, the words seemed stiff and inadequate. From the kitchen window that morning, I watched Nick teach Molly to ride a bike, and I heard her shriek and giggle as she wobbled on training wheels. I told myself that we were already a family; we would weather whatever life brought. It didn't matter what I said or how I said it; the impact would be the same. But I couldn't bring myself to begin, and the day passed with me saying nothing. When Susan and her family arrived for a Sunday barbecue, I was still mentally juggling sentences, planning and revising what to say.

Susan and I mashed ground beef into patties, sliced veggies to grill, and Susan complained how lazy her girls were, how they were old enough to help but didn't, never set a table or washed out a sink. I heard the cadence of her voice but wasn't really listening. I was picturing the future, the way my little world was about to change. Nick was outside, manning the grill, making small talk with Tim, and feet thundered upstairs where Molly and Emily played. Julie and Lisa lay prone in front of the television watching some teenage reality show. And while Susan danced with food, I drifted, thinking about Rose's wedding, imagining my own. It would be in August, small and intimate, including only half of the police force and dozens of colleagues and close friends. I wondered what I'd wear, what would be appropriate, how much I would show by then.

And there it was again: the truth. There was no escaping; I'd have to make my little speech. I stood in my house, surrounded by the people I loved most, nervous and tongue-tied, knowing that it was time. I couldn't wait anymore.

Out back, a gentle breeze blew the wind chimes on my patio. Tim opened a beer for Susan, guffawed at something Nick said. Nick turned as I opened the sliding door, and suddenly I felt woozy. I swayed, steadying myself with Nick's pale blue gaze.

Then, knowing that I was carrying more than just a tray of burgers, hoping I could keep my dinner down, I headed out back to join the others. I thought about the name Oliver, and wondered whether Molly would get her wish.

The house looked smaller than I remembered. Smaller, and much more forlorn. Standing at the curb surveying the property, I half-expected to see myself at six, bursting out the door and running down the hill to the stream, or burying myself in mounds of crisp fallen leaves. Or at ten, hiding in secret shaded spots in the garden where no one could find me. Or at sixteen, sneaking out on crisp fall nights to meet Kenny Birch, the high school track star who lived next to the gated property on the corner. Who, it turned out, cheated on me with that trashy redhead in my trig class, Stephanie Laing.

Oh, Lord. Why was I remembering all this? I hadn't thought about any of these people in decades. But now, from all sides of the street, memories came swirling. Old Dr. Hennigsman, who lived across the street and always wore a three-piece suit, even when taking out the trash. Professor Hogan, who smoked nostril-searing, pungent tobacco while sitting on his porch swing, arias charging full-throttle from his window. Hilda, our plump housekeeper, her waist-long caramel-colored hair coiled into a gravity-defying knot, trimming rosebushes in the side yard. And my dapper dad, eyes twinkling, rushing off somewhere magical with a cheerful kiss and dazzling smile.

Stop now, I told myself. Don't revisit the past; those times are gone. You're here to deal with the present. I closed my eyes and took a deep breath, steeling myself for the walk up the path, reminding myself that I was not a child anymore. I was a grown woman, no longer vulnerable to the house or to the demands of the man who occupied it. Years had passed since I'd lived here. Decades. I had my own life now, my own home and family, a second child on the way. Being here was no reason for my stomach to churn or my hands to go clammy. What could happen? After all, he was just an old man.

Molly let go of my hand and raced up the path to the veranda steps. Six years old and high-spirited, Molly had little tolerance for standing around. "I'll ring the bell," she called.

Fine, I thought. You ring it. Because if you don't, we'll have to stand here while I get up the nerve. Which might take days. Weeks. Oh, Lord. What were we doing here? Why had we come? Yes, okay. We'd come because my father was a widower, alone and eighty-three. And Molly was his only grandchild. And I was his only daughter. But still, I hadn't seen or spoken to him in years. I hadn't wanted to and still didn't. Our complete estrangement suited me fine. In fact, I tried my best never even to think of him. Life was easier, more normal, that way.

Of course, there had been times—entire years—when I'd thought of him ceaselessly. His handsome, contagious smile; his twinkling, playful eyes. His deep reassuring voice. His boundless promises. His endless lies.

Eventually, I'd stopped spending energy on him. With the help of an interchangeable stream of sitters, housekeepers and maids, I'd managed to survive my mostly motherless childhood, had finished college, married, divorced, adopted a child. I'd built a career, gotten engaged again, become pregnant. Hell, I was forty-plus-one-or-so years old. I bore no resemblance whatever to the skinny, self-conscious, apprehensive and often disappointed kid who'd once lived here and unconditionally, usually at her own peril, adored her father. Through long years of repeated disillusionment, I'd turned so far away from my father that when I'd been making a list of wedding guests, I'd automatically omitted his name. I'd never even told Nick, my fiancé, that my father was still alive, let alone that his house was only a twenty-minute drive from ours. I'd acted as if I'd had no father. And that had been fine.

Until now. Somehow, despite my strongest survival instincts, here I was, at my father's door, my six-year-old daughter at my side. A warm October breeze rattled the brilliant leaves of a dozen ancient trees, sounding like applause. As if the trees were clapping, welcoming me home.

Molly pushed the buzzer, removed her finger and immediately pushed again. And again. And again.

"Molls—" I grabbed her hand before it could make another jab. "Don't ring so many times. It's rude."

"But Grandpa's waiting. He's expecting us."

Grandpa? She'd never met him, yet she seemed instantly comfortable with the concept. Grandpa. She was going to visit her grandpa, as if it were a normal thing to do. I wondered what she expected, how she pictured him. How would she greet him? And how would he react? Would he scoop her up in still strong, suntanned arms, charming her with a broad grin and baritone laugh? Would he lure her with a jangle of gleaming gold coins and silver dollars?

"Wait a minute." I squeezed her hand. "Give Grandpa a chance to get here. He might be upstairs."

Her eyes turned to the door, waiting. And my mind wandered. Somewhere close by, dogs barked furiously, cloyingly. Across the street, a large buffed man in a black T-shirt and jeans stood under a weeping willow tree holding a huge dog, maybe a mastiff, on a leash. Was he watching us? He seemed intent, staring at the house, eyes darting away when I looked at him. But why would he be watching us? He wasn't; he was just a man walking his dog, gazing across the street while waiting for it to sniff a tree trunk. So, where was my father? Why wasn't he answering the door? And, when he did, what would I say to him? How should I greet him?

My stomach fluttered and wrenched, and I put a hand on my belly, as if reassuring the baby. I didn't want to be here. When Dad's next-door neighbor, Lettie something—Kinkaid? Yes,

Lettie Kinkaid. When she'd called, I should have told her that she had the wrong number. That I'd never heard of Zoe Hayes or her father, Walter Hayes, or any Hayeses at all, ever. Or that Zoe Hayes had moved away, leaving no forwarding address. Or that she'd died; that, in fact, I'd buried her myself.

But I hadn't said any of that. Instead, I'd asked what was wrong, what had happened. She'd pointedly asked when I'd seen my father last, and I'd felt my face get hot, embarrassed by her chastising tone, a stranger's assumptions. She must have wondered what kind of daughter I was, neglecting an old widower. She must have thought I was an ingrate, a self-absorbed superficial brat. Living so close, not seeing him at all. Ignoring the poor man in the winter of his years.

Afterward, I'd considered pretending that the call had never come. That I didn't know he was ailing. But in the end, I'd been compelled to listen to the stranger who lived next door to him imply that it was my fault that my father hadn't been eating, had become fragile and occasionally disoriented, had been ill with the flu much of last spring and hadn't played cards in months.

"No cards?" I'd repeated.

"Not even with his usual guys, hon. Not a single game."

My father was avid about few things; one of them was cards. Any kind of game that he could bet on gave him pleasure, but card games were a way of life for him. He'd play anything. Gin. Poker. Blackjack. Even Canasta. So when Lettie'd said that he'd not played a single game, I knew the situation was serious. Emotions became irrelevant; the duties of blood prevailed. It was time to go home.

And so here I was, waiting for the door to open. We waited. And waited. The neighbor's dogs kept barking, fraying my nerves. Fidgeting, Molly pushed the buzzer again. Then she climbed the stone railing that ran along the long veranda, jumped down and ran beneath the weeping willow branches on the front lawn. I watched her, recalling my early years, and gazed beyond her along the street of aged rambling homes, the gold and red hues of century-old trees, the mix of color and shadow.

Mount Airy was hilly and overgrown with foliage. Overripe. Stone houses hunkered under the shadows of leafy branches; the ground was dotted with moss and freckles of light that penetrated the shade. The people here were racially and economically mixed, an eclectic population of all professions, educational levels, religions and cultures. There were even some authentic hippies, still around from the sixties, still running a food coop. My father hadn't selected the community; he'd landed here by chance. After his gambling binges had finally left us broke, his grandmother died and left him the house in her will.

As a child, I'd thought the house immense. Now, though, I realized that its formality, not its size, was what had made it seem formidable. Corinthian pillars lined the porch running along the sides of the house. On the south side, a wide, once flawless lawn sloped down to a wooded creek. I knew the terrain well, remembered darting among those pillars as a child, pretending, as a teenager, escaping from life. I'd climbed up and dashed down the hill, splashed on slippery rocks. Now the pillars were chipped and cracked, the porch sagging, the garden overgrown. The wood on the shutters was rotting and the lawn neglected, bursting with weeds. My father had completely let the place go. I wondered if he'd cut me out of his will. Or if someday all this—the massive decaying house, the large untended property and the responsibility to care for it—would be mine. I shook my head, dismissing the thought.

Where the hell was he? What was taking him so long? I'd called the day before to confirm the visit. I was sure I'd made the time clear. Mentally, I replayed the phone conversation.

"It's Zoe."

"Zoe?" He'd sounded hoarse and baffled. Well, it had been years.

"Yes."

Silence. Apparently he hadn't been any more thrilled to hear from me than I'd been to call.

"What can I do for you?"

What could he do for me? As if I'd want anything from him. "I thought I'd stop by and see you tomorrow."

No response.

"How's the morning?" I suggested. "About eleven?"

A pause. "Eleven o'clock?" I could hear him breathing. "Okay."

And that had been the extent of it. No "How are you?" No "What's new?" Not a word of happiness or shock or horror that, after years of silence, I'd suddenly called. Just a casual okay, agreeing to see me at eleven o'clock. So, it was ten past eleven. If he was expecting me, where was he?

I stepped off the porch into the untrimmed hedges and peered through smudged front windows. No sign of movement.

What was going on? Maybe he hadn't heard the bell. Or maybe he was outside, in the back. Or on the phone. Or lying dead in the bathtub, or on the bathroom floor, paralyzed from a stroke. I'd once heard of a woman who'd lain like that for days until someone found her. By then, she'd died of dehydration, not of the stroke. Stop it, I told myself. Dad is perfectly fine. Okay, I argued back, if he's so fine, why isn't he answering the door? Obviously, something was wrong. Besides, Molly was running out of patience. We couldn't stand there waiting indefinitely. It was time to move.

So, holding hands, we set out on the slate path that circled the house, overgrown foliage tickling our legs. We passed the neglected vegetable garden, thigh-high with weeds. I tried to open the mudroom door, the hidden door off the driveway, the elongated windows along the porch. All were locked and rusty. No sign of my father. Finally, dreading the descent, I led Molly to the always damp and moldy rear stairwell and started down, hoping she wouldn't have time to notice how slippery the walls were.

"Eww," Molly declared. "My sneakers." Her favorites, the yellow pair, had already squished into mud coating the steps.

"Careful. Don't slip."

"Mom, this is gross."

"I know. Try not to think about it." We descended another step.

"Yuck."

Clutching her hand, trying not to slip, I led her downward, remembering the squirming clump of worms I'd once encountered at the bottom of the stairwell near the drain. A single ray of light bounced off the wet concrete wall; the rest was shadow and slime, smells of mildew, damp earth, decay, something rotting. What the hell were we doing here? Why didn't I just take Molly and go home? An image flashed in my head: my father lying unconscious on hard linoleum; and I knew we had to go on. Stop whining, I scolded myself. Just keep moving. I took another step down. One foot, the other. Molly followed slowly, reluctantly. Four, five, six steps down.

At step seven, Molly simply stopped. "I'm not going, Mom." Her voice was firm. Even in the shadows, I could see the finality in her eyes.

I squeezed her hand and gave it a tug. "Molls, we can get in the house this way. Come on. It's just a few more steps."

"No way." She stamped her foot as an exclamation point, splashing my legs with slime. Perfect, I thought. So far, it was a fabulous homecoming.

"Molly, please." I was begging, sounding pathetic. "There's a way to get in down there."

Her jaw was set. Immovable. "I don't want to get in. I want to go home." She stamped her foot again, splattering more muck.

"Molly, we have no choice. We have to look in on Grandpa. Then we'll go home. I promise."

She stood her ground, refusing. Molly was strong-willed and persistent; arguing with her would get me nowhere. So, as I had when she was a toddler, I reached out, scooped her up and carried her down the steps, praying that my feet wouldn't slide out from under me, wondering if the worms were still there and if we'd land in a soggy, writhing mass. Carefully testing each step, I held on to Molly, ignoring the chorus of her whines and the repeated thunk of her wet sneakers against my khaki capris.

Finally, we reached the bottom. The air around us clung clammy and dank; the sunlight had disappeared. Something thick and moist was sucking my shoes, and I didn't dare look

down. Shadowy webs and encrusted cocoons coated the basement door. I took a breath, balanced Molly on my hip and,
praying that my father hadn't removed it, remembering briefly
Whopper, our long-deceased golden retriever, I kicked the spot
where the doggie door used to be. It swung open easily, sound-
lessly, not even rusted. I knelt, tentatively balancing Molly's
weight on my thighs, and pushed the panel open again. Molly
clutched my neck, gaping in disbelief.

"Molls, it's not as bad as it looks. I used to go in this way all
the time." I didn't mention the dread evoked by that memory.

She tightened her grip. "I'm not going in there."

I looked at the doggie entrance, the muck surrounding it and
the darkness beyond. Frankly, I didn't blame her. I didn't want
to go in either. Still, we had to get into the house, and, without
breaking a window, this was the only way I knew of. But I
didn't want to force her to go in. I couldn't. Instead, I gave her
a choice. "Okay, here's the deal. I've got to go find Grandpa to
make sure he's all right. But you don't have to. If you want, you
can wait outside."

"What—out here?" Molly glanced back up the dark, mucky
staircase, then down at the door. "By myself?"

I was about to say that I'd take her back upstairs and that she
could wait on the porch, but before I could say another word,
she dived forward and flew through the opening. All I could see
of her were the muddy soles of her bright yellow sneakers.

And so, muddied, disheveled and more than a little dis-
concerted, I'd come home. Molly had been unable to
unbolt the lock from inside, so I'd had to crawl
through the muck and slither through the doggie door after her.
Finally inside, I got up off my knees, brushed crud off my legs
and hands, gave Molly a quick hug and flicked the light switch.
One dim bulb came on at the far end of the basement.

Molly scowled. Apparently, her visit was not going as
planned.

I didn't blame her. The basement air was chilly and mildly
rank. Rotting garbage? Dead rats?

I squatted beside her in the shadows, wiping smudges off her face with soiled fingers, making them worse. "Molls, I'm sorry. This visit is all messed up. Hang in there a little longer, okay? We'll go—I'll take you for ice cream as soon as we find Grandpa."

"I don't want to find him. I don't like him."

"Well, we still have to find him and see how he is."

"I don't care how he is. I hate him."

Oh dear. I wondered if I'd traumatized her, if she'd forever associate the word "Grandpa" with dank slimy stairs and chilly dark basements. Actually, to me, the description didn't seem far off.

"Mollybear, Grandpa's an old man, and he might not be feeling well. We have to make sure he's okay."

She glared, defiant. But she let me take her hand, and together we started across the expanse of darkness under my father's house. The basement was an open underground space, unbroken by walls. We stepped around support columns, piles of newspapers, stacks of cartons, mountains of luggage, mounds of old clothes. We passed hunkering silhouettes—the water heater, a tangled mass of pipes, the furnace. The guts and bowels of a big old house. I told myself that I was imagining the crawling sensations on my arms. No spiderwebs were clinging to my face, no whispers tickling my neck, taunting me with secrets I couldn't quite remember. No shadows flickered in the dark corner near the cedar closet. I hurried Molly through the clutter, around discarded furniture and broken appliances, barely escaping the grip of a familiar uneasiness I'd thought long forgotten. By the time we reached the stairs we were almost running, and near the bottom of the staircase, afraid to look back, I felt certain we were merely two steps ahead of some deathly embrace.

My mouth went dry. I clutched Molly's hand and sped up the steps. Panicking about something nameless and unseen, telling myself I was being childish, I literally dragged Molly up the steps. We flew, but, as in a nightmare, the staircase seemed to elongate before us, each step seeming steeper and farther away, harder to climb than the last. With each step, Molly got slower, her breath faster. She was upset and tired; I was being insensitive, expecting too much of a six-year-old. I forced myself to slow down, grasping her hand until, finally, we made it to the top of the narrow, creaking steps, and, relieved to escape the basement, I pushed open the kitchen door.

Even before we'd stepped onto the fading linoleum, though, I'd stopped breathing, stunned first by the sight of my father, then by the knife and the widening pool of blood.